THE

PERPLEXITY

OF

ENGRAM

A FUTURISTIC FABLE

John F Russo

John F Russo

John F Russo Fictional Novels

The Perplexity of Engram
(A futuristic fable)

Enjoy Angela Fournier
Adventure Thriller Series

in

Tabula Rasa – Book One

Darkness After Midnight – Book Two

Compromised Interests – Book Three

Le Journal – a Novella – Book Four

Other titles in this series coming soon!

Whiteburn – Book Five

(Including excerpts from Le Journal)

Books2Read:

https://books2read.com?ap/8prE7z/John-F-Russo

Website: johnfrussoauthor.com

Disclaimer

The Perplexity of Engram is a work of fiction. Names, characters, places, and incidents are the products of the author's imagination or are used fictitiously. Any resemblance to actual events, locales, or persons, living or dead, is entirely coincidental.

ISBN-13:

Paperback: 978-1-734645705

E-book: 978-1-734645712

Dedication

A thank you is not enough for my sincere gratitude to my beautiful and loving wife, Lori, who worked by my side and gave me the opportunity and encouragement, and courage to reach a life time goal of writing. Without her support over these short 18 years, I would probably be driving a 1967 VW and forced into being a greeter at Walmart. Thank you Baby!

To my wife and my family, I dedicate this first book to you.

A worthy mention: *to my characters who daily waited patiently for me to fire up the computer so they may dictate their intent and allowed me to share in their misery, their joys, and their humor as some days we laughed out loud, while others, we had to clear the moisture from our eyes. To you, I thank you for your direction.*

Special Acknowledgement

A very special thank you to Claire MacIntrye, for not only granting permission for the use of the Marine Building as my Androicropulous, but she also furnished a fabulous photo for my use.

Thank you so much for your consideration.

To my friend and editor, Charles 'Papi' Thomas who had to endure all my mistakes, I thank you.

Introduction

This futuristic fable inspires man's resilience after being re-born through computer propagation some 15,000 years into the future. Without the plague of religion and the locust of governments to impede their dreams, discoveries and decisions, they cope with life and nature on their terms.

They embody the quintessential spirit for all to succeed without prejudice. They display their humor, their love, their passion and their fears, while others prefer the treachery of the past to despoil these dreams. Hardships are overcome with the camaraderie and respect that is afforded to every man, woman, and child.

Each character voices their own story which unites man's re-birth on a new world – EARTH 15,082 AD.

Content

Act I - Discontent

Act II – The Awakening

Act III – Welcome to Inception

Fore Warning

There is no need for a Preface to this truth.

We are our own breath of destruction. We are living and dying the Prelapsarian Era. We choose of our own free will to kill, maim, destroy, deface, lie, cheat, ridicule, humiliate and disrespect our fellow humans with no recourse or candor.

Our inner sanctum of life is probed, prodded, dissected, recorded, analyzed, categorized, and in some cases, the cause of our demise.

Our religions are based on fear, greed and impropriety.

All of our governments have failed us!

They have created a moral precept to govern, manipulate, and quench any deceptive contradiction they imply.

We are being held hostage mentally, emotionally and physically.

John F Russo

Prologue

The Journal

"The discovery of this journal, the reading and comprehension of information transcribed within its pages, can only have one positive outcome. The negative outcome, and worst possible scenario, would be that an invasion from Aliens has claimed your world, and as they systematically destroy anything of value, they accidently came across this journal. More than likely, they neither understand what has been written within these pages, nor do they care. Mankind has lost its soul and probably depleted its last breath of air. This Journal, as man, will become dust.

The positive, and I hope the actual discovery, is that man has now taken upon himself to procreate, self-regulate, govern, and take on the challenges of developing a better world.

Please learn from our mistakes!

In the 21st and 22nd Centuries, scholars believed that the Prelapsarian Era would have been the summation of conflict throughout vast areas of the globe. The continuing conflict of the Middle East over land and religious issues pre-dated even the Julian calendar. The Asian population explosion that threw countries into turmoil over water rights, food regulation, and boundary disputes, should have exploded into massive destruction. The immigration, health, and governmental control laws that defined the North American Civil Rights Revolution caused severe internal strife and mass amounts of bloodshed; it sheared the countries not only from north and south, but from county to county. Any one of these conflicts would have been enough to change the face of the earth. But the nuclear bombs stayed safe, the missiles did not fly, and the armies were at stand down. No, it was Mother Nature herself that precipitated the fall of man.

There were warnings!

The subduction of the Juan de Fuca Plate under the North American Plate was showing more activity than any previous scientific documentation. Reports of abnormal shifts in weather patterns from around the world had the news channels buzzing, while the science community, on high alert, dealt with facts, not conjectures. The most astute scientists who were studying the ramifications of plate displacement gathered at a summit, and it was of their opinion that engineered the survival of man.

Most governments collaborated with these scientists some did not. As the data poured into the International Center of the Humanity Defense Console 'ICHDC', the time line for action kept getting shorter. The expense of engineering an 'Ark' like the biblical Noah was cost prohibitive as no one knew what would be considered safe passage. In response, the scientific community drafted a plan to fortify at least one solid structure in each city with a computer matrix that would protect all internal and external interferences. They also picked these safe havens for what they deemed most likely to survive a major catastrophe. These safe havens were a time capsule for future off-spring, where computers safely and carefully maintained DNA samples of the surviving few scientists and the selected DNA from computer profiles of its citizens.

Computers wrote survival guides called the 'T-series'. These books were distributed to all of the sequestered sanctuaries and set with a DIN number referring to its standardization in populating information and format. Not all of earth's knowledge was included in these books as each source had to be combined to re-start the world as we knew it.

A Tabula Rasa for mankind!

As predicted, the shift of tectonic plates moved more than 180 centimeters, compared to the usual three to four centimeters, thereby causing massive earthquakes, eruption of volcanoes of which the largest reaction was at Yellowstone National Park. It blanketed the sky in ash and blocked the sunlight for decades. The trigger of these movements set the stage for every other plate to collide and volcanos to erupt around the world. The Axial Seamount, a mere 480 Km from Cannon Beach, Oregon and only 1400 meters below the surface of the sea, boiled the ocean with its magma. The desert of Afar, Ethiopia was the birth place of a new ocean as the African and Arabian plates split in half. The earth as we knew it changed in every possible configuration!

Geological teams across the globe, at least the ones that survived, were instructed to check the atmospheric pressure and radiation levels daily, weekly, then monthly, and finally yearly, but without fail, all in vain. We lost satellite contact with the remaining voices around the globe. This end of time was of the Gregorian calendar 2192.

We at the 'International Community of the Humanity Defense Console' wish you all good luck. We are hopeful that the computer systems have been faithful to their task.

John F Russo

The Engram (Engineered Responsive Analytical Monitor) is programmed to handle all tasks and assist in the rehabilitation of the human life form.

If we have presumed too much for the computer or the catastrophe was so heightened that we miscalculated the outcome, look to the North American Legacy for Human Survival (NALHS) as they professed the earth would heal itself in time. They took refuge in the many government silos around the world. The scientific community was not in alliance with their ideals, but a treaty was signed by the 355 participating governments as a safe guard, in case their assumption transpired.

We examined every possible scenario. The NAHLS Coalition has knowledge that needs to be incorporated in the T-book series. We have implemented a safe switch in each known region that may prevent adverse conditions to the development of human life. Once life has been restored, the Engram will delineate the division between resources, habitat, and reproduction. Its energy will be derived from, what we call, Neuronal Stimuli Compression (NSC). In its dormant period, little energy will be consumed; as earth's conditions favor reintroduction of creature establishment, it will absorb energy from its surroundings. Our prediction for introduction of life as we know it could span up to 15,000 years or beyond.

The dawning of a new civilization ultimately depends on the resourcefulness of its citizens."

Dr. Marion Michaels
Chief Science Officer of ICHDC

Act I

Discontent

The Fourth Rising

It was the beginning of the *Fourth Rising of the Blue Moon* and everyone in Belcare was basking in the energy, absorbing as much as they dared, before the words were shared by the Engram. It was duly noted in the scriptures that the Engram required unaltered neuron energy. They were not to overindulge as this could lead to optimal denial of future favors, and no one wanted to challenge the Engram's wrath.

The Grounders, as the Belcarians called Nalhsians, were believed to be the only clan allowed to bask longer; their pinkish, thin skin, and red-rimmed eyes mandated more nourishment then the Belcarians. It was only fair. They were the ones responsible for keeping everything in order, and properly functioning, that is, they were the sub-servants of Engram law. However, there were whispers that the Nalhsians were the true heroes of the eco system and with that adulation, they were often asked to appear at communal unification ceremonies. Their favors were in much demand, but unfortunately, the timing of the ceremonies was not as kind to the Nalhsians as all would have liked. In truth, the citizens of Belcare owed them a great debt!

Books T1 – T10

A grey-haired man, known as *Din1289*, of medium height with a portly girth mostly hidden by his shoulder to ankle tunic stood on the upper level of the Androicropulous, transfixed at its beauty, remarked in his usual oratory fashion.

"As far back as the first Transition Series entry, all have been at peace. The Engram guaranteed prosperity and salvation as set forth in the first T1 book, *Gestures and Commands*. As a student of ancient studies, I, Din1289, have read the verses and set to memory all ten books with each implication that might befall us if order was compromised and the risings were allowed to reshape."

Everyone was excited to be part of the fourth and fifth risings including Din1289, as this time of year offered the freshness of air that drifted from the mountains, and even though flowers and trees were always in bloom, there was still a feeling of re-birth. These two particular risings were the gateway for the introduction of the *Sixth Rising of the Twin Moons*. This special rising had only been documented five times since the keeping of the books. Hence, the celebration of this fruitful time, with the full blue canopies of Belcare's notable trees and the luminous waters filled with a cornucopia of yellows, reds, and soft browns, yielded such excitement.

"Yes...a wondrous time indeed!" elated Din1289 as he swung on his pudgy feet. He continued, "I have heard the whispers that one of the Clans had diminishing ideals about our benevolent beliefs. We cannot let their acquisitive manner influence our nominal numbers of our fold. As I stand on the upper level of the Androicropulous and marvel at its unique composition, I am caught in awe of the exceptional location for benefiting from all of the information one needed to satisfy their continuous training and self-regulatory compression. This is such a magnificent structure."

His hand traced the peaks and crevices of its towering multi-columned entry.

"The beauty of the carved-scripted blocks and opulent archway beset with the rays of the sun welcome our citizens to pass through its revolving doors. It is our gateway to all we know and understand. A place of learning for the most respected of our peers. I tell no misconception or boast any infatuation onto myself, the truth be told, I am a learned man and a keeper of these books. I am the Din Master."

Upon entering the Androicropulous, Din 1289 had a thought. *The Nalhsians had no capacity for digestion of self-regulatory compression; therefore, on these lunar events they had free will to travel about and to admire their arduous works of labor. I recount on one of these past revelations a chance meeting. I had personally met one of the Grounders, a mere boy by his size, whose name, I believe, was Relaeh. His speech, I presume, was not of ours, but he seemed to be attuned to his environment and his surroundings. It was by chance we met, at the steps of the Androicropulous after an Engram revelation. He seemed perplexed, but also, at the same time, predisposed to enter the Androicropulous. No Grounder has ever stepped forth into this most reverent place.*

I exchanged pleasantries with him and showed him the placard illustrating direct restriction on Grounders entering. He appeared to understand and left with no further incident. I spoke of this with my peers and they too agreed that it was a peculiar action, but since no harm was done, we simply went on with our readings.

Relaeh as a Young Man

Relaeh was the name he heard from the time he could remember. Jesting, his friends in Nahls referred to him as a 'mutant topsider', but it was only his close friends that could speak in this jocular manner. He was taught the language of the Nalhsians and had been protected since he was a small boy by his mentor, friend and father figure, Master Leumas. Relaeh thirsted for knowledge of the Belcarians, but was harnessed by Master Leumas who advocated patience, and instructed him of the inner workings of the Nalhsians, their social order, the science of man and his complexities, and a commanding vocabulary of the Belcarians. Before Relaeh entered the festivals, Master Leumas chalked his skin and laid lines in red about his eyes, a type of ritual, as it were, and protection against the sun's intense rays before the rising of the blue moon.

Although Nalhsians were very much respected, they nonetheless, were forbidden to colonize with the Citizens of Belcare. The purity of all blood lines was imperative to the survival of all, as interpreted from the T books. This was something Relaeh did not understand, but truly felt in his beating chest, that someday, all would be equal. It was obvious to him that his shape was more likened to the Belcarians, (Topsiders), than the taller and wider physique of the Nalhsians. Even at an early age, he had grown to a standing height of 178 cm, but wished he could be at least 188 cm. His young friends, the twins Dugar and Regor, were at least 200 cm and much wider between the spread of the arms. He felt although, even as a child, that he possessed good shape and strength for moving things, leaping from the ground, and stepping like the wind. Master Leumas had taught him well. The young Relaeh had great capacity for understanding mechanical instruments and could manage the ancient excavators of the ground.

As an adolescent, he could support himself between long cables that stretched between two landing positions; he had no fear of heights and often swung from support columns to test his adventurous character. Master Leumas would scold him on his precipitateness, but at times, when Master Leumas was hidden in the shadows, he would smile with delight as Relaeh displayed his aggressive playfulness. He reveled in the thought that Relaeh, when he became a man, would embark on a wondrous journey.

Clan N13 and Inception

Clan N13, as they called themselves, found they were neutralized to the influence of the blue moon's energy and the Engram's revelations. They had escaped during one of these revelations, but some bore the disfigurement, as the distance of travel in the restricted zone was prohibitive for one of many years. They spoke freely amongst themselves of past traditions, present surroundings, and future idealisms. They kept their isolation as an outcast clan to a point of mysticism. Their claim to the hidden truth could not be mentioned from the lips of supportive clansmen of Belcare. N13's existence and whereabouts was unknown by the Masters and ordinary citizens of Belcare.

Clan N13 divided on their escape to explore the treasures of their new world. One of the clans lived freely in the hidden valleys of the far mountains at water's edge, and caught what they needed to survive and nothing more. They called their home *Inception*. They were not warriors but hunters; although, the younger men believed they could hold their own, as witnessed by their physical games.

The Clan of Inception kept the ancient art of planting the land, and brought forth fruit, vegetables, and a sturdy selection of crops to which they fed themselves and their four-legged animals. They mastered the melting of ores and turned them into utensils for hunting, cooking and fishing. They also devised a cistern system that cleansed their drinking water gathered from the crystal-clear blue sea. Their trees, covered in green foliage, afforded them shade and protection from the afternoon sun. Their huts were made of thick bamboo and dressed in many colors made from crushed berries, the color of which indicated the prominence of each elder and his family. Some of the clansmen built their huts to stand on stilts at water's edge to take advantage of cool breezes that blew on shore.

Leinad, the leader of Inception, was a man of many years with long greying facial hair, weathered face, and kind blue-green eyes. Even though at the time of their exodus, his years were not many; he now walked with a distinctive limp. His daughter, Eittam, was a young twenty-three years and a ravenous beauty with dark complexion and eyes as deep in color as her father's.

This day, Leinad sat at his table reading his journal when he heard the swish of footsteps. He looked up and turned to see Eittam as she entered his structure. He hailed, "Ah, my daughter, you are as beautiful as your..." and before he could continue with his inveterate verse, Eittam interrupted him.

"...Mother. You say so, but I cannot gaze upon my own likeness. Your truth may be misguided."

Leinad laughed, "Would you then possess my eyes for your adornment, or take the word of truth to solace your impertinence?"

"Father, you make my face flush with such words".

"Then, my dear, it is the truth of an old man that you must hold nearest to your heart. Now, what is this whisper of intent from the boy, Bocaj? Is he the one to harness your mischievousness?"

"Father, he makes unusual eyes with me and I have not returned his favor. He is much more suited to my minor, Aivila."

"Well then, my daughter, would you like me to speak to his father, Councilman Nephets?"

"No... I will confront the matter on his return from the inner world."

Androicropulous - The Revelation

As the sun slowly set, it illuminated the full moon that rose above the Androicropulous. The crowd began to assemble for the great lunar revelation. The Engram was the authoritarian who governed all of the revelations. As the magic of the music filled the Androicropulous with a soothing rhythm, the symphonic sounds added to the glorious colors of the descending sun. The Androicropulous' lights flashed in waves further enhancing the festive mood as everyone took their place and locked arms. They hummed and swayed to the music cleansing their mind for ingestion of the regulatory compression.

The citizens enjoyed this feeling of euphoria, the peace that settled their minds, and the relief from built-up anxieties. This compression carried them through to the next rising, and then it would all start again. As they anticipated the arrival of the Engram's energy, their chanting heightened everyone's awareness and readiness to begin. Suddenly - all was silent. The stillness broken only as a whisper—the whirring of the oxygen fans. A few moments past, and then, a scintilla of light, followed by a chiming of bells. "Ahhhhhhhh!" The crowd collapsed in deep euphoria.

Within the tarriance of time, Din1289 and his fellow Belcarians were rejuvenated to their conceptual senses. They lifted themselves from the ground and their minds were at ease. The citizens of the dome city of Belcare joyfully recounted their experience with each other as if they alone, had manifested this revelation. Their satisfaction and clarity of their limited memories were now, once again, etched into their cerebral consciousness. They light-heartily continued with their business of the day.

Androicropulous

After the revelation, Din1289 continued on his way, past the still intoxicated masses to the great revolving metal-encased doors of the Androicropulous. Stopping once again, he marveled at the masterly design and workmanship of their predecessors.

"To have forged these incredible masses of elements is beyond comprehension. We have no tell-tale stories of these wondrous works in any of the T-Series books. Maybe the Grounders had the knowledge and tools to construct these opulent structures. But, if that were the case, why would they not be building now, and instruct us on these..." He paused for a brief moment of jovial indulgence and then continued with his foreplay. "Why would we want to build when we have the Grounders? They are much more adapted to that sort of work then we."

He continued to scrutinize his surroundings and voiced his opinion as if he were an ancient fore-teller.

"The Transition books were not the only books on display that one reflected on." He spun with his arms out-stretched, and said, "We are a learned clan. There are many derivatives of the T1-T10 books that freely expressed the path of rectitude. How could one deny or even think about denying what was set forth before us?

Our displays of the *Speculant Books* are of immense popularity with our more, common folks and their children."

He proceeded onward to the Great Hall where his colleagues continued to gather after the revelation. The doorway was wide enough to fit four councilmen side by side, even with their girth; the massive carved doors stood at least two men high. The room was a light grey in color with a lengthy platform and several podiums simply placed, adorning its polished face. The main seating, dressed in padded fabric, tiered upward in a semi-circle for clear visual and oratorical awareness for all present. Din1289 entered his most beloved place.

"I bid you all good will..." He paused in speech, stepped up to the podium, and turned to face the group.

"It was a matter of discussion before the occurrence of the blue moon invocation that we, the cadre of our citizens, needed to establish a periodic instrument that demonstrated our cumulative experiences. A time-piece, as it were, to be constructed on the great square, so all could describe their periodic adjustments sequentially by equal segments."

His peers agreed with excitement.

"On the other hand," he paused as he looked around and then continued, "...as translated in T2.17, a time-piece would or could add anxiousness to the community; it was so advised, not to introduce such a device."

A lull commenced in the audience, he then proceeded.

"We talk of time, but of no relevance to our daily existence. I know, being Din1289, that it has been 1289 periods of passings since the T1 books were inscribed into my care in these, our great halls. But, what is that in relation to? The number of moons that have appeared, or the number of revelations, or the number of completions that I have awakened after resting? If we assume that each *Keeper* lived a passing of twelve moons, multiplied by his resting days, carried forth by his Din numerical value... well, I can see even now, I am perplexed beyond my normal contemplations. And if a commoner, with his diminished capacity for intellectual stimuli would set his eyes upon such a piece... I cannot imagine the consequences."

His peers stood and applauded. They all agreed to drop the subject of introducing such an adversary to their peaceful community, and that the continued readings of their T-Series books were only meant, for their eyes only. Thus, another period of time was concluded.

Belcare

Belcare was located high above the waters, south of the North Gorge. Fertile flat lands laid south of the warehouse district and beyond them, the treacherous sand fields stretched past the circumference of the energy dome. Majestic mountains rested to the west and east. It was said, that beyond the great rock formations of the west, lay a wild body of water that extended as far, in all directions that one could see. This was only a whisper as no one man had seen this truth.

John F Russo

The City of Belcare:

12

Bocaj – The Journey to Belcare

Bocaj, Councilman Nephets' second son, his first being swallowed by the great sand many years prior, was afforded the respect of an eldest son. At a mere twenty years, he stood 176 cm tall with a brawn physique. He contributed daily to the ongoing survival of his clan. His swift stride and dedicated aim had won him admiration from all. He had an argumentative personality, though not founded on arrogance or hearsay, but on truth. His belief was in seeing to understand, and his determination to set forth and follow his seed was only compromised by lack of age and experience. He, therefore, felt a need to ask his father to let him lead an expedition to the northern mountains, were he could gather knowledge that books and introspect could not foretell. His desire at this tender age was to return to his father's homeland and guide those who wished to follow, to the freedom of Inception.

After being granted permission from the Council of Elders, Bocaj and five fellow hunters made ready to traverse the unknown, the unknown that only a very few had survived.

On the morning of departure, Leinad handed Bocaj a magic stone wrapped in a crimson sash to keep it safe and dry. Leinad peeled away its layers of protection and said to Bocaj, "Use this to find your way. When you dip down into the valleys your direction will become disadvantaged. Dig a hole in the earth and find a broad leaf that you may position into the hole. Pour water from your sack onto the leaf so it may hold the water. Find again a lighter leaf. Take this rock and stroke this needle in one direction." Leinad demonstrated, and then said, "And lay it gently on the leaf. Be patient and then follow its direction. When you are in a clearing, you can use the stars at night or the sun during the day to guide your way. Be careful, Bocaj. Do not let your whereabouts be known."

After grappling each other's' forearms, he bid farewell to his father, and then Bocaj and his fellow travelers set out on their journey leaving the village behind.

Aivila, Leinad's youngest daughter, approached Bocaj just outside the village. She stood in the water-soaked ground and reached for his knife. She trimmed a lock of her fiery-red hair and handed it to him. She smiled, gazed upon his eyes, and turned onto the path back to the village. Bocaj tightly held her locks in his fist as he watched Aivila disappear over a small ridge. His fellow travelers smiled but did not utter a phrase.

Master Leumas – the Philosopher

Master Leumas, a Nalhsian of great distinction and admiration, had the misfortune of a poorly designed body. His stature was incredibly short for Nalhsian standards and much more on the pudgy side. He walked with a waddle like that of the quacking birds found around the ponds of the Topsiders. But what he lacked in stature, he more than made up for intellectually. His astute and sagacious mind propelled him into the realm of Oracles. Respected by all, his mere presence was illumination for his followers. As the Master of Studies, it was his duty and right to teach the new breed of Nalhsians their rites of passage.

There was a mystery in the air that everyone in Nalhs felt. The elders requested that their off-spring be prepared in matters of negotiation, customs, language and social awareness of the Topsiders. Without the authority to actually study the Topsiders side by side, each time there was a revelation, Master Leumas instructed the young students to go above ground and observe the masses, but not to be so obvious as to spark any questions. At certain ceremonies, they were able to study the Topsiders first hand, and then returned to Nahls to speak of it in a study group.

Circulation was the key so as not to attend the same ceremonies, thereby observing their mannerism at each setting. The outcome was always the same, friendly, forthright, but as one of the students remarked, "To me, they seemed a few stones short of a sack." And all the class would break out in cachinnation. Even Master Leumas had been seen to raise his cheek-line into a bubble. It was true that the Nalhsians were well advanced in their evolution, far more than that of the Topsiders. The Topsiders, however, were unaware, and in some circles, incapable of the thought that the Nalhsians were superior to them.

Master Leumas – The Friend

Many years ago, during one of the revelations, when a majority of the Nalhsian students were either being honored by the fashionable ceremonies or just observing on their own, Master Leumas was on one of his many strolls down an abandoned air tube. He liked the solitude that it provided. He was able to re-charge his thoughts without being stopped every few feet with unwitting questions from the younger generation. Although, he most graciously stopped to answer even the most extraordinary question, as there could never be an inappropriate question when someone thirsted for knowledge.

It was on one of these insular occasions, deep in thought and deeper into an abandoned tube that he noticed, ahead, something strange in form but it seemed to move, like a body endures when laboriously breathing. He approached prudently; hunched over more than he thought possible. Suddenly, the cry of a child reverberated through the tube and then a 'gasp of air'. He stopped, and pondered; *Why was a juvenile cry coming from such a large object? Perhaps - a hurt animal?*

Master Leumas proceeded even more tentatively. And then, within a staff distance between them, he saw it. *The cloak, the cloak,* he murmured in his mind. *This cloak is familiar. I have seen this cloak before, but that is impossible!*

He knelt down beside this strange object. Gently, he dusted the sand away and opened the fringe of the cloak. Before his eyes as true as nature itself, a woman and a very young boy, laid still.

Bocaj – The Journey

While Bocaj and his men traveled along a narrow path, he instructed them to walk in each other's footsteps so as not to betray their numbers to anyone who may observe the imprints of their passage. He also instructed his artist friend, Kire, to record landmarks, so if necessity manifested, they could easily recount their bearing.

Along the edge of a swift river, they stopped and observed. At this time of the season, the milky white blanket covering the mountains was melting, so caution dictated their manner of crossing swiftly moving waters. Bocaj raised his hand and grabbed his keepsake that hung around his neck; he felt it necessary to share a memory.

"While on a hunt, we chased a large brown beast to the edge of the waters. Thinking we had it trapped, we raised our bows, but in a flash, the beast stepped into this rushing water and escaped from our arrows. We followed the river for a night and a day, to perhaps get a second chance. When we finally came upon the beast, it was crushed against the rocks. It might have escaped our arrows, but the mighty river revenged our intentions. Let us go up river to see if we might drop a tree or find a flat-tail's wooded cave to cross." Bocaj's moral was well understood; neither man nor beast could escape Mother Nature.

They had not traveled far before they observed what Bocaj was imagining. A deep motionless pool lay in the wake of a swift moving river and as the forces abruptly turned, a series of large boulders was embedded with the branches of a flat-tail's endeavors. The underlying current rushed the narrowed passage, gushing with great force as it crashed downwards into the angry pools. The waters swirled within its elements landing upon the lower rocks before it continued on its way.

The men dragged a couple of smaller branches over to the obstruction to bridge the waters and use the cave as a stepping point between the boulders. It appeared as if the river had precariously placed the branches in a swish of movement. Bocaj was happy with the placement and motioned to his men to carry on.

Bocaj's thought was to stay as close as they could to the great water's edge but not down on the soft sand that divided the great waters from the forest. He knew at some point they would have to head towards the rising sun, and then, follow the magic of the needle.

After three days of travel laid behind them, the terrain began to get steeper, and the valley light was shortened by the mountains. When they left the flat lands and approached a forest, the roundness of the trees was of the size they had never seen before. At one point, they all joined hands and failed at completely encircling the diameter. Bocaj and his men agreed that they would make substantial housing, at least ten men high above the ground. If lashed together with rope and vines, they could create walk-ways, and secure safety from roaming beasts, while on a hunt. Their ideas kept circling around and around. They made a notation on the drawings for future exploring and possible settlement. This was an exciting adventure. They were all very pleased with what they had found. They knew their clan would regale in their enthusiasm as well.

Din1289 – A Class Play

One of the many duties of a Din Master was to attend school events. Din1289 particularly enjoyed these outings as it was a propitious opportunity to witness the teachings of the young citizens of Belcare.

Nearing his destination, he thought. *Today the young students will present a play, written by their own hand I may note, of the upcoming special event, The Sixth Rising of the Twin Moons. It shall be interesting to watch them capture the truth of our revelations through the eyes of children so young.*

Walking through the doors of the school house, Din1289 was greeted by the Monitor-in-charge and escorted to the open space where the play was about to begin. Din1289 took his seat and as he looked around, he was amazed by the number of parents who occupied the room, and how many took delight in seeing their off-spring perform such a significant piece of their heritage.

The lights dimmed and all were quiet as the curtain raised from the make-shift stage.

Act 1:

(Stagehand)

Two blue discs rose across the yellow painted backdrop. A voice out of view began to speak.

Narrator

(A young boy attempted a man's voice)

"Welcome all. We the people of Belcare gather..."

The class began to assemble in a semi-circle and held hands.

"...to be inspired by our Engram. We revel in the energy provided by the 'Sixth Rising of the Twin Moons'..."

The children closed their eyes and lifted their heads to face the moons.

Narrator

"...as we await his instructions."

Music started to play, softly. The children swayed with the music.

Children

(collectively)

"Hmmmmmmmmmmmmm"

Monitor

(In the shadows, softly)

"1...2...3..."

The children stopped humming, waited, and stood still.

Din1289 noticed that some were a little impatient, and fidgeted with their garments.

Monitor

(In the shadows, softly)

"1...2...3..."

The Monitor held a switch, and flashed the stage lights off and on. The children that had bells rang them and rang them. After all bells stopped, they collapsed to the floor.

While most of the class was laying there in silence, two children, a very young boy and a girl, got up and went over to their respective parents. The little girl announced to her mother, "I don't hear anything, Mommy."

The Mother shyly bent to her daughter, "Shhhhh darling, it is only pretend."

The children jumped to their feet and all began to laugh.

The play ended. The Audience clapped with approval.

The lights came on in the theatre and everyone stood to congratulate the children.

Din1289 most amused and with a bright smile on his face, ventured over to the little girl who got up during the performance. He bent down to her size, shook her hand and said, "What is your name little one?"

The little girl responded, "Eve."

Din1289 thought that was a very strange name and said, "Eve, what... what an unusual name. It is the same forward as it is in reverse. Did you not hear anything when you were at the big building, Eve?"

Eve said with a little whiney, "Nooooo".

Her mother held her close and said, "Sure you do my love. Remember, we all talked about it."

Facing Din1289, the mother said, "It is such an honor to meet you. I hope the actions of our little girl do not upset you? She is so young and does not quite understand as yet."

Din1289 replied, "Not at all." He reached for the mother's hand. "She is very sweet and I will look forward to seeing her, perhaps in the theatre of the Androicropulous?"

At that, Din1289 bid his farewell and thanked the Monitor for such an outstanding play and of such celebratory conviction for their entire heritage.

The walk back to the Androicropulous had Din1289 in a quagmire of thought. *When I touched the girl's hand I would generally feel a displacement of neurogenic energy, a slight pinch or warmth attached as our hands met. I do not believe I felt that, nor from her mother. It is possible I was so wrapped up in the performance and the adulation that I just missed that transfer. But so, as it being relatively close to the last revelation...* Din1289 decided to put it out of his mind, for the moment. His world, The Androicropulous, loomed in the near distance.

Eittam and Aivila

On Aivila's return from the low lands, and her brazen bid of farewell to Bocaj, Aivila entered her sister's chamber and said, "I bid you good will, my sister."

Eittam looked up and with a smile said, "And to you, my love. What matter do you address me with today?"

"I am curious, my sister..."

"Yes, it is good to be curious," interrupted Eittam and then, "...and where have you been to have such foulness spoil your garments?"

"I have been down at the low lands bidding farewell to Bocaj. You are not disappointed in me are you?"

"Why would…"

Interrupting her sister, Aivila said, "I know I am only of eighteen years, but if you do not prefer Bocaj, I would chance his gaze."

Eittam paused and thought… *Maybe now I will have no need to confront Bocaj on his return.* She then said to Aivila, "My sweet, loveable, little sister, I do not gaze upon Bocaj. He is more like a brother to me. And if you are bound with joy that he is the one that you will want to have children with, then my sweet sister, you must follow your heart."

Emotionally, Aivila said, "I know you are the eldest and your heart must be satisfied first…" Aivila dramatically fell to the ground at her sister's knees, rested her head upon them, and confided, "…but I cannot control the urge that stirs up inside of me."

"And Bocaj, has he gazed upon your eyes?"

"I cut my hair and gave him my fiery strands to carry with him. He did not throw them down but grasped them tightly."

"Ah, my little sister, I think you are growing up. I have no intent of gazing upon ones' eyes if my stomach does not feel the twist of my loins. It seems you are beyond me in this matter."

Eittam and Aivila laughed and hugged each other.

"Now, my almost a woman, sister, you better clean up before Father starts asking you questions that would surely redden the face of most young girls."

Relaeh

Relaeh, a young man of twenty-four years of Nalhsian time, had recently completed his mathematical and structural design applications courses at Nalhs University. He had learned so much from his tender years until now. He found great humor in his pre-adulthood nuances. This new mathematical language pleased him greatly. The Nalhsians were the most intelligent people he had the pleasure to study with. They had ancestral knowledge that had been passed down and etched in many volumes.

His friends, Dugar and Regor, also attended Nalhs University. Regor was studying the nervous system and its reaction to stimuli using sound waves to impregnate memory perception. Regor's teacher was a woman whom Relaeh had never met but had heard whispers of Her vast knowledge of the old world and Her spiritual sense of the future. Dugar's interest was in applied behavioral consciousness. The twins seemed predisposed with what was happening to the Belcarians and tried to comprehend the magnitude of what controlled them. The three boys had created an immeasurable bond. Although the twins were his best friends, he loved and owed everything to Master Leumas. He had given him knowledge that no other could. He considered Master Leumas his Father.

Madame Noir

Madame Noir had aged, if at all, gracefully. She appreciated everything that Her friend had done for Her more than words could describe. As She sat in Her chamber, She reminisced of the talks they shared, the people they loved and missed, and of a little boy who was now a man. She knew of this young man's thirst for knowledge and his sense of adventure. Soon too, he will be gone. She momentarily struggled with Her braces, but still, She felt so alive. She knew She had a gift; some whispered She was their Oracle. Her knowledge lent well with Her friend and at times, when they read together, they would lift their heads and stare at each other as if they were reading each other's minds. Perhaps they were. A smile would broaden their faces, and then they continued with their reading.

They worked on many projects together. He had a laboratory built for Her special needs where they spent countless hours improving upon what was before and what might be in the future.

Daily Her thoughts questioned Her choice of obscurity that denied the warmth of a little boy. She was skeptical of what the end result might be. Would there be shame, regret, denial, or worse indifference? She needed to discuss this with Her friend.

Her friend, Leumas, had saved Her life more than twenty-three Nalhsian years prior.

Kire – Twelfth Night

By the twelfth night, Kire finally sat down and began to record his biographical accounts.

He wrote: I am thankful for the opportunity to have been allowed to participate on this adventure with Bocaj.

Although my friend and I share the same age, he seems in some ways, many years beyond me. I trust and respect him for his many accomplishments. And now it is my turn to facilitate the journey with drawings and writings for future admiration.

By the second day of travel, Bocaj related a story of his past whilst hunting. It was very philosophical in meaning as we were starting to become more knowledgeable of our surroundings. The elders had taught us their old language and as we gained our own understanding of our current developed language, we can then translate their message, and recount our experiences with much more detail and influence. I have noted in my text, that even Bocaj sometimes slips with his new teachings. I have therefore, amended where necessary to achieve the greater good, so our off-spring may be enlightened by what may transpire.

After three days of traversing dense foliage, we came across trees of massive height and girth. We clasped our hands together and tried to encircle the trunk, but failed at doing so. They were of reddish color and had thin green needles. They were unlike our long wide-leafed trees that bore fruit, as these did not. Nonetheless, their sheer size would allow us to bridge one to another and create residencies twenty plus meters in the air. Our clansmen who have claimed interest in observing and ascertaining usefulness of plant life for our clan would greatly appreciate our find. As a quick note, there seemed to be an absence of intrusiveness from insects.

We had been following a river line that Bocaj was convinced would lead us to the great vast water to our west. By this day, the twelfth, we have sighted a body of water as Bocaj had predicted and in an exhale of exuberating emotional excitement, one of our hunters yelled out "EUREKA!" By no means did we understand. Bocaj quickly mimicked with, "Yes, EUREKA, EUREKA!" We all started shouting, "EUREKA, EUREKA" and then floundered on the ground like a catch of fish. Bocaj insisted I put in writing this name, Eureka, for this spot, on my map.

Before we descended from our position of great expanse, we saw, to the magic needle's sunrise, an ominous rock formation with barren slopes and an apparent jagged rim forming a mouth with many missing teeth. A slight breath came from within and disappeared into the skies. A site that will need to be explored more in greater detail.

Master Leumas and Madame Noir

Master Leumas, after finishing his class on Old World Geography, went to his chamber where he noticed a message on his 'Holographic Wave Anon Console' (H-WAC). It was from Noir. She was in need of his opinion on a delicate matter, when his time allowed. He thought the message was a little strange, as it was the first day of the week and usually they shared their encounters on the third day. He quickly encrypted a reply that he was on his way.

The labyrinth of hallways, moving sidewalks, and descending decks would take Master Leumas an hour to arrive at Madame Noir's laboratory. He coded his route into his personal *Anon*. This afforded him swifter exchange between decks and not the burden he would have endure to re-enter his code at each transition. At 59:06 Master

Leumas' Anon flashed when he approached Madame Noir's lab. It in turn notified Her H-WAC of his impending entry.

Upon entering, Master Leumas had urgency to his speech and uttered, "My dear friend, what is of such importance? Are you of ill health?"

"No, no," quivered Madame Noir. "I am... at a crossroads in deciding what I should do."

Master Leumas, relieved, questioned his friend. "In what may I ask? I cannot recount a time when I have seen you so..."

Madame Noir cut Master Leumas short with a gasp, "Leumas." She paused momentarily and as she gathered her composure, She started to converse a little calmer. "Please sit." She motioned to him a comfortable chair that she knew was to his liking. "There is a lot on my mind. Where to begin..."

Master Leumas, knowing his friend was in deep thought, tried to make light of the situation. With a smile, he said, "How about what you want to discuss first?"

"Yes, yes. Let me begin with this. My concerns are for Trebor and of his journey that we both know he will soon want to embark upon. Next, meeting him, do we explain our relationship, enlighten him on who he is and why the Nalhsians call him *Relaeh*, or do we conspire with chance to take its course? Do we tell him the meaning of the revelations, the consequence that could occur if we are not careful and diligent in our pursuit? We cannot protect him anymore. He needs to find his inner soul.

"You have done masterfully in your teachings with him, Leumas, but for him to grow into the man we both know he must be, I am perplexed," stated Madame Noir.

Master Leumas knew that one day this very scenario would unfold. He had these same conversations with himself. Madame Noir had been anxious for some time now, he felt, knowing Her love for Trebor, she had watched him turn into a man. And Her concerns were of truth and needed to be satisfied.

Master Leumas cleared his throat. "My dear, Noir, it is true that Trebor needs to gaze upon you before he steps into the unknown. I have given this much thought as I know you have. I believe at this time, he should be introduced to you as my friend, my associate in human, environmental and astrophysics studies, and of course, as The Guardian of our old world sacred books. Let him be enamored with your presence as we all are. Then let him decide if he needs to pursue additional truths. Otherwise, this knowledge may cloud his mind and distract him from finding the truth. He is a man of years but his heart is still of a young one."

Madame Noir forced a smile. "Leumas you are a fine man and teacher. I do not want to foreshadow his discoveries or create doubt to his destiny. We shall do what you propose."

Master Leumas felt his friend's admissions had, for the time being, been satisfied, and said, "I shall request to Trebor an introduction to a most learned colleague and friend, and we shall together, investigate his intent of discovery."

Master Leumas set his arms about Madame Noir and relinquished his lips to Her cheek. He turned and took leave of Her laboratory.

On the return route to his chamber, Master Leumas decided to deviate from his earlier direction and chose a lesser traveled pathway; one he hoped with only minor interruptions.

He had a lot to consider.

Din1289 – Lack of Tingle

The Belcarians had passed the half-moon sighting and Din1289 had not been able to get the children's play out of his mind. Truthfully, it was not the play, but the lack of a tingle from the mother and that of the little girl with the strange name. Din1289 wondered. *What was the girl's name? Oh yes, Eve.*

He thought he had a memory of one other, many passings before this one. He could not completely adhere to the memory but as he pursued it, it started to come clear. *Yes,* he thought, *I know it now. The woman was my intern who was studying to be the next Din Master. She just disappeared one day. No one knew of her whereabouts. There could not have been any harm to her as we know not of violence. I remember now, when I touched her hand, there was no measureable heat or tingle either. I hope the same implication does not befall this little girl. But, I think at the next revelation, I shall keep a more investigative eye on this little one, to make sure no ill breath shall distort her being.*

Kire – 30 Days Out

Kire recounts without pontification.

"It has been 30 days since we left our home. The trek has been easier than in the beginning, since we landed again on the sand before the great waters. We had to pitch branches about us to protect us from the wind. The water is much colder and angry. It beats upon the rocks with giant plumes of spray. There are hills of white sand stretching as far as one can see. We do not investigate these hills, because tales have been told by our fathers recounting their experiences with man-eating swirls that can swallow you all as one.

"We have fished in the great waters and have gathered meat from wild animals, which we placed upon fire and adorned with the berries and fruits we have collected along our travels. Our flints remain hard and true and there are many branches washed upon the sand to kindle into fire.

"We are resting a couple of days before we set off to the direction of the needle. We have not seen footprints other than ours. The skies are grey and open upon us with great force. We miss the warmth of our home."

Aivila and Leinad

A full moon has passed since Bocaj lead his team of hunters to find the city of Belcare. Aivila, anxious about Bocaj's safety and his expectant arrival back home, wandered over to the end of the dock where Leinad was repairing netting for the next day's outing.

"My dear, why so forlorn?" Leinad asked.

Aivila twirled her hair and fledgling asked, "Father, how long of a journey was it for you and the clan on founding our home?"

Leinad thought this a strange question and her wimpish manner was not of her. "It took us four full moons to find our home. Why do you ask?"

"Were there any great beasts that preempted such a lengthy journey?"

Leinad sadly recalled his memories, but nonetheless said, "We were in discord. We had lost some of our loved ones in the sinking sands. When I attempted to reclaim them from the swirl of sand, I suffered an injustice to my leg from the energy of the dome."

"I am sorry, Father for tormenting you, I just... well rather I should say, I am concerned for our travelers that they might enter upon unknown danger that would limit their swift return."

"You are considerate of their journey. I am proud of you for your interest. This is something a woman does not accept too readily."

Aivila spoke abruptly and offered, "Father, we women understand full well of our purpose and what must be done. We accept these transactions as a matter of growing our families and securing our homes."

Leinad almost dropped his needle and thread, and apologetically said, "My daughter, I meant no disrespect but... what are you truthfully asking of me?"

Aivila hugged her Father. "I wish to gaze upon the eyes of Bocaj and I am troubled with his distance from me."

Leinad started to laugh. Annoyed, Aivila responded, "Father, must you jest with me?"

"Aha, I might have known that you had an underside to these puzzles and beguiled wile. I see now how you manipulate me for your desolation."

"Father, it is not quite as you say," retorted Aivila.

"My darling, daughter, if you are of desire to gaze upon the eyes of Bocaj, what of your sister?"

"She has no desire to gaze upon Bocaj. I have spoken with her and she is in agreement with me."

Leinad stood forth right and tried to sound displeased. "So now I am cast away from the decisions of my family. You and your sister have taken your sides before I am aware of these transgressions." Leinad hugged Aivila and shared in a humorous tone. "Ah you and your sister will put me under. Truth be told, I have spoken with your sister about your intent. I was expectant of your conversation with me. I will speak to Nephets if you wish?"

With a charming smile on her face, Aivila thanked her father for understanding the ways of women.

Master Leumas and Relaeh – Planned Introduction

As suggested in the conversation between Master Leumas and Madame Noir, they had to set a meeting to introduce Relaeh to Madame Noir. Master Leumas summoned Relaeh for an informal exchange of interest to set the stage for this upcoming enlightenment. Relaeh, unaware of this deception, entered Master Leumas' chamber.

"Good will to you, my Father."

"Relaeh, and to you as well. Please sit and let us commingle our thoughts."

Relaeh always enjoyed their casual conversations, but usually by the end, Master Leumas somehow left him with another antidote to test his judgment.

"How have your studies transpired? Do you believe they will serve you well?"

"Yes, of course, my Father, but I know I have barely been acquainted to the facts of life and the mysteries of the universe. Why do you ask?"

"I know you have heard whisper of Madame Noir. I believe your friend Regor has had the opportunity to have studied under Her guidance."

"Yes, quite right. He has the utmost respect for Her superior knowledge and that Her privacy is upheld as She wishes. I would imagine if that were not the case, She would have no time to conduct Her own experiments. I, for one, would be a constant annoyance to Her."

"Yes, I believe that as well," chuckled Master Leumas in jest. "What do you say I arrange an encounter for you to be introduced to my esteemed colleague, Madame Noir? She is aware of your desire to explore outside of the Nalhs habitat. She thought a chance to reflect on what may transpire would enhance your journey."

"I...I would be so honored. I know not what to say."

"That is a first for you to not have a legion of replications to induce," replied Master Leumas humorously. "I shall set the introduction for seven days from now. Let us gather here and we shall amble together as my Anon will gain us entry to all levels."

Questionable Excitement

Relaeh was extremely honored and excited to be given an audience with Madame Noir. On his journey back to his chamber, he thought, *I have many questions to ask, but I hope they will not sound infantile. I must tell Regor and maybe he can instruct me on the order of my questions as he had an opportunity to study under Madame Noir.*

Another thought came to him as well. *This is the first time I have been able to leave Master Leumas' presence without an antidote to unravel. Hmmmmm, what has he conceived to bring this honor upon me? Perchance this is a test of my spirit or perhaps my teachings? I will ask Regor of his impression.*

As Relaeh was set to contact his friend Regor, his Holographic Wave Anon Console (H-WAC) chimed. It was Regor.

"Good will, my friend. Dugar telepathed me; he felt your excitement. He is in his chamber on the 12th deck and I am on the 86th deck so I did not pick up on your anxiousness. What has transpired?"

All Nalhsians were telepathic. The twins had been working with Relaeh to open his extra sensory channels and to feel the electrical stimuli that fed emotional responses.

"Good will to you as well, my friend. I am not surprised that Dugar could feel my excitement, since we are only two decks apart. I have been granted an audience with Madame Noir."

Regor knew it was of joy and not sorrow, but failed to realize, it was of such magnitude. *"I am so pleased for you. She is a stunning person, with incredible knowledge that is beyond our scope of understanding. Did you know that She has the gift of extra sensory perception as us Nalhsians?"*

Relaeh, a little baffled, questioned, "She is not a Nalhsian?"

Regor, sensitive to his friend's bewilderment, said, *"No, She is like you. We thought Master Leumas might have revealed this to you? We never thought that you did not know otherwise."*

Relaeh, now completely confused, interjected, "How can that be? From where is Her origin?"

"I do not know. I am as perplexed as you. No one has conveyed this information to me, but I remain respectful of Her intentions."

"Of course, my friend, one does not slew the truth of another. I... just... why would Master Leumas keep sacred this truth from me, if She is one like me...?"

"My friend, do not let your anxiousness distract you from your jubilant encounter. Only a few have been granted such an epic gesture."

"No, I will try to conceive my thoughts as before, but now, they seem so infantile to even bother you with a retort. I will converse with you and Dugar tomorrow, after I have time to reflect on this."

Relaeh signed out of his H-WAC, sat in his lounging chair and stared off to nowhere.

"Dugar, did you perceive my conversation with Relaeh?"

"Yes my brother, I could not add anything more than what you have done. We will confer tonight so we can be tolerant of Relaeh's feelings tomorrow."

The Awakening of Eve

It was the morning before another revelation and Din1289 thought he would take a position behind the great doors of the Androicropulous in order to catch a glimpse of the little girl known as Eve, and her mother and father.

Secretly he hid and in the shadows, thoughts conjured, *This is a satisfactory vantage point, and if need be, I could rush out to protect her from harm's way. Although, I cannot fathom what that might be. And, do I possess the courage to do what must be done?*

As the midday sun approached its end, the crowd gathered, the music played softly, and the lights waved throughout the Androicropulous. The chanting started with the joining of hands and then silence... moments passed, and then the flash of light and the beautiful sound of bells. Din1289 was reveling in the spirit of the revelation as everyone collapsed in euphoria. Even though Din1289 was indulged in the moment, he did sense that more than one family did not hold true the same body awareness as the others.

A slight hesitation or maybe stiffness he thought. Something was different but he could not quite put... All of a sudden, Eve lifted her head from her mother's side.

WHAT was this? Recovery had not manifested itself as of yet, but there she was, oblivious that she was being watched. And too, another, a boy! What was this misalignment? Can it be so? Can the new off-spring be tolerant to the Engram? How will I be able to explain this to my peers? What will happen? I need to summon a convergence immediately." He paused. *"I need to calm myself, calm myself, calm myself,"* he repeated. *"I have many more passings ahead of me, how shall I be instrumental in my teachings? It could be the will of my peers to replace me, take away my privileged authority. Perhaps, if no words are relinquished... No, I cannot entertain such foulness. I need to reflect on what I have seen. Maybe then, I will clearly see my future path.*

Din1289 gathered his books and paper and headed down to the great chamber. He sat there in silence waiting for his peers to gather as they did after each revelation. *What shall I say? They will expect some new transcript to be contemplated. How will I begin?* He thought for a moment. *What if...?*

A voice from the great doors rang out, "Good will, Din Master."

"And to you as well, Erodec," he said replying to the familiar voice.

The young intern, Erodec, had been given the honor to study under Din1289. He mastered the ability to recite verbatim all ten books, but needed the guidance to understand their implications and resolve.

"What shall we discuss today, Master?"

Din1289 paused before he spoke, "I have a challenge for you, and of course, the councilmen, when they all arrive." *These moments will allow me to gather my thoughts.*

"A challenge would be good, sir," said Erodec noticing that his Master seemed more engrossed in thought as he did not answer him. *I believe Din Master is preparing a notable inquiry for this challenge. He is more distracted than I have ever seen him.*

All the councilmen had finally gathered and were waiting for Din1289 to commence.

"Good will, my friends and colleagues. I am considering a challenge for you to submit a reflection on a hypothesis that 'All men are created equal'. We will base the hypothesis on Books T9 through T10. I am especially interested in Erodec, as he will undoubtedly need to conspire with you all, as his confirmation has not had the legions of time to develop. I would like to see the positive, but also the negative to this hypothesis. Erodec will extract the information and place it before us."

Interrupting, Erodec said, "But Master would that not contradict our Great Engram and all our teachings in the T Series books?"

"Not at all, Erodec. We must place each teaching in its order and use each instrument of conveyance to extract exactly what the good books teach us. The writings are before us, but we need to be able to defend them, if an occasion arises."

The Councilmen looked around at each other in slight confusion and then the eldest of the council, Atir, said jestfully, "And by whose hand would an uprising be assembled? We are of one clan here and the Grounders have neither the ability nor desire to instigate such a thing."

The cadre always enjoyed these jocular intercourses between Din1289 and the body of the council.

Chuckling as well, Din1289 continued, "Yes my fellow colleagues and Atir, you speak the truth. I did not say uprising, I said if an occasion arises. As I said, this is a hypothetical quest, not to upset our teachings, but to reinforce them. Now let us conger a time... in considering an appropriate interval shall we agree upon the conclusion of the Sixth Rising of the Twin Moons? We all gather here, as usual, and we will let Erodec summarize his, and of course, your findings."

Atir motioned to speak, "And what of the festivities planned for the sixth rising? This is a very special occurrence, one that will not be seen for twenty generations."

Din1289 readjusted his thought and said, "Yes Atir, you speak the truth, let us prepare the paper and chance a conference after the sixth rising."

The council stood and gave adulation to the challenge set forth by Din1289. As they gathered in groups and spoke amongst themselves, Erodec went over to Din1289.

"Excuse me, sir, but I am perplexed. How should I begin?"

Din1289 looked up and said, "Well, pick yourself five of your peers that you feel have the most influence and form a committee. I would start with Atir. Once you have exhausted your inquiries, exhibit them to your colleagues and then prepare your findings."

"Sounds very logical, sir. And thank you for this opportunity to confirm my patronage to the Council."

Din1289 nodded. *This will give me time to resolve my issues. I will talk with Atir so he may keep me abreast of Erodec's findings.*

Delayed Journey

Kire wrote in his journal: It had been a daunting week with torrential rains and stiff winds. We had managed, with great perseverance, to find the end of the land. Water surrounded us in each direction, except the one we had just traversed. It was of opinion that we follow the water's edge to the sunrise of our instrument and attempt a crossing at a point of lesser distance.

We have migrated through lowlands, but as we traveled to the rise of the sun, we were faced with increased elevations of sheer rock face on parallel sides with rushing waters below. When we put to our eyes the sliding tube invention, we could not see an end. We have encountered large islands betwixt the great walls of stone that had risen in equal height to our standing position. We have cut vines to interweave with our ropes to elongate them. Tomorrow an attempt will be made to lower a man down the rock face, tethered to our device, and then swing him like a spider casting a web to the other side. Bocaj insisted that we test the strength by pulling on it, three men to each end. Amid the gravity of this exercise, with no mocking intended, we shared a humorous tale as Bocaj and his team pulled my team of three through our camp into a cistern of mud. We all had great gaiety, which was most craved after such a tumultuous week.

Prelude to Introduction

It had been one week past. Relaeh prepared his questions one more time and took leave of his chamber to meet up with Master Leumas. His talk with the Twins had him more at ease, but he still had not talked with Master Leumas of what he had learned. The questions were swirling in his head and usually he could conjure an answer, but today, he could not think clearly. He did not know what to think, and as the Twins had told him, just relish in the moment and spirit of meeting Madame Noir. He respected their instruction of being positive and not to dwell on what might not be.

Master Leumas had programmed clearance into Relaeh's personal Anon chip so he could transfer without pausing at each deck for a retinal scan. Master Leumas had complete authority to reprogram anyone's personal Anon chip. Doing so always saved travel time.

Relaeh felt thankful for this opportunity as only a few had been offered this audience. Relaeh arrived at the precise time Leumas had instructed. Leumas' H-WAC chimed as Relaeh was about to enter.

"Good will to you, Relaeh. I trust you have completed your questions for Madame Noir?"

"Yes, my Father, and for you as well."

"Excellent, are we then ready to set forth?"

Master Leumas sensed tepidness to Relaeh's reply. Not his usual casualness... perhaps a sign of maturity or even awesomeness has overwhelmed his zeal.

Along their journey traveling on the moving sidewalks to the Endeavor elevator, Master Leumas' personal XP Anon chip set the Centronic Security Systems to all green. The Endeavor, the fastest elevator of four in this sector, transported them down one hundred and fifty decks below their current position. The first one hundred decks swished past within moments. The next forty decks began to be almost recognizable, and as it approached the last ten decks one was able to see 140, 141, 142, until finally a slight hiss from the electromagnetic discs slowed the elevator to a perfect landing. The elevator revolved 180 degrees and presented its passengers to the required deck, one hundred and fifty. They stepped out.

Master Leumas placed his hand on Relaeh's arm and asked, "I have sensed apprehensiveness with your manner today. Are you of ill health or is it a preconception of what may transpire today?"

"I say with truth, my Father, I have no preconceived interventions. I have had thoughts of unworldly discord but have reconciled my languish to comfort the situation and bring forth the enlightenment of the day."

"Very well Relaeh, let us go forth to fulfill your destiny."

The Awkward Lesson

This was the day that Madame Noir had held in Her heart. Although, apprehensive of what may transpire, She was willing to suffer through yet another anguish to realize the truth.

She wondered, *What shall he ask of me? I cannot impose anything I do not know, nor yet, should I hold back on what I do know. I will let him direct the questions that summon his heart.*

The H-WAC chimed and Master Leumas led Relaeh into Her private chamber.

There was a sense of tension but it quickly dissipated as Relaeh pranced in with his usual lively gait. Master Leumas telepathed Relaeh's delight to Madame Noir who immediately eased the frowning strain in Her face. She cordially offered Her hand to Relaeh. Relaeh was quick to respond but as he was in motion, he viewed the braces on Her legs. Tubes of liquid continued to flow backwards to a low humming pump. He clasped Her hand in his. It was soft, probably the softest flesh he had ever touched. They remained conjoined hand in hand without saying a word to each other.

Master Leumas made his attempt to break the silence, "Madame Noir, this is Relaeh, and Relaeh, I would like you to meet our Guardian, Madame Noir."

Leumas waited and waited as the two gazed into each other's eyes. Relaeh finally understood what his friends had been trying to teach him, and in a fleet of a moment, it all came clear.

Relaeh, realizing Master Leumas' stare interjected, "It is such an honor to gaze upon your eyes."

At that, Master Leumas and Madame Noir expelled a gasp, and with huge smiles on their faces Master Leumas said, "I am sorry for falling short on your studies, but the term 'to gaze upon one's eyes' is reserved for one's intent to seduce a lover."

Relaeh reddened in the face. "Oh my, please, please except my apologies. I had no idea..."

Madame Noir smiled and kindly responded, "No apology is necessary. In fact, I am flattered. It has been a lifetime ago that one has cajoled me so. Please sit beside me and let us commence our discussion."

Madame Noir asked Master Leumas to ready some hot water and herbs, and offered some biscuits of unique mellifluous flavor.

Relaeh complimented, "These are delicious. Of what are they made?"

"They are a blend that I have cultured in my lab," replied Madame Noir.

"We have not studied such providence in our biology applications."

Master Leumas voiced, "Well, I can have you take a course in Home Economics."

"Home Economics? I have studied Old World Economics and Social Economics but have not heard of Home Economics. Does the matrix vary with this course?"

"Relaeh, you make my belly lift with gaiety. Home Economics was an endearing term in the first world for a study class that women took. It prepared their way in managing a home, their families, mending torn garments and preparing of sweet delights and fresh cooked meals. They used a burner system that heated food, and then garnished them with delectable vegetables from their gardens."

"And this would happen every day?"

"Yes," said Madame Noir, "And sometimes on special occasions, the man of the house would adorn the table with flowers for his beloved wife."

"And would these provisions be mandatory?" asked Relaeh, confused.

Master Leumas was quick to reply, "Only if you had intent of gazing upon her eyes."

At that, Madame Noir and Master Leumas subjected themselves to feverish, spontaneous exhilaration.

Master Leumas apologized to Relaeh for his uncontrollable burst of gesture, but concluded, he has not held himself in such discomfort for a very long time.

~

The mood of the chamber was not what Relaeh had envisioned. He was pleased that his good friends, the Twins, had spoken truth to help in this jubilant concourse.

"Now, Relaeh," said Madame Noir. "Leumas tells me you have interest in exploring the outer worlds?"

"Yes, Madame Noir."

"And how do you plan to proceed with materializing this adventure?"

"Well, Madame Noir, I am not quite sure. I was hoping to get some insight from you."

"Are you planning on venturing out to the topside and learning of their social behaviors, or do you have aspirations of something greater?"

"I have tried to gain entry into the Androicropulous to possibly learn of what has been, and then direct my intentions thus."

"I will tell you this. What is in the T-Series books will be of no help to you at the present. I suggest you plan a greater destiny and gain knowledge from what will transpire."

"Why are we not allowed in the Androicropulous? Is it not a great hall of learning, a place where man may assemble and speak of truth?"

"You are asking many questions that you will come to know. First, the Belcarians believe we live in dirt burrows and still count as high as our ten fingers. They understand only this: we are the keepers of their breath! They have not tried to acquire knowledge of our being, because their program does not allow them to."

"I plead no disrespect, Madame Nolr, but how did you make the transition to Nalhs? You have, as I, their stature but we do not possess their required participation in the revelations to exist."

"I met Leumas a very long time ago when I was studying as an intern for a master Belcarian. Leumas brought me through the Portal during a revelation, to understand the complexities of Nalhsians and to offer their assistance in restoring the Belcarians to a, shall we say, a more productive society. When I approached the Din Master with questions of the revelation, he would not listen to what he called 'contradictions to the Engram'."

"I believe I have met this man. It was outside the Androicropulous, after a revelation. He stopped me and motioned to the pictograph that visualized 'No entry by Grounders'. This was confusing, as they did not seem to be aware of our name."

"It is not their fault, as they have no conceptual knowledge of what went before. They have been programmed to live their life as instructed to the moon cycle."

"But that is no life!"

As quiet as Master Leumas had been through their conversation, he now interjected, "You see, my son, you have already been enlightened. Now before Madame Noir tires, what shall you need of us?"

Jesting, Relaeh said, "A way out of here..."

"That is not a matter of frivolity but of grave concern," countered Master Leumas.

"I meant no disrespect. I have no awareness of what lies before me or where I shall point myself?"

Madame Noir spoke up, "I am told of a clan that escaped some twenty plus years ago. Their heading was south along the coast of the old Pacific Ocean. I have no knowledge of their whereabouts or their servitude."

"I thought that whisper was a mythopoetic tale?"

"No, it is the truth I speak. You will need charts and compass, and a couple of trusted men," invoked Master Leumas.

Madame Noir added, "'The Sixth Rising of the Twin Moons' is in a month's time. The festivities will be abundant and it will allow a shadow of mystery. Prepare yourself and we will speak again before your journey. Now I am tired, you have a lot to discuss with Leumas and to settle your supplies."

"Madame Noir, I...I", unable to express his emotions, he bowed his head to Her.

As Master Leumas and Relaeh stood to depart, Madame Noir asked, "Relaeh, may I inquire on a more personal note... do you have one that your eyes gaze upon?"

"No, Madame Noir, my studies have not allowed the presence of one."

"Then your heart has not found that joy," She stated.

"My heart?"

Madame Noir touched his heart. "Here, you will feel the tightness when you gaze upon the eyes of your love and then your head will be light as a cloud. We call this love."

"And then the flowers?" he asked.

They all chuckled and took leave of Madame Noir.

The Great Gorge and Micja

Kire filed a report: Five days ago we thought we would have failed in our mission. The shear depth of our position to the disturbing waters below, plus the distance from us to our proposed landing, seemed insurmountable. But, success was in our sight as we created our spider's swing and propelled our best climber, Micja, to the island's rock face. It was not without anxiousness.

Our first attempt failed, as we held on too long with the surplus rope, and as Micja reached to grab the other face, he was jerked back and crashed into the wall of stone. For a moment he was still. We waited, and then he signaled us to start the swing again. We were all relieved to see this. On the second attempt, Micja was able to grab the other rock face but the stone peeled from itself, and as he was falling backward, we quickly pulled in the excess rope as he would have truthfully, been under water. The third was successful. We swung Micja further than the other two attempts, knowing, if he did not secure himself to the other rock face we would be unable to gather the rope quickly enough.

When his hands grasped the rock, he only had the length of a man to raise himself. Quicker than a morning yawn, he had propelled his stature to stand flat upon the rock. I had not seen anything like that before, nor have I heard a man being called as another. His, as strange to me, was *Goatman*.

Bocaj's idea was to have Micja tie his end to a tree and then hand over foot, hanging precariously upside down, draw another rope-vine to where Micja was standing. We were then able to string parallel strands top and bottom, and covered the bottom strands with stepping logs. We repeated this same method to pass from this island to what we hoped would be the main land. I think we all had expectations of Bocaj's tale of the great beast falling into the rushing water and being crushed by its force against the rocks. I think Micja, more than we, had that feeling.

We, once again, started to follow the direction of the magic needle. Bocaj decided since the land was of subordinate rolling mountains, we would stay true to its direction, and if confronted with another great body of water we would stay to the sunrise side of the needle. Each midday and nightfall, I have lain rocks in a cluster to mark our trail, but not so conspicuous as to attract attention. I have also scribed thus on my map for our return.

Inland had been warmer than at the water's edge, and at times, we had to strip down to our walking pants. We had been fore-warned in our fathers' tales of the beating sun, so we brought an extract from our plants that refreshed our skin.

Our walking stride has been with determination. Bocaj has been patient of my observations and my need to transcribe them to paper. He has promised we shall share time for such recounting. I have made mental notes of the flowers we have seen in order to put them to paper when we next make camp.

There is such beauty in this valley. I could stay here forever!

Invitation to the Grounders

Master Leumas left a message on Relaeh's H-WAC that his Anon had been programmed for him to join Master Leumas in his chamber as soon as possible.

Relaeh arrived with great speed. Master Leumas' H-WAC chimed announcing his arrival.

Master Leumas, very surprised, asked, "How did you traverse the walk-ways with such speed?"

"I felt your wish before my Anon activated. From the moment of our meeting with Madame Noir, my awareness has become much clearer and I am able to detect your inflection for need in your voice."

"Very good, Relaeh, you are becoming as you are meant to be."

Relaeh, not sure exactly what that remark meant, said, "Of what is your urgency?"

"We have an invitation from Din1289 to attend the Sixth Rising of the Twin Moons. He seemed more matter-of-fact that we needed to send representatives to witness this phenomenon. They are preparing as we speak; turning it into a grand festival. He wishes our thoughts as soon as possible, as there only remains three weeks until the rising and the next revelation. I believe this would make for an opportunity to research their plans, which we can add to yours. What do you think?"

Relaeh paused for a moment digesting his father's need.

"If I go as you suggest, he might become alarmed at my stunted growth, as I believe, he thought I was very young and had not reached my intended stature. But, if Dugar or Regor go, we can communicate telepathically. They could be my eyes."

"That is a marvelous idea! I will summon the Twins and give them instructions on what to plan and where to set objects that might conceal your disappearance. No one would be the wiser. Will you take some warm water and herbs with me, Relaeh?"

"Of course... there is something I wish to ask you, Father."

"My heart is yours."

"I had learned before our meeting with Madame Noir that She was not of Nalhsian decent. I could not find Her origin, as I was told She was like me."

"Yes, continue." *What will he ask me?* Thought Leumas.

"I have not known a mother or father like me, and please, with no disrespect and seeming insensitive, as I love you as my father, but... is She my mother?"

"It is truth as I say; Madame Noir is not your mother."

"Thank you, I was troubled since you did not speak of Her as in my likeness that if She was, She did not want to love me."

"My boy, I tell you this, She does love you as much as a mother does for her own. She has not been as healthy as you saw Her last week. You have given Her new hope and Her wish has been not to bring any more hardship to you."

"Hardship...?"

"Madame Noir could not care for you in Her condition so She thought it best that you only know of me. She has watched you grow and at times we took great pleasure of watching you swing from the great wires as we hid in the shadows."

"But you, yourself, gave me notable disregard as a young boy for doing as you mentioned. And yet, you tell me you both found great pleasure in watching?"

"As your teacher and protector, I wished you no ill will if you would have taken a fall. I would not have forgiven myself if you had. You will understand of this double standard when you have little ones. Trust me."

Before they could continue Master Leumas' H-WAC chimed. The Twins had now arrived.

Din1289 – Prelude to the Sixth Rising

Din1289 thought it was of good gesture and of opportunity to send a message to the Grounders to ask for their advice and their participation in the sixth rising. He had recounted his notes from a conversation with his woman intern some twenty legions past. She spoke of a highly developed society living beneath the ground that shared, amongst other worldly knowledge, extra sensory perception. At the time, he would hear none of this, as it went against all of the Engram's teachings. But, he had seen for himself the default of letting the Belcarians procreate amongst themselves. He thought maybe the Grounders could perceive non-believers, which would relieve him from the responsibility of having them compressed. Their detection would add to his favor and then guarantee his position as the Guardian of the Great Books. A case could be made in the great hall for stricter reinforcing of the revelations and future implant upgrades.

Din1289 thought it wise to have one of the fathers of the young children in question, Salocin, to be in charge of decorating the dignitaries' platform, as this would give his man maximum exposure to the Grounders.

The sun was setting, which meant the Grounders should be able to absorb the rays without damage to their delicate skin. They usually wore peculiar adornment about their eyes that reflected the sun from entering. *Those poor people,* he thought.

As he went over to talk pleasantries to Salocin, he noticed two tall Grounders coming his way.

"I bid you good will," declared Din1289.

"And to you as well, sir. I am Dugar and this is my twin brother, Regor."

"I am Din1289; I am Keeper of the Great Books and Scholar to the cadre of Belcare."

"We have been instructed of your position," replied Regor.

"And this is, Salocin, our manager of decorations."

"It is also an honor to be introduced to you as well, sir," Regor said recognizing the man.

Din1289 could not detect any obscure difference in their meeting of Salocin. *Maybe when the sun lowers even more, and they remove their adornments, will I then be able to detect a subtle gesture of acknowledgement.*

Din1289 started to impress the Twins with his grandiose ideas for the decorations and festivities. He directed their attention to where a musical ride would be in motion for the children. He pointed to where an assortment of brightly covered awnings devoted for showing wares from different haberdashers would reside. And of course, intermingled with them would give rise to assorted delicacies for everyone's delight.

Dugar asked, "And where will this fine platform be located?"

With a floundering wave, Din1289 positioned his thought. The Twins followed his intent and then Dugar said, "The time of day that you intend will be unfavorable for our dignitaries. May we suggest in shade of the Androicropulous, thus not distracting from the festivities, but merely exchanging side for side?"

Din1289, who seemed obviously careless of this consideration, thanked Dugar for his guidance in re-positioning the platform, and instructed Salocin to amend this discourse. Din1289 asked that perhaps one week before the rising, they could find time to resurface for further inspections. They both agreed and headed back to Nalhs.

John F Russo

Meeting in Master Leumas' Chambers

The Twins, Dugar and Regor, with Relaeh and Master Leumas were all sitting in their mobility chairs. These chairs were unique to their sector as Relaeh, when just a junior, designed the first anti-gravity air chair that gravitated on one spot. His most recent design allowed one to move around a room with simple word commands. It was easier for Master Leumas to reach his taller cabinets without having to resort to old-fashion stools. He never felt comfortable on those anyway. At times, he summoned Relaeh to fetch different apparatus for him when Relaeh visited. Master Leumas thought that maybe Relaeh designed these chairs so his trivial incidents would not be bothersome to Relaeh. But in any case, he loved his chair.

Regor had everyone's attention. "I have met the man called, Salocin, at his union several years ago. I had not perceived any difference in him, but his wife did not possess the Engram's strain. That I am quite sure."

Master Leumas added, "And Din1289 has never insisted that we attend any revelation. We are welcomed at our leisure."

Dugar shared his opinion. "The position of the stage has never been an issue. I believe he knew the correct position as he frivolously waved his arms to the opposite side of the Androicropulous, while he precisely indicated the positioning of everything else."

As each had questioned their visit, they turned their gaze to Relaeh.

"My friends, I believe there was no intent of misalignment of the stage, but that it was a pretense to bring you close to the man called, Salocin. I believe Din

Master has gazed at others like me and Madame Noir, and now, is perplexed in handling the situation if more of us are not with the Engram strain."

Master Leumas gasped..."Are you suggesting he has witnessed a Miracle, my son?"

"A miracle for us perhaps, but not necessarily for the Keeper of the Great Books. The last account I have of the people of Belcare is four generations, with Din1289 being of the oldest generation. There are no 'Old People'. We have our elders here in Nalhs. They are taken care of respectfully, in each sector, so they may engage in conversation with the young ones. They have their dignity and choice of multiple events to attend. So, perhaps the young mothers of Belcare have bypassed the Engram's strain? And perhaps, they continue with the revelations as not to bring attention to themselves and their family?"

"Interesting theory, my son. How can we entertain this anomaly?"

Dugar and Regor responded almost simultaneously.

"When we go topside the week before the sixth rising, let us involve ourselves in further conversation with the men, and perchance we can meet their women and children."

Regor said, "I will strike idle conversation with Salocin as I was a guest at his union. Perhaps something will come of that."

"Yes, very good," added Relaeh.

They were all excited as they shared their intuition of the intent of Din1289.

Master Leumas explored a thought, "And what of the Din Master? What will be his reaction to this conversation? Will we put Salocin in danger?"

"I know of no danger that could befall this man," rationalized Relaeh. "If there is a suspicion and, as Regor has implied, he already has the Engram's strain. Maybe a readjustment, but no harm at this point."

Master Leumas was happy with their conversation.

"What information do you have of a planned route for Relaeh, Dugar?"

"We have thought of this. When we return we will mention to Din Master that because of the grandiose celebration that he is mustering, more of our elder Nalhsians would like to attend. We will transport them from the Portal in our machines so they can make the distance with little discomfort. We appropriate one extra that Relaeh can use to slip away into the shadow of the Androicropulous. We can have it packed with supplies for his journey."

"Excellent!" replied Master Leumas. "I shall gather a party of dignitaries, but I shall not convey our intentions. There is no need to influence others. You all have done well. Let us conspire after you have returned in two weeks' time."

They all agreed, and then Master Leumas turned to Relaeh, and asked him to fetch some warm water and herbs. And from the top shelf, if he would be so kind, there were some sweet biscuits from Madame Noir.

Kire – Amazement

Continuing his recounting in his journal, Kire wrote:

After another three days of travel we had hit another body of water, though much smaller as we saw many islands scattered throughout. We headed to the sunrise side and continued our trek in search of Belcare. We passed several monoliths protruding high from the flat lands covered with a blanket of white that concealed their barren nature.

To our sunset side lay more water with a multitude of islands spotting the surface, but as we continued to traverse this diverse land, none were more beautiful than the fields of brightly colored, bell-shaped flowers. They had six petals on a long stem with colors from the rainbow. White, yellow, red, purple and pink waving at us as we passed by. As I took a moment to sit beside them, I was able to capture the entire vastness before me - a sea of color with a majestic mountain in the background. Such beauty - such a wondrous sight!

We had departed from our village almost two full moons when we spotted an immense, translucent semi-circle, looking like a bubble in water, but transfixed to the ground, and it rose to great heights. Bocaj estimated that we needed two days of good strides to land us at the edge of this sphere. We would then set camp, gather our thoughts and wait for the revelation to transpire, to gain our entry. As foretold by Leinad and Nephets, *'You must wait until the light passes from the ground, and then strike as quickly as possible before the light recharges. The sun will be low in the sky and the moon will reflect its light, allowing you to advance in the shadows without detection. Once inside the perimeter, set up camp in the woods, and from there, cautiously observe before making any contact'.*

I shall make another posting when we have secured our camp on the outside of this sphere.

The Status of Erodec

Although Din1289 had been very busy with the celebratory plans, he remained in contact with Atir. He had witnessed no abnormality from the exchange between Salocin and the twin Grounders. He still, however, craved to learn of any genetic defects that might have occurred during DNA incubation by the scientists who were following Engram's protocol.

There were only seven more passings before the sixth rising and the grand revelation. Erodec was to have substantial documentation of his findings by this elapsed duration. The Din Master thought it was best to secure an encounter with Atir to reconcile any deviation that might have been brought to light before Erodec went to Council. Today would be a good day as tomorrow would bring the Grounders back to have overview of the progress.

After he rose to the residence floor of all bachelor councilmen, Din1289 waned to the end of the hallway and knocked a peculiar set of strikes upon Atir's door. Atir answered with expectant eyes but quickly re-focused upon engaging Din1289.

"I bid you good will, Councilman Atir."

"And to you, Din Master."

"May I step in and have a word on the progress of our young intern, Erodec?"

"As you please, Din Master."

Din1289 entered the room and noticed the slight furnishings offered to Atir. He thought, *How did he fall out of favor? I cannot recount any injustice that would afford these conditions.*

"You live modestly, Atir."

"I have no need for self-indulgence. I eat, I read, and I sleep."

"Perhaps a chair of more cushioning for reparation of your weary bones?"

Atir articulated a nod of his head and said, "I will accept with gratitude if you so desire."

"Let it be so, Atir. You shall have a cushioned chair so that you may read in comfort. And perhaps one that falls back with a rest for your feet. I shall see to it. Now, my intent on this visit. Has Erodec impressed you with any findings?"

Atir sat down on his only wooden chair, while Din1289 theatrically strutted about.

"He has confided in me that many years ago an intern under your care vanished without any trace. I remember her, a very bright and inquisitive young woman. Her name escapes me, but nonetheless, he has divulged whispers that she was not of the Engram strain."

Din1289 stopped in his stride and replied, "I know of the woman he speaks - Noiram. And yes, she disappeared from my sight. I could not find any clues to her whereabouts. I do not have knowledge of her lack of the Engram strain though. How did Erodec come about these findings?"

"A young man has ways of persuasion when not encumbered by civil unions. I shall leave it at that."

"Yes, and does he have suspicions of others?"

"He mentioned a children's play but had not confirmed any misrepresentation as of yet."

"Very well indeed, I look forward, I mean, we all look forward to hearing his report. I will not infringe on your hospitality any further, I bid you good will, Atir."

Din1289 left Atir's modest space and headed straight for the Archives of Reproduction and DNA Diagnostic Studies.

Perhaps with aid from the diagnostic team I will be able to render, if possible, the exact location in the development stream that is misaligned to the calculation set by Engram. If by chance Erodec has not thought of this quest, I may offer in defense of the Engram - human error! What reference of me knowing if Noiram had a missing strain?

Din1289 was not quite himself as he reached the main foyer and descended the stairs that lead to the Archives.

Meeting - One Week Remaining

The next day's sun had set sufficiently for Dugar and Regor to comply with Din1289's wishes to return for final inspection of the platform. They stepped onto the pathway from the Portal, just as a young man in a black robe, with an obvious devotion, swirled past them.

Dugar made a jesting comment, "I had no conception that the Topsiders could move at that speed."

The two continued their jocular observations as they approached the well-decorated platform. Din1289 was not in their immediate view, but saw Salocin, kneeling, in obvious concentration as he added some final touches.

They approached. "Good will to you, Master Salocin."

Startled by Regor's deep voice, he stood quickly pinching his finger on a misaligned wreath. "Ur...good will to you both. You startled me."

"We had no intent. We apologize for our inconsideration."

"No, not a...I mean..." He hesitated, "I have words for you, but cannot divulge these whispers here."

The Twins were concerned for Salocin's unrest, and obvious moisture about his head. Regor sensed Din1289's presence walking towards them and interjected, "Yes, it has been a long while since I was first invited to your union. I trust all are doing well? And may I impose, are you of children?"

"Yes, I have a son."

"Very good, Salocin. Is he taking of his father's trade?"

And before Regor and Salocin finished their conversation, Din1289 was upon them.

"Good will, Din Master," saluted Dugar.

With a smile, he replied, "Good will to you both. I see Salocin is keeping you of interest."

"Yes, I had the opportunity to witness his unity and was asking of his welfare."

Dugar imparted with his observations, "The platform has transpired nicely and the setting is in alignment with the Androicropulous."

"It is I that must acknowledge your keen sense of placement. We would consider no displacement of your dignitaries. And how shall they arrive?"

"We will transport them in our machines to just beyond the back of the platform, if that is in accordance with you?"

"Ah... your machines, will they not harm our inlays of stone?"

"If you are referring to our great *diggers*, they have not burrowed a hole for six generations. We will, however, present our dignitaries in our machines that ride on a cushion of air, Din Master."

"Oh, yes of course, I was merely jesting with you."

"And we enjoyed your intent."

Modestly, Din1289 suggested, "Shall we peruse the common sites where a more serendipitous visualization will be performed?"

"We would appreciate your time if you so intend, but we do not want you to indulge us for our mere merriment. We sense your need to attend another engagement. We can conclude our promenade after your revelation."

"Very well, I bid you well."

Din1289 turned and headed back to the Androicropulous. *I need more time in the Archives. Those Grounders seem content with the proceedings... cushions of air?*

Dugar and Regor casually strolled through the scattered tents; they sensed a watchful eye upon them. When they rounded the last structure, out of the shadows, a whisper of a voice spoke out.

"Follow me so we may speak in private."

Secret Unleashed

The men of Nalhs followed the faint whisperer through the shadows of the festival grounds, crossed a boulevard of lined trees, and past a cluster of precariously constructed habitats. The figure momentarily stopped and looked side to side. A finger was placed to the lips, and then, a wave of a hand, as the figure darted across the open space and disappeared behind a large and more secured building. Being of much larger mass, Dugar and Regor had to squeeze between the sides of the brick buildings. They turned the corner and confronted their secretive admirer. She stood three quarters to their height, with slight build and medium length hair. Her face was illuminated by a stray light beam that peeked through the foliage next to them. She had kind eyes.

"I am Einna, the wife of Salocin. I trust there will be no reprisal, for I must speak truthfully. I am without the strain that inflicts our people. There are a few of us, mostly women that talk amongst ourselves, who are free to think and remember from our beginning. Our children also seem to be free of this control, which has us all worried for their safety and continued growth. We believe our husbands will follow us and be able to function without this intrusion of compression. But we need to go beyond this encampment to live our lives as free citizens, no matter what may befall us.

"I could tell when we met at our unity that you sensed me different and I was afraid that you would find it binding to inform the Androicropulous of such. You did not. I trust you now more than ever and beseech your help."

Dugar and Regor had been telepathing back and forth as Einna was speaking. They had already acknowledged her rectitude and motivation for urgency.

Regor leaned closer to her, "We understand your solicitation of us and we will hold binding your truth. How many in your fold would consider such a transgression?"

"We have fifteen as we speak. There may be others but their trust is not yet binding to reveal any consideration."

"Do you have a mother or are you first generation?" asked Regor.

"I have a mother but she has no intent on traveling with us. She is afraid of the unknown and recites her age as a deterrent."

"And what of the others?"

"There are six couples, and three children. One of the couples is with child."

Dugar asked, "Your husband, Salocin, he wished to speak to us. Was this his intent?"

"I love my husband very much and he loves me, but I have not mentioned this to him face to face. We women have conspired to save our families and our husbands. They are good and kind men."

"The upcoming celebrations could host multitude of deviations, but to engineer such a movement in the prescribed time might not develop as you wish. Let us recount our theories to our confidant. We will conspire to bring about what you ask," said Dugar.

He, and his brother Regor, slipped out of the shadows, past the tree lined boulevard, and back to the ceremonial grounds that led to the Portal.

Salocin Seeks Help

The thirty-meter wide pathway was lined with trees and bushes on each side with dimly lit lights atop poles of ornate design. There were many pathways from the Androicropulous and the central park. They spread out like spokes adjoining a central hoop (the growth rings of the Engram) and then three times that again until the boundary of the translucent sphere. Each loop was named from the Androicropulous as *Peace*, *Truth*, *Conviction*, and *Serenity*. The boulevards were laid out as points of an octagon with the center spoke, which started as 1st Boulevard, and thus to the right until the last, 8th Boulevard. As the Androicropulous was slightly askew of True North, it was, however, in direct line to Magnetic North. Dugar and Regor were engrossed in telepathic communication as they walked down 2nd Boulevard, to where, a short distance ahead laid the entrance of the Portal. Unexpectedly, Salocin stepped out from behind a tree. They stopped suddenly.

"It seems I have startled you, as you did me, I apologize."

"Of no consequence," replied Regor.

"And what would be your intent, good sir?" inquired Dugar.

"I need to ask, and as I have spoken to other men, I know it is not my own abnormalities that test me. But I, we have strange dreams that do not reflect our natural character or our influence. These images manifest themselves shortly after a revelation and intensify until a re-compression. They occur not just at night, as you witnessed one taking hold of me this very day."

"What do you imagine?" asked Regor.

"We all imagine the same scenario; we are holding onto a... I have no name, but it flashes fire from its end. We have made no account to its purpose, but men beside me fall with anguish on their faces and many exposures about their body with blood spurting out. Smoke fills the air and the grass blades are saturated with our liquid. I have no understanding of these images."

Dugar asked very intensively, "The ages of your friends, are they as you?"

"Yes, maybe a moon passing on either side."

"You have confided in us of what we have great interest. We are in much appreciation for your candor. We will develop a matrix for you and your friends, and if we can arrange approval, we will invite you to our labs."

"We cannot be seen entering your Portal. It has never been done."

"Let us investigate the treaty to ascertain permission."

Salocin nodded his head and vanished among the shadows and shrubbery. The Twins, in obvious delight, entered the Portal.

Erodec Interviews Old Woman

Erodec, in his haste, brushed against one of the tall gentlemen from down under. His adornment about the eyes fell askew. He hurried to the other side of the ceremonial grounds to speak with an informant before her husband returned from work. She said she had news of a children's play. Erodec took the Din Master's challenge with great enthusiasm and figured he finally had a chance to flaunt his talents. He wanted more than to sit and nod his head in agreement to what had been said. He would show them all the aspects of their heritage as instructed by Din1289. He took the steps two by two, crossed the wooden passage and readied himself before knocking. It was not unusual for one of the Council to come calling as it further entrenched the teachings of the Engram.

Erodec knocked on the door in a peculiar rhythm. A face appeared in the glass door and quickly opened it. Erodec was welcomed in.

"Good will to you, madam."

"Yous comes abot te girrl?"

The voice muttered in a strange dialect that Erodec had never heard.

"Why yes, you said you have knowledge of misgivings from a children's play attended by our Din Master?"

"Iz twas there. Iz cleanse te floors. He touched te woman ans her girrl. Iz could sees he had no flicker froms either. He tries to hid te fact but Iz could sees, Iz tell ya, Iz could sees, he knew they was diff'ren."

"And perchance was there another occasion you might have noticed this difference?"

"Aye, at te steps. We was readen' and te mother stars droppen' and te kid fellow before time. That's all Iz got."

"Do you have their names?"

"Te little one is call Eve, but Iz think she has a noder."

"I thank you for your time, madam."

The woman, stood at the doorway and watched as Erodec took his leave. He was uneasy about offering her account and wondered how she missed the gene pool. Next, he had an appointment with the Data Reclamation Center. He was not so concerned on what DNA had been implemented but what was left out. Perhaps they would have an accounting of missing strains. He knew of the young man there, as he was an intern as well. They had crossed paths before.

Secret Admiration

The night air was fresh and the approaching moon had not yet set itself high in the sky. The shadows danced on the old building as the dim street light reverberated. At the bottom of a stair well, one small light cast an ominous illumination upon the entrance.

Erodec charged down the stairs and whipped open the door. The room was long and gray with two rows of wooden benches on either side that shared unusual deviations. At the end, a wood-framed glass door carrying half fallen letters, stood as a sentinel of what was inside. He knocked softly and tried the handle, but it was locked. A muffled voice from inside asked, "Who is it?"

"Droenal, it is I, Erodec."

Droenal unlocked the door and let Erodec step inside. He shut the door behind him and replaced the lock.

"I bid you good will, Droenal."

"And to you, Erodec. I was surprised to hear from you. It has been a while since we gazed upon each other. I thought you might have forgotten about me?"

Erodec stepped closer, "I have not forgotten your gazes. My time has been preoccupied by a challenge from my Master." Erodec stepped even closer. He placed his hand on Droenal's arm and pulled him to his chest. Droenal placed his arms about Erodec and their lips pressed together.

Droenal whispered, "I have dreamt of this."

They held each other tight for a moment and as they released Erodec inquired, "Have you found of what I asked?"

"Is that all you want of me?"

"No, my friend, but I have only a few days left to amend my findings before I consult further with my colleagues and then present it to the councilmen."

"Well, I have found some ancient discrepancies over two generations ago, but nothing current. Will that help?"

"I was hoping for something more current, but let me have their names."

"Names? I only have numbers. But if you have the people or a sample from them, we can easily match their DNA."

"I have neither. Have you heard whispers of clansmen not participating in the revelations?"

"Well, our group does not attend at the Androicropulous as it is not required to do so. We still have need for the compression, but we prefer to join hands over at my place, and then fall into a pile. You should come over. There is a lot of gaiety afterwards."

"I can imagine, Droenal. I must take leave now and recount with my colleague to find a different direction."

"Don't forget me."

"I won't."

Erodec made haste to the Androicropulous and Atir.

Camp at Sphere

Kire continued in his journal:

We made good stride and have set camp a safe distance parallel to this anomaly. Bocaj had thrown a spear into its wall. We watched as the spear sizzled and then puffed into nothingness. Not even an ant size piece could be recovered. If too close, our hair stands on end, which brought us to our knees with exuberant cackle.

We are quite high above the water's edge. Bocaj wants to travel the length of the sphere towards the waters, to see if there is another route that we may take without discovery. Perhaps we may swim under it. We shall see tomorrow.

I have long waited to just sit and put to paper all of which we have encountered on this journey. Bocaj is a true leader. We are thankful for this opportunity. We know not what will be waiting for us on the other side. I shall for today sit, and draw my most precious of memories. I will need berries to paint the brilliant colors of those bell shaped flowers.

Truly beautiful! He scribed.

The Twins Recount

It was early in the morning when Relaeh's H-WAC began to chime. He found it very humorous to see the holographic images of Dugar and Regor as miniatures.

"A very early good will to you both."

"And to you, our friend. We have unexpected news for you. We have talked with Master Leumas this morning and he wishes a summit in his chamber as quickly as possible."

"I shall be on my way."

As soon as Regor's image vanished, Relaeh's H-WAC chimed again. This time it was Master Leumas. *"My boy, we need to meet as soon as possible."*

"Yes, my Father, I have received a message from Regor. I am on my way."

"Make haste, your Anon is cleared for travel."

The H-WAC chimed again, this time it was Madame Noir. *"Have you heard the news, Relaeh?"*

"Not yet, I am on my way to Master Leumas' at this moment."

"Good, meet me at my lab afterwards."

"Yes, Madame Noir." He signed out and barreled out his door.

What could have changed so dramatically, to be rushed around so early? What were the Twins up to last night?

. . .

Master Leumas' H-WAC chimed as Relaeh appeared in the doorway. Regor and Dugar were already sitting in their mobility chairs, and Master Leumas had the hot water and herbs set in trays.

"Good will, gentlemen. I trust your reconnaissance proved worthy."

"More than imaginable," replied Dugar.

"Yes, we met Salocin's wife Einna peering through the shadows. She has admitted to her lack of the Engram's strain as well as five other friends that wish to travel outside of the Engram's hold," reported Regor.

"There may be more..." added Dugar.

"Boys ... slow down. As you see Relaeh has barely cleared the sleep dust from his eyes."

"We beg your indulgence, Master Leumas." Regor continued, "We met with Din1289 for a moment as we sensed he was in a hurry to be elsewhere. We spoke with Salocin, who was in fear to talk at that time, as Din1289 was approaching us. As we left the platform, we strode down by the tents that were being set up for the celebration. And out of the shadows spoke Einna, Salocin's wife. We met her at a safe spot where she indicated that she was only one of a few that she knew of, to be without the Engram's strain. She said she wanted passage through the energy field to life beyond Belcare."

Dugar added, "There are fifteen in their party, six couples, three children, but one couple is with child."

Regor continued, "As we were approaching the Portal, Salocin appeared and asked for help with these dreams that he and a couple of his friends were having. They were very disturbing and felt they were incapable of stabilizing, except for the immediate timing of the revelations."

Master Leumas interrupted, "Are the friends of Salocin the same as spoken by his wife?"

"We have no knowledge, as Salocin had no recount of our conversation with Einna. They are of the same generation."

Relaeh spoke up, "Are you saying that Salocin has no knowledge that his wife is without the strain?"

"No, we believe he is aware and also, his son is without the strain."

"A boy, as well as the women... very interesting. We are then to assume that the boy is fourth generation and appears to have no strain, as he was conceived by his natural parents. But I have met first generation boys and girls the same age as of Salocin's son. So the Engram is still producing his heirs to gain the energy from their very souls. The more nero-energy generated from the citizens, the stronger the Engram is perceived," stated Master Leumas.

"And, what of the treaty, Master Leumas? Can we interfere for the good of the people?" asked Dugar.

"It is recorded that we, as Nalhsians, cannot interfere unless life and peril threaten their continued existence. And as you can see, the population continues to grow."

"What of me? I am not Nalhsian, it is plain to see," shared Relaeh.

"There can be no mistake," laughed Dugar, as they all did.

"You are, Relaeh, you are their Relaeh!" admitted Master Leumas. "We will discuss this with Madame Noir as well. Now tell me, Regor, about these dreams from the men."

"I believe they have a cognate gene from the past. This gene is manifesting itself, probably due to the induction of the energy levels now built up by the Engram, as you stated. This gene could become highly developed to a point where they assume the personalities of the very ones that occupy their dreams. It could demonstrate in an anxious or dangerous situation.

"We would like to transport them to my lab and work on a matrix to stimulate this gene under a controlled situation."

"Of what disturbance do you imagine they possess?" inquired Master Leumas.

"We believe they are warriors." conceded Dugar.

"Warriors! We know of no wars for generations and generations, possibly 12,000 years! When our ancestors signed the 'Humanity Defense Coalition Treaty' in the 22nd Century, all 355 countries approved the 'Order of Defense', which guaranteed propriety for all mankind. If arms were to be utilized, it was for the protection of earth."

The Twins and Relaeh were stunned to hear this from Master Leumas.

Choosing his words carefully, Relaeh said, "I beg your indulgence, my Father, but how do you know all this?"

"It has been written and kept in secrecy, that is until now, for which I apologize for such an outburst of emotions. Your tender ears had no need of hearing this knowledge. Not yet."

"As you then suggest, Master Leumas, we are in year 14,200?" asked the astute mathematician, Regor.

"No, the Nalhsian calendar would be 15,082, which is of the same Gregorian calendar of old earth," replied Master Leumas.

Dugar made a comment, "The inscription above the Androicropulous has the numerals 3 5 5, as you inferred. What might we deduce from that?"

"I believe it was one of the founding buildings utilized as a *League of Nations*," shared Master Leumas "...maybe a safe haven as well. We have no authority to enter into Androicropulous, not us Nalhsians..."

They all looked at Relaeh and smiled.

"Now tell me more about these dreams," enticed Master Leumas. "I am very disturbed to hear this."

"They speak of flashes of fire coming from something they are holding, and men beside them falling in pools of liquid drenching the ground," replied Dugar.

"If we remove these men from the energy of the Engram, do you think it is possible these genes would subside, and then they could resume a productive life?" asked Master Leumas.

"It is possible but we will have no knowledge of the transition until we form a matrix and study the results," insisted Regor.

"If we draw samples of each man, and label as such that their anonymity is secure, and encrypted the name with number in that fashion, I will allow tests to be performed. I will cite the inquiry as of grave circumstance for the well-being of humanity. This must be carried out in strictest confidence."

"Thank you, Master Leumas. We shall make an attempt to re-establish contact with Salocin in a prudent manner."

"And what of the exodus?" asked Relaeh. "Should we proceed or re-schedule to incorporate the six families? The sixth rising is such a festive event, it would shadow our movement. If we wait for another rising, would it not increase risks?"

"Let us conspire with Madame Noir," replied Master Leumas.

"She has requested a viewing from me after our meeting. Should we all join Her to recount what has transpired?"

"No. Relaeh, you meet with Her first, and if She requires our presence we shall most hardily comply. Now take leave of us. I wish to secure our arrangement with Dugar and Regor."

Master Leumas scrutinized all that had been said through his Anon Lap Recorder. There can be no mistake made against the ancient treaty, but he acknowledged a need for intervention. Dugar and Regor waited patiently as Master Leumas summarized their plan.

Madame Noir Tells All

Relaeh's Anon worked perfectly as he shuffled between moving walk-ways and elevators. The Endeavor propelled him into the depths of their sector, as if it knew he had a pending appointment with the most Delicate of Nalhs. The Endeavor stopped, the capsule rotated 180 degrees, and Relaeh stepped out, but this time to Madame Noir's private laboratory.

Madame Noir had been listening to the conversations from Master Leumas' chamber telepathically. She needed to hear what Relaeh's intent was regarding his mission. Her H-WAC chimed as Relaeh was let into a holding office. He was surprised that he could not walk directly into Madame Noir's lab. Madame Noir waited until the entry door closed and then Her private door hissed open.

"I am sorry for the inconvenience of the outer office but Leumas insisted on strict security."

"I believe him to have assumed correctly, Madame Noir."

"I know you have heard today of knowledge that is still digesting in your mind, but I do not want the state of affairs to interrupt your plans of discovery. How have we proceeded thus far?"

"I am in good control, Madame Noir. All arrangements have been met, the air machine has been secured, and provisions have been hidden from view. I just need directional indicators and a chart, as you said you would provide."

"Yes, good. Now, I query your dedication to your mission in light of what has transpired. Are you as dedicated to your mission of discovery, as Regor and

Dugar are in producing answers for the very few that solicited their aid?"

"I am as you say. I am fervently dedicated on my discoveries and what they may change or aid in developing our combined futures. But, if I am to believe by some intervention that I am expected to ignore the fate of these few for the good of all? Well, I cannot within my heart forsake those who have asked for help just for my own gratification. There will be time for my discoveries and possibly these few good people will help me on my trek."

"This is the answer I was hoping for. You have matured to be who you were meant to be. You are the *HEALER*. You are their Healer, their light to the future. I bow to you, Sir."

"Madame Noir, I don't understand."

"Please sit... many years ago I was an intern to the Din Master. He instructed me on the ways of the Engram. I was granted an interview with Leumas, and as we spoke, I realized that the Engram was created to re-introduce mankind to a safe environment, not to encapsulate them. We, as people, were diminished to a microscopic spot on a glass slide. Our DNA was transcribed into bits and bytes for computer analysis and then mixed and matched to form the behavioral patterns that the Engram perceived as worthy individuals, that is, if the world survived."

"Then what of the Nalhsians? They have ancient knowledge. They have generations still alive. They are not like the Topsiders."

"No, they are not, but they used to be. They were a faction that believed in the earth and that the earth would heal itself. They took refuge in underground silos and from there, they built the infrastructure that you see today. I have visions of a journal, which I believe now, was meant for your eyes... and mine. I know not where this journal resides but I am convinced you will be the one to find it."

"Am I a concoction of the Engram?"

"No, you are third generation, born of a mother named Tomei and of father called Nephels. My husband and I were their best friends. We tried to escape together with twelve other groups. We were the outcasts of Belcare. We were the *Nationalists 13*."

"How did you and I encounter Nalhs while others did not?"

"My husband had our baby in his arms as we all had to run like the wind to cross the sand fields. You had let go of your mother's hand to run free. A sand hole opened up and you fell through. I grabbed your hand and was pulled through with you. The next I remember is seeing a welcoming face telling me everything will be alright. I could not move."

"You saved my life, and I am the cause of your confinement to this apparatus and yet worse, to live without your own child to hold." Relaeh, without hesitation, dropped to his knees and wrapped his arms around Madame Noir. He held Her and he wept. "I have done you such injustice; words cannot describe my forlorn heart."

"This was not my intent of recounting the past and one that I feared would take place. You are of my heart as well. You need to be strong for us both. You need to be strong for the people you have inherited. This is your journey Trebor! You are the Healer, their Relaeh!"

"My name is, Trebor?"

"That is your given name at birth, but in all of our hearts, it is still Relaeh. Relaeh the Healer!"

"And of Master Leumas, he raised me, he taught me as his own. I perceived that Master Leumas was not my real father, but out of respect and probably the need for companionship, I imagined him to be."

"He is a good man. He is my savoir, our savior, and my friend. He is so proud when you call him Father."

"What shall be my course of action?" Relaeh paused, "I shall postpone my mission of discovery and lend a hand to Dugar and Regor for they may need a 'topsider' to direct their intentions. And of you, Madame Noir, what may I do for you?"

"Hold true to your heart of our conversation today. After you have pleased the intentions of Dugar and Regor, reset your mission of discovery... and for me, find knowledge of the whereabouts of my family."

"I would be honored, Madame Noir."

"And Relaeh, one other request..., could you call me Mom?"

"I would be flattered and it would give me great adulation to call you Mom, Mom."

"It is you now making my eyes water. I love you, my Son. Now go and see what mischief you can populate."

"Yes, Mom."

As Relaeh took leave of Madame Noir, his stepping was as if he was as tall as his friends. There were still many more questions, but in all good time. His revelation was internal and expandable, not like the Topsiders who were internally diminished by the Engram. He had to save his people!

Din1289 – A Dream

Din1289 awoke abruptly. His night clothes were dripping wet and his face was soddened with moisture.

"What... what, that cannot be? Children get back!" He shook his head and realized he had dreamt the second act of the unwritten children's play. In his awakened state, he proclaimed: "Why did they get up and leave? They crawled upon the ground as a hurt animal, searching for a safe haven to hide and wait to mend. This is not our teachings. We are no husbandry dedicated to inflicting foulness upon our flock! We must start again, for the young, so they may be satisfied of the endearment the Engram holds for them. We are not ready for pagan worships and contradictory ideals. We need to grow our populous in the manner that has been prescribed. We must adhere to the books' teachings and not delineate from them. Who knows better than I!

"We need stronger attendance at the revelations. We need of our fellow Belcarians to see and believe that their search for sanctuary is here, not beyond our walls.

"I will use this speech at the great hall. I will mesmerize them with my oratory insights. They too need to believe again and not just sit and nod their heads. We shall not succumb to an invasion of non-believers!"

John F Russo

Eittam's Premonition

The soft yellow-orange moon was nearly full, and there was another chasing it of almost identical circumference. Eittam had been awoken by a startling vision, which had uneased her. She put on a robe over her natural state and walked down to the dock. She stood at the edge where her father prepared the fishing nets. The sea was calm and the breeze reassuring. Her arms were crossed about her as she gazed into the night sky. A voice behind her broke the silence.

"My dear, why are you about at this early hour?"

She remained vigilant in her stance.

"Oh Father, I had another vision... a young man running in a field. The grass neared his waist but his stride was hard and with determination. His arms were well-formed and he pumped them with each stride as to add more wind to his back. I felt the anxiousness about him, but I could not make out his face."

"Was it Bocaj?"

"No Father... but similar in size... older, with a mature aura."

"Where was he running to, or was it from?"

"I believe to help. My images are getting cloudy, I cannot see anymore, I'm sorry, the vision has left me."

Leinad placed his arms about his daughter and comforted her. "Your mother had visions. She felt we had no choice but to leave Belcare to start fresh, no matter what the cost. Her life was our cost and my sorrow."

"But you had another woman, you had Aivila."

"Yes, that was out of convenience not love. We had to grow our clan. Her husband, her lover died trying to forge the great gorge. He was a good man. They never had children and she asked if I would sire a male for her. At last, my destiny was not to have a boy, but another girl, your sister Aivila. And to add to our existing grief, she died upon child birth. I believe in my heart she is happy. She gave birth, and then joined her true love."

"Father, I do not believe you are cheering me up."

"Eittam, I apologize. I long for your mother, and when I see you as you are, you are of her. You do make the sorrow lessen."

"Father, I love you and thank you for my sister. I shall try to get some sleep. I believe Bocaj, on his return, will have happier news for us. Good night, my Father."

"Good night, my daughter."

Master Leumas' Chambers

Relaeh sped towards Master Leumas' chambers as fast as he might and still managed to keep his feet on the ground. He shall not divulge what Madame Noir had spoken to him. This was not the time. There were more pressing issues at hand and he wanted to be part of the 'new' revelation. Master Leumas' H-WAC chimed almost as soon as Relaeh had reached the doorway.

"At what speed are you traveling, young man?"

"I came as soon as our meeting was over. I believe you have all reached an itinerary for developing the course of action but let me infuse my thoughts so as not to distract from your plan. I have decided to not pursue my discoveries until after we have secured safety for the six families and to help in any manner to correspond with the Belcarian men who are of difficulty. Let me be your eyes and ears to expedite your matrix for these men. I can conceal my image with disguise and be like a topsider, so as not to arouse any curiosity."

They all smiled and Dugar added, "Our dear friend, maybe we know you better than you know yourself. We knew you would not flatter yourself with your discoveries, knowing we could not accomplish this task without you."

"You are already implicated in our plans," stated Regor and then said, "We are family, my mutant topsider."

They all found the gaiety in this summation.

"First step Relaeh... you need to summon the friends of Salocin..."

"I apologize for this interruption, Father, but Dugar and Regor said that Einna and the women were going to attempt to escape from Belcare this very rising. In light of what is transpiring, we need for them to participate in the revelation, as their disappearance would arouse suspicion and possible collection. If we could delay their escape until at least the next rising, Dugar and Regor might have a matrix designed to minimize that warrior gene in the men."

"That is very plausible, my son, but what if this revelation develops the gene more, and they become violent?"

"We have no recourse, as there is no time for my friends to possibly obtain the knowledge with the revelation only two days from now. Salocin indicated that right after a revelation they are calmer, and then the madness intensifies as the days grow in between the revelation."

"That is true, Relaeh, you speak wisely. Did Madame Noir give you an elixir?" jovially asked Regor.

"She enlightened me, shall we say. Dugar, would you confess that the young intern of the Din Master was of my height and possible looks?"

"You could be disguised as such."

"Then I offer to you, my friends that I dress as he, with adornment about my eyes with a miniature Anon built in, and with your help, telepathically, we search for Einna. Father, is it possible to obtain a cloak as worn by the intern?"

"I believe I can arrange this for you."

"Good, then tomorrow's sun will take me topside and we will begin this quest."

"Relaeh..."

"Yes Father, I will fetch the sweets on the top shelf," interrupted Relaeh.

"Thank you, but my intent was to tell you, I love you as a Son."

Erodec and Missing Names

The night had slipped away from Erodec. He had planned to invite conversation from Atir that night, but thought otherwise. He also needed time to prepare his synopsis of that day. Rest was what inspired him now. The sun's light would highlight the intensity of his discoveries.

. . .

The light filtered through the slates of his window and shone with warmth on his eyes. Erodec was pleased that his chamber had natural light shining through. He hated drabness and wondered how Droenal could endure his occupation in his present surroundings. *When I become Din Master, I will move his office to the Androicropulous where the windows are grander and bright. And if he is closer, I will not have to lurk in the shadows to acquire information needed to maintain civility in Belcare.*

With his thoughts formulating, he quickly dressed in his usual robe, affixed his eye adornment and headed to Atir.

The sun warmed his back as he approached the Androicropulous. He paused for a moment as he gazed at the inscriptions surrounding the arched doorway leading inside. They all were different and he questioned the artists' motivation in structuring such profound images. He pushed on through the revolving doors and headed over to the rising platform. As he stood and waited for the platform doors to open, the Din Master stepped to his level from the floor below.

"Good will to you, Erodec. You must be out of wind to arrive here at this time."

"Good will to you as well, Din Master. Of what do you speak?"

"I thought I saw you moments ago crossing the fields at the festival tents, heading in opposite direction to where we stand."

"Forgive me, Din Master, but you must be mistaken. I have merely completed my journey from my chamber as we speak."

"I duly apologize for my assumption. The stress of this celebration must be clouding my mind and my eyes. And how does the challenge proceed?"

"I am delivering my findings to Atir this morning and shall consolidate these into an oratory form by our scheduled symposium."

"Well done, Erodec. I look forward to a stimulating debate. Good will to you."

"And to you, Din Master."

The door of the rising platform slid open and Erodec stepped inside. He pressed the button for Atir's floor. *What did he mean debate? Are we not solidifying the truth of the Engram? What collaborator may he discover from the floors below?*

Erodec arrived at the Councilman's floor. He walked to the end and tapped a peculiar knock upon his door. Atir opened it; this time his eyes danced with excitement.

"Good will to you, Erodec. Please step in."

"Thank you and good will to you as well, Councilman Atir."

"Do you have findings of notable remarks?"

"Yes... but first, I had a curious conversation with the Din Master moments ago in the grand hallway. He envisioned my person crossing the festival fields as I stood at the entry to the rising platform. He also mentioned a stimulating debate on my paper. Was this challenge not to enforce our teachings of the Engram?"

"Let us comment on your findings first. Have you news of any discrepancies that perchance would stimulate debate in the Council chambers?"

"I do have some incongruities that might spike debate. I have knowledge of approximately 130 numerical challenges, or possible disappearances, or merely incidentals that occurred two generations ago. I cannot ascertain names, as my source only has archives numerically. And, if we were to implement this conjecture, would we not be ridiculed?"

"What of the little girl?"

"Again, the source would be scrutinized as unreliable; as truth be told, I barely comprehended the words from her mouth."

"So as it stands we have not accomplished what the Din Master set as a challenge? Or have we? The Din Master set this as a hypothesis. Let us be bold and challenge him on the teachings. We can use your information on all three assumptions. The missing numerical variants, the misunderstandings of the little girl and, and most cleverly, the acquisition of a substandard creation. For what purpose could possibly be gained by the Engram for creating a mutant Belcarian? We could summon your sources and have them as witnesses to your findings. It does not matter if we prove misgivings as long as there remains doubt."

"But I have promised anonymity to my sources other than the mutant."

"Well, my friend, it is up to you to assume ridicule and lose position with the Councilmen."

Relaeh Disguised

The sun had lifted the shadow from its face and was beaming forth the energy to Belcare. Relaeh had emerged from the Portal and was heading towards the last known location of Einna. His cloak flowed with his swift movement across the festival fields and the tree lined boulevard. He emerged and then immersed between the parallel buildings and stopped short of the last brick. He peered right and then left. The yards were full of sun-soaked foliage and rows of overturned dirt. A figure knelt at one of the rows planting seed as the sun filtered through. He walked slowly and methodically, not to arouse suspicion, but with dedication as a councilman would in approaching a new constituent.

"Excuse me, madam. I am in search of Einna, wife of Salocin. Do you know her whereabouts?"

"Oh, Councilman you startled me. I believe she is in the outer field planting with some of the other women."

"Thank you. Will we see you at the Androicropulous in two risings of the sun?"

"Most certainly, Councilman. We enjoy the energy that our Engram delivers to us."

"And the festival, will you and your family partake in the frivolity that the Din Master has devised?"

"Oh yes, Councilman, we look forward to it."

"Good, I will look forward to our next meeting. Good will to you."

Flushed at having a conversation with a Councilman, she said in return, "Oh thank you, sir. Yes... I shall speak of you to my husband. Thank you, sir."

Relaeh set course to the direction indicated by the woman.

I have only been out here once. This is beneficial to re-acquaint myself with the surrounding area. Much has changed since I was a boy of fourteen. The trees have grown in size and some foliage has been replaced by corn fields. This will give me adequate coverage in a month's time, when the stalks will be of greater height and fuller to hide my air machine.

How can the councilmen wear these tunics? They are hot and choke my neck. I surmise they have need to dress differently than their fellow Belcarians. They are not supposedly endeared to infatuation, but we all know they crave veneration. So meaningless without benevolence!

Relaeh approached a cluster of women mingling underneath a fruit tree. Two small children were playing a short distance away.

"Good will, ladies," said the imposter, Relaeh.

As they looked towards the man who was wearing a tunic, they collectively answered, "Good will to you, Councilman."

"This day is ripe for your pickings, I perceive?"

"Yes, Councilman. May we help you search for something of importance?"

As Relaeh approached closer, Regor acknowledged that the woman known as Einna was standing to the left of four other women.

"May we be so bold and ask your intentions, good sir?"

"It is such a beautiful day I thought I would take a stroll and muster the fine women of Belcare to partake in the grand festivities that our Din Master has planned for the sixth rising."

"Is it not strange that one such as yourself should indulge in a personal invitation, and to come such a distance?"

"I have, as we all do, a concern for your welfare in participating at this festive revelation. I believe it is imperative that you and your families need to be recognized as true believers in the eyes of our Din Master. Your perception of me may raise concern, but your lack of presence might endanger future travel plans. As my colleague and friend, Regor mentioned, it is most important that your attendance be observed."

Einna stepped forward.

"Good, sir, you look as another, but I perceive a different persona." She approached even closer.

"Good, sir, you are conversing in riddles. We five women are as one belief, one that we hold true, as I believe you do."

Relaeh removed his shaded adornments.

"Oh my. . ." Einna dropped to her knees while the other women stood in awe. "You are The Healer!" The other ladies dropped to their knees as well.

"Please ladies, this is not my intent. Please get up so not to arouse anymore suspicion. I was unsure if all of you were of the same belief. I apologize for my garish introduction."

"No, sir, we beg your pardon on our limited perception. What is your will of us?" asked another lady, named Rajean.

"There has been an inquiry of magnitude that requires a need to reschedule your plans. We understand your commitment, but would advise to discard your journey until possibly the next revelation. We believe it is of grave importance that you be seen with your families, as you have done so in the past. And please instruct your children to remain as still as possible during the recovery session."

Einna replied to Relaeh's request and said, "If we reconsider our movement will it not add more risk as the seventh rising will not have the same impact as this coincidental mingling of the Twin Moons and the revelation? And what about Yuda? She is in her sixth month... would it not increase her chances of miscarriage during our exodus?"

"I do not see one among you, which you describe as been pregnant?"

"She works at the Reproduction and DNA Diagnostic Studies Office at the Androicropulous," replied Rajean.

"You will need to speak to her of this intent and one we will need to address when the time arrives. I suggest as the days progress that you search out suitable foliage as disguise as close to the rim loop as possible and stock them with your needs, a little at a time. We do not want to give way to suspicion. I have an extra Anon incorporated into this symbol for you."

Relaeh reached into his tunic and pulled out an unfamiliar device.

"This will keep us informed of your whereabouts and to be able to communicate with you."

Relaeh handed the device to Einna. Its round shape had four divisions: one solid spoke running top to bottom with two other spokes adjoining the center spoke from its outer ring. He illustrated to Einna and the other ladies on its use.

"It is very simple in its use. To converse, press the space on the left; to activate the visual accumulator in the center, press the right button; for emergency, use the bottom left. The bottom right is of no concern to your movement. I have designed it so you may adorn it about your neck. We will send a signal to it, which will warm your chest; if it is safe you may respond. If questioned about this adornment, say you bought it from a haberdasher at the festival. We will have multiple designs available, but without the activations. Do not show these activations to anyone including your husbands at this point in time. They will be informed as we get closer to the seventh rising."

"You are incurring great risk in coming to warn us. For that, we are truly grateful. My father whispered on his death bed of a figure dressed as a Grounder trying to enter the Androicropulous many moons ago. He promised me we would not be enslaved forever, but to wait patiently for a sign. Please forgive our impetuousness for not believing."

"And how did you realize I was the one? I, myself, have only recently been informed of my aspiration?"

"You walk with an aura of a man of destiny!"

"I shall hold true to my heart your loyalty and forsake any harm that may approach my body to bring about your freedom. This was afforded to me; I shall return it to you."

Relaeh Escapes Detection

Relaeh took leave of the women as they grouped together to eye the auspicious piece. Relaeh's intent was to find Salocin to procure DNA samples from him and his friends, which Regor and Dugar needed to start on a matrix to identify this abnormality.

"I shall be of more concern, as the mid-day hours will host discerning eyes," he telepathed Regor.

Relaeh slipped between the buildings on the back side of town where the glare of the mid-day sun produced little shadows. Moving quickly, he passed a flickering street lamp, where upon, a figure emerged from a doorway at the bottom of a stairwell.

As the figure turned, a flash of a tunic appeared in the corner of his eye. In haste, he stumbled on the first step, dropped his notes, and then scurried to reform. Reaching the top step, he hailed loudly, "Erodec!"

Relaeh turned down a tree lined boulevard, out of view and without response. This boulevard was one of the spokes that lead from the Androicropulous, to the south side of the festival tents. It was imperative that he sway among the flapping tents without detection.

There were many workers hammering stakes and drawing lines. There was only one more day before the revelation and the Sixth Rising of the Twin Moons. He needed to find the inflicted men quickly; his disguise would not support him much longer. Regor related to Relaeh that the grand platform was complete and not to investigate for Salocin at that location.

The sun had reached its peak and the warmth was bearing down. The collar was tightening like a noose around his neck. "Where am I to seek him out?" telepathed Relaeh.

Searching among the other decorated marquees, he noticed a man dropping down to his knees with his hands about his eyes. He approached, "My friend, are you in need?"

Regor informed him, *"That is not Salocin."* Relaeh dropped to one knee to comfort the man in need.

"Are you of ill health?"

The man raised his head. He had moisture about his eyes. "I fear my mind is playing unscrupulous tricks on me."

"Are you a friend of Salocin?"

"Yes, Councilman."

"I need to speak to you and Salocin, and your other friends who suffer from this infliction. Where may I find them?"

"Councilman, how do you know of such things?"

"I am not who I appear. I am a friend of your situation and we need to proceed immediately. Again sir, where may I find your colleagues?"

"Salocin is installing grates at one of the delight gazebos on the main thoroughfare. Three are hauling lines on the major exhibition pavilion and I know not of Taeman."

"As I do not know your other three friends, I implore you to summon them back to this tent, as I will go for Salocin. Lend me your smock and cap. Now go and hasten directly."

The festival grounds were in a state of flurry to make ready for the grand celebrations. Relaeh slipped easily in his new disguise among the many workers preparing for the event. There were many rows of *delight* gazebos lining the main thoroughfare, which Relaeh had to scan, each and every one, so Regor may identify Salocin. Midway down, he darted into a gazebo as he heard, "Erodec...Erodec, I finally caught up to you."

Erodec turned back towards the recognizable voice. "Droenal, good will to you. What do you mean?"

Relaeh started to re-adjust shelving already put in place as the two stood before him.

"I called you out moments ago as you passed by my office."

"I do not understand your intent. I have not been your way all day."

At that exact moment when their conversation formed in depth, Salocin entered the gazebo where Relaeh was re-adjusting the shelving.

"What are you doing man? I have already set these in place."

Regor instructed Relaeh that the man questioning him was Salocin. The two standing in conversation on the main thoroughfare paused in their conversation when they noticed indignation towards another.

"My good men, perhaps a mistake has transpired, but a calmer approach should justify a resolution. I know we are all excited to indulge in our forthcoming celebrations. Now place your hands together and resolve your issues," interjected Erodec.

As the men clasped hands, they bowed their heads towards the Councilman, acknowledging his prominence and words of wisdom.

"Now Droenal, of what do you accuse me?"

"Moments ago I hailed you but you did not respond."

"Trust me, my friend, as I pledge to you, this is the second time that I have been accused of being somewhere I have not. Who dares impersonate my being?"

As Droenal and Erodec were recounting of what had transpired, Relaeh drew Salocin near and whispered, "I am a friend of Regor, we need to converse with your other friends immediately."

Erodec noticed this whisper of reconciliation out of the corner of his eye and shared, "Good gentlemen, a resolution without indignation, Good will to you both."

Erodec and Droenal turned and slowly walked the thoroughfare towards the Androicropulous. Regor telepathed Relaeh on his 'topsider resolute'.

"We must return to the mid-tent where your friends will meet us."

"Who are you?"

"At this moment, that is of no concern. We need to take DNA samples for Regor and Dugar so they may design a matrix to help in your disadvantages."

Kire on Bocaj

Recording the past events, he wrote: We traveled to water's edge and found no discernible means of undermining the entrance to Belcare. The fish in the area stayed clear of the energy dome for at least 80 meters. Without our skinned canoes, we had no ulterior plan for observing the circumference of this impervious sphere. We did, however, indulge in a cleansing of our bodies. The water was fresh in temperature but not as reticent in our words as the great waters at Eureka.

Today, back in camp, we started assembling our supplies to make ready for tomorrow's embarkation to Belcare. We were told to be prepared, for when the sun sets and the moon rises that is the time to make haste. There was no exact time, as each revelation was based on this occurrence.

Our base had been set at 100 meters from the sphere hidden among trees and foliage. As we know not of edible fruits or animals for hunting in the sphere, we have stocked our supplies as necessary. Bocaj's intent is to make contact and befriend whom we might have encountered, and to take refuge in their huts out of view. We shall then peruse the village at night to summon those who wish to leave with us. I shall continue our findings and observations after we gain entry to the Belcarians' bubble.

Nalhs – Regor's Lab

Relaeh had managed to secure DNA samples of five men. It was getting too risky to find Taeman. There would have to be another attempt made after the revelation. Regor thought perchance, not securing Taeman's DNA might give comparisons in structure against the others on hand. The five would have been at the end of their enlightenment and their most vulnerable impact of the warrior gene. Taeman's would be at the beginning of the compression, with the most energy being absorbed by the gene from the revelation.

Regor was adjusting his Pleiotaxy Cohesion Traxor to analyze a known gene of relative normalness. Relaeh made the mistake of asking Regor what he was doing.

He explained, "After I analyze a responsive gene, I inject samples of the five for comparison, and then try to decode their genes to match that of this known sample. I call this Electromagnetic Parabolic Praxis. A procedure I created to delineate the pathogen causing separation along a curved digitized parabolic line of known value, whereby the separated gene stands parallel to its compounded isotope, allowing me to attach or detach electrical energy impulses in their altered state. I can apply as much energy as needed to any particle and observe the reaction for genetic mutation."

"Oh!" sighed Relaeh.

"The machine isolates my sample into points along my curved path, by which hereditary characteristics are separated from their chromosome structure, whereby I attach (cohesion) impulses and the Traxor records all value." Re-stated Regor, somewhat simplified.

"Right... I think I will converse with Dugar on what design we will implement to obtain samples of Taeman. Good luck with your, ummm, research."

Relaeh never thought he could have too much knowledge, but Regor had proved him wrong.

"I shall file that information in the back of my brain for my next stimulating conversation with Master Leumas. Unfortunately, he probably understands Regor."

Important Strategies

Relaeh knew Regor was very capable of solving whatever they needed to locate and reverse the mutant gene in those six men. He telepathed Dugar to conspire a plan; the next day at the Sixth Rising of the Twin Moons would be difficult to isolate anyone. Dugar agreed with Relaeh that it was imperative to facilitate plans as soon as possible and to meet him in his chambers.

I wonder, if the men were together as warriors, was it then their solidarity that brought the women together, and did they have previous knowledge of such unions? But, that would be impossible odds as they are all third generation. Could it have been the mutant gene that searched out each other and then band them together? If the latter is the case, Regor might find it impossible to isolate that gene. Or, could there have been human interaction that knew of the strain and acted sanctimoniously for their devise? Or even more plausible, if someone knew an uprising may transpire, then a military type force would be beneficial for their assumption?

Relaeh was pondering all possible scenarios as the rising elevator arrived at Dugar's deck. He did not take the moving walk-ways but decided hard surface would be quicker.

Dugar's H-WAC chimed as Relaeh approached. He stepped in.

"Good will, my friend. Please sit. Regor tells me you were curious of his work and then found it confusing."

"Yes, I am not adapted to that sort of science; although, I was developing ideas that might rouse the peculiar gene into perspective."

"What that might be?"

"Without sounding insensitive, would an alliance with a military force dictate a reason for someone to alter or relocate these mutant genes into vials for propagation as protection from an uprising? Why would six friends, close in age all possess the same strain if it were not for purpose?"

"I understand your theorization but from whom and why? There is peace here. There is no logical reason for a military force."

"I believe you are right, Dugar. It was a flash in my mind and not well thought out."

"Shall we continue with tomorrow's intention?"

"Yes, Dugar. I need a deviation from these absurd thoughts."

"I have obtained a program for tomorrow's festivities. It begins at mid-afternoon with a parade that will start on Conviction and 2nd, down 2nd Boulevard to Peace, surround the Androicropulous to 1st Boulevard, and then turn thus down the main thoroughfare culminating at the festival grounds. There will be children dancing to the Androicropulous' music; platforms will be pulled along the route with various enactments, preposterous figures prancing on each side, and a walking collage of the entire heritage of Belcare."

"You say preposterous figures... what may they be?"

"Most are taken from the children's *Speculant* story books. Birds with feathers scattered around, painted faces, shoes to fit a giant, my pants on you," jest Dugar.

"What? You do jest. I tell you truthfully, I had the chance to be of your size, but turned it down because I wanted my head closer to the ground and not in the air."

They both enjoyed the bantering back and forth.

"We have no image of Taeman unless he stands as one with Rajean. How are we to detect him?" asked Relaeh.

"Did you not give her an Anon?"

"No, I gave it to Einna but with all the activity, one does not know the situation of their person. Taeman could be separated from Rajean, one side to the other."

"They are with child. One of them must be near to encourage performance," suggested Dugar.

"When I met Einna, Rajean and the other ladies, there were two small children playing in close proximity. I cannot recount their faces but possibly their stature."

"You had an Anon direct you to Einna, as my brother confirmed her. Swipe your code into my H-WAC and we will replay your meeting with her and the others, and perhaps the Anon picked up on the child's image."

"And I do not understand why Regor remarks with such statements about you."

Again they enjoyed another jocular interaction. They scanned the meeting between Relaeh and the women, but only from a distance was the little girl's face partially highlighted. They tried enhancing her image; her golden hair hid her basic features.

"If I dress as I was, perchance the little girl would recognize me?"

"I believe you have out worn that tunic, as I perceived, from the disdain in the intern's voice. Your eminent collection would most undoubtedly be drawn."

"Yes, you are correct again, my friend. I will need to succumb to another disguise. You and Regor will be as dignitaries with Master Leumas; then I must perform as a preposterous creature. I shall take leave of you, my friend and work on a suitable character of disguise."

As soon as Relaeh took leave of Dugar's chambers, he inscribed this message on his Anon to Madame Noir: "I am in need of your direction as soon as possible, Mom." And before Relaeh could seize an elevator...

"You are cleared to my chambers. I await your presence," responded his Mother.

Home Economics

It took Relaeh a half an hour to arrive at Madame Noir's Chambers and during that time, he re-examined his ideas for disguise, as well as formatted the logistics for his next day's strategies.

I believe Regor determined to succeed in his endeavors and Dugar will be preoccupied with arranging all the air machines for the dignitaries. Master Leumas will be setting schedules for securing his fellow colleagues and possibly a speech to applaud Din1289's efforts for orchestrating such a fine event for the citizens of Belcare. It is of his style, although, I perceive that Master Leumas has a disdain for the Din Master. They do have a history; however, Master Leumas has not shared any judgments upon Din Master's character.

When Relaeh arrived at Madame Noir's chambers, Her H-WAC chimed to his perceived presences. He walked in and said, "Good will to you, Mother, I trust you are doing well?"

"Yes of course. What is your plight that I may assist you?"

"I am in need of Home Economics."

She chuckled, "Home Economics, Relaeh?"

"Yes Mom, I need to attach garments together for tomorrow's festival so I may go undetectable to anyone of authority."

"Oh, you need a sewing lesson?"

"If that is what you call it, then yes."

"Very well, what is your idea for a costume?"

"Costume, Mom? I need a disguise so my person can mingle among the citizens as I search for one of the six."

"Then a disguise it shall be. What is your intent on character?"

"I would like to color my face to look more like the Topsiders and possibly facial hair to hide my features. I shall need a white tunic large enough to stuff with padding and pants to match in color. I was thinking cylinders of red a meter long attached to the bottom of the pants and a tall hat of the same color. Upon my chest and back of the tunic I will cut out an eleven point board leaf of one of their indigenous trees, also in red from the same material."

"And why do you need the extra length of your pants?"

"I have an idea for *altitudinous* preposterousness."

"Very well, Relaeh. Let me teach you how to sew."

Revelation Day – Peace Symbol

The sunlight sifted through the trees and reflected off the insignia of the Androicropulous' golden beams so intensely that it appeared as if the sun was radiating from within. The crowds were gathering to mark their spot along the route of the parade. The vendors were laying their wares about the tables as the delights, with their sweet smells, were arranged in their baskets. Some citizens were milling around the haberdashers buying peculiar adornments as fast as they were placed on the tables. These adornments could be slipped over fingers, hung around your neck, sewed on tunics and bags, designed into multicolored garments, and as insignias on men's hats. Some thought it to be the foremost loop that surrounded the Androicropulous with 1st Boulevard, the main thoroughfare, ending at its entrance, with Boulevards 4th and 6th joining hands at the Grand Park.

One of the citizens asked the haberdasher, "Of what name shall we call this truly distinctive design celebrating this day's events?"

"I have been instructed if a name be desired, we shall call it *Peace*."

Not a more beautiful day could be welcomed. It was perfect.

Revelation Day – Last Minute Details

When the sun reached its apex directly overhead, the Din Master re-adjusted his sand-glass for a reference time to meet his fellow councilmen and the dignitaries of the ground at the stage that was now positioned to the left of the Androicropulous. He thought he would wear his red tunic, as not to be inharmonious with the other councilmen, but as his position should so be declared.

Master Leumas was scribbling the last notations for his benevolent speech of the Din Master regarding his unselfishness in devoting his valuable time to prepare this glorifying event.

Master Leumas mustered a chuckle, "That could be misconstrued in a variety of directions."

Dugar had the air machines in position to gather the Dignitaries of Nalhs and to transport them to the decorated platform. His commissionaires were in attendance to assist the elders in boarding and departing the air buses, and of general need that might arise. He had inquired to Relaeh of his whereabouts as they were nearing departure. Relaeh informed him he would leave from the Residence entrance rather than the Commercial docks, as he needed to blend in at the beginning of the parade. Regor had just arrived at the docks.

Revelation Day – The Parade

When the great doors of the Portal opened, Dugar and Regor positioned in the first air machine, lead the entourage of dignitaries down Conviction. Master Leumas sat comfortably in the back of the open cockpit enjoying the sites as they swished south on Conviction, past 3rd Boulevard and then right on 4th Boulevard to their final destination, the rear of the decorated platform.

Dugar positioned his air machine pointing opposite the direction of the stage. Closing his eyes, the machine leveled to the ground and the swishing abated; the other drivers followed suit. The commissionaires helped their elders while Dugar aided Master Leumas from the air machine, up the back stairs of the platform, to his designated seat. Dugar and Regor sat directly behind him. Master Leumas thought, *These seats are not as comfortable as Relaeh's mobility chairs*.

They all awaited the arrival of the Din Master.

The crowds had lined the streets and waited patiently for the parade to begin. Relaeh had secured his *preposterousness* by the time the Residence elevator opened its doors on street level. With his hat on, he had to bend at the waist to clear the door opening.

The participants were engaged in formation as if they were awaiting Relaeh's personage to appear. Other preposterous characters were inspiring the crowd. Relaeh joined their intent as the Din Master waved his arms like that of a conductor; the music introduced the beginning of the frivolity of the day.

It had been a decade since Relaeh had risen to such heights. He still had his balance and his legs were much stronger than as an adolescent. The crowds cheered as he passed by. He had no intent of adulation; his goal was to find Taeman. Luckily the platforms moved slowly. He was able to scrutinize each parent and child combination, and from his great height, he was able to peruse both sides of the moving platforms.

As the dancing children rounded the corner to Peace loop, Dugar's internal Anon scanned the dancers. He perceived no identification. Then the first platform appeared. He scanned one side but had to wait until the platform rounded the corner completely in order for him to have a clear access to the opposite side. Nothing. He telepathed Relaeh, *"Where are you? The first platform has already rounded the corner."*

"I am alongside the fourth platform and have not made any contact."

The second platform followed the first, and as it straightened out, Dugar scanned its darkened side. Nothing there either. A yellow dancing bird and a brown terrifying beast engaged in unnatural merriment as they lead the third platform. Relaeh quickened his step, and in doing so, he inspired the crowd. The dark side of the third platform revealed itself to Dugar.

"I've found her. Her aura is as previously scanned from your Anon at your meeting of the women. Quickly, her father is beside her wearing garments of a hunter."

Relaeh advanced his step but needed to cross to the dark side of the platform to make contact. The crowd cheered his joyful stepping as he resembled a crane hopping over lily pads. He caught up with the hunter in full view of the dignitaries' platform.

He called out, "Taeman?"

The little girl known as Eve recognized Relaeh's voice. She turned her head to her father and said, "Daddy, it is the Healer!"

Relaeh was perplexed on his discovery; he tumbled into Taeman.

The crowd hushed in anticipation as did the observers on the Councilmen's platform. Dugar stood straight up and telepathically inquired, *"Is that you as the tall man dressed in red and white?"*

"Not now, Dugar, I am a little predisposed."

The crowd encapsulated the two characters. The Din Master stepped to the oratoric enhancer and said, "Please citizens, give them air. Attend to their needs, carefully."

"We shall be in touch, Taeman, good will to you."

"And to you, sir, and thank you."

"For falling on you, making you bleed, or creating a display?"

"You know why, sir."

The crowd helped Relaeh to reform his costume without further incident.

"Erodec, see to the tall man's health when he rounds the Androicropulous. He is of splendid costume. I would like to ask his intent of such a civilized design. Our coincidence of color should afford him an audience. What do you say, Leumas? Is he not showing a gesture of commonwealth?"

"It is true, this design does inject more intent than a yellow bird."

"Sarcastically put, Master Leumas," telepathed Regor.

"Droenal, would you not say the tall man reflects well his impersonation?" said Erodec.

"I believe we may unmask his mystery soon," replied Droenal.

Fearing for his friend's discovery by the intern Erodec and his friend Droenal, Dugar spoke up. "I shall help you collect him, Erodec. He may be suffering from altitudinous discomfort with his head being so high in the air."

The three men took leave of the platform as the first moving platform rounded the back of the Androicropulous.

"Relaeh, you must de-mount from those vertical tubes as you pass the main stage. I will set the air machines to elevate as to cause a distraction. Hide as you need," telepathed Dugar.

"Shall we collect him on the loop as he passes 4th Boulevard?" asked Dugar of Erodec.

"Yes, he should be easy to hail, even with this crowd," replied Erodec.

As the three stepped out onto the Peace loop, the air machines rose and bumped into each other in a random pattern. The crowd reacted to the clumsiness of such machines and hailed in gaiety. Within a blink of an eye, Relaeh relinquished his vertical tubes and dropped beneath the main platform. As the third platform loomed discovery, the tall man was nowhere to be seen.

"What...? Where did he go?"

Erodec frantically started to look under the moving platform; he nudged the entertainers from their posts, but without luck.

"This impersonator has disappeared, again," he said.

"Did you see him?" questioned Erodec of Dugar.

"No, sir. I had to re-settle the air machines," replied Dugar.

"Droenal? What of you? Have you seen the tall man?"

"Nothing, as you," he said bewildered.

Frustrated, Erodec and Droenal headed back to the main stage.

"Did you collect our tall man?" inquired the Din Master.

"I am sorry, Din Master, but he seems to have vanished."

The Din Master broke out in laughter, "A man of such great height vanishes from plain sight! Maybe he lies on top of the moving platform in ill health from his fall?"

"I could not ascertain his whereabouts, Din Master." Erodec and Droenal shared inquisitive glances as three dignitaries from Nalhs sat, somewhat pompously, on their hard wooden chairs.

As the collage of Heritages, being the last group of festive display, dispersed among the many canopies of vendors and haberdashers, the last congratulatory words from Master Leumas could be heard throughout the festive park lands. "And last, but not least, we honor your Din Master regarding his unselfishness in devoting his valuable time to prepare this glorifying event."

The crowd responded with cheers and whistles as Leumas returned the oratoric enhancer over to Din1289.

The Din Master turned to Master Leumas, "Will you be staying for the revelation and for the Sixth Rising of the Twin Moons?"

"We shall be honored; a wondrous sight for both observations. We will amble down to the festival canopies, so as not to be a distraction to your citizens."

"Very well, Leumas, we will be gathering shortly as the sun is setting below the tree level. Our citizens will be enjoying much merriment after the revelation, I can assure you."

"We shall languish in the moment as well, Din Master."

"That is three double entendres today, Master Leumas, you are doing well," Regor recounted telepathically.

From under the main platform, Relaeh telepathed, *"Are you saying my Father, perchance, has an unknown career as a stage Maestro?"*

"His delivery is quite astute," jest Dugar.

"If you three do not unleash this conveyance, my sides will be in need of Madame Noir's stitching."

They all enjoyed a truly inside joke...

The Twin Moons

Everyone was in place of observation that needed to be for the Engram's compression. The synchronization of their recovery to the councilmen was impeccable. Belcare, for the moment, was unified.

. . .

The Din Master, Atir, Erodec and Droenal joined up with Master Leumas and the Twins. Relaeh hid from sight his tall man's disguise in the air machines and adorned another costume while the Belcarians were in their recovery session. No one was the wiser.

Relaeh hastened to meet up with his friends, but he stopped first to speak with Taeman, and little Eve. He bent down to her.

"Whisper in my ear if you know who I am."

She whispered, "Relaeh."

"You are correct. Now I want you to keep that a secret otherwise harm might come to me. Can you do that for me?"

"Yessss."

"Good, my sunshine."

He stood up. Taeman and Relaeh were in costume of the same hunting clan. As they approached the dignitaries a woman stepped to Erodec's side and hailed him.

"Good will to you again, Councilman. I instructed my husband of your gentle inquire and delightful gesture the other day."

Erodec and Droenal instantly crossed eyes. He withheld the desire to create a debate in front of the Din Master.

"Ah, good will to you again as well, madam. I trust you are enjoying the day?"

The woman almost froze on the spot but continued as she eyed the dignitaries, "Yes, yes we... we won't keep you from your duties."

"Then I bid you good will, madam."

Regor, Dugar and Master Leumas sensed a troubling moment for Erodec, but reveled in yet another mischievous encounter by Relaeh.

The Twin Moons rose with spectacular illumination as the crowd was awed by its magnificence. Their brilliance filled the face of Belcare. The trinkets about the necks of the citizens dazzled in their movement; shifting shimmering rays glistened upon every conceivable surface.

The children danced with delight as did the preposterous creatures of the parade. Everyone was feeling the luminescence of the moment; however, lurking in the cast of the deep shadows to the south, was the band of hunters from Inception.

Bocaj and his men had never witnessed these buildings of stone. Their height matched the great red trees of the south. They were in awe as they lost fear of discovery and wandered transfixed in a state of euphoria. They had sheathed their bows and arrows before they rounded the side of a massive structure. The opulent archway directly in the middle was adorned with sashes of color, and flickering light, and then, the noise of alternating pitches saturated their ears. The same sound as created, at times, by the string of their bows when an arrow was released true. And in the night's sky, two bluish moons shone so brilliantly you had to make your eyes as slits as not to burn them. No one seemed to bother with their presence.

Another clan of hunters came into sight and Bocaj thought it unusual for them to be without weapons. From where they stood, they witnessed two men, much taller than the rest with a pudgy older man by their side. *They are probably protectorates,* Bocaj thought. Another group had long coats; one was of red color, possibly the leader, as he seemed to lead the rest. When they approached a haberdasher's table, Bocaj noticed a familiar piece. He picked it up. A hunter from the other clan noticed and stepped to Bocaj's side and he commented.

"Do you like the symbol?"

He spoke with an air of influence but he dressed as they.

"Yes, my Father and his friend have one."

Relaeh detected an older inflection of his spoken language, *strange*...

"Really, they must have been here earlier as we do not have many left. Would you like one?"

"I'm afraid we do not carry wealth with us. We can offer a leg of meat or ripened berries."

The three Nalhsians picked up on Relaeh's wonderment.

"It seems we have the same preference in this refinement. Let me offer it to you as a gesture of good tidings."

"Gentle, sir... that would be a kindship indeed. Until we meet again I offer my forearm to yours." Bocaj instructed Relaeh on the grappling of friendship.

The night did not end without notice as the Din Master caught in sight, a passage of exchange between two men dressed as hunters. He had not witnessed such an exchange for over twenty legions. *Why now? Even if they were as one with the custom of character, they were not of age to recount this action.* The Din Master summoned Erodec to bear witness as he might find adulation from the council to his astute perception and determination in observing two men of unknown origin.

"I shall..."

"No Erodec, we shall not prejudice our moment of triumph at this time. Observe and trace their direction. The light of the day will expose their identity. Their whereabouts will be known only to our eyes, to be used as we may see fit."

"I shall do as you ask, Din Master."

Dugar and Regor watched interestingly.

Insights

As the night drew to a conclusion, Relaeh inquired to Salocin and Taeman, if he may walk with them and their families.

Bocaj and his men were mingling among the tents of vendors, but decide it would be prudent if they withdrew from the frivolities, so as to not draw any more attention to their persons. There were large groups of citizens still engrossed in merriment to conceal their departure.

Bocaj instructed his men in a whisper, "Let us take leave and observe as we pass of any stalkers. We have many questions to unravel of tonight's encounter."

Erodec and Droenal remained in the shadows of the foliage of the Grand Park.

Dugar and Regor informed Relaeh of their intent to transport the dignitaries back to Nalhs, and asked if they should leave an air machine for him.

The Twin Moons were high in the sky. The street lamps were unsure of their purpose as the luminance from above remained constant; only on the back boulevards hidden beneath the protection from the trees, had shadows appeared with any assurance of importance.

Relaeh and the two men conversed, while trailing their families stride. Relaeh started with idle chatter, "Please indulge my awkwardness, but if I may recite your family's tide. The family of Taeman, little Eve, and I believe, I have had the pleasure of meeting your wife, Rajean."

"Yes, that is correct. My daughter's given name is Evelyn Rose. But she is such a flowering petal that some get confused and call her Rose from the flower Taeman grows."

"Yuda, the one with child, her husband is...?

"Jacor," invited Taeman.

"And of course, Salocin and your wife Einna and your son's name?"

"Adam," informed Salocin.

"And where is Einna? She does not walk with us."

"She remains at one of the tents of delights. Did you partake in the sweet pleasures? She made them of her own accord."

"I did, they were delicious. I may transcribe a recipe to her that I encountered not long ago."

"She is always in search of refinements to her pastries."

"Taeman, you said Eve's given name is Evelyn?"

"Yes."

"Whereby did you conceive such a name?"

"My wife felt even as she grew inside of her that she deserved a name to bear witness to her birth as an enlightened soul. She sees and feels things differently than the rest of us, well that is except Adam," remarked Taeman.

"Adam is another enlightened soul, as you say?"

"Yes, I foretell that Adam and my daughter Evelyn Rose will someday aspire to greatness."

"Thank you for your indulgence. I have another to ask."

~

Einna had recently finished her collection of her sweet delights. In the distance towards the Androicropulous, two figures displayed themselves clearly to her, but to the direction of their stares, they were undetectable. She activated her visual accumulator and remained still. She watched while the two charged another position. Whatever they were concealing, or from whom they were being concealed, were no longer visible. They left their position in the shadows and strode on one of the Grand Park's pathways. She turned off her device.

Conspiracy Theory

The sun rose with another bright smile unaware of the underlings that transpired from the previous night. Erodec had awakened early and was already stepping through the hallway at Atir's domicile. He knocked upon Atir's door with his usual peculiar rhythm.

Atir answered, "One moment please." He quickly put a strange object in a bureau drawer underneath one of his tunics. He shuffled over to the door. "Good will, Erodec."

"Good will to you, Councilman Atir. I have some disclosures to inform you from our last day's events."

"Please, do come in and sit. Would you like some hot water and herbs?"

"Yes, Councilman Atir that would be very satisfactory."

"You sound concerned more than informative."

"Yes, the Din Master enticed me with adulation from the council if I pursue his wishes. But I believe his intent was not to flatter my person but to decompose my stature."

"Why is that?"

"From this challenge he has afforded me, I have read and re-read books T9 and T10 as instructed. I mean no disrespect to our beliefs, but if you remove a few repetitive phrases, and you were not a believer, you could construe these teachings to be of reverse to what we know as truth."

"Go on."

"Maybe, I am just confused, but over the last week there has been someone impersonating my person. As we stood on the Grand Park grounds last night, a woman approached me as if we had a conversation, of which I have no memory. I smiled and nodded as in acknowledgement, but I could tell in her face, whom she assumed was me, was not who she recognized. She bid her farewell and left."

"Is there more for your concern?"

"Yes, I already spoke to you of our Din Master's misconception of seeing me elsewhere, and then, my friend Droenal said he hailed me passing by his office, which was in the opposite direction to where I stood. I feel a conspiracy is upon me. For what, I know not. Last night as two men sported unusual greetings, the Din Master was most ecstatic on my witnessing this and suggested I follow their intent."

"And did you?"

"Droenal and I discussed this new enticement and agreed that as no discourse was evident we would just continue our stroll through the park. There were personages of many costumes and to become suspicious of one small group as they sauntered with no care of collection seemed not foolish, and I mean no disrespect, but paranoid."

"But you recounted of someone impersonating you. Is that not being paranoid?"

"I believe it is the orchestration of the Din Master to unnerve me before we gather to disclose our findings from this challenge."

"That is a strong accusation you say, especially from such a respected man. How will you proceed to procure evidence to support these theories?"

"I do not know. That is why I petition you for construction of influence that I might direct my energy."

"I see. So what will you tell the Din Master on your noncompliance in following the strangers?"

"I will say, that when we rounded the Androicropulous they vanished, just like the tall man, yesterday. Maybe there is a black hole all of these aberrations slip through."

"I apologize for my lightheartedness, but I do not believe the Din Master will accept a black hole theory."

Erodec visualized the humor as well in his last statement. They gathered cups and drew hot water and herbs.

A Humorous Retrospect

The twins and Relaeh had a restful sleep, but now it was time to get down to work. They had all gathered in Master Leumas' chamber and were enjoying a recount of the festive day. Dugar and Regor were reminiscing of watching Relaeh, claving with his vertical tubes strapped to his legs, stirring the citizens to heightened merriment and dropping as a languish bird from the sky upon his prey. Master Leumas was once again holding his broad stomach from the humorous depiction, while Dugar illustrated Relaeh's awkward collapse upon Taeman.

"You may jest but I had no option. The little girl, Eve, recognized my voice and gave me up," retorted Relaeh in his defense. "I had to do something. We were approaching the main stage."

Regor spoke with moisture running from his eyes, "My friend, we could barely contain ourselves, and the Din Master could only think about how coincidental it was that you both had red in your disguise."

"It was coincidental. In my defense, I had no preconceived knowledge of his choice of garment."

"And then the Din Master asked Master Leumas of his impression, and I quote, "It is true, this design does inject more intent than a yellow bird."

"Yes, well perhaps the disguise was a little garish, but I had no intent of being a yellow bird as Dugar implied. It served its purpose."

"That it did, my son, and many years of jocularity as well. I shall dry my eyes and then let us continue on today's business. Regor how goes the research?"

"I have not been able to isolate the gene as we speak. My algorithms have been working all night to find the common denominator. As soon as it transfixes onto one we will then, perhaps be able to restrain it."

"Very good, we look for an answer soon. Dugar, what of you?"

"I have located the coordinates of our unknown guests. I recorded their aura as Relaeh was in conversation with them. I tried to trichotomize this information to establish past or present growth stems, but unfortunately Relaeh's aura must be of stronger amplification, which interfered with my results."

"What do you mean, Dugar?"

"There was very little difference in temperature values thus rendering the experiment unacceptable."

"Do you not recount the experiment we did at the university with you and Regor?"

"Yes, but we are twins so our heightened heat index would be accounted for. We still had separate emanations that established our different identities."

"Perhaps if we encounter them again, we can solidify a truer value for you to run the tests again."

"As you wish, Master Leumas."

"Now tall man, what do you have in your hollow legs?"

"Father, I shall manufacture an announcement of your change in careers, and that you will be available for unions and other discreet avenues for whimsical pleasure."

"Haha! You honor me with what I know very little, but I am enjoying your precipitous innuendoes as always."

"I meant no disrespect..."

"None perceived, my son."

"As you all perceived my intent yesterday as flirtatious, it was not. Regor has Taeman's sample; my contact with the young hunter was extra ordinary. I did sense strangeness, like a shadow drifting over me when we spoke. He mentioned his father and a friend had one of the Peace Anons, which in itself is not strange, but it was the way he recounted as a past vision, and the grasping of the symbol in his hand. We have had these communication devices for generations, and I know not of one citizen of Belcare who is in possession of one. So are they an aberration caused by the twin moons rising, I think not. I do not believe in creatures from the past rising in our present. I also had words with Taeman and Salocin and asked them to heed the words of their wives, as we will be in contact with them."

"You are of determination, my son, and I applaud you. I shall add this to our discoveries. I have learned of turmoil in the ranks of the councilmen. I know it gave you great pleasure, Relaeh, outwitting the intern; although, I have come to believe he might be at risk. He will need some guidance but I believe a figure that will help our cause in the future, not hinder it. He will be put on display by his Din Master in front of the council. We will wait and see the outcome. Now, as for the aberrations, I believe they are from the free world, the world beyond this dome. Relaeh, he could be an ally when you depart on your discoveries. Keep that in mind. The question is, should we attempt to make contact or should we sow the seed into our six families to ascertain their intent?"

"What if they have the same warrior gene as the ones we are testing? Putting them together could combine their

125

resources and then incite a need for the Nalhsians to defend Belcare," conjured Regor.

"I do not believe that theory, my friend. I realize we had a short introduction, but they seemed more inquisitive of what was going on around them, not to capture for spoils. One of them carried paper displaying drawings, I presume, he imagined from sight. That is not a warrior."

"Very good observation, Relaeh."

"I agree, Master Leumas. I replayed my Anon last night and it is as Relaeh says, the drawings were in his sack."

"Then what should we conclude from their arrival? Let me pass this on to you. How did they know the schedule of the revelation to pass through the energy field?"

Bocaj Inside the Dome

Bocaj and his men were well hidden in the foliage of the southern rim. They had remained awake, recounting their experiences and impressions that very night. Sleep finally came to them as the twin moons passed overhead and out of sight behind the trees. The morning light brought renewed energy and purpose.

The men organized themselves as they did each morning, sitting around a small fire to heat water, and sharing a morning bite before embarking on strategies.

Kire was very excited to share his observations.

"The colors are so distorted from what is on the outside. Even now, as I peer upwards the trees have a blue cast to them, not green as ours. Do you think they believe this to be of true value?"

"I do not know, Kire. I would assume if they know not of the real world, then this world is true to them. And what of the imposter hunter? What say you, Micja? Is he true in spirit?"

"I believe as we are sitting here, he is as he says."

"I agree," interjected Kire. "His eyes are as true as yours, Bocaj. If I would disregard your forehead and mouth, and peer into your eyes only, you would be as close as one as I have seen."

"And what of the other hunters? I watched as they all disappeared on the other side of the curved building. Do you believe they would be choice of contact?" asked Micja.

"I believe we need to conceal our whereabouts for a few days. Perhaps at night under guise of shadow should we venture into areas that might deem useful to us. Did any of you observe their tradition of garments? If we remain as we are, I believe we will give our identities as true and then what would perchance of us then?" shared Bocaj.

One of the other hunters spoke up, "I have noticed no tracks along the rim of this dome. If we stay as close as possible to its side, we shall fair well. I believe they are in fear of the dome, so they stay clear of its energy."

"Well spoken, Retu. You are a wise hunter," acknowledged Bocaj.

Their smoke from the fire dissipated within the trees. They were well versed on survival in the forest and of not foretelling their whereabouts.

127

Council Appointees

The Din Master had outlined in a memo to his cadre before the fifth revelation that the city was in need of the appointment of three men to unrelated positions, as their clan had grown and now necessity was upon them. He listed his recommendations, but if the councilmen had others in mind, they had their free will to nominate them in the voting process. None had been added.

Salocin was chosen as the municipal official that would handle all departments of construction and damage control for Belcare. One of his duties was to procure and install the constant visual aids throughout the city to maintain compression for his fellow Belcarians. Today, he and his fellow workmen were occupied with dismantling all of the festival provisions. Each must be categorized, charted, and stacked in a systematic order for future celebrations in the south warehouses along Serenity. It was a demanding process, as care was essential in handling some of the more delicate floral exhibits that must be returned to the Arboretum and Taeman.

Taeman was given the chief botanist declaration. This appointed position promoted the continual support by the council to increase the awareness of the Engram's support for the beautification of Belcare. With his appointment came the consulting on the establishment of the grand gardens along the west rim. The proximity of the main gardens to his laboratory was a short westward stroll along the outer loop. He enjoyed his office space as his south windows overlooked the serenity of the forest.

Jacor secured the title Material Manager, whose offices were located next door to his friend Taeman and within the same building as Salocin. He was one of the few Belcarians that had direct interaction to the reclamation, handling and storage of goods, created by the Nalhsians for the Belcarians. His complex work required him to fill all material deficiencies that effected the growth of Belcare as set out in Book T4. He was very thankful to the councilmen for this position.

As the three friends worked in close proximity to each other, they often shared mid-day meals at the rear of Salocin's office, on the deck that he had built for such occasions. They all enjoyed the quiet and isolation that it provided. Each of the appointees had been given associates to work closely with them.

The irony, that all six men were good friends went without notice.

Once in a while, the women left the fields to accompany their husbands in mid-day festivities.

Madame Noir and Master Leumas Conspire

The previous days had brought many questions that needed to be answered. Master Leumas was in Madame Noir's chamber reiterating the contents of what had transpired that might have been out of Her telepathic range. She had already processed the conversations that all four had in Master Leumas' chamber, but thanked Master Leumas for his concern. Master Leumas had sent Her Dugar's reproduction from his Anon of Relaeh's folly, which they both enjoyed watching together. Decisions, although, had to be made.

"Leumas, you believe our visitors are from beyond this dome?"

"Yes, and I believe that they might be off-spring from your clan."

"Why do you believe so?" She asked eagerly.

"Relaeh mentioned that when he spoke to the leader, he seem to recognize the Peace ornament. He spoke of one such piece with warm regard. I believe when we were first introduced, you were as an intern, that I gave you such pieces, unfortunately of weaker significance, and asked that your men hold them true to their hearts."

"I am sorry, Leumas; it has been what seems three lifetimes ago. I completely forgot that transaction. Oh my! Do you believe they could be of my clan?"

"I cannot foretell any other possibility. And Relaeh also mentioned a strange shadow that he felt encase his body when the two spoke. He is becoming more sensitive to abnormalities as he gets stronger in his intent. He is the one that developed the plan we witnessed, and I might add, with no regard for his own safety."

"He is coming of age. His enlightenment will be well embraced by others, for that I am certain and proud."

"I believe that as well, Noir."

"How shall we proceed with our guests, Leumas? Shall we gather them here in Nalhs? I could introduce myself to evoke a response."

"I suggested to the lads that they sew a seed with the women of interest and let them initiate first contact. Until Regor develops a counter active gene, or is able to isolate it, our contact should remain limited. The woman, Einna, has an Anon symbol, so she will be able to stay in contact with us. We all agree that the visitors do not present a risk of intent to harm. Now, one other concern at hand is Erodec, the young intern. He has been given a challenge to uphold the teachings of the Engram with both positive and negative ramifications. He has uncovered several discrepancies in the biological makeup of some of Belcare's citizens. Should we introduce more evidence for his theories, or let him flounder?"

"I heard you speak in favor of the intern with his possible alliance to our quest, but without trial there cannot be any reward. He is still only reporting facts and has not yet digested the reality of these abstractions. If you agree, let us endure along with him; we shall be there, if need be, to raise him up and fortify his convictions."

"You are wise as always, Noir."

"Not always, if I would have known Relaeh's heart, I would have introduced myself much earlier."

"You cannot speak as such. It was meant to be as designed. It has given him a determination more than I thought possible at his age. You have inspired a boy, who now walks as a man."

"Leumas, my friend, you are too kind."

"I only speak the truth. I shall take leave and gather the boys to ready for engagement into unique situations."

"Leumas, let me know as you do, if our visitors are from my clan. My heart aches for knowledge of their situation and whereabouts."

"I shall without hesitation, Madame."

John F Russo

Possible Suitors

Leinad's hut was sparse in content but surrounding him were objects of truth that endeared his convictions. A thick journal with tattered pages, read daily long ago to his children, laid comfortably on his table top. Another object adorned the head of his bed. A crimson sash hung with conviction cradling a circular artifact. His nightly ritual centered upon this symbol, as testimony to his lost love. His longing, anguished with the pain of loss, had suffocated his dreams of happiness, to witness, night after night the vision of the sands devouring its prey. His only consolation was the truth of heart of his daughters Eittam and Aivila. They alone, each morning, resurrected his spirits so he could govern as a man of integrity, of wisdom, and of fairness. Most of his officiating had been concerned with growth of the community, rather than civil disappointments. His respect had been earned through hard work and devotion to his people. The truth was... he was loved by all.

Eittam and Aivila were involved in preparing their morning delights when Leinad entered the chamber of fire. The air filled with the smell of pleasantries as Aivila pulled fresh baked pastries from the brick oven.

"My dear daughters, you harvest a smell that will challenge your suitor's convictions for eternity."

"Here, Father, some fresh picked berries to adorn your pastries. I fear our suitors will not pass your judgment lightly," jest Eittam.

"And what of my Bocaj? He most certainly will be honored in our home. Correct, Father?"

"You speak as if the boy has already gazed upon your eyes. The last we spoke it was *your* intent. I will have to offer him consulting to prepare him for you. I am afraid his journey will not gain him enough experience for your dealings," laughed Leinad.

"Father, if my insolence is of age, then I suggest to you that when I lock him into my loins, I shall insist upon him if he would like to speak to you, he shall never return," retorted Aivila.

"Ahahah, and that is what I speak of, my daughter. I trust Bocaj will have to be a man of strong will to suffer your insolence."

"Father, we all share certain heartiness in our desires. We only have you to thank for that," slyly inferred Eittam.

"Then I shall require heirs of such precipitous manner as you," indulged Leinad.

"I believe Aivila will harness Bocaj, but I feel no such certainty for my fate."

"It is conceivable that your heart will travel from here, Eittam. Maybe it is the runner in your dream?"

"If he is made of solid stature and not just an aberration, I would consider such gazing. I shall change our direction of thought; I had a feeling that Bocaj and his men were safe and have entered the domed city. I feel great power from within."

"We can only hope good speed to him and his men and that they find what they must to harness this need of discovery. They belong here to help in the construction of Inception," interjected Leinad.

"I believe he will endow us with great wealth, Father," imparted a spiritual, Eittam.

Plan for Garments of Taste

Master Leumas had instructed the boys to join him in his chamber. Regor had excused himself as he believed he had isolated the warrior gene. Dugar and Relaeh waited patiently for Master Leumas to adjust his notes from his earlier conversation with Madame Noir.

"Lads, Madame Noir and I have conferred on the direction we are bound to investigate. We shall, at the moment, leave Erodec to his fate with his councilmen. His ideals will not be alone, so if recovery is pending, we shall quickly booster his opinion.

"We also believe that the women of interest should initiate contact with the visitors. In truth, at the present, there appears to be no threat to their person, so we need to devise a plan to first, to secure the visitors whereabouts, and second, quench any desire to question anything more than they have already done or seen. The visitors will need garments of similar fashionable taste, much like exhibited by the Belcarians. We can introduce these with the weekly freight to Belcare and address them to a vacant warehouse where we will instruct Einna to distribute the garments to them."

"My Father, if we arrange this distribution and scheme in your fashion would it not seem fabricated and then alert the visitors to some possible harm?"

"What would be your plan, Relaeh?"

"If we, as you say, arrange shipment to the warehouse, but let the visitors ask Einna of where they might invite garments of the citizen's taste. Einna could inform them that they would gather garments from their husbands and place them at the warehouse for their use.

If the leader is as calm as he seems, he will not detect treachery from us. All we need to do is have the women in a pretend state of gathering fruits from trees near their location. I believe the men will contact them without the fear that they have been discovered."

"And how, my son, have I taught you such movements of espionage?"

"He has always possessed a mind of twisted and bent state," taunted Dugar in a sly manner.

"Father, it is not all me, I have had help in the art of secrecy and placing a veil over one's eyes, I should say."

"That is what is called touché," remarked Master Leumas.

"I did study the ancient art of swordsmanship, Father."

"We did not play with ease as children, Master. Relaeh was a very proficient adversary even with his stunted growth," jibed Dugar.

"We learnt many arts of self-defense at the academy, of which Dugar is in need as we speak," laughed Relaeh.

"Do you two ever have a conversation without jesting so irrepressibly?" asked Master Leumas.

"We try not to, Master. It is part of our love for each other," insisted Dugar.

Dugar placed his arms about Relaeh and hoisted him from the ground.

"Put me down, you over stuffed Nalhsian."

"Children, you need to converse with Einna, as we have no prediction of what the intent of the visitors are?"

"Yes, Father, we will inform her of our conversation and her need to remain innocent of any implied treachery.

135

As you remarked before, the visitors could be the citizen's facilitators in abandoning Belcare for their own discoveries."

The two boys took leave of Master Leumas' chamber. They headed to Relaeh's chamber to transmit an energy tone to Einna.

The Haldon and the Growing Populace

The Haldon was a unique piece of equipment designed by the Nalhsians for communication between the citizens of Belcare. It was gifted after the fifth revelation, as a prelude to the upcoming festival of the twin moons. It was presented to every household of Belcare and to government offices for use in their everyday communication, whether conducting business or for personal use. Din1289 opposed this Nalhsian technology, as he felt it would undermine the authority of the council, and the purveyance of such, could lead to idol worship. In passing of the vote in favor, the council, led by Atir, deemed it essential to further develop the forward growth of Belcare. The citizens were able to easily insert their needs to the Office of the Material Manager without the bothersome need of vouchers. This made Salocin happy, as his job became much easier, to not have to collect paper or create the waste that the old system demanded. The Haldon was also more responsive to the associated needs of the people. Salocin thought that maybe one day there could be portable units that people could carry with their person.

As Belcare was growing in population, their deficiencies became more recognizable. As more of the fourth generation was being procreated between man and woman, and not of artificial insemination from the Engram, healthcare was the topic women spoke of most often. It was true the Nalhsians did operate a clinic for minor accidents; but with respect, the women of Belcare believed they needed to rally in support of larger care units in front of the council. This also displeased Din1289, as now they were inferring the council was not devoting their resourcefulness to the reality of the wishes of the people. Din1289 thought that this had the potential of being a thorn in his side, but he reveled in the security of the compressions brought forth by the Engram.

Din1289 knew it was a mistake to introduce procreation by the people. There was much less unrest nearing the revelations as now; and with some fourth generation off-spring not containing the Engram strain, his desire for encapsulation would need to be greatly increased to maintain control. His immediacy to inform the council of his concerns could coincide with Erodec's findings, and with this support, the possible collection of these rousers, which if injected with the Engram's sensibility, would maintain the benevolence of Belcare.

Two more passings of the Sun and we will have our debate, thought Din1289. *My opponent's opinions shall coincide with our teachings or else he will feel the engagement of his own demise.*

Intent of Sports Field

The midday sun had brought pleasure to the six friends of Belcare who were sitting upon the structure built by Salocin. They enjoyed the casual conversations and the camaraderie that was afforded to them by the council. They often spoke of the pleasant meeting they had in the council chambers, partaking in warm water and herbs and delicacies provided by the Din Master, as he enlightened them of future appointments for the integral operations that needed to be set in place.

They strived to recount their friendships as they grew from adolescents to manhood, but could not quite conceive any relevant images of such events. Nonetheless, they felt their friendships would endure all passages. With the introduction of the Haldon, every indication was prospering for the future of Belcare. The community as a whole could revel as one. There was no need to relate stories from one to another verbally as such truths underwent misrepresentation by the ending of its telling. Now they instructed, matter-of-factly, the correct interpretation instantaneously. What a marvel, indeed.

As they were sitting enjoying the day, Taeman, encountered an idea. "My friends, give me reason why a sports field north of the city, say in between 1st and 2nd, in the forest adjoining the North Gorge, could not be constructed. I can handle the materials, Taeman can introduce plants and other foliage of color and Salocin can approve the construction?"

"That is a splendid idea! I believe the council would consider it as an asset to the well-being of its citizens. Although, if my memory serves me correctly, I believe that location has been allocated for future home sites, but the forest just to our left between 4th and 3rd, could be a suitable choice," remarked Salocin.

"We could meticulously separate the underbrush from trees of maturity, and then use the trees to assist in construction and benefit from the discard by fabrication of furniture. We could seed a new strain of plants we have been cultivating called *Tulips*. They are very colorful and would form well as dividers along pathways," infused Taeman. "How shall we proceed?"

"I will instruct council of our plan today in hopes of gaining support, and then, purpose the beginning to be within the rising of the next full moon," stated Salocin.

The men all gathered around to visualize their ingenious idea for the health and well care of the citizens.

Divergence

Master Leumas sat perplexed; he searched his mind as if an answer was waiting to be discovered.

There has to be a logical sequence that we can follow without seeming as if we are delaying our duty to the Belcarians.

He tapped his Anon to inform Relaeh and Dugar of a closed session on recent developments. He was confident that Relaeh and Dugar possessed the cognizance for this type of interference without perception of intentional repugnancy. They responded with astute diligence.

Master Leumas' H-WAC chimed as the boys hustled to Master Leumas' devotion.

"Good will to you, Father," announced Relaeh.

"Good will to you, Master Leumas," affirmed Dugar.

"And good will to you both."

"Of what purpose shall we devote our attention, Master Leumas?"

"Sit, please. These Belcarians are an interesting clan, no doubt. I have learnt of a community plan to develop a sports field in the south by southeast sector of Serenity Boulevard. They have requested a bladed *digger* to level the field and another to remove trees from their proposed area. I generally am not involved with this type of request, but the location precipitates our action. As described by Dugar, our guests have concealed themselves on this very track of land for redevelopment. If we allow this request to be exchanged through the normal channels, I fear our guests will be exposed before we have concluded our business."

"What do you propose, Father?"

"Well, that is the reason I have summoned you two. Your minds work in a direction I have no concept of."

"I believe that is a compliment, is it not?" smiled Relaeh.

"Of course," chuckled Master Leumas, and then he said seriously, "We need to delay the acquisition of such equipment, so we may inform the visitors of their need of re-location without it coming from us. That is the best intent as I can relay."

The boys smiled with delight as Master Leumas again was in need of rescue. The boys pondered the situation.

Relaeh spoke up first.

"I do believe the women have not made contact as yet. We could instruct them of this revelation, and hasten their delivery of the garments to the warehouse."

"Perchance," questioned Dugar, "could we not deliver garments of workmen, thus protecting their identity with implied garments, but also offer work for further disguise? This could infuse them into society without notice."

"Dugar, you are learning something from me. Let me add... if Dugar, since he has privilege of their identity, attends a preliminary meeting of the contractors of the council..."

"And we previously inform Einna to our intent...," interrupted Dugar.

Master Leumas shared his opinion before Dugar could finish, "We cannot seemingly be involved with such treachery."

"Indulge me, Father; I see where Dugar is going. We send Dugar as the Nalhsian representative for structural reformation. It could be his choice to ascertain certain workmen, who he believes have endurance and integrity to accomplish what the contractors required. He is not instigating revolution, but testifying of what we believe of their fortitude to have had the ability to navigate the energy dome."

"We have the ability to announce over their Haldon, the recruitment of such resourceful men to accomplish the desire of the council. We know very well there are few men of this stature in Belcare," declared Dugar.

"Let me summarize, my Father; you have a perplexing look upon your face. First, we send a note to the contractor of this project of an impending meeting. This will slow the requisition for machinery. Second, we inform Einna that there is a whisper of intent of construction near the visitor's hide out and that the women have devised a plan to keep the visitors' identity secret and a way to observe Belcare in safety."

"I agree with the first intent but why would Einna want to help these men she just met?" questioned Master Leumas.

"You speak the truth, Father, let us revise this plan. We send the note to the contractor; we go back to the original plan of their haphazard meeting in the forest. We let Einna be the judge of character and possible intent of the visitors. We shall be able to monitor their conversations via her Anon. If she believes in their righteousness, she may inform them of the women's intent on exiting Belcare and summon their help. The voluntary placement of workmen's garments could still transpire if that direction of thought did not unfold. Dugar, after the meeting, could suggest his ability to announce recruitment of workmen of capable substance over their Haldon, and then establish a work camp or residence in one of the vacant warehouses next to the site. Einna could then re-contact the visitors of this opportunity."

"That sounds more plausible, my son," said Master Leumas with a lamenting tone.

"Father, how did you become privy of this information? Would not the Din Master have to sanction this endeavor?"

"The Din Master is above this type of Belcarian community interaction. Let us say an old ally remains constant with relative news of the goings-on of the council. Not more can I divulge at this time."

"Are you saying you have a spy in place on the council?" suggested Relaeh.

"You might infer that, I cannot possibly comment on the accuracy of your assumptions."

Dugar and Relaeh enjoyed a moment of merriment with Master Leumas' comment.

"Then, Master Leumas, how have we become privy of this information without divulging your source?" asked Dugar.

"Once council has approved the construction plan, a requisition for materials and machinery will be submitted from their material manager to our liaison. He or she will submit that form to our central council for allocation. And then, I am afraid your device must take over," insisted Master Leumas.

"Dugar, did you not have an internship on the Engineering board?" asked Relaeh, very well knowing the answer. "And for the Belcarians to proceed they will need to consult with our Engineers on electrical, wastage and water consumption."

"Yes, go on," replied Dugar.

"Your friend, that you occasionally gaze upon her eyes; is she not an Engineer and sits on that Board?"

"I see where your twisted mind has alluded to," lightheartedly replied Dugar. "You want me to use my influence on the woman of my dreams for your needs?"

"Not my needs, my friend, she is too tall for me," laughed Relaeh.

"There you two go again..." scolded Master Leumas, but with a hint of shine in his eyes.

"I shall discuss this with Ruvana," invited Dugar.

"There, Father, all is solved. I shall instruct Einna of our deception."

"You never seem to disappoint me. You always leave me in a state of awe..., I seem speechless," said Master Leumas.

"Father, I sense slight sarcasm in your speech."

The Ladies Chance Meeting with Bocaj

The men of Inception had kept to their word of staying out of sight, but they were starting to get a little wanderlust. They were unable to do all their exploring at night and needed to replenish their supplies of berries and fruits. The day-light hours only afforded that luxury, so it was decided they would divide into three groups of two to lessen discovery. Retu took one man and traveled as close to the dome as possible; Micja took another and went straight through the center of the forest, while Bocaj and Kire ventured to the extreme right, which was the closest to detection.

They all were still under the guise of the forest and the overgrown foliage when Kire motioned to Bocaj of three large brick buildings to their right, where he saw some men sitting on a ground dock. Kire thought, maybe at an earlier time, the water level must have reached these buildings and precipitated the need to build such a dock. Then, upon the waters receding, the deposited soil remained, thus a dock also remained in such proximity to the ground. The docks in Inception sat above and stretched out into the water for a reason. He could not fathom another explanation. They slipped by without detection.

Retu's pathway was unencumbered by brush alongside the dome's growth ring. He had distorted vision through the dome; he could only identify the structures of large trees as everything else blended together. He thought they would be extremely visible to the citizens if one so chanced the wrath of the dome. If they moved quickly enough, they could take refuge among the side bushes to escape detection. They passed a large stretch of sand.

Micja and his counterpart went straight through the thick of bush and trees. They had to be very careful as to not create excessive noise that might alarm someone near. They were taking a great risk; one that a hunter did not consider lightly.

Mindful of detection, Retu approached the edge of the forest and the beginning of the gardens; he could not detect their position of insertion from the outer world. They had done well at concealing their entrance. Retu was respected for his acute sense of awareness. He was the eldest of the six men and had almost Bocaj's life plus half again in age over him. He knew he was not a leader as Bocaj, but his instincts prevailed well for establishing maneuvers.

Retu instructed his man to lay low as he scouted the open space between them and the fields of berries. It was clear. He motioned his man with two fingers pointing to his eyes to keep observant as they passed through to the berry bushes.

In front of Bocaj, the field ended with rise to orchards. Even Micja had the privilege of being hidden by the orchard on his path. Retu decided to go beyond the berry fields to the stalks of corn. They had experience in crushing the kernels into a powder and then making flats or using as a mash to support fruits and berries. He thought these gardens were well laid out and he felt safe moving slowly among the corn stalks.

Micja made an easy transition from forest to orchard, but his path was not as secured as he would have liked. They attempted to brush up the long grass at the forest's edge to conceal their passage; their prize awaited their picking.

Bocaj and Kire's route was still shrouded with heavy foliage. When they neared the orchard, their infiltration into it was smooth and without detection.

"Let us go deeper into the orchard," whispered Bocaj, "...we will be able to climb the limbs to pick from the top so the citizens will not notice our spoils."

The fruits were round, deep red, and tasted delicious. Bocaj thought of the pastries at the festival and immediately knew where their fruits had been harvested. His father, Nephets, had not spoken of such delicacies that abound inside the dome. He had a different perspective of the inner city than his father or even that of his uncle, Leinad. He had witnessed a calm collective society, free from any social order, and integrated with multiple skin color and facial characteristics unknown to his sight.

Since Kire had the position in the branches, Bocaj caught the fruits and stuffed them into their leather pouches. Bocaj was about to stuff another, when he flattened to the ground upon hearing voices from close proximity caught his ears. Kire, upon viewing Bocaj, remained motionless. The voices came closer. Detection was imminent, Bocaj had no recourse. He stood up proud and gave a bowing gesture. The ladies stopped with a gasp!

"My kind, ladies, we mean no disrespect to you or your orchard. We have come from afar and are in need of fruits for our salvation. We ask that you might so indulge us and we will take our leave."

"Kind sir, we perceive no ill harm to our person or our orchard. I have seen you before, at the festival I believe. Your costumes were in much delight of my husband," warmly noted Rajean.

"Was it your husband I had words with, madam?"

"No, he was another," replied Rajean.

"I gave you pastries," interjected Einna.

"Yes, madam, they were delicious, thank you for your kindness."

"You say you come from afar?" queried Einna.

"Yes, madam."

"How is that possible?" asked Rajean.

"With patience, my good ladies, with abundance of patience," proudly related Bocaj.

"When you say afar, you are not referring to the north side of Belcare?" inquisitively asked Einna.

"No, madam, we are from a land two full moons away."

"And you made this journey to our little society for what gain?" innocently queried Rajean.

Kire decided to descend from the top branches. He felt anxious towering over the ladies as they periodically viewed his station. Micja and his man remain crouched out of sight.

"We heard tales from an early age of this magnificent city of the north. We had to discover for ourselves the truth of these fables."

"And have you found your answers?"

"Not all, madam, but as you can see..." Bocaj gestured at his garments, "...we were not prepared for such influence and fear that our presence could be construed as other than our true intentions."

"Yes, you speak the truth. We only wear your attire during festive occasions, and I do believe a continuance of such fashion might instill a dilemma to your observations," stated Einna.

"May we suggest, kind sirs, a distraction from inquiring eyes? We could gather garments of more befitting a workman and deposit them at forest's edge," kindly enticed Rajean.

"The old warehouse, Rajean, has a dark cellar where they could exchange their garments without regard. If we lay them here, they may become of notice by chance, as we fell upon these gentlemen this day," said Einna, being of concern for their safety.

"Oh, Einna! You are of truth; we could gather the other ladies and each carry a piece of garment and drop them off on the way to take lunch with our husbands. We could hide them well in our satchels and then pick fruit on our return home," added Rajean.

"Good ladies, why would you risk such embarrassment for our need? We are but strangers," interjected Bocaj.

"We may have need of your knowledge, good sir, and your help," implied Einna. "Give us two risings of the sun to gather such things. And how many will there be?"

"There are six of us, madam. Madam, we hold true to our heart as we believe you will hold true to yours," Bocaj paused "Madam, this adornment about your neck..."

Einna, startled at his discovery, acknowledged a response, "Yes?"

"My Father has one, but of larger size as to fit a man's hand."

"You speak of warmth in your voice, good sir. May you rest your eyes upon it again," responded Einna.

The ladies retreated to the direction of their home, while Bocaj and Kire headed through the orchard to where Micja had been in hiding. They all headed to the outer boundary and disappeared in the forest.

Einna felt a warm tingle upon her chest. She pressed a button.

"*Ladies, you did well and very convincing,*" congratulated Relaeh.

"Shall we set our sights upon the grand theater?" jest Rajean.

"*You might have a new career in your future. Do you feel their intent is just?*" inquired Relaeh.

"Yes, my Healer. The leader has eyes as true as yours," shared Einna.

"*We shall arrange for shipment of the garments and a note of your hand to be placed where you indicated. Thank you, ladies.*"

The ladies were beaming with delight as they continued on their way.

The Nalhsian Representatives

Salocin had gathered his friends to meet two representatives of Nalhs. It was important that they emanated a sense of good will, even though they had received approval from Councilman Atir. The need for cooperation was still apparent between them and the representatives. Salocin decided that with the shade provided by the grand trees, an informal atmosphere would be best served on the deck of the main floor. *A convincing arena to showcase their vision,* he thought.

The two representatives were escorted to the waiting idealists on the back deck. As the door swung open, Dugar recognized them immediately.

"Good will, Salocin, I had no knowledge it was you and your friends that were instrumental in producing this fine project."

"Good will to you as well, Dugar. The same applies to your manifestation upon our request. I am very pleased that it is you that stands before us."

Dugar introduced a Board Member of the Engineering Department, Ruvana who would be asking questions of the proposed sports complex.

"Good will, good sirs. I am impressed with Dugar's reaction of learning of your involvement with this project. I am also impressed with your choice of holding our meeting among nature's own and the compassion for our needs to be shaded from the day's intensity. Let us begin. I have brought a plan of consideration for your perusal to identify the key issues involving such an endeavor. I do believe you are the first to conjure such a scheme, for which I congratulate you.

"There are some main issues that need to be addressed. First, the energy to power a common facility, the possible usage after the sun disappears, the need for reclamation of waste, the recycling of water to maintain flora, and the desired material to create a pleasing presence as one with nature. I have outlined these under the heading Structural Amenities.

"Second, work force. We can assist you in recruiting workmen of substance to aid in the development of your dream. Do you have any such persons in mind?"

"We only have knowledge of us six, who possess any type of desire to hail this task at hand. Taeman is a botanist who will instruct placement of desired foliage and flora. Jacor can expedite all material importing and placement, and I have some knowledge of construction," replied Salocin. "So with your aid in securing workmen to assist in our chores would be greatly appreciated."

"Very well, I will assign that task to Dugar, as you have already built a presence. We may require a foreman who can handle the equipment you require. I believe Dugar also knows of this hidden talent in one of you.

"Last, there will be a need for residence or work camp that our workers can maintain hygiene, prepare their meals, rest and enjoy their time off. Do you have such a provision, or are we in need of developing that also?"

"We have an empty warehouse, conveniently located to our proposed site that could be quickly converted to living quarters as you described, madam Ruvana," related Jacor, politely.

"Very well, I am under the assumption, Jacor, that you hold the position of Material Manager?"

"Yes, madam... and my assistant, Sirius."

"Just the two of you? Do you have anyone else who may assist you in attending to the needs of the workmen without you being distracted from your duties?"

"Our wives may participate. They are wonderful cooks, they tend to the gardens and they possess capabilities of maintaining control in unique situations," insisted Jacor.

"Very well. Good sirs, do you have any questions that have not been fulfilled?" asked Ruvana.

"When shall we begin?" inquired Salocin.

"We will prepare a preliminary supplies and materials list for our liaison officer and send a recruitment inquiry over your Haldon for workmen of suitable demeanor. I shall personally select a qualified foreman that will satisfy your desires, and shall we say without implications, forthwith," announced Dugar.

"We are excited to begin this project, Dugar, and thankful for your input and madam Ruvana," politely emphasized Salocin.

With an air of accomplishment, Dugar imparted, "Then we shall bid you good will."

The men once again gathered in excitement over their successful meeting with the representatives of Nalhs. Dugar and Ruvana strolled along 5th to Conviction and on to the Portal.

"Ruvana, you were undeniably outstanding. Your professionalism controlled and manipulated each question and concern. I believe I am fortunate in having you in my life," shared Dugar.

"Did you believe I would have been of lesser stature?" jest Ruvana.

Dugar, responded tongue tied, "Uh...no, I mean you are a woman of awesome character and devotion..."

Ruvana interrupted him, "You better say that." She placed her arm in his. "For you, I would do it again, and, is there any other question of importance for my consideration?"

Dugar knew he was out of his league of social dalliance and thought it wise to remain silent.

The Great Debate: Erodec vs. Atir

The councilmen had gathered to hear the complexities of the challenge set forth by the Din Master. Atir had taken his usual position in the front row, center, as Erodec was situated on the left of the podium. Droenal was seated across the walk-way in front of Erodec. The Din Master was shuffling papers at one of the podiums waiting for the last councilmen to take their seats. The symposium began.

"Good will, my fellow Councilmen. As you are very well aware, we are here to rebut the hypothetical challenge of our teachings. I have laid this challenge onto our intern, Erodec, that he may summon the advice of our more knowledgeable councilmen, but also to have his free will to analyze all discoveries that might have presented itself in this discourse. I thought to merely sit and listen, as we have become accustomed, would serve no justice. I then shall subpoena the idealism of Master Atir to join Erodec as opponents to further demonstrate this implied hypothesis."

Atir responded with acute calmness while Erodec's eyes, if not attached, would have fallen onto the floor.

What! What has he just announced? What plan has the Din Master on conjuring the interplay between me and my collaborating colleague, Master Atir?

Atir stepped to the podium and acknowledged the accolades from his councilmen. He instructed them to quell their enthusiasm with a wave of his hands. Erodec approached the other podium with a single applaud.

"I shall mediate on behalf of the council, but we will hold an open forum upon deliverance of warrant views. Let us begin. Erodec, if you would be so kind as to introduce whichever side you propose," invited the Din Master.

"Good will to you all. I would like to express my gratitude to our Din Master for giving me this opportunity to establish my sincerity, and to possibly..." with a jestful inclination in his voice, "...coerce your vote as an equal on the Council."

The councilmen remained stoic. Droenal suppressed a cheer. Erodec searched the room for any hint of life.

"Then I shall begin with the hypothesis. Our research was limited to the T9 and T10 books as dictated by our Din Master; therefore, a true detailed analysis of the complete teachings of the Engram is not possible. We shall diagnose the value of disclosure in my findings. I must interject at this point, that my thesis was planned as a straight investigative discovery and not to be offered as a rebuttal, as we now have before us."

The Din Master thought Erodec was doing quite well at this point.

"I shall state the facts, and then, if Master Atir wishes to counter such facts, then, I guess we will have a debate."

Still no reaction from the councilmen.

"I have uncovered a discrepancy of 130 numerical summations that have vanished in thin air. It is true that they could be due to faulty blending and therefore discarded as potential citizens..."

That's it Erodec, drown yourself in disbelief and rhetoric, thought Councilman Atir.

"...but upon further investigation I was able to match these numerical codes and combine the citizens' reproduction charts, as pertaining to this sequential period and given names upon birth. I have before you..." Erodec waved the papers in the air, "...a list of names of persons who have vanished!"

The councilmen reacted as if the sun had fallen out of the sky. Cajoles and jeers filled the room; hands waved aimlessly. The Din Master pommeled his gavel upon his desk to regain order. Never had he seen such an outburst. He banged and banged...

"Please, councilmen, calm yourselves..." Banging, and banging again. "Councilmen please... well Erodec it seems you are able to stir these gentlemen after all. Please continue," insisted Din1289.

"As I was saying, I do not have all their names, but enough to pose the question of their disappearance. And I have an eye-witness to the possible missing strain now inherent among our fourth generation citizens," incited Erodec.

"Atir, can you refute these claims?" asked the Din Master.

"Thank you, Din Master. These discrepancies may be true, but according to your mandate, the challenge was 'Are all men created equal'? I fail to understand our young intern's intent with these discoveries. In my learnings, I have not found one who is not as the same as we all here. I do believe the eye-witness our beloved Erodec is speaking of, was herself injured at birth, and thus has an assuming flaw of intellectual disparity. I therefore recommend that without scientific involvement from the Grounders, our 'vanished' citizens remain conjecture. Our teachings award us the ability to debate, but our sanctuary within the realm of the Engram reinforces our status as defenders of the good books." Atir concluded.

The councilmen cheered in the favor of Atir, of his oratory skills, and as a true defender of the great books.

"Very well put, Atir. I believe our challenge has been justly met by the revelations that have transpired. I congratulate our adversaries in a fine performance. Do we have questions from the floor before we adjourn? No, then kind gentlemen"...Din1289 displaced his gavel, "We are adjourned. Good will to you all."

Atir was flocked by the Councilmen as Erodec and Droenal slipped out without notice.

"What was the intent of that fiasco?" inquired Erodec of Droenal, "I believed they wanted the truth. The truth that our society is changing and soon the Engram will fall out of favor with our citizens; and then what? Are we to implode from within? Atir turned on me; that was not what we discussed. Is he the saboteur of my stature? What of my station now with the councilmen? What shall I do, Droenal?"

As they neared the revolving doors of the Androicropulous, they heard a voice hailing them from the direction of the great hall.

Regor's Isolation of Chromosome

Dugar and Relaeh were waiting at Master Leumas' chamber for arrival of Regor, who had shared the promise of inspiring news. Master Leumas, as well, had privileged information concerning Erodec's castigation from the council. Dugar and Relaeh were involved with their usual bantering.

"I thought you told me you had a casual relationship with Ruvana?" questioned Relaeh from overhearing Ruvana's *consideration* statement.

"I do... I thought I did. We have not discussed anything like what you are implying."

"Dugar, Dugar..." Relaeh shook his head back and forth, "...you are sly, but not enough. She will have you on your knees begging her to gaze upon your eyes."

"That is not our custom," retorted Dugar.

"I was speaking metaphorically. What is your impression, Father? Has Dugar's bachelorhood reached its limit?" jest Relaeh.

"My, my boys! Although Dugar, Ruvana did sound somewhat questioning of your intent," sighed Master Leumas.

"Not you as well, Master!" said Dugar, not wishing to admit Relaeh's observation implied truth.

Saved by the chime of Master Leumas' H-WAC, Regor stepped into the chamber and witnessed two men smirking and his brother with a discouraging frown.

"Good will, my friends. I see you recounted Dugar's Anon and his..., I shall invert that to, her conversation with my brother," laughed Regor.

"Brother, you are supposed to stand up for me," insisted Dugar.

"I would, but your speech was silent. You should give in to Ruvana's way. She is smart, well respected, a stunning beauty of Nalhs, and most important, for some reason she desires you. It could be worse, you could be like Relaeh, he's never pressed lips with a woman," incited Regor.

They all enjoyed great merriment over Dugar's dilemma.

"Now my fellow conspirators, I have concluded that the warrior gene is of old manifestation but the introduction to the six men is relatively new. Possible contact could have been accomplished through injections, or taken orally as in digestion of a pill form, or hidden in food, or liquid substance.

"I have isolated the chromosome and have a series of tests aiming at bombarding the protein with corresponding energy neurons as applied by the Engram, while attempting to encircle the protein with sticky neutralizing plasma. The samples I took from the men after the revelation are multiplying every hour and then compounding exponentially. The sample taken from Taeman before the revelation is mutating at a much lesser growth rate," shared Regor.

"When did you take the samples of the men, Regor? After the revelation?" inquired Relaeh.

"While they rested in their recovery state."

"And what of the samples I procured, are they invalid?"

"Not at all. I need a comparison, as well as a delivery system, for when I can contain this warrior gene," reassured Regor.

"I am relieved you are having some success."

"Success will only be achieved if we can effectively treat these men."

"Very good, Regor. Dugar, have you arranged necessary provisions with our liaison officer?" inquired Master Leumas.

"Yes, I have personally checked the inventory for workmen garments, utensils for the camp, bedding, and all purveyance needed to sustain our guests. And there was an over-stuffed chair with a rising foot rest slated for Atir by order of the Din Master that I thought strange."

"The Din Master was probably securing Atir's perceptions shall we say," hinted Master Leumas with slight sarcasm.

"I should add, Master Leumas, a letter of Einna's hand is embedded in the garments out of sight of the Materials Manager, Jacor."

"And, what of I, Dugar? When do I get to power these great machines you so thoughtfully entrenched for my benefit?" hissed Relaeh.

"Such tone, you know you desire to mix and mingle with the Topsiders. I can tell as we speak, you are anxious to spin a track," laughed Dugar.

"Ah, at last my friend, you have found my true course. I am to be a builder of playing fields."

"Well boys, let us leave the theater of your intent to the one that portrayed our poor intern as an agitator. I have knowledge that our intern failed to impress the councilmen and that Atir effectively secured the teachings of the Engram as a, some might say, spiritual revival. Although Erodec appears to be dejected, a source that he believed to have questionable authority has now come to his aid."

"Father, how do you know all this? The council meeting was this very day, and yet you know the concluding consequence before they rise from their seats."

"My, son, all in due course. My position affords me certain gratitude that you will inherit when that time arrives. Now back to topic. We shall inspire this advantage with appropriate discourse for Erodec's inquisitive mind. I believe you all have plentiful burden to occupy your intentions for the next few weeks, therefore I will challenge Erodec in my own subtle way.

"Keep this in mind as you translate your intentions, we have no knowledge of the leaders name. How will we focus on our visitors without seeming vulgar? Will the women play an imperative roll in communicating dialogue from us to them, or are you, Relaeh, going to assume the role of disguised contractor? Let us not rule out that our inventive

Relaeh has knowledge of all the men of Salocin's gathering. He also has represented himself as a kindred spirit in the eyes of the leader. My challenge to you lads, how do we proceed without jeopardizing our treaty with the Belcarians? Accumulate your investment in your combined learnings to ascertain a positive approach. I wait your discovery of direction before we apply such maneuvers."

"Yes, Father."

"Yes, Master Leumas."

The boys took leave and agreed to meet for dinner that night in Relaeh's chamber. Dugar inquired if he may invite Ruvana as she is now an ally. Regor and Relaeh agreed that an unbiased, fresh view would only add to their instructed direction as implied by Master Leumas.

Visitor's Decision

Each canopy was well hidden in each of six directions among the foliage as Bocaj and his men sat around a small fire in the center of their camp.

"Bocaj, I was not afforded the conversation between the ladies, and you and Kire, but am I to assume you believe their intent is of truth?"

"Yes, Retu... they mentioned a need for our help when I relayed to them of our journey from afar."

"And I detected the women were pursuing this exchange on their own benevolence, without discussion offered to their husbands."

"Why do you say so, Kire?"

"They mentioned of gathering garments of workmen from their husbands and hiding their disposal of such before they took lunch with their husbands."

"But, they also commented on taking lunch and then proceeding to the orchards, which would imply their husbands were in between the old warehouse and the orchard. As Kire and I approached the orchards, there stood three buildings coincidentally, to our right. Kire remarked of the men distracted in conversation who were sitting upon a dock. Their garments were not the design of a workmen's uniform; however, there were two of lesser notability," recounted Bocaj.

"This is your observation of the women's desire to procure our attention for their instrument?" inquired Retu.

Bocaj shrugged his shoulders, "I envision no inkling of discourse."

"They spoke with sincerity from the heart," added Kire.

Micja, who was siting patiently, weighed each discovery as foretold by Bocaj and Kire, and implied, "Do you believe their husbands are of danger?"

"Why would you question their stature?" asked Bocaj.

"As I crouched, I was privy to your conversation. There was no malice towards their husbands. In fact, there was a joy in taking lunch with them; therefore, I perceive the women have all their interests binding to their reference of aid."

"Hmmmm...I conceive your perception, Micja. I have chosen wisely my comrades for this journey. Then what do you all say to our continuance of securing our garments of workmen next dusk as the sun leaves the sky? The moon will offer little light to guide us, but our instinct shall instruct our direction."

They all replied to Bocaj's decision, "Aye!"

Dinner at Relaeh's

Relaeh's dinner guests had all gathered around the table in his chamber. He had prepared an outstanding spread of farm-raised fish atop a wild-rice blend with a delicate spreading of green, orange and red vegetables. The table was set with four appointments. Semi-sweet nectar filled the lightly rimmed, tall-stemmed translucents. A bouquet of flowers sat in the center, and its aroma drifted as magic to each place setting. Regor, Dugar and Ruvana were astounded with the well-appointed table.

"Relaeh, where did you conceive such decorum," asked Regor.

"Home Economics," jest Relaeh.

"Home Economics?" questioned Dugar.

"Madame Noir relayed Home Economic instructions for decorating a table."

"Your Madame Noir is a very wise woman," complimented Ruvana. "Perhaps a training course for all Nalhsian men is in order?"

Relaeh perceived a gesture that Dugar may need to instill, sooner than he thinks. He enjoyed a moment of jestful delight.

"By what means did you resource these delicacies, Relaeh?" inquired Ruvana.

"It is very simple to accomplish if you have the imagination to press the correct buttons on the H-WAC Culinary Digester."

"Yes, we women of Nalhs understand the use, but how did you, as a man, develop this direction of events?" again questioned Ruvana.

"My Father, Master Leumas, always prepared such delights. I would presume his instruction was from Madame Noir. Other than that, I am without words."

Regor started to ROAR with laughter...

Dugar questioned his intensity to such a viable answer.

"It is not the instruction of knowledge that I am racked with such amusement, it is that Ruvana has now left the two of you in silence."

They all conceded that perhaps such merriment was of observance. The dinner finished with the fine delights offered by Madame Noir.

Dugar began to share his plan to his friends.

"I believe if we can instruct the women, as Jacor implied, they will have influence over the visitors. Ruvana and I will only be of reference for their actual endeavors of construction, otherwise we tempt the judiciary process as invoked by the treaty. You, Relaeh are free to instigate any discourse that Master Leumas agrees."

"Your words are of truth, Dugar; my intention is merely to assist and observe. I do not choose to distract any progress that the women might have assimilated with the visitors. Let the women instruct us on their findings and if there will be a need for our interjection, then at that time. It also depends on Regor's diligence in procuring an antidote for that gene. I shall remain as your contractor preparing the site for their sports arena."

"I see the women as the key collaborators," said Ruvana. "They have control over their husbands and understand their needs, and they seem to have developed a spirit with the visitors. They are willing participants in this trialogue of interest."

"Relaeh, how much time do you require to work the field?" asked Regor.

"I believe I can have the ground prepped and utilities roughed in by the end of the third week."

"That only leaves a couple of days before the next revelation. I shall endeavor to complete my task before then."

"I shall instruct the excavators to be mobile and in place in two days. That will give the visitors time to discover their garments, and the letter disguised from Einna instructing them on their course," stated Dugar.

"If I may use my office to assist in document preparation, it would aid in any inopportune delays," offered Ruvana.

"Very well, my friends, I will inform Father of our plans this evening. I know he will welcome all we said. He has great respect for the treaty and I of him."

Tomorrow's light will afford the four instigators renewed energy and clearer heads. The friends said good night and parted ways.

Dugar's Distraction of Freight

Dugar had awakened early this morning to meet the challenge of supervising the arrival of the requested inventory in Belcare. He met up with Jacor and his assistant, Sirius, who were already dividing the contents into sections for distribution.

"Good will to you both," animated Dugar with a wave of his hand.

"Good will to you as well, sir," replied Jacor as he picked up his bill of laden to show Dugar what had been partially deposited from his requisition.

"I see we have been afforded the materials to begin installing the quarters for our workmen," acknowledged Dugar. "Where will you locate their premises, Jacor?"

"We receive all commissioned materials on our ground and first floors, depending on size and timely distribution. The old warehouse occupies the identical floor plans, so I concluded that the first floor of the old warehouse would be an appropriate destination. All the utilities are in good working order, which will make the transition convenient."

"What of the cellars? Are they convenient?"

"I would not direct any use of those, as most of the space is designated for pipes, electrical panels, and huge columns for the support system of the building. There is no real natural light, as the cellar windows are small and above a man's height. Well our height, not yours," smiled Jacor, hoping he had not disrespected his Nalhsian representative.

Jesting, Dugar replied, "Perhaps then a condo maybe constructed to serve our needs when attending events topside?"

The two men jointly enjoyed a jestful moment.

Dugar, noticing a pompous chair, said, "And this is for Councilman Atir?"

"Yes, Sirius and I will deliver it when time permits."

"As I am available at present, may I suggest, to limit the wastage of time, you and Sirius deliver the chair while I peruse the rest of the inventory. I comprehend your stacking system and if you allow me to continue in your absence, time will be well spent."

"Sir, your consideration would be most acceptable, and greatly help our day's scheduling. With all of this new construction and purveyances, our abilities are being stretched."

"Very well, Jacor. Are security systems prevalent on the old warehouse?"

"We have no need of such apparatus."

"Then I request that I shall endure as you, and you may transit your chair to Atir."

The two men readily agreed, and Sirius furnished a lorry, where upon, they deposit the chair for Atir on its flat platform. The cab was cramped even for the two Belcarian men and Dugar wondered who the mechanical engineer was that designed such an ill form of transportation. *Perhaps it was a student project of Nalhs?*

. . .

The track of the lorry was of modest width, allowing it access to otherwise laboriously narrow pathways. They pulled parallel to the rear docking platform of the Androicropulous and placed a four-wheel dolly on top of the dock. The lorry's platform was considerably shorter than the dock, so rolling directly onto the dock to the commercial doors was not a simple task. Each man took a side to raise the back of the burdensome chair to dock height, and as one held it in its bearing, the other ascended the adjoining stairs to position himself in a precarious balancing pendulum. They managed to slide the chair and plotted its four sturdy feet solidly upon the dock. They straightened their strained backs; their adrenalin was pumping as they lifted the chair to the awaiting dolly.

The rising freight platform, on the inside of the Androicropulous was wider, higher, and longer than the passenger platform, so the accommodation of the chair and the two men was inconsequential. They felt a wave of uncertainty as they arrived at the Councilman's floor, but proceeded steadfast down the long hallway to his chamber. When Councilman Atir answered the door, the two men were dazed with apparitions, and had no coherent acknowledgement of Councilman Atir.

"Jacor...Jacor...Jacor," hailed Atir. Slowly Jacor responded to his calling. "What has happened?" questioned Atir.

Jacor looked up to witness a familiar face and with a waver instilled in his voice, he weakly said, "I apologize, Councilman Atir. I believe we may have fostered a virus that manifested itself whilst struggling with your chair at the dock."

Concerned, Atir offered, "Will you take of water to calm your attack?"

"Yes, that would be kind of you, sir. Again I apologize for our perception of anything less than professional. I cannot fathom the intent of the virus flaring up in such a manner."

"Well, as no harm has embodied your stature, Jacor, let us hope these sudden attacks do not complicate your response to duty."

"I believe we are of our senses as we speak. Your new chair has arrived, Councilman Atir." Jacor gestured to its grandeur. "I believe you will find solace lounging in its grasp."

"Yes indeed. Our Din Master has bestowed such a unique piece of construction to glorify my restrained opulence," conjured Atir.

After setting the chair in a somewhat eminent location, the two men took leave of Councilman Atir. As he sat in his illustrious addition, he thought of the attack that overcame Jacor and his man. He wondered how the men would be able to harness such an occurrence and still maintain consciousness.

~

The two men arrived at the warehouse, still shaken by what had just occurred. They sat perplexed. Although relieved it had passed, they wished Councilman Atir had not been a witness. Dugar perceived an injustice had manifested itself upon them.

He strolled to their side with tentativeness. Compassionately, he inquired, "My good fellows are you of ill health?"

Jacor raised his head and with a slight smile and said, "We believe we are. I know you are aware of our predicament. We just had an episode at Councilman Atir's chamber. He was most indulging and concerned over our continuance of this day," reflected Jacor.

"Did he question the intrusion of manner?"

"Not exactly," professed Sirius. "He was more concerned of our ability to be able to maintain our duties."

"He did not inquire of your health, a fever, an ingestion of ill-timed fruit or such?"

"I mentioned a possible virus, he administered us water, and then he questioned our response to duty. That's it," recounted Jacor.

"I see. Well, have you adjusted from this virus?"

"Yes, we feel better but this wave that engulfed us was more extreme than anything we have previously experienced." Sirius nodded in compliance.

"Well, in your absence I managed to account for all of the arrivals and placed them in their appropriate designations. Tomorrow another influx of freight will devour your time. I suggest you take to your homes and rest before tomorrow's arduous task."

"We shall do as you advise, Dugar. And thank you for your understanding and diligence in managing our tasks of the day," respectfully replied Jacor. "We shall situate the lorry and then be on our way."

"May I experience the maneuvering of this machine into its storage?" asked Dugar.

Bocaj - The Warehouse Note

The sun had set low in the west as night befell the City of Belcare. It was a moonless night; the stars were the only prevailing blurred illumination. Retu guided his band effortlessly towards the three large sturdy buildings that resided beyond the edge of the forest. The two on the left had visible dim lights perched over their perspective doorways, offering assurance as a protectorate. Beneath the middle building, a strange machine protruded into the night's air. The last building on the right remained in darkness, with no signs of movement encircling its domain. The men moved cautiously, barely smothering the blades of grass as they proceeded in silence. A wisp of air flaunted with the ends of their long hair as one might toy with a lover. It was a night ready for seduction; they took the cellar door as theirs.

Bocaj quietly instructed his men to discard their fashion of dress and to take up the workmen's garments. As they sorted through them, Kire found a note addressed to the "Kind Leader"; he passed it to Bocaj.

Kind Sirs, we have fashioned together your garments of workmen with several changes for your convenience. Our husbands have intent of constructing a sports field adjacent to your structure that you now occupy. We understand that a tall man, different than us and another as we, will require workmen to assist in this endeavor. If you are of such intent to remain in Belcare, this opportunity awaits you. We are of knowledge that this warehouse will be converted into workmen's quarters. We believe as you, that secrecy of our previous introduction remains as such. Our husbands must not have any inkling of our earlier conversation. Their safety requires thus. The tall man and the other are trustworthy as we. When our paths cross again we will gladly accept introduction.

Kind regards,

Ladies of the Orchard

Bocaj read the note aloud to his men. They sat for a moment while the implications had time to summarize in their minds.

"By the intent of the note, I am in firm belief of Micja's interpretation of our conversation with the ladies. Their husbands have befallen some sort of retribution upon their stature. Therefore, we shall remain at distance of forming friendships for their safety, but we shall observe any transgression that may harm the unity of our ladies from the orchard. Are we all in agreement?"

The men again aligned themselves with Bocaj as the leader and visionary of this expedition.

"Very well, let us enjoy the solitude of our surroundings, and at first light we will gather as instructed outside of this building and respond for their need of assistance. I believe we have found an opportunity to further enhance our discoveries. Good will, my comrades, until daybreak."

~

In the depths of Nalhs, Dugar related to his brother the imperative acceleration of discovery for isolation of the warrior gene, as the intensity and the simple exertion of labor is crippling the men. Dugar also noted that Atir made no inquiry to what caused the men to fall in their state. *Interesting,* he thought.

The Visitors' New World

The sun peeked above the mountains and cast the seduction of the night away. There was coolness in the air but a refreshing scent dominated its wavering. Relaeh had taken a different path to the old warehouse than Dugar in such as, their meeting, witnessed by others, must not seem to be contrived.

The visitors had gathered at the rear of the warehouse awaiting acceptance by, as noted, the tall one. As the tall one approached, Bocaj recognized him as one of the sentries who was guarding the pudgy one. Perhaps he was not a sentry, but a mere observer of the events that unfolded that night. There was so much to learn of this multi-cultural society. Although his men represented many facets of facial configuration, they had no tall ones amongst their citizens.

Dugar approached the waiting men.

"Good will to you all. I am Dugar from the Society of Nalhs. I trust you have gathered from the inquiry we posted on the Haldon. You all appear to be of sound condition for the task at hand. Shortly, I will introduce you to our contractor who will instruct you on your duties. There will also be six men of honorable position that instigated this endeavor to whom some of you will dedicate your time. I will remain in close alliance with the designers of this project, our contractor, and the Board of Engineers of Nalhs. In case you have questions of duty or what may befall you, I suggest you make all inquiries to your foreman or myself. Here comes your foreman now."

When Relaeh reached the men, he was immediately recognized by Kire. He leaned toward Bocaj, "That is your acquaintance from the park without his facial encumbrances and bushy eye hair. I recognize his eyes... as yours, Bocaj."

"Observe his intent," whispered Bocaj.

Relaeh stepped directly to Bocaj and extended his forearm just like Bocaj had instructed him at the Grand Park. The men grappled.

"I am Relaeh, your foreman on this project. I shall attempt to memorize your names. You are...?"

"My name is Bocaj."

Bocaj took the lead in introducing his men one by one; Kire, Micja, Retu, Songa, and Tavlo.

Relaeh continued, "Welcome, we are all early in arriving before the designers of this project, so let us inform you of our intent."

Relaeh motioned with his hand the area of designation for the sports complex and then instructed them on moving the boxed up freight and thick flat panels into the old warehouse.

"First, we shall construct your quarters. There will be another shipment today with considerable volume to sort. We will coordinate schedules with the other group upon their arrival."

As they approached the cargo doors of the old warehouse, just above the entrance, large letters appeared but were slightly hidden by the growth of ivy. Relaeh brushed the ivy aside with a fallen branch. Inscribed was 'C B C'.

"Interesting," announced Relaeh. "It appears your building has been inscribed with its own monogram. We shall call your quarters then, CBC."

Inside, the area was quite large with abundance of open space. Pipes of different assortments pierced the floor to the cellar, and also continued upwards to the floors above them.

Relaeh instructed that nearest to the pipes they would partition walls for privacy and hygiene, and on the opposite side, cabinets, sinks, and instruments of heat, would be installed. In the center, a large chamber for their mutual relaxation and on the opposite side of that space, in between each set of windows, partitions would be constructed for their private sleeping quarters.

The men of Inception had experience in building huts and docks with binding of ropes and vines, but never with an instrument of light beams. Relaeh detected their hesitation and assured the ease in learning this technology. Most of the partitions were pre-assembled and snapped together with the proper insertion hardware.

Before the sun took its position directly above them, the men had their new accommodations set in place. The next shipment provided the essentials to furnish their habitat. Two of Bocaj's men assisted Jacor and Sirius to sort, and then, they delivered the inventory to the proper location, while the others installed the refinements.

The day went well, even though it was consumed by the construction of the workmen's quarters; their conversation, other than instructions, was held to a minimum. They worked hard, which afforded them one more day of leisure before the excavators (diggers as the Belcarians referenced them), would be introduced on the work site. Relaeh and Dugar had bid their farewell as had the men of position from the next building. The visitors had their secured privacy set before them.

They remained silent as each perused a different admiration of their efforts. The partitions had brilliance of color without having to find berries to place upon them and each room could be interchanged with another to support ones taste, as Relaeh had inferred. The latrines were not holes in the ground but an apparatus attached to the wall where one sat in leisure. As you entered a room, a Bio-instrumentation Monitor sensed your biorhythms and automatically adjusted room temperature and lighting; words they had never heard, now had function. They had never seen comforts that insulated them from their cross boards, that let a man slumber effortlessly. When one lay at rest, this thin pad sensed your body weight and warmth, and then adjusted to your comfort level; if the levels were not acceptable to you, only a few words were required to re-adjust ten degrees in either direction.

Songa and Tavlo aided Relaeh in attaching water and waste pipes, to which they were amazed to watch as he waved his hand in close proximity whereupon water rushed from a round tube. With simple commands, he changed the temperature of the water to his liking.

Each man had been given a transparent card of unknown material, with a lanyard attached and were instructed to use as they deemed fit for further garments at local haberdashers, and dining pleasure at local eateries, at least until they were introduced to, Home Economics.

Their eyes had been opened to a new world. Leaving this behind would be difficult, but their love still remained entrenched in Inception.

A Guided Tour

As the light of the day penetrated their windows the men of Inception awakened to more astonishing discoveries. As they stood naked in their personal foundation tube, a passing of light surrounded their entirety and within seconds their bodies were sanitized. After, half of the translucent tube opened and released them to the privacy of their quarters. There, they were faced with a choice of garments to start the day. The colors were abundant.

They assembled in their large chamber; the astonishment of their discoveries was still eminent. Today would be a day of more unexplainable wonders as they were afforded time to explore on their own.

A knock on their door startled them into the present.

"Good will to you all," announced Salocin. "Let me introduce you to my wife, Einna and her friend, Rajean. They have prepared a morning meal for your delight. I shall take leave and begin my reports. If you have any other needs, I will be in the last building of the three."

The men bade farewell to Salocin and set to properly introduce themselves to the ladies of the orchard.

"Your kindness and attitude has overwhelmed us. We have not words of gratitude that can be expressed truthfully of our hearts," shared Bocaj. "Our eyes have seen what our minds cannot fathom. This world of yours would not be imagined in our thoughts of the night."

"As you have the freedom to imagine and recount past events of your growing adolescence, most of us do not have that privilege. Our memories are only shadows that must be re-introduced by the Engram at each revelation. We have no endearment associated with past events as you. That is why we crave to be free; to recount our past events and imagine a future. That is the joy we seek, as you are astonished by what you see here."

"Rajean speaks the truth. Observe what you may, but hold true to your heart that you do so as free men," insisted Einna. "We believe, as we stand before you, that one of us will lead us from this anonymity of our soul, to go forth and create our station in life as we believe."

"We shall remain true to your cause and will observe accordingly," reassured Bocaj.

With a hint of jest, Einna responded to their choice of garments, "Although, kind sirs, you look handsomely in your new garments, may we suggest a coordination of more subtle intent. As the sun rises and strikes your fancy, it may blind the residents of Belcare with your combination of color."

"If you are to be seen as us," suggested Rajean, "...the shades of purple, red and blue are meant to accent other more mute colors, but not to be worn in conjunction with each other."

"I like the vibrancy of color," insisted Kire. "They illuminate our visage."

"That they do," smiled Einna.

"Shall we then re-adjust our garments of more subtle intent, Rajean?" inquired Bocaj.

"Unless you plan on replicating a preposterous creature of a circus, I would definitely consider re-adjustment."

The men acknowledged their indiscretion of intent and voluntarily re-dressed. Kire invited displeasure but bent to the ladies' will.

As the men returned one by one, the ladies assured their choice of attire. Only Kire had to retry. Finally they were all set.

"We have been instructed to guide you through Belcare, if you so choose, or you may use your free will to observe," said Einna.

"We would accept most graciously of your time if we would not be of hindrance," said Bocaj.

"Shall we begin with the laboratory of my husband?" invited Rajean.

"We are at your discretion."

The six men divide in two groups of three, as each lady strolled in between each group. They first observed the workings of Taeman and his assistant, Jang. He instructed them on where certain type of plant or tree would be placed according to the master plan of their project. Kire noticed a particular flower and inquired.

"What a beautiful flower. What is its name?"

"It is called a Tulip. A new strain germinated in the labs of Nalhs."

"But I have..." Bocaj nudged Kire in anticipation of his recount of seeing fields of the wondrous plant on their journey.

"...have not seen anything so colorful."

"We shall plant numerous plots around the new sports field," informed Taeman.

"May I help with your intent, as my stature would be of little use to the main development?"

"That would be most helpful, Kire. I was set to ask your foreman of a possible recruit. Mister Bocaj, do you have any objections?"

"Not at all. Kire would be a fine recruit."

"Kind sirs, shall we venture further?" remarked Rajean as she pointed to the door without requiring a reply.

As they strolled past Salocin's office, they noticed benches and table appointing a wooden structure.

Curiously, Micja inquired to the intent of such a structure. He was informed that it was called a deck and no, not a dock, as a dock was over water and a deck was built over land. Its efficiency was sometimes aesthetic and other times functioned as a social area of gathering when shoes worn by some ladies were not suitable for contact with grassy areas.

"So," questioned Micja, "...the ladies require such a structure for their needs?"

"Correct," replied Einna.

As they continued their stroll westward along Conviction loop, Bocaj noticed a store set with, what appeared to be, tools for depictions. He commented to Kire that a visit would be essential for imagery descriptions of their journey. They ventured in. Kire's eyes jousted with every inconceivable vision surrounding him.

"You sketch do you, Kire?" asked Rajean.

"Not with this fashion," excitedly replied Kire. "But perchance my future will hold outstanding imagery to glorify our discoveries."

Kire used his transparent card to obtain essentials to produce what he perceived in his mind. They took leave. This, so far, had been an outstanding day. Next door, beyond the steps of a lower floor, a young man dressed in a black tunic ascended from the office of Genetic Archives.

Calm before the Storm

"What do you perceive this morning, Father?" asked Eittam curiously as she approached the dock to where her father was overlooking the waters.

"The sky, my daughter. The sky is unusually dark where the water meets in the far distance. If you squint your eyes, a greyish column like that of a tail, meets the water's edge. I have noticed since standing that it appears to have gained in size and perceives to be getting closer. Earlier this morning it was only the white of my small finger and now it seems to have dropped down to include some pink."

"Do you believe we are of danger?"

"I have no knowledge of its course. Not in two decades have I seen such a thing. We have endured black skies and white strikes that have produced thunderous noise but I have not seen a tail."

"Shall I summon Nephets? He still has keen eyes."

"Yes, go my daughter, and ask of him to investigate this abstraction with me."

During Eittam's departure in fetching Nephets, Leinad noticed a slight rise of water on the dock's markings. This was not new during a storm, but the bay before him was comparatively still, and beyond the sand bar the seas were a meniscal light chop with barely a wave turning. He thought, *What name would we call this foulness?*

Nephets approached and hailed, "Leinad, what purpose has your daughter summoned me for my sight of eyes?"

"Look to where the sky and water meet..." Leinad pointed to the direction, "...what do you make of that?"

Nephets took note and then cupped both hands together as if his hands were a sliding mirror invention.

"It appears as a greyish tail spun from...from...the sky. It touches the water and then they are one, but only momentarily."

"Have you seen such a sight, my friend?"

"Never! We have endured many things together, but never have we witnessed such a phenomenon as this."

"And look at the dock markings. We are calm, and yet the water is rising without provocation," remarked Leinad questioning his own years as a seaman.

"Father, I believe we should announce to the villagers to take refuge on higher ground and to protect their person with banana leaves and hefty branches."

"Are you having a vision, Eittam?"

"No Father. But my stomach is anxious and my breathing is short. It would be of no harm to secure higher ground for a few days to witness this outcome."

"I agree with Eittam," said Nephets. "Without our hunters here to help us elderly and the little ones, our resources are limited to just a few able men."

"Then let us set forth to go hut to hut, and then to the refinery so they may secure what need be. Eittam, seek out your sister and inform her of our intent. We shall need to build temporary structures to shelter our provisions on the hillside, and have everyone fill our clay pots with fresh water, and bring dry sticks for securing fire. Summon the men and women from the fields to secure our boats after they harvest what they can from the crops. I shall not leave until all have secured safe haven. Now go and spread the word."

The two set off to do Leinad's business. He hobbled to his hut and gathered what he may of his previous life. His walking stick was as old as his last journey, but it still heeded well at his limited pace. His amenities were few; his unique symbol, her crimson sash, and a journal written by her with instructions on how to rebuild their lives, were his only endearments. His treasures, ones that he would never give up - upon his life.

Madame Noir's Cream

Master Leumas had been sitting with his friend at Her lab. Looking up from reading one of his entries on his Anon, he noticed a strange look on Madame Noir's face.

"Noir, what is wrong? You look pale," inquired Master Leumas.

"I do not know, my stomach, as if I received a blow that has knocked the air out of me."

"Let me help you to your chair. You have been pushing yourself. You know if you stand too long you sacrifice your energy," passionately endeared Master Leumas.

"I was just doing a final analysis of *the Revitalization Cream* for Relaeh. Nalhsian skin is thinner; I do not want to suffocate Relaeh with the Nalhsian blend."

"I have noticed subtleness about your eyes. Are you testing your cream on yourself?"

"You are too aware of my presence, Leumas, my friend. It was just a dab, but thank you for noticing." She mustered a smile as the sickening feeling subsided.

"Would you take of water, or warm water and herbs?"

"I favor warm water and herbs please, Leumas. You are so good to me. I cannot impress upon you my endearment for you."

"You only speak of such kind words while I fetch you your warm water and herbs," chuckled Master Leumas. "And your cream, will it repair Relaeh's skin if exposed to the piercing sun?"

"That is its intent and possibly the nuisance of insect bites. His skin, although more resilient then Nalhsians, remains without the constant exposure that one develops over time in the outer world. In my lab studies, the repair of skin tissue exposed to typical sun radiation manifests quite quickly. He should have only need to apply it once, but real application will be the true test. And then we will need a Nalhsian to test my theory. Perhaps you would be of willing subject?" jest Madame Noir.

"If I need to suffer in the audience of the Din Master while he spouts of alliance to the Engram, I shall not participate, but thank you for thinking of me," cordially denied Master Leumas.

The two rested as Madame Noir recirculated her life fluid through her dialyzer. She was thankful to be able to stand, even temporally, with usage of this machine, but She longed for the days of unrestricted movement.

Kire Defuses Erodec

Erodec raised his head as he conquered the top step, which placed him in the middle of the visitors.

"Good will, Citizens," announced Erodec, trapped between a group of six men and two ladies.

Startled by the figure in a black tunic, the ladies replied, "Good will to you, Councilman."

"I see you are taking a leisurely stroll on this glorious day?"

"Yes, Councilman."

Erodec tried to conger past thoughts from his memory for knowledge of the six gentle men at the ladies' sides. He noticed that they were dressed in the workmen fashion of Belcarians.

"Have we had the opportunity of introduction?" asked Erodec.

"We have not been properly introduced, Councilman, but we have laid eyes upon each other at the Grand Park," informed Bocaj.

"Yes, I believe I recall now, you were dressed as hunters."

"We are hunters," stated Bocaj proudly.

"From along the north rim of town," indicated Einna.

"From the north rim?" questioned Erodec.

"Yes, they hunt and trap for the local market," interjected Rajean.

"Yes, that is when the Nalhsians allow for re-stocking of game," replied Bocaj with a jovial intent.

"Quite right, good sir. I imagine you are held at their mercy for your contribution to our society. And where do you reside, as I believe, I have not encountered you in this district before?"

"We prefer the solitude of the forest, Councilman."

"I see, and now, you appear to be in a different array then your hunting garments?"

"We have been recruited from the message posted on the Haldon for workmen to aid in the development of the sports field. Since re-stocking of the game takes time, we volunteered to continue our support for the citizens' interest," replied Bocaj.

"Very well indeed..."

As Kire perceived the next question could induce a level of discomfort for Bocaj, he stepped into the conversation before Erodec had time to summon such thought.

"Please excuse my interruption, Councilman, but may I speak frankly with you?" Kire placed his hand on the Councilman's arm and drew him aside. The others stood with slight confusion on their faces.

"Please excuse my brashness, kind sir, but I noticed at the Grand Park you were with another gentle man of fine features as yourself. As I am a historian of such, it would be my pleasure to adorn you both with a private sitting for portraiture."

"Truthfully?"

"Yes, we are at this time procuring essential pigments that I may record on parchment a visual recounting of the development of this project."

"And you would have time to glorify our image on parchment?"

Kire felt he now had Erodec's full attention.

"The allotment of time would not be detrimental to your busy schedules as your refinements have no need of character adjustments, kind sir," flattered Kire.

"Well...?" Erodec searched for a name of this gentle spirit.

"Kire, sir."

"Very well, Kire, we shall take great pride in assisting you in your endeavors as your friends are contributing as good citizens as well," stated Erodec as he spoke with an air of infatuation. With a broad grin about his face, Erodec turned to the waiting group and declared, "Well, good will to all of you gentle men and to you kind ladies. Oh, Kire, where would your interest lie for our future sitting?"

"I shall discuss an appropriate location with our foreman out of harm's way, and if I may presume of Madam Einna's kindness, she shall transmit my findings to you."

Einna smiled with acceptance as Erodec lightly stepped on his way.

"Where did you come up with that tale?" questioned Bocaj.

"I perceived the next question could have been awkward to resolve, and with his slight inflection of speech, I interpreted an opportunity to dismantle his direction of thought with a proposed adulation of character."

"Your talents hold me at awe, Kire."

"I am also in awe of you, Bocaj. Where did you learn of our words so soon?" questioned Einna.

"I listened well to the tall one, Dugar, and to our foreman, Relaeh."

"And when do you propose to redeem this masquerade of adulation, Kire?" asked Rajean.

"I believe I remarked on obtaining permission from our foreman when safety was not an issue."

"You are cleverly disguising your intent as a misfortune manifested by another," noted Rajean.

"You should be a councilman, Kire; you speak as they do, with no real intent but plentiful promises," laughed Einna.

"Truthfully, my sketches remain of nature, as I have never attempted to put to paper a face or stature of man. I have recorded wild beasts with hunters gathered, but with a wildness of brush strokes, without detail of eyes or tender features," admitted Kire.

"Then perhaps you could honor Rajean and myself with an ageless portrait in a natural setting, as we have no inhibitions to imagination for you to develop your skill with tender features," beckoned Einna.

"And Yuda, I believe, would cherish an informal depiction in her state of pregnancy. May I foretell that the rest of our friends would set to claim an opportunity to showcase their awareness for their husband's adulation?" incited Rajean.

Bocaj and his men stood in astonishment as the Ladies of Belcare requested the talents of Kire to flatter their image for prosperity. Perhaps Kire's charm was best suited for feminine encounters, as the men of Inception reddened in the face of the ladies' implied intent, and Kire remained unabashed.

Regor and Master Leumas' Plausibility

Regor had requested a meeting at his lab with Master Leumas, Relaeh, and his brother Dugar. There was immediacy in his replication over the H-WAC that sounded alarming. Relaeh and Dugar had arrived before Master Leumas as his distance and troublesome canter required more time.

They stood in a room full of dials and gauges of all assortments. Some dials turned, some flicked off and on, while others slid up and down. Some gauges were in stacks of four to six and had needles moving from side to side. Some displayed digital impulses, and others varied between raising fluid levels and flashing ascension of light, and then repeated. Tubes and thermal beakers either sat in their attended stations or upon instruments of heat. Glass partitions isolated the scientists from fatal inducement of air borne particles and slithering globs of matter.

Regor's desk was a mound of miniature discs, books and journals; some written by Regor, some by other scientists. The room was bright and the white walls eliminated any persistent shadow. Multiple centrifuges lined a complete wall, and above them, more dials and switches. To Relaeh, the space seemed confining although the room must had measured twenty meters long by about the same in the perpendicular direction. And beyond this room were many more he saw through the half-glass partitioned walls.

Master Leumas finally arrived and as Relaeh noticed, slightly winded.

"Father, are you of ill health?"

"No, my son, just of ill shape. I hurried here from Madame Noir's lab. I'll be fine. Now, Regor why have you tired an old man?"

"I have disturbing news, Master Leumas. The micronucleus, being the smaller of two nuclei present in a healthy ciliate protozoan, is being drained of its iron deposits electromechanically, and then resets with the compound we call the warrior gene. It is as if a myoelectric impulse that can stimulate nerve endings to operate prosthesis is controlling the men with involuntary actions. I also believe this is the format used by the Engram to control the citizens of Belcare."

"This is disturbing news on how it is affecting the men, Regor; however, I believe this is a break through for us to isolate it. If the warrior gene is feeding off the ciliate, then let us induce a replica of non-consequence like a placebo charged with a magnetic induction, which will attract the disdained gene. We can introduce millions of isotopes of near identical elements within our placebo and as they mirror the warrior gene, the aggressiveness will be diluted, and we simply flush their systems," concluded Master Leumas.

"In theory, that does sound plausible, but we will have to run tests, and then bombard them with light energy to ascertain their effectiveness," reiterated Regor.

Sitting patiently while the two men spoke a foreign language, Relaeh finally inquired, "I am excited for you, but with no disrespect, what I am doing here?"

"You are witnessing the future of Belcare, my son. After Regor finalizes his findings, you will be the conduit of freedom for these gentle souls. As you will be working closely beside them, your involvement will be invaluable in documenting their moods, their energy, their speech patterns, their cognizance, their stamina, and anything else you deem essential to their change of habits."

"We will teach you what subtleties to be aware of, and as Dugar visits their offices, he also will be able to transmit data to us for each comparison," said Regor.

"Tomorrow morning, the excavators will be delivered to the construction site. I will be needed topside to initiate the design of the project. When will you require our attentions for instruction?" asked Relaeh.

"That will be as we learn of our experiment's truth. I apologize for not having a forth coming time for you," replied Regor.

"We shall do what we must," insisted Relaeh. "I have reset the time of departure from Belcare at this next rising. I believe the ladies of Belcare will influence the men of Inception to aid in their exodus at this time, as well."

"Whereby did you gain knowledge of their citizenship?" asked Master Leumas.

"While I was instructing them on the water system, one of them mentioned they had nothing in *Inception* that compared to our technology."

"Very good, my son, that is the knowledge we crave, to be able to re-establish communications with distant clans."

"I also noticed that Bocaj, the leader, wears the symbol about his neck. I have programmed another of identical character, for which I will substitute with his. I believe he will be in need of communication with us as he attempts to return to his home with our citizens. I will not instruct him on its use until we gain knowledge of their intended departure," said Relaeh.

Dugar finally stood to inject his schedule for the upcoming events.

"Relaeh, I have instructed the engineers moving the excavators topside tomorrow of certain supplies to transport with them. One of the flare boxes will be empty to hide your person. They have no knowledge, so let the machines rest before popping out."

"Popping out ... as a child's toy? Shall I also be in costume as the preposterous creatures from the parade?"

"You have worn so many, the surprise would be of your natural intent," returned Dugar.

"You will miss me when I take to my discoveries, my friend."

"You speak the truth. That is why I must embrace with as many innuendos as I may bear," infused Dugar.

"Perhaps by the time of your return, Dugar's humor may be interrupted by the cries of his little one," implied Regor, not wanting to miss out on any sabotaging opportunity.

"Brother, you so misrepresent my intentions with Ruvana."

"It is not your intent, my friend, it is Ruvana's intent you must watch out for. And, I only tell you this as a friend," said Relaeh joining Regor's humorous intent.

"You boys are impossible. I cannot recount such slyness when you were all pulling at my pant bottoms," scolded Master Leumas.

"Father, it is our jocular persistence that keeps our minds sharp for any retorts under dire pressure. We have heard you as well, interject subtleties of humor against your friend, topside; therefore, I conclude you are our source for such humor," snipped Relaeh.

"AH! You got me as well. I shall need to brush up on my insubordination for your union. That is, if you can find one that has a taste for infantilism," retorted Master Leumas.

Once again the lads and Master Leumas merrily concluded their business with love and affection.

John F Russo

The Citizens of Inception Dig In

The soft breezes of Inception had been overturned by a cooler more determined blow. The seas from afar had developed white caps as the swirly dark nemesis approached the village.

The lush, green grasslands rose to gentle sloping hills while a meandering brook divided its design. Beyond these hills laid the fruitful orchards, delicate gardens, and fields of crops. Family huts with outside fire pits resided near to the creek, and in a shadow's distance, the usual center of attention, the *long house*, but not today. The villagers had been busy building make-shift lean-tos scraped into the hillside, and used everything from cooking pots, broad-axes, spears, and by hand. They sharpened bamboo poles and pounded them into the ground, at an angle to the hill, to drain water off their banana-leaf roofs and to protect their bunker from flooding. The villagers heeded the words of Leinad and Nephets—they had saved them once before.

The geographical location at water's edge had served the village well, if compared to traveling the treacherous trail many miles inland through the canyon to the grazing fields. A journey not well suited for Leinad. Eittam and her sister Aivila had lived on the water all their lives and enjoyed the natural freedom of the water washing over their divested bodies. They dove for assortments of crustaceans almost every day. But now, their paradise was looming with potential harm.

Eittam and Aivila had secured a bunker midway up a thirty-meter hillside. They set into the hill, step landings, and secured a rope to a solid stake by the side of their bunker for use by Leinad. His troubled walking necessitated the course his daughters took for their loved father. They knew that when the rains came, the wet grass would not hold their weight but act as a child's slide making it difficult to ascend to their stronghold.

Eittam had taken her father's treasures, bound them in cloth, and deposited them into their protective enclave. Leinad was helping others, as much as he could, with their provisions. His daughters, after securing their needs, helped the women of the traveling hunters with their young ones to ascend the incline of the hill. Nearly all were in place.

Nephets and his wife, Tomei, joined the village herdsmen to secure the animals further up the canyon, where the grazing fields were of higher elevation, away from the creek bed. The journey was not fit for all, but they had endured many times through conditions of greater consideration. The rains had not yet arrived, so their footing was stable along the creek side.

Although everyone was huddled fairly close together, it was not the same as taking food to the long house and sharing amongst your friends. Inception was a free society of idealistic beliefs. Their Principals were simple and few.

No man may take from another without agreement of restitute with article of equal worth.

No man may bring harm to another in words or by hand.

All are of equal status and intent and each must render assistance to one less privileged due to unforeseen circumstances.

All must strive to learn and accept those whose capacity is challenged.

Be of strong will and determination to do one's best for the good of all.

These were the core values instilled by Leinad and Nephets, as their lead, and had been the conviction for all to follow.

Inception had seen increasing growth in agriculture implementations and mining, with the arrival of three of the original thirteen clans. It was only by chance, in different surroundings, that each had met. The families had grouped together, set a course and forged their way to the water's edge of Inception, again by chance. Their shared heroic adventures over mountain and desert terrains, always incited great stories over the fires of the starry nights; each memory as clear as the night itself.

But tonight would not be one of those nights, nor for the next few nights, as the sky was turning grey and a hint of mist was developing in the air. Leinad sat at the waters' edge and watched the scurry of bodies lining the hillside. He was engrossed in thought. He was thankful that the arrival of the new citizens held the same belief as his, and that they complemented the growth of Inception.

They had among them a fine hunter named Retu, who had volunteered to assist Bocaj on his journey. Nephets was relieved to hear of his recruitment to Bocaj's band. Leinad thought if Bocaj was here, he might have led the animals to the higher grazing ground, rather than his friend, Nephets. He knew his friend was of strong will and determination, and his wife Tomei was still strong and agile. She had great speed, not only for a woman, but as fast as any man. Bocaj took after his father and mother with all of their goodness and features. Nephets should be proud to have borne a son such as Bocaj. As boys were in

196

Nephets blood line, girls were in his. As he thought of his conversation with Aivila and her desire to gaze upon Bocaj's eyes, he could not help to think that Bocaj would be his son as well. He only hoped Bocaj was up to the challenge of a strong-willed woman such as Aivila. She would make a wholesome life partner, and one who would give him a grandson, possibly more than just one.

Leinad was startled into reality as Eittam called his name.

"Father, why do you sit looking so perplexed?"

"I was gathering thoughts of our fine community and how well everyone participated with the chores at hand. Not one was idle, that is except this old grey beard."

Eittam sat beside her father.

"Father, you are not old. Your life has not been beset with ease. You have suffered greatly with the loss of my mother and the indignation to your leg. These injustices take a toll on one's soul and bite at one's determination. You have created a fine home for Aivila and me and one you should be proud of. I know you have great concern for the approaching storm, since you have no recount of the past to enlighten us. But, we will endure. Now come have a meal with us."

Eittam stood and helped her father to the upright position. Arm in arm, they walked down the boardwalk to their hut. Eittam assured her father that their pending discomfort would be short lived.

John F Russo

Construction Day – Belcare Field

Relaeh was up early and had displayed his person stuffed into a safety box that was secured to a pallet destined for the sports field. The discomfort lay only in the box as the gliding excavators were cushioned with air. He thought of the ancient excavators that required ten men for each to maintain as it bored through rocks and deposited it's after-matter in bins trailing behind on tracks of steel. How technology had changed and he was happy it had.

The flat-land excavators rode on air and transmitted sound waves to either remove a summit of earth or create a basin. Its guide-sensors leveled ground with the precision of a physician's knife upon his operating table. The arbor excavator was the most fun to operate. One simply glided to position near the crown of the tree, and with its extended articulating arm, grabbed the refuge, while a laser light dissected each limb. The visual accumulator attached to the arm sensed any heat source that emanated from human aura before depositing off-cuts to the ground. Precision and care were essential to keep the laser in line with intended dismemberment. The controller adjusted the intensity of the beam for each strike, as misalignment could burn a hole in anything it touched. The comfort of the cushioned cabin resembled more of Relaeh's chamber chairs, rather than a machine of destruction.

Relaeh waited, it seemed an eternity, after the machines came to rest before he popped out of the safety box. There were no crowds cheering him on or sounds of laughter, but only the stillness of the early morning and the awakening of the tweaking songs of birds. There were no birds that flew freely throughout Nalhs, only their mantra from the aviaries that were softly introduced each day.

As Dugar and Ruvana approached the intended sports field, Relaeh hid a symbol in a side pocket of an excavator. Shortly, the men of Inception would join them. Relaeh noticed as his friends walked toward him and the sunlight backlit Ruvana, how beautiful and natural she was. Her garments draped over her with flowing exuberance, capturing every curve. From her hooded protectorate that fondled her unencumbered head, to her full-length tunic that swayed in her determined stride, she commended respect. *Dugar was a fortunate man*, he thought. He only hoped Dugar realized what a wholesome partner she would make. And, as Regor jestfully implied, perhaps a little one; one that might bare Relaeh's birth name, Trebor.

Relaeh brandished the spots before his eyes as he visualized the harmony of his friends interwoven with his purpose of healing the citizens of the new world. His impetuousness at times, likened him to a vacuous spirit; the truth be told, his purpose was of such magnanimity that death itself could not cheat him of his persistence.

As Dugar and Ruvana neared Relaeh, he flaunted a smile of familiarity and said, "Good will, to my favorite couple. I presume you are both well?"

"Good will to you, my favorite instigator. Yes we are both of good health," snipped Dugar.

"Dugar! Why are you so impertinent to your friend? He is just asking politely of our well-being," scolded Ruvana.

"His intent is far more reaching then you assume, my dear."

"And what might that be?" she questioned.

"Uh, ur..." Dugar stumbled yet again and looked for the correct answer in his friend's eyes.

Relaeh smiled and spoke as briskly as possible.

"He believes my wishes may compromise your dating ritual and therefore distort your sensitivity to a rational development of mutual awareness thus leading to an undetermined destiny that could have manifested into a more spiritual understanding if I were to keep my intent as an aberration in my mind."

Well done my friend, telepathed Dugar. *Now let us see if she has an answer to that?*

"Oh Relaeh, that is so sweet! You have such fondness and respect for our relationship," sentimentalized Ruvana.

"What!?" exploded Dugar, out loud.

"I remain as others who hold Dugar dearly, that all his wishes may propagate forthwith," said Relaeh as he accepted a hug from Ruvana.

You are choking me with your innuendos, my friend.

"Could we please proceed with the matters at hand?" insisted Dugar.

"Yes, Baby," said Ruvana as she quadrated her Anon for visual conception of the planned excavation.

Dugar sensed the intensity in Relaeh's eyes, as if he were to burst with exhilaration by Ruvana's last remark.

As Ruvana expanded the quadrants on her Anon, the men of Inception gathered to witness, in awe, a transparent manifestation of displayed lines of intersection that held words without pen or parchment and foliage that hung in midair. Ruvana explained the juxtaposition of each element, and then swirled the image to lie upon the ground identifying the field in its true dimensions. The men of Inception, out of instinct, jumped back at this marvel. Dugar and Relaeh ventured out onto the image with pins of different gradation in hand and placed them in the ground as the visualization rendered each location for marking - they did not notice the hesitation of the workmen. Relaeh questioned Ruvana on a particular marking called a *mound*.

As the visualization remained laminated, the men of Belcare approached with the same cautiousness as the workmen from Inception. Ruvana diminished their hesitation with reassurance and sorted through the length of pins, grabbed a hand full and instructed Taeman and Kire to do the same. They walked out into the tridimensional matrix and placed them about to establish the inset of the plots for Tulips and other foliage as imagined by the men of Belcare.

Relaeh looked up from placing pins and with a hint of a smile, he watched Dugar admiring Ruvana as she instructed the others on placement so Relaeh may excavate the field with precision.

"I sense you perceiving my view. I will not deny the energy that surrounds my heart in spite of your feeble incorrigibleness," remarked Dugar as he turned to Relaeh.

Relaeh accepted Dugar's intent with a nod. As the two stood side by side, they glanced over to the estranged men, who now had clenched in their hands more pins for placement. Relaeh called them over so Dugar could assist half of them, and Relaeh took the others to the purposed site of the common facility. The men hesitated before embarking on the field with its display of tridimensional hatchings. They stood in wonderment, looking about them, and rotated with arms spread as if to gather its knowledge, as a child gathered raindrops on a summer's soft rain.

Relaeh enjoyed watching their intent, as the technology of Nalhs once again made a strike at the influence of Belcare. He took his time with instructing them on the markings of the pins and placement, so they could grasp the importance of allegiance with Nalhs for future development.

"As the matrix indicates, place the green tip pins following the green lines for wastage, the blue tips are for drinking water, the red will be for power banks and the purple pins will be for reclaimed water, as used throughout the field for watering of foliage and plants. As you can see, a building will be sitting above all our underground utilities that must be installed prior to construction.

"Before we begin, Bocaj, I noticed your symbol about your neck. If you give it to me, I will endear a safe pocket on the air excavator so my sensors do not try to bury you," jestfully implied Relaeh.

Bocaj, with slight intrepidness, relinquished his symbol to the trusted foreman. Relaeh began the task of adjusting controls, to synchronize with each color of pin, to achieve the desired depth. The men watched in awe as Relaeh formidably attacked the ground, systematically placing each trench at just the precise location and depth. The only sound was the *swoosh* of the air turbines as the *sound waves* made no sound at all, but vibrate the ground with pulsating decisive incisions.

Standing at 4th and Serenity, Din Master watched excitedly from the safety of distance, as the foreman maneuvered the machine with perfection. He had no conception that a worker of Belcare had such knowledge, but then, he was not a man of the field with abilities of that kind. He was thrilled to see all the men working as a unit for the common good of the citizens of Belcare. There could be no mistake to the Engram's intent for unification and solidarity among its people. He thought, *they will all come together to defend the truth.*

Looming Storm Taunts Leinad

The stalled storm had caused a false sense of security among the villagers of Inception. They had removed themselves from the hillside after a week of looming weather. The blackened skies taunted Leinad like an animal stocking its prey. He stood at waters' edge and gazed out over the sea. Bolts of light flashed in the distance and slapped the sky with thunderous innuendos. It crept closer, then stopped, and waited, as if eying the movement of its intended victims. Nephets and Tomei had returned to the village, and they too stood beside Leinad and gazed at the intent of their nemesis.

The breeze remained chilled. The waters turned on the opposite side of the sand bar and rose as a horse in battle and then crashed to the soft sand. Their bay remained somewhat calm, in defiance of what was approaching. The water level had moved another inch higher, but without threat or consequence to the village's fresh water creek. All waited in limbo for their stalker to unleash its war cries; it beat on its drum of thunder as it hurled its lightning bolts, and pierced the veil of the water's innocence.

When the fishermen ventured out into the bay to retrieve their traps, the storm moved closer, and as they retreated to shore, the storm stalled to seemingly re-energize.

"By what intent has this storm such malice for our people?" asked Leinad.

"I have not seen a force demonstrate such wildly controlled insistence," remarked Nephets.

"Does it desire a human sacrifice to satisfy its hunger for death?" mocked Leinad.

"One cannot presume the desire of mother nature's beast-child to superstitiously accept the sacrifice of a virgin's innocence. It eyes us all, my friend, it eyes us all!"

"Then how shall we prepare any more than what we have done? Shall we burn our homes to escape its spoils? Shall we pack our belongings and head inland to start anew? Or shall we stand and fight?" Leinad's last statement struck a chord of resistance and spiritedly said, "Let us build a wall across our boundary from one hillside to the other, over top of our water-way and reinforce it with boulders and rocks."

"And what of water being trapped on our side, would it rise and flood our burrows?" questioned Nephets.

"We add gates to rise as we need, but to keep lowered for the initial impact from the villain's intent. What do you say Nephets, is this a strategy to prove effective?"

"As I have witnessed the action of our warrior's intent, I believe no energy spent by us would be of waste."

The men set forth to initiate their defensive plan and called a meeting in their town hall. After an influx of questions and re-design modifications, they all agreed on the construction of their wall. Men and women scurried to cut thick bamboo, gathered vines to weave into rope, filled their carts with rocks, and dug holes for planting the poles.

~

Eittam had been bedridden in her chambers with a fever she thought she inherited from one of the children. Rarely had she been affected by such nuisance, but this time, in her weakened state, as she drifted through her subconscious, extraneous clandestine demons ravished her stature. Aivila vigilantly had been placing cold cloths about her feverish skin as well as dabbing the moisture that dripped from her natural awareness. When she shivered with cold, Aivila disrobed and lay with her sister to warm her body.

Three tortuous days embattled before Eittam's body calmed from shudders and violent tossing. Aivila sensed her sister's ease, and had prepared a hot water mixture of vegetables and fish. Patting the remaining droplets from Eittam's forehead, she opened her eyes to the smiling face of Aivila. "You gave me great concern, my sister. I have not seen you in such a state." She helped Eittam adjust her head cushion. "I have prepared nourishment for you."

Weakly, Eittam said, "Thank you, my love. I sensed your nearness to me, which gave me strength as I denounced the evil penetrating my visions. Is Father well?"

"Yes, at the moment. He and the rest of the villagers have built a great wall across our boundary nearest to the sea for protection against that menacing storm stocking our presence," informed Aivila. "Have you seen others in danger, my sister?"

"I sensed Bocaj in looming pain, but not of harm, and others facing death with egregious creatures. I believe it was a true vision and one not of implied fever," recounted Eittam.

"My sister, I agonize for your visions and my Bocaj. Is his grief for others, perhaps one of his band has fallen to harm?"

"I believe so, but then the befallen man vanishes into air inexplicably," offered Eittam.

"Take food, my sister. I have scented a warm bath when you are ready to indulge in sweetness."

"Aivila, thank you, you will always be the light of my soul. You say Father is well, for the moment?"

"He has been fighting the demon within the storm as if it was a vendetta against his person solely. Nephets has been a calming influence, but Father rages with intent that the storm is toying with him. And when you took ill, he blamed the storm for your injustice. I am worried about Father's balance of mind."

"Help me with my bath, Aivila, and then we shall go see him together."

Aivila extended her arm to her sister as they made their way to the awaiting sweetness. Stepping in, Eittam submerged her tired body in the caressing waters and rested as Aivila soaped her hair and then gently rinsed the evils away.

~

Leinad had been working tirelessly on his project. He pushed and pushed with unintentional delirium to divest the spoils away from his menacing albatross.

He will not win, he thought. *I will stake my life on it.*

The rays of the day were felt through the greyness of the sky but now it had tipped its vestige and gave way to the preying monster. Aivila and Eittam slowly approached the fortified rampart.

Aivila called out, "Father...Father!"

As he turned, he saw Eittam standing and getting along, albeit slowly, but nonetheless, without fever. He grabbed his staff and rushed to her side.

"My dear!" He kissed her forehead. "...You have put the scare of death in us. Your sister has endured your presence throughout these last few days. I..."

"Father," she said interrupting Leinad, "...by which hand do you embark on such toiling? This fortification is massive and you speak words intended for an adversary of man's likeness onto a storm with no response?"

"Daughter, I hear what you say but..." he raised his staff toward the direction of the waiting storm and waved it with intensity, "...he tests my fortitude, my very being as he delivers strikes of white over our heads."

Calmly, Eittam said, "Father, you have done all one man can do. Our villagers have set your desire before us. Now it is time to chase your delirium with much needed sleep. Nephets can post sightseers to warn the village if the brew manifests itself. Nephets, you too need to put this behind you and get some rest."

"It has ears, Eittam! It watches us, every move we make; it counters us, like a game."

"I shall take into consideration of your lack of sleep, my loves, but you are best suited to handle any atrocity against our stature after you have slept. Now go, both of you, not a word."

The two drained men listened to Eittam's words and hobbled down to the boardwalk and off to their respective huts. Eittam and Aivila arranged for sightseers to rotate throughout the night and to clang the bell if danger approached the village.

Eittam turned to Avila and said, "I have seen the anger of this storm. We need to be very watchful for Father and Nephets. They cannot be left of their own devices. I fear they will take upon themselves to do what no man can. Do you understand, my love?"

"Yes, my sister, I will relay your warning to Tomei so she may keep a watchful eye as well."

"Let us take food to Father, so he may rest with a full stomach."

Passing of the Word

Within a few short weeks, Relaeh and his consortium had managed to set all pipes, removed hindering trees, and lay the foundation to begin the common structure. He also had exchanged Bocaj's symbol with another of exact likeness. Meanwhile, Kire had played in the dirt with Taeman, planting his treasured vision... Tulips.

The Din Master had dropped by on several occasions to witness the rapid advancement of the sports field. On this very day, he once again was in awe of the transformation that had taken place in front of his eyes. He approached Salocin and congratulated him on this fine addition for the citizens of Belcare. The Din Master requested of Salocin that with such timely improvements, the dedication of the field to the citizens of Belcare, be scheduled the day after the revelation. He also requested if he would please inform all who were involved, to gather for this festive event. Salocin agreed to spread the Din Master's words.

The Din Master took leave of Salocin and headed down Serenity past the warehouses, made a right onto 5th, and as he was about to cross Conviction, Erodec and Droenal approached from the direction of Droenal's office.

"Good will to you, Din Master," recited Erodec.

"Good will to you all as well. Have you taken upon yourselves to witness the progress of the sports field being constructed?" wondered the Din Master.

"We have made inquiries of the scheduling, and have been assured that by this revelation, all will be in compliance with the master plan," shared Erodec.

"And what of the matter we discussed? Have we procured necessary documents?" inquired the Din Master.

"We have made progress by cross referencing between several departments as you invited."

"Good, keep this information close to your being, as I feel its discovery could undermine our intent of exposure."

"We have uncovered another issue of more substantial interest," offered Droenal with concern.

"Truthfully?"

"Yes, a minuscule amount of substance was removed from RDDS archives several generations ago, but we have no knowledge of its present whereabouts," informed Erodec.

"Let us not speak here in the open. I have requested to Salocin that the day after the revelation shall be an opportune time to dedicate the sports field to the citizens of Belcare. Bring your documents to my chambers after the dedication. We shall gather our thoughts in a more welcoming environment. I bid you kind souls good will."

"And to you, sir."

As Din1289 retreated to the Androicropulous, Erodec and Droenal headed to the warehouse district to meet up with ladies, Einna and Rajean, who were in the process of cleaning the workmen's chambers. The men had been very respectful of their new environment at the CBC building. The visitor's daily cleaning ritual had left very little for the ladies to amend, thereby only needing finishing touches to translucents before they took leave. As the ladies rounded the corner to the street, Erodec and Droenal approached.

"Good will, Councilman. Are you following up on our note from Kire?" asked Einna.

"Yes, and to inform you of the Din Master's intent of dedication for the sports field following the revelation."

"We had not heard of the dedication being so soon. We have not spoken with our husbands, as I assume they have knowledge of this intent?" inquired Einna.

"I believe the Din Master was in conversation with your husband, Salocin, regarding this matter this very morning. Therefore, I would like to request from Kire a date of portraiture following this dedication, and where we might take full advantage of the beautiful surroundings they have worked so hard in developing."

"I believe he will be most relieved to remove his hands from the dirt and acquire his brush to slip through his fingers," shared Rajean.

"Then ladies, we will leave the appointment in your hands and we will expect a summoning from Kire for this delightful engagement."

The two men distanced themselves from the ladies, traveled along Serenity, and past the impressive edifice of the common building.

The ladies decided they had better inform Kire and the other workmen, of the impending dedication, and Kire's appointment with the Councilman and his friend after the dedication.

Salocin stood alongside Taeman, Jacor, Relaeh and the men of Inception as he discussed the Din Master's plans. The ladies strolled over. Politely, Einna interrupted her husband, and started to recount Erodec's wishes.

"Kind sirs, we beg your pardon, but we have just removed ourselves from the pleasure of Councilman Erodec. He informed us on the intent of the Din Master to dedicate the sports field to the citizens following the revelation, and Kire's destiny with brush and paint following that."

"Yes, my dear, I was just informing our friends of this scheduling dilemma. It appears the construction might not be completely finished in this short of time."

"If I may," interrupted Relaeh. "...we have one week," stumbling, he reworded his phrase, "...six passings to finish. Jacor has already informed his liaison officer of Nalhs to supply the finished interior of the common building. If we all arduously apply ourselves, we can have this project finished. Our power banks will offer us light in our darkened hours, and ladies, if you can muster some help to keep our workmen fed and hydrated, I will oversee any additional provisions needed for an extended stay away from our homes."

Rajean picked up on Relaeh's true intent.

"I will muster the other ladies to pack anything they feel will aid in this extended stay. As the night air cools, I will instruct of warmer garments as well."

"My husband, I will need to speak to Kire so I may transmit his decision to the Councilman," added Einna.

"Well then my friends, we have a project to finish. I suggest we ready ourselves for a staggering journey so we may oblige the Din Master," instructed Salocin.

Relaeh and the ladies briefly gathered together to confirm intent. Einna took Kire aside.

Relaeh stepped over to his air machine out of hearing distance of the crew and the ladies.

"Dugar...Regor...did you hear the news?"

Dugar replied. "Yes, my friend, and thank you for keeping your telepath open during the conversation. We believe we have a serum to mask the reaction of the outbreaks, but will not have an antidote ready in time of their departure. Regor has set the serum in pill form that I shall give to you this night so they may start to control their episodes. Master Leumas suggests you might have a word with the leader, Bocaj, on the infliction demonizing the men, who will be joining him on his journey back to Inception. The ladies seem well aware of your intent and the need for supplies. I will bring a compass and maps with me for Bocaj and instruct him on their usage. They should be able to cut several weeks off of their journey. I hope, in time for Yuda's delivery in Inception."

"Very well, my friend, I will also instruct him on the usage of the symbol. We have a lot of variables we need to control for their safe passage. Once the energy of the revelation drops its shield, they will be on their own to secure safety on the other side. I worry about Yuda, being with child, to make the distance without injury to herself or her unborn." stressed Relaeh.

"Ruvana has been working on a stretchable brace to support the unborn for the journey," shared Dugar.

"I imagine it would be adjustable to fit any size of roundness and of height?" inquired Relaeh humorously.

"Truly? You will not be satisfied until we have joined in union?" retorted Dugar.

"Sorry, need to go..." quickly replied Relaeh with a smile upon his face.

Relaeh Informs Bocaj – Sports Field

The darkness had transformed into a brightly lit arena for the scurrying of bodies. Lines had been laid upon the field, flower gardens had been tested for water pressure, delivery, and automatic setting, walk-ways had signage placed appropriately, and the tiered seating had been temporarily set.

As the moon approached its highest ascent, indistinguishable shadows accessorized the vacant storage sheds at the rear of the newly constructed sports field. Relaeh engaged Bocaj as they leisurely strolled towards the outer field.

"I beg of your indulgence as I have many words to impart upon you. I have intentionally replaced your symbol with another, as I trust your intent for the citizens of concern. You and your men have proven to be resourceful and sincere in your discoveries, and I...we believe you hold their safety in the highest regard. Your symbol is activated to send and receive messages, to visualize situations, this button is to send an emergency signal, and the bottom right button is a tracking signal attached to our monitors in Nalhs. The one you see around Einna's neck is also activated with her knowledge. One of your challenges will be to monitor their husbands. They have been dealt an injustice to their person for which we are desperately researching a cure. At the moment, they do not know of these devices, as we were unsure of whose intent to inflict this injustice, or from whom their guidance is controlled."

"Of what nature is their injustice?" inquired Bocaj.

"Our scientists believe it is an ancient warrior strain introduced into their blood stream without their knowledge. We are still investigating the reasoning and intent of such action."

"Will they turn on us?"

"We do not believe so, as long as they feel the love and camaraderie shared by their wives and the friendship you all have developed. I have personally inquired to the health of Moltov, as he faced an attack at the festival grounds. I believe my sincerity helped him recover without displaying any violence. Or, it could be possible the strain has not fully developed. We are still not sure of its catalyst."

"We sensed from the ladies that their husbands were in some danger, but they did not specify the nature. We knew the ladies' wish to leave Belcare because of this injustice."

"Not only that, but also in fear of their off-spring. There are many questions to be asked, Bocaj. I am sure your journey will allow time for these to be answered."

"Will you be joining us on our journey?"

"No, my discoveries will have to be determined at a later date. My friend Dugar will be transporting equipment for your use tomorrow at first light. He will instruct you on its usage. Bocaj, I have become fond of you and your men, and I trust your journey to your homes will be successful and without incident."

"And of you, as well; maybe our destinies will cross again in the free land."

"Let us not speak freely in front of Salocin and his friends until the day of the revelation. We do not want to antagonize who may be responsible for their injustice," warned Relaeh.

"I shall hold our conversation true to my heart."

"We still have much work to do, so Bocaj, let us join our fellow workers."

As the two men had been engaged in conversation, the friends of Einna and Rajean had been busily setting up temporary accommodations in the CBC warehouse, so their husbands may concentrate on the construction of the sports field.

John F Russo

Formidable Friendships

The early dawn peeked over the mountains as the rays of sun began to illuminate six couples and their children, who were comfortably resting on their Bio Thermo Insulators (BTI) lying upon the floor of the great room. Retu was the first to rise, as always. He stepped over their overnight guests on his way to the culinary digester. Looking through his sleep-threaded eyes, he perceived Einna, Rajean, and Narfinia had already begun to prepare the first meal. Yuda, Siena, and Kasha had set the table and started to organize their provisions that they hurriedly manifested the night before.

"I bid you fine ladies good will," sleepily commenced Retu.

"Good will to you as well, sir," replied Rajean.

"I am usually the first up to prepare for the others, but I foresee my tardiness has forced your response to duty."

"Not at all, Retu. It is our pleasure to aid in all that will progress your schedule without disruption," replied Einna.

"Our husbands have not been afforded the opportunity to assist in such a fine project with such dedicated men. All of us ladies perceive the maturing of friendship that will be required to fulfill our mutual discoveries," shared Narfinia.

"If I may speak for the others, we have been greatly surprised of the candor displayed by all we have met. Our initial intent was to only observe your society, but your kind words and interest has overshadowed any doubt we may have perceived. We are in full agreement that your presence in Inception will be seen as instrumental in developing our little society. I am from another clan that by chance fell upon Inception. We were greeted with respect and now have become one with its citizens, as we believe you will."

"I have not had the opportunity to work alongside of you, Retu, but my husband Jang, the assistant botanist to Taeman, speaks highly of your friend Kire's interest and dedication," added Siena.

Kasha, wife of Moltov, questioned, "Are you all of partners?"

"Not all. I am a proud husband and father of three children..." Retu indicated by his hand the height of each child, "...the eldest, a boy, perhaps not much longer, as he is insisting on going on hunts with me. My other two are my rays of sunshine, eight, and the youngest two. They take after their mother."

Yuda questioned. "Your second eldest, I presume as to your reference, is a female?"

"Yes."

"I believe I will be in need of her assistance if she so pleases," said Yuda as she rubbed her tummy.

"I tell you with no disbelief, she will welcome the opportunity."

The other men of Inception have now gathered at the sitting of a beautifully arranged table inset with fresh flowers. The friends of Salocin had also risen to accept the light of a new passing. Rajean instructed them on their placement around the table. There were thirteen glasses filled with freshly squeezed orange nectar placed about them. Bocaj noticed the miscount.

"Kind ladies we accept your favor of the morning, but I do detect a miscalculation in the number of servings present."

Just then, Relaeh bustled through the door with a broad grin about his face and sunshine in his eyes.

"Good will to all my fine new friends. I gather everyone had a pleasant resting and are eager to start anew?"

He sat down without an answer at the prearranged thirteenth setting. He raised his glass to salute each other—watchfully.

Bocaj, however, insisted on answering, "I shall speak for myself. Those pads of 'therm...a...bio' invention have rested each and every sore muscle in my body."

"Ones, I had no knowledge of," interjected Songa humorously.

The whole room exploded in jocular explanatories reflecting their well-being. As Dugar and Ruvana approached the sports field, the cachinnation could be heard arising from the CBC warehouse. Dugar telepathed Relaeh, and questioned the intent of such boisterousness. Relaeh's reply was interrupted with jocular intermissions; he finally answered. "We shall be there momentarily."

For Dugar and Ruvana, their wait was short in coming as they watched the workmen, some in pairs, others in three's, but no one walked alone as they approached the field. Relaeh finally appeared from behind the pack with determination in his stride and a grin flushed his face.

"Are you of sweet nectar, my friend?"

"Not the sweet nectar that you envision, Dugar. But our good gentle men, with the help of their wives, have been administered their first session of hope in their orange nectar."

"Our hopes for a mere acquaintance, seems to have blossomed into formidable friendships," shared Ruvana.

"I believe the construction of this sports field truly reduced the flaring of infliction. And now with this formation of friendships, let us hope the tension may lay idle," said Relaeh.

"I shall go to the ladies and instruct Yuda on the harnessing of this apparatus," said Ruvana as she excused herself.

"My friend, is it just I who perceives a development of caring for the ladies from Ruvana?" inquisitively asked Relaeh.

"I believe you to be correct. She has a fondness for the ladies. Maybe she sees their strength, and their devotion to their husbands, and to each other."

"As you and Regor are my brothers, I find myself drawn to Bocaj in a familiar way. I believe his aura is of kindness, respect and determination."

"Much like you, my friend," replied Dugar. "I shall miss you when you take leave on your discoveries."

"Alas, it might not be as soon as I predicted. A cure outweighs my perception for discovery."

"Has everything been set in place?" inquired Dugar.

"Yes, I had Einna instruct Kire to deliver their provisions and hunter paraphernalia to the outer shed nearest the forest line last night. For the next two nights, the ladies will infuse the supplies with their requirements."

"Good, I shall affirm with Bocaj on the instruction and on the usage of the compass and maps."

"Dugar, I would also include Kire and Retu. Kire has been documenting their journey on parchment and Retu is a respected hunter of his society."

"As you wish. The more knowledgeable on the workings of the instrument can only aid in their journey."

"I will recommend Tavlo to join Taeman and Jang on finishing their planting project. He is of solid means and determination; he may ease the burden of labor. His hands are the size of yours," laughed Relaeh.

"I will take that as a grand compliment, my little friend."

As the men joyfully departed, Relaeh headed to the tiered seating to help in final assembly, while Dugar summoned Bocaj, Kire and Retu. Ruvana had made way to the workmen's chambers and knocked on the door.

"Good will, fine ladies, my I enter?"

"Yes, please, Miss Ruvana," respectfully said Rajean.

"I have a life gift for Yuda."

Yuda appeared from the main table with the last of the utensils needed to be placed in the hydro-static cleanser. The other ladies joined in to view Ruvana's gift. She removed it from under her outer wear and placed it upon the lounging room's table.

The ladies took refuge on the soft lounging furnishings. Ruvana placed the apparatus next to Yuda and coarsely adjusted its straps.

"Yuda you will need to remove your clothing so I may make a final adjustment to fit you perfectly. We do not want anything to happen to your unborn before he or she has a chance in your new world," insisted Ruvana as she patted Yuda's baby bump.

The ladies of Belcare, as the ladies of Inception, had not been harassed with fear or condemnation, but were full aware of the beauty of their exposed tenderness. Ruvana instructed Yuda to lift each leg, one at a time to slip into its webbing and then placed, with the help of Kasha, each lead around her back, lifting the tummy support upward, then pressed each strap together one on top of the other. As Yuda grew in mammary size each flap could be adjusted individually, and then the other two leads crisscrossed in front to support her nourishment, and yet again folded into each other behind her neck.

"How does that feel?" inquired Ruvana.

"Madam, I cannot thank you enough. It feels very supportive."

"I have one of similar design but for different intent," announced Siena unabashedly.

"You are so bad, Siena," jestfully remarked Kasha. "That is why you have a child; there are too many missing flaps."

"Actually, did I not let you borrow it, Yuda?"

"Yes, Siena, but I do not believe that was the cause of my impregnation," beamed Yuda.

"When we get to Inception, Siena, I want to trance my husband with its powers," insisted Kasha.

"Maybe the ladies of Inception require garments of display for their husbands," invited Rajean.

The ladies enjoyed their moment of intimate interplay, as Yuda modeled this gift of life from Ruvana.

"Miss Ruvana, we know the journey will be difficult but we all hope you and your man, Dugar, will be able to one day, join us in celebration in Inception," warmly invited Einna.

The ladies all agreed, and one by one, gave Ruvana a hug for her support in contriving a life support for their dear friend, Yuda. Ruvana had unknowingly fostered an endearing friendship with the ladies, out of shear unselfishness, to help their cause. The ladies held hands and agreed to be lifelong friends no matter life's intent.

Inception's Relief

The last several weeks had held everyone in Inception on heightened alert. Their nerves were frazzled as the looming storm played with their senses and judgment. Fortunately, when the daylight broke above their eastern horizon, there was calm in the sky. With their flood gates open, Leinad and Nephets stood on their dock, looking out to sea. Their nemesis had disappeared and the light blue sky was waiting to be warmed by the sun's rays. At waters' edge, only the natural lapping soothed the buried columns of the dock—the bay remained calm. Outside the sandbar, the dance of the wild horses angrily beating the ground had been replaced with an idyllic sonnet, metering each wave with precise rhythm.

During the awakening of the citizens, one by one, they too, marveled at the calmness of the sea and the intensity of the blue sky. The impending horror had been stripped of its guise. Now all may return to normal.

"I have never before been privy to the salacious nature of the intent of this storm," reflected Nephets.

"Aye, I have no imagination that could visualize the fierceness that had lain before us," stated Leinad.

"We are left in wonderment, my friend."

"You speak the truth, Nephets. Now it is time to reorganize our citizens so we can carry on with our commerce."

"I shall gather my wife to fetch the animals from our higher grazing grounds. The herdsmen will be relieved to come home," said Nephets assuredly.

"Very good. I shall aid the citizens with their transition back to their huts, and have the smelters reopen the foundry. Nephets, have Tomei satchel some fresh berries and vegetables for the herdsmen; perchance they have consumed their supply."

"We shall return within a week if all goes well," said Nephets as he took leave from the dock. He traversed along the boardwalk and past the rampart to his hut's sanctuary to where Tomei was waiting. She had perceived their journey and had made ready their provisions. Nephets stepped inside. Tomei seemed predisposed as she instinctively prepared fresh berries.

"Are you of ill health, my love?"

"No... It has been over three months since Bocaj has left on his journey. I long for his smile and peculiar ways."

"He is a proud hunter and displays good sense. He will be fine. We were only a few more years than his when we ventured through the unknown," shared Nephets, vying for agreement.

"He was a boy yesterday and today a man. Aivila has spoken to me of her course of gazing upon Bocaj's eyes on his return. Even though she has not known either mother or shares the blood of Noiram, she has her determination. I suggested we would honor her request and welcome her as a daughter, even more than we do now; however, Bocaj is also determined and his sights may be of different direction."

"And her reaction to your truth?" questioned Nephets.

"As a hunter herself, with perfected aim. She stated she has always loved Bocaj, even as a mere child. She is committed that her love arrow will be true and that she will provide many babies for our delight."

"Hahaha, yes I see our delight. I foretell if this union comes to pass, they will be off discovering and we shall have the pleasure of instructing their little monsters."

Nephets, as always, relinquished a smile upon Tomei's face. He voiced a thought.

"My love, why do we not prepare enough provisions as to rest in the high pasture for several weeks? It is of no consequence if we return next week or three. The grass of the high land will be of benefit for the animals. We can gather the herdsmen wives and children, and sponsor a reprieve from these last several weeks. I predict the children would enjoy the adventure."

"Very well, my love. I shall inform Eittam of our plans as she holds all of our interests so dear to her heart," insisted Tomei.

"She is of her mother," replied Nephets.

"I cannot count the nights that I lay awake recounting her unselfishness in trying to save our son, Trebor. My heart tells me she is not lost, but my mind's truth moistens my eyes with the thought of losing them both."

"I too, my love, and I know Leinad feels the pain every day, not only the injustice to his leg but the heart of

Noiram. He has indicated to me, that without Eittam and Aivila, his life would not be."

Tomei left her hut in search of Eittam to instruct her of their intent to camp at the upper pasture land. She noticed the citizens had been busy securing their huts and Inception had started to return to its normal activities. Eittam and Aivila had reopened the children's school, while the children's parents reestablished their routines. The village was bustling with energy in the wake of the preceding weeks. Tomei entered the school house.

"Good will, Eittam and Aivila."

"Good will to you, Tomei. How may we serve you?" asked Eittam.

"We want to inform you of our intent to camp at the higher grazing land for several weeks. And please inform Leinad as well. Aivila, I spoke to Nephets of your course with Bocaj. He is in agreement of your intent, my love, and wishes all to go well," happily informed Tomei.

The ladies shared a hug before Tomei took leave of the school house.

"Our family's wishes grow, my sister. Now it is up to you to convince Bocaj of your intention," jest Eittam.

"I shall capture his eyes and his heart," stated Aivila with determination.

"I have no preconceived premonition that you will not hold true his heart, my sister," lovingly shared Eittam.

"Now my children, we have five Principals that we, the citizens of Inception hold true to heart. Who shall recite one of them?" questioned Eittam as she gazed over the room for a show of hands.

Aivila, on the other side of the room, instructed the older girls on mending garments and encouraged them to use their imagination on creating new designs for festive wear.

The Seventh Revelation et al

The Din Master always rose early on festive occasions, and this being the seventh revelation, was no different. He decided to inform the citizens of Belcare, before the revelation, of the next passing's celebration and dedication of the newly developed sports field. He would honor the men responsible, the men he and Atir had picked, as the officials representing Belcare's interest. At the ceremony, he would include the other citizens of Belcare who volunteered their time as well. He presumed a notable mention should be made of the dignitaries of Nalhs, who helped sort out the details of such an endeavor.

. . .

As the sun's rays drifted through Erodec's window, he out-stretched his arms past the shoulders of his friend, Droenal. Droenal, sensing his lover's movement cuddled closer and pulled Erodec's arms to his chest. The two laid there in a harmonious awareness of intimacy as the sun warmed their nakedness.

. . .

The CBC warehouse lay dormant and barren having been stripped clean of essential utensils and its exuberant visitors. No longer could there be heard the jocular explosions, or tales of danger that once filled the warmth of the rooms. The furniture was left to neutralize to a default temperature and the walls desensitized to a mottled grey. As the stories remained, "The images faded into the breaking dawn."

. . .

Beyond the sports field, the newly constructed utility shed had been abandoned of instruments of hunting and provisions of necessity. Only the remnants of construction and future maintenance materials took up residency. The chirping of birds defied the once bustle of industry, while calmness and tranquility now filled the air.

Only the whisper of speech and the softness of step could be recognized, drifting, following the band of travelers while they observed the boundary of the energy field. Retu led while the ladies were followed by each man of Belcare spaced between the men of Inception. Einna had tethered Adam to her being as Rajean had done the same with Eve. Siena carried her one-year-old girl in a frontal brace, allowing Kire to assist her in her movement; Bocaj finalized the row. Retu motioned for the regiment to stay clear of the approaching sand fields upon nearing the thinning of the forest. Just beyond the clearing lay the berry bushes, and then, the safehold of the corn fields. He remained as a sentry as each crossed, one by one, to the safety of the brambling bushes. He then restored his lead to the direction of the full-bloomed corn fields that hid their personage. There, they huddled with packs and refreshments, minimizing any conversation; they waited for the drop of the energy field.

During their previous night's dinner, Bocaj revealed the plan to the men of Belcare, the wishes of their wives to escape from the grasp of the Engram, and to set their spirits free from persecution. They, the men of Inception, were their instrument of conviction and determination. The hunters' village lay within two full moons of Belcare, where they would be welcomed as free men. Their contribution could be as Belcare, of course, minus the influence of Nalhs. The men of Belcare rallied with the decision of their wives; they were the responsible force for creating and binding their group together. Any misconception of intent was not apparent with these men as seen through Bocaj's eyes. He agreed with Relaeh that someone else held the control. The group remained cheerful and focused as they waited for the sun to gaze upon the full moon's face. They had performed as a unit before, and now, that unity would save their lives.

. . .

Relaeh remained in his chamber with his friends Dugar, Ruvana, brother Regor, and his Father, Leumas. They had not graced the awareness of the seventh revelation. Their chat was minimal as they patiently waited for word from Bocaj.

. . .

The Din Master looked out over the gathering crowd at the steps of the Androicropulous and noticed his official, Salocin, and his family was not present. And where were the others that worked so hard on the sports field project? He turned to Erodec and in a soft voice said, "Erodec, where are the workers? Can you account for them with your vision?"

Erodec scanned the crowd with precise focus, trying to match the faces to his memory. He could not. He informed the Din Master of his inability to locate the friendly faces of question.

"Erodec, take Droenal by your side and flush out our absentees. They must be here for their adulation."

"Yes, Din Master. We will first check the warehouse as this seems to be a gathering focal point for all. They are probably induced with accomplishment and have miscalculated the approach of the revelation."

The two men took leave and headed south on 4th to the final loop, Serenity. It was only two passings ago that they had an inspiring conversation with the ladies concerning their upcoming portraiture by Kire. *What befuddles them now?* They round the back of the old warehouse and rat-ta-ta on the door. No answer. Droenal tried the handle, the door pushed open with ease. The great room was barren.

"Droenal, look in their chambers," said Erodec horrified.

Erodec peered around corners expecting a vision of mortality, but nothing emerged from its glaucous walls. Droenal hailed out with similar boisterousness as each chamber was abandoned. When Droenal searched the last chamber, at the edge of a cabinet peering out in idleness, a corner of parchment beckoned discovery. Droenal dove over the resting boards and carefully opened the cabinet door. Staring back at its aggressor, in true likeness, Erodec and Droenal were portrayed in a field of Tulips, decorated in a sea of color with a majestic mountain in the background. Erodec, who was swirling around the warehouse, sensed Droenal's quietness. He hailed Droenal loudly, but it was returned with a meager testament. As he slipped through the doorway, Droenal stood motionless; peering down at something he was holding. Erodec stepped to Droenal's side to inspect his findings. Before him, a beautiful portraiture of the two of them as they sat amongst flowers of each color, with a detailed discovery of nature, captured without prejudice. Inscribed in the lower corner, they read, "Let not your perceptions deny another's truth." Signed: Kire.

The two men gazed into each other's eyes with astonishment. Steadfast, they searched for answers in their consciousness. As moisture rose to their vision, they took hold of each other as the tarriance of time had no consequence, only truth would determine their dedication.

As they related in each other's revelation they carefully rolled the portraiture and left the gracious chamber of enlightenment. The platform of the Androicropulous seemed an eternity away. Their hands quivered with both excitement and obscenity, as they defied the servitude of injustice implicating their person. The citizens of Belcare needed to adopt an alternative. Strutting upon the platform, the Din Master questioned their findings. In a word, Erodec hailed, "Vanished!"

They all dropped to their knees as silence filled the air of the Androicropulous, and then, the scintilla of light followed by a reverberation of bells...the veil dropped!

"RUN, RUN, WE MUST ALL RUN - RUN FOR YOUR LIFE!" yelled Bocaj.

Jacor steadied Yuda as she grasped her unborn; they ran for their life in the illumination of the moon. Rajean, picked up Eve, held her tightly to her chest, and ran faster than she ever thought possible. Little Adam took three steps to every one to stay alongside his mother—the wind guided his feet. Kira pushed Siena and her baby with determination, "RUN, Madam Siena, RUN...I will not leave you behind, RUN." The sand pelted their faces and latched to their sweat. Tavlo hailed loudly, "ONLY 50 meters, RUN Ladies, we can do it, PLEASE, RUN FASTER!" Jang and Songa ran side by side, distributing their load between them as the other men, already burdened with provisions, laboriously crossed the line of doom to the safety of their previous camp.

They all collapsed in a pile of joy, as the scintilla of light struck the ground aft of them and re-staked its position of prominence. Moisture obstructed the eyes of all, as the shear astonishment of determination and direction of their new friends, had given way to hope. They lay in a state of euphoria as they gazed, for the first time, upon the true brilliance of the full Moon. It welcomed their freedom. They quickly dust themselves off and danced and hugged each other in unabashed merriment. Bocaj activated his symbol and acknowledged to Relaeh, "We are ALL safe."

Relaeh's chamber exhaled in an exuberance of emotional excitement! Their translucents clinked with sweetness of success as the liquid caressed their lips and tickled their throats.

For Bocaj, his men, et al, it had been three months on this journey of discovery. They had accomplished, for now, what they had promised to do and for the future generations of Belcare.

Erodec and Droenal Conspire

The ease of time passed as the Belcarians once again, joyfully recounted the liberating experience of the revelation. The spacious platform allowed its diminishing dignitaries to rise and influence the crowd of the good word of the Engram. Erodec and Droenal slipped away under the guise of excitement. The Din Master, forcing a smile upon his face, congratulated the other Councilmen. It was as it had been written.

The young Councilman and his friend headed to the privacy of Erodec's chamber. Their stride was of determination. After they closed the door behind them, they stalked about, not knowing where to begin. Finally Erodec said with astonishment.

"If it were not for our knowledge of Kire and the others, I would not have imagined what has occurred before us. And if you were not by my side to witness of what has transpired, I would declare my insanity and commit myself to a room of unaltered consequent. Truly, everything that has gone before us has been of purpose and great design."

"I believe as you, my friend. We have to formulate a plan to determine our future and the future of Belcare. Who can we trust?"

"I am perplexed as you, Droenal." He paused. "The foreman, he illustrated great control over the men working on the construction of the sports field in alliance with the tall one. Maybe he has the key to unlock this mystery."

"By what name did he present himself?"

"I know not, Droenal. I know not of his residency, either? Who is he?"

"Maybe he is our imposter!"

"My imposter? Could it be? Perchance he has resourcefulness to implicate such design? But, by what command? He is not a leader of the community; he does not share a Councilman's seat..."

"He is a Ghost!" interrupted Droenal, "...perchance from the missing DNA records, the escapees of the second generation?"

"I could almost agree, except we are similar in age. If he is a ghost of the second generation, his age could not be concealed. If he is of the third generation, then he is of mother and father and not as I. Regardless, he possesses the ability to transform and then within moments of discovery, he vanishes!"

"He has magic like the men at the festival. They put a pea underneath a cup and move them about in such a manner that discovery is impossible."

"Are you implying he is of three persons?"

"I know not his travel or of his heritage, Erodec. He looks like us but transpires where he deems necessary."

"A man of many colors and personalities, indeed! If he be the one of such design, we could collaborate with his sensitivity to remedy the injustice beholding all of us. If the Engram is our sole being and controller, why have we not been witness to his likeness? The Din Master must be the only one who has shared that vision. I doubt he will conspire with us, as he is a devoted man of the written word. Ah, alas, my head hurts with indecision, Droenal."

"We shall overcome this together."

Erodec rubbed his sorrowful eyes. "We need a plan, and that I am sure."

There was a moment of silence while the two men gathered their wits. Droenal stood in amazement.

"What of the tall one? Dugar is his name. When you set forth to request the attendance of the tall preposterous creature from the parade, he offered his assistance. What would have transpired as a simple encounter to direct the wishes of the Din Master, turned out as before, with our hands empty. Vanished! Maybe it is he who possesses the magic and not the foreman. He created the disturbance of their air machines as the gambler redirects our vision of the cup and pea."

"You are wise, my friend, perhaps we are implying the wrong deduction in favor of the foreman, and have missed in establishing the true honor to the man from Nalhs. It is said they have wisdom beyond our comprehension, this could explain all of our misguidedness."

"How shall we proceed, Erodec?"

"We shall solicit the aid of Dugar by instilling in the Din Master the imperative nature to discuss our findings of the missing 401.11 substance. He must respond in order to maintain his present authority," stated Erodec.

"He did request that we meet at his private chamber after the dedication of the sports field to discuss our findings. What do you suppose he will do now without the organizers being available?"

"I believe he will claim all the adulation for its success and not quiver a moment."

"I believe you speak the truth. Shall we get more comfortable before the sun begins to awaken our citizens?" queried Droenal.

Laying in the quietness of Erodec's chamber, Droenal asked, "What of the image Kire displayed on our portrait? Do you believe such a place exists?"

Night's End

The Din Master was appalled with the one word oratory of Erodec, "Vanished!" He headed to the old warehouse to see for himself. The dimmed bluish cast of the full moon lit his way as he approached the darkness of the warehouse. The door was unlocked, so he pushed through. The ceiling light illuminated a reddish cast, as it perceived the intruder's aura. The walls varied in a kaleidoscope of color, unsure of its destiny. The figure darted from room to room, nothing, not a clue to their whereabouts. Frustrated, he left the hollowness behind. The sports field was vacant but it was ready for the citizens of Belcare.

During his isolated walked, he pondered, *I shall give a grand speech indicating the cooperation between the Council and the Nalhsians. I shall deem it Belcare Place in honor of its citizens. Maybe Belcare Landing, or Belcare Sports Facility, or BC Place for short, or...I will think of it tomorrow. Erodec and Droenal have some explaining of their findings. I am eager to learn of such misdirection.*

. . .

The iridescent twinkle of the clear night's sky soothed the pain of injustice that occupied the former men of Belcare. They sat in peace with their families and friends around an intimate fire. Bocaj placed in their drink another pill to further mask any anxiousness. They indulged in this tempered relaxation. The men of Inception wasted little time in setting up camp and laid out their newly acquired BTIs. *No more cold grounds or discomforted*. A gift from their friend Relaeh was truly welcomed, and with enough to pass along to the citizens of Inception. The peculiarity of its diminished size, once opened, could comfort a man and his wife.

Tomorrow's light would bring challenges of new circumstances from a new world that they would confront together. Their eyes grew heavy as their minds explored their imaginations.

. . .

The gathering at Relaeh's finally came to pass. As he laid in slumber, the excitement of disguise, the challenges of discovery, and the endearment of friendship rested on his mind. He had a smile on his face, but an aching in his heart.

ACT II

The Awakening

The Awakening Begins

The men of Inception had plenty of practice striking camp, but today, they milled about re-organizing packs for better distribution of weight before their friends awoke to the crystal clear morning. One by one as the warming sun kissed their faces, the citizens of Belcare stretched and yawned to the smell of the flavor of outdoor cooking. Retu was in his element. With a broad smile, he mixed and blended his concoctions with a swish and a swirl over the charcoaled fire. Ooh's and aah's broke the silence as the smells drifted over the heads of the awakening guests.

"My friends, it is time to taste my cooking without the aid of your culinary digester," proudly invited Retu.

As each gathered around, Retu placed his delicious mixture upon his newly acquired, almost weightless plates. His guests digested with delight at his masterful culinary skills. Their early morning departure was continually delayed as each had to manifest in their minds, a different sound, or color, or smell. Their senses were awakening to a new dawn of discovery. It was magical!

Bocaj smiled with well-being as he and his friends assisted their future citizens of Inception. Tavlo, who had being privy of the workings of the compass while they were in Belcare, now instructed Salocin and Sirius on the usage of the compass and how it related to the parchment called a *Map*. Relaeh had related to Bocaj of Tavlo's strong yearning for mathematical equations, as he had perceived Tavlo's intent while they assembled the inner workings of their warehouse, and also during the assembly of the tiered sitting benches. Collectively, they all had a special talent to share with each other.

With the use of Kire's sketches and his notations, Tavlo plotted their swiftest course to Inception.

"We will head straight south along the inner waterways, through the valley of the flowers and cross your suspended bridge over the great gorge, and then, instead of traversing to the wild waters of the west, we will implement our modern technology to continue through the uncharted low lands that are beset between these two mountain ranges."

They were all in agreement, as the least amount of rugged terrain would set well with the ladies, especially Yuda.

With provisional packs hoisted upon the backs of the men, the ladies carried the much lighter BTIs, garments for two days of journey before the need to re-wash, and containers of liquid refreshment. It was their beginning of a new life as they happily followed Retu and Tavlo.

Yuda's life brace allowed her the security to keep even pace with her fellow travelers. Kasha started everyone singing a humorous, traditional Belcarian three-part harmony as a passing of time.

. . .

After they had spent two full days in the heat-stricken windless valley, they welcomed the relief of the cool breeze that brought much needed moisture. In only two days, they had shared the experience of blazing heat, and now, as the dark heavy clouds gave way to falling moisture, it penetrated every segment of their body. They gleamed with excitement. Eve stuck her tongue out to capture its moisture and suckled its nourishment. The constant of Belcare was quickly being replaced by natural beauty and elements. They set up camp under the protection of emerald-green canopies with views of distant protrusions that rose majestically from its earth, and mysteriously puffed an occasional plume of white mist.

The third morning brought freshness to the air as they once again bore their burdens and forged south. By midday, they had entered the valley of the flowers, now known as Tulips. Taeman and Jang joined Kire in the excitement of witnessing the natural placement of these wonderful flowers. They too, agreed with Kire of the unparalleled beauty that beckoned one's spirit to remain in their midst. Perhaps, on another journey, they would be able to tame the origin for future studies. At present, their destiny was cast.

Heading in a southwesterly direction, they rounded the heel of the inner waters, where Kire added words of interest not known to the Belcarians. As Inception had enjoyed a periodic time piece, and had adopted ancient adjustments of calendar, he thought it was necessary to school their new friends in this enlightenment.

"We no longer speak of a *passing* as between the sun to the moon, but as a day. Each day is divided into 24 equal segments known as hours, and each hour is divided into 60 minutes, where by each minute has 60 seconds. I know this is confusing, but it does get easier. With this same logic, seven days equal a week and four weeks, thereabouts equal a month, known as your *moon risings*. We have twelve months in a year, no longer called a *legion*."

"How did your citizens come by these instruments?" queried Einna.

"It had been written in Leinad's book, and as he deciphers the knowledge contained within, he discharges to us. His daughters, Eittam and Aivila, teach our young ones these enlightenments," answered Tavlo.

"By what chance has he been afforded this knowledge?" questioned Rajean.

Bocaj interjected, "Our fathers carried this knowledge with them when they undertook their escape."

"Are we to build upon this knowledge?" asked Salocin.

"Yes, this is ancient knowledge that has been passed down. When you gaze into the night sky, each set of stars tells a story that relates to our movement upon earth," said Tavlo. "As the earths distance changes between the sun, and the relationship between the stars increases or decreases, our passing of the months indicates different seasons."

"We have no change of seasons, as you call them, in Belcare. Every passing... pardon me, every day was as the one before. I do not have knowledge of any periodic time piece," insisted Salocin.

"Maybe your councilmen have decided not to introduce such a time piece as part of their control over its citizens. We call it a sundial," elaborated Bocaj.

"Why would they entertain such a folly?"

"I have no reply to your question, Rajean," admitted Bocaj.

"Do you not have books of interest in the Androicropulous?" asked Tavlo.

"Not as you suggest. Or not that are on display for the citizens to query," said Einna.

"You say we now have four seasons. Are they divided equally as well?" asked Taeman, trying to digest this new revelation.

With a slight hint of humor, Bocaj replied, "Well, it depends on your tolerance to cold and location. If we remain where we stand, cold will be upon us soon. When we arrive in Inception, we will enjoy a moderate temperature during our winter months and warm to hot weather for ten months."

"So this will increase our growing time, uh season, as we have in Belcare," said Taeman.

"Spoken as a true botanist, my husband," smiled Rajean.

"I have noticed at first, redness to my skin and now it turns to brown." said Siena inspecting her arms.

"We are in the summer season of this area, and as you stay longer in the rays of the sun, your skin will change in color. Do not tempt the rays, as your skin will be afire," warned Kire.

"I like this color," she insisted. "Perhaps I should shed my garments to devote my wholesomeness to these rays. Look Yuda, my shade is as yours."

"We will have time to enjoy our journey after we have crossed our suspended bridge. It is a treacherous fabrication that served us well, but I question its sturdiness for the weight in which we carry. It took us three days to arrive where we stand from the great gorge, so I am estimating four to five days as we are laden," informed Bocaj.

Their journey seemed to shorten each day, as new discoveries were brought to light. As each enlightenment sprung to the forefront of their awareness, they desired more to be part of Inception. There was so much to learn. Their nights were now spent, not just gazing upon the stars, but engaged in understanding their meaning.

Erodec Exclaims

Erodec had maintained an anonymous stature for eight passings since the awakening of the discourse of the seventh revelation. His chamber had allowed him the seclusion to manifest a litany of scenarios without the absolution of one. Droenal had appeared on occasion to question Erodec's condition, but it was suggested his solace was not yet ready. His function as an intern to the Din Master, the protectorate of the T-series books, was threatened; this caused great suffering in his mind and his duty. Thousands of pages he had set to memory, for what intent? For the truth that lay in the brush strokes of Kire's portrait, or the disappearance of his fellow workmen? Or, the truth that set them as puppets to the desire of the Engram, and the treachery of his fellow councilmen? Which truth was he to realize? An optional existence beyond the energy field did prevail. This truth he believed.

Droenal thought that eight passings was enough for Erodec to understand his direction of intent, and to initialize a response. He knocked on Erodec's door with the suggestion of authority.

"Erodec, it is I. We need to speak, let me in," he demanded.

Erodec got up from his chair and let Droenal in.

"Thank you, my friend. It is time for us to talk."

"Yes Droenal, I believe I cannot endure another passing sitting in this chamber."

"Good! That is what I came to hear. Let us forge a plan, a plan that will question everything we have been told, a plan that reverses our instructions in the great books, and a plan to aid the citizens of Belcare in their exploration."

"You have been busy planning your own escape, I do believe, Droenal?"

"No, just to instill in you and your duty to the citizens. If not you, then who? The Din Master visited me at my office and inquired why we had not met with him after the dedication? I instructed him that an illness had come over you."

"Thank you, my friend. I have been in thought. Of the many questions in my mind, I believe as our original assumption, Dugar of Nalhs must be our first inquiry. I am, as you say, feeling much better after this stay of solitude."

"Then let us go now to speak with the Din Master of our previous findings. Perhaps he will have instruction for us?" insisted Droenal.

The two men departed Erodec's chamber and made haste to the Androicropulous where the Din Master was usually preoccupied. The day was as always, pleasant, but now they visualized everything with greyish overtones— not at all like Kire's portrait. They ascended the steps of the Androicropulous and then charged the weighted revolving doors to the waiting rotunda that directed its visitors to the grand hallway of the auditorium. Sitting off by himself, they saw Din Master engrossed in one of the T-series books. Erodec and Droenal quietly confronted him.

"Good will, Din Master," emitted Erodec, softly.

Looking up from his readings, and upon identifying the familiar face, the Din Master cordially replied, "Good will to you, Erodec. I trust you are feeling of better health?"

"Yes, thank you, much better."

"And you, Droenal. How is your health?"

"Very well, Din Master, thank you for inquiring."

"By what circumstance have I been afforded this gathering?"

"I beg your indulgence for not collaborating with you after the dedication, as my illness severely hampered your invitation. Respectfully, we would entertain an audience with you as your schedule dictates."

"Very well, Erodec, shall we retire to the seclusion of my office since it is directly above us?"

"It would be most welcomed, Din Master."

The three withdrew from the auditorium with watchful eyes following their intent. Since the Din Master's office was only one floor up, they took the marbled staircase. The door of Din Master's office was of heavily-carved wood with depictions of sea animals and creatures of stoic nature; they entered. The Din Master strolled behind his elaborate desk and graced the red-padded chair with his presence.

"I believe our earlier conversation ended abruptly with implication of an issue of more substantial interest. Could you be so kind as to elaborate?"

"Yes, Din Master. Sir, we did as you instructed on cross referencing between several of our archival departments, including Droenal's. I was able to persuade Councilman Yannis' wife Landora, at the RDDS, to reveal through the numerical values obtained from Droenal, the sequence of births that corresponded to the 130 missing second generation citizens and then cross referenced those with birth announcements registered through our citizens' documentation department. But as we researched, the differences in DNA representing our known Councilmen, a reference number of 401.11 was somehow removed from encrypted files by someone of high authority," informed Erodec.

"And what is this 401.11?"

"We are not sure of its value or its intent, but Landora confided that a value that low must be from an ancient society."

"Who could have gained entrance and for what purpose?" incited the Din Master.

"We do not have knowledge of that either," added Droenal. "We presume someone from Nalhs might have knowledge of the transaction or the meaning of this substance."

"We do have knowledge of the tall one, called Dugar, who might be able to enlighten us on this quest," shared Erodec.

"It may explain the disappearance of 130 of our citizens and the workmen from our sports field project," elaborated Droenal.

"You have not heard... it was not only the workmen that disappeared, but our citizens of position, Salocin, Taeman, and Jacor and their families are missing as well," enlightened the Din Master.

"WHAT!" exclaimed Erodec.

Beacons of Hope

From the depths of Regor's lab, his fellow scientists heard the overzealous cry of "EUREKA!" Regor hailed loudly as he finally broke the genetic code for the warrior gene. It had been a grueling several months of laborious sacrifice with sleepless nights and drowsy days. His last experiment quantified his results of isolation and degeneration of its multiplying influence. He pondered his next step to secure the serum in an appropriate form for travel and delivery into the men's system.

Injection would be the preferred delivery but as their travels are of concern, possible breakage of vials or misdirection of the needle without instruction, could be a major factor to a suitable design. A gel capsule would be fine, but they would need two a day to one syringe. They would not be able to mix it in sweet nectar, but swallow in whole...that would be of certain distaste. The heat factor could also play a role. Hmmmm, either the serum or capsule would have to be chilled. How would they be able to control that?

Regor invited Master Leumas to his lab to discuss the good news, but also to conspire on an appropriate delivery system. He also informed Dugar and Relaeh on his H-WAC of his discovery. Dugar sent his brother a "Congratulations" telepathically and Relaeh replied with excitement over his Anon. Dugar and Relaeh agreed to join Regor in his lab immediately.

After fifteen minutes of travel, Dugar and Relaeh were throwing their arms about Regor's stature. The room was filled with cheer and "well done!"

"I had complete faith in you, Regor," admitted Relaeh.

"Relaeh speaks the truth, brother. I believed in your ability to solve this injustice."

As they were reveling in the jubilant news, Master Leumas entered Regor's lab.

"Well done, Regor. I believe my faith in your ability was not of question."

"Thank you, Master Leumas, but my concern now is how shall we deliver the antidote to the men and then administer such? The serum must stay chilled before entering the blood system as a temperature rise will weaken its effectiveness."

"At what temperature must it remain?" inquired Master Leumas.

"At 12.22 degrees Celsius."

"Our air machines are capable of inducing that through our condensate chillers," factually replied Relaeh without hesitation.

"And how will you know their whereabouts?" asked Regor.

"I programmed Bocaj's symbol with a tracking signal."

"At what distance and what terrain does it heed true?"

"I have been tracking their progress for the last eight days; however, when the terrain dips low, I lose the signal."

"So, Relaeh we are in need of a celestial beacon to maintain transmission of his signal." stated Dugar.

"Do we have such a device?"

"Ruvana was speaking of such a device the other day. It was in reference to what we speak of today," happily shared Dugar.

"And…?" invited Relaeh.

"She and her colleagues have had one developed for years, but have not had an occasion to deploy it."

"How are we to set it in the sky?" asked Relaeh.

"It has a fusion thruster that will propel it into the air beyond the gravitational pull of earth," informed Dugar.

"Perchance my question was confusing; we cannot penetrate the energy dome. Again, how are we to set it in the sky?"

"A question indeed, Relaeh. We will need to ponder on that for a time," said Master Leumas.

"One other element to consider, Master Leumas; I cannot guarantee the stability of the serum for an extended period of time. We must act as soon as possible," explained Regor.

"Dugar, do you know the whereabouts of Ruvana at present?"

"Probably in her lab, Master Leumas."

"Very well, inquire if you may drop by to witness the size and ideal scope of engineering such a feat. Perhaps she has an answer to our question. I shall remain here with Regor and sort out the logistics of transporting the antidote to the men. One question, Regor, how many of your original pills where given to Bocaj to administer?"

"Twenty one days. They had three days before they left and now eight days on their travels, which only leaves ten more days until the manifestation of the gene will once again be without protection."

"Relaeh, Dugar, you heard Regor. You have less than ten days to raise this beacon and to make contact with the men. You have a challenge set before you, good will my sons."

"Yes, Master Leumas." Dugar and Relaeh took leave of Regor and Master Leumas and headed to Ruvana's lab where she was waiting for their arrival.

The Weaver II was an intermediate elevator, compared to the Endeavor. Its travel was not as deep and used mainly for midrange travel between decks 21 and 99. Since Regor's lab was located on the 86th deck, only nine more levels above his would be necessary for them to ascend. It only took minutes for them to arrive at Ruvana's lab. As Relaeh's Anon announced their arrival, Ruvana waited with a loving smile on her face. It had been several days since Dugar and Ruvana had seen each other, as both had been very busy.

"Good will, my love and good will to you, Relaeh."

"Good will to you, Ruvana," replied Relaeh as Dugar walked straight for Ruvana and placed his lips to her forehead. They shared a quick embrace and then turned their intentions professional.

"I gather the celestial beacon is the reason for both of you to be here?"

"Dugar implied you have such an apparatus that could keep us in constant contact with the citizens out in the new world."

"Not just one, but several, so we might triangulate positions around the globe without losing contact on the other side of earth." explained Ruvana.

"And how might they be released from Nalhs?" questioned Relaeh.

"They cannot. That is why we sit in silence from possible contact with others. The treaty will not allow us to interfere unless the citizens of earth are threatened."

"Please indulge me, Ruvana. If the citizens of earth are in peril, we can interfere by any means to defend their lives?"

"Correct."

"Then I propose the citizens of Belcare are at great risk if we do not intercede with the administering of Regor's antidote," expressed Relaeh.

"You must secure that assumption through Master Leumas and his Council before we are allowed to set beacons of communication in the sky. You must know, doing so allows us to monitor any and all communications derived from those beacons. In the ancient world, war broke out over such a maneuver by one of the Americas as they listened to conversations from other governments and the earths' citizens," enlightened Ruvana.

"But this is for the protection of our citizens," insisted Relaeh.

"I agree, but you should know the possible consequence based on what has transpired in the past."

"As I am of Belcare, and I have been somehow instructed to heal the citizens, I place my trust in Nalhs to always ensure the safety and security of the citizens of earth, as you do today. It is with this co-operation, I believe will hold true to all, for the betterment of all," declared Relaeh.

"My friend, you sound like a true Councilman, and I say this without prejudice. You do warm my heart that we all will be equal through the eyes of all."

"Dugar, Ruvana, I will die with this truth upon my lips."

"Well then, Ruvana, how shall we proceed to help our friend accomplish what he must do?"

"We need to be on the outside to set the beacons into flight. Let us approach Master Leumas, as I believe he already knows of the questions we will indulge him with. Let him make the decision," stated Ruvana.

"How large or small are these? Will they fit into a personal air machine, or will I need a commercial loader to transport them into position?" asked Relaeh.

"For expedience, two commercial air machines; one can be used for storage of extra guide lines, launch pads, inclinometers, and Anon guidance systems, so we may control its trajectory. The beacons measure five meters so the other transporter should handle their size. It must be fitted with an articulating arm to assist in positioning. You will be in need of assistance to set the correct degree of angle and mounting position, so they will adhere to our coordinates in orbit. There are six of total to be launched," informed Ruvana.

"Then I shall be his assistant as the representative of Nalhs," insisted Dugar proudly.

"Do you believe that I am going to let you two have all the fun? I have wanted to fire these off for years. I shall assist you as well, Relaeh. The ladies are my friends, so this is my contribution for the legacy for human survival," declared Ruvana.

With their plan in hand, the three departed Ruvana's lab, stepped onto the moving walk-ways to the Weaver II and descended back to Regor's lab on deck 86. As they entered, Master Leumas was about to leave.

"Father, we are glad to see you are still here. We have a plan and request your consideration in facilitating its outcome."

"Proceed, Relaeh."

"Ruvana and Dugar have committed their expertise and determination to aid in establishing communication beacons globally. We need your permission to possibly set a Portal beyond the energy dome, and to transport our air machines to the outer world for positioning of the beacons for launching. We are in full agreement and belief that the treaty would not be compromised, as this action would save the lives of our citizens."

"You are asking of me, Relaeh, which I cannot grant alone. I will need to consult with the other Councilmen of Nalhs, on the legality of such a maneuver. Nonetheless, I do feel the imperativeness as you all here. You have demonstrated your concern for the citizens, of not just Belcare, but of all who might be living on the outside and those who will come after them. As time is of essence, I would wager your intent would be to install a Portal beyond the energy field, using an extinct air shaft that might exit beyond the sand fields. Would this be an accurate assumption?" stated Master Leumas, instructively.

"Umm, yes Father. That is an accurate assumption for which we had planned."

"Very well, I shall gather my peers to question your plight and secure your permission. I would also imagine you would require a temporary permit to set this in motion without delay? Would that also be a correct assumption, Ruvana?"

"Uh...yes, Master Leumas. The Physical Engineering Department would require such a permit to access a Portal for transportation and installation."

"I thought as much. And Dugar, I would imagine your representation and facilitation would be in accordance with any legal aspect that you three should encounter?"

"Yes, Mater Leumas. My accounting of this matter would most definitely endorse and solidify any question of intent that our elders and the treaty could manifest."

"I could not have said that any better, Dugar. I believe you have an order without restriction waiting for you, Madame Ruvana. Now, what are you all still doing here? Be off."

Relaeh wrapped his arms around the pudgy man from Nalhs... his Father, his mentor. The three inspiringly pranced from Regor's lab.

As they made-way on the movable walk-way, Relaeh said, "I believe my Father just gave us instructional words that we might not have conjured if it was not for his direction. And..." he turned to Ruvana and said with great pride, "...Ruvana, my Father called you Madame Ruvana."

Beaming, she said, "Yes, I perceived his intent and I shall not let him down."

"I have only heard one other bestowed with such admiration and that is Madame Noir."

"Stop, Relaeh, you are making my face flush and moisture conjures in my eyes."

"My dear..." Dugar placed his arms about Ruvana, "...You are respected by us all. And for me, you have captured my heart."

"YES! That is what I have been waiting for," loudly hailed Relaeh.

The three interlaced their arms as the moving walk-way brought them closer to their dreams. Their stature among the citizens of Nalhs had been recognized with Master Leumas' gesture. Forever more, Ruvana would be known by her peers as Madame Ruvana. An endearing moment shared by the future of mankind.

Shake and Roll

The citizens, led by Bocaj, stood at the entrance to the first of two suspended bridges that crossed the mighty gorge. The rushing waters below suggested a hypnotic illusion if care was not taken to look forward whilst nearing its rocky edge. The strands of rope and vine appeared to be as stable now as when they intertwined them on their first crossing.

Bocaj honored Micja to step forth without pack, but with a tether, and instructed him to tie it off around a large tree. Upon the second man's arrival, return for his pack, as he only wanted one person at a time to cross on the stepping logs. The time allotted for this procession would be tedious, but Bocaj thought necessary for everyone's safety. The weight of each man with pack was almost equal to half-a-man again. Each person had a tether placed around them with a loop over the newly-stretched life line.

After each mother took to the stepping logs and safely reached the other side, her husband with child, followed. Bocaj and three of his men still remained to cross. Kire stepped gingerly across the stepping logs without incident. Micja, now with his full pack, crossed as tepid as Kire, again without incident. Songa got the go-ahead from Bocaj as soon as Micja touched the other side. Bocaj watched nervously as Songa secured each step before taking another. He stepped onto the island safely. Bocaj untied the rope from the securing tree behind him, as Tavlo pulled the slack. Bocaj treaded onto the stepping logs. A breeze rose from the gorge below and swayed the bridge with slight intention. Bocaj, hand over hand, step by step, ensured his placement before advancing. Tavlo reeled in the slack without throwing Bocaj off balance. It was team work as the others watched nervously. Finally, Bocaj plotted his foot upon the rock island and all relax with a sighed, "Phew!"

One more gorge to tackle before they could continue to the south. Bocaj offered his plan again, as everything went well on the first crossing. Micja, again without pack, tested the validity of the stepping logs as he crossed the second narrow bridge. He tied off the life line as he had previously done and signaled for the first to cross. Tavlo, being a man of determination and girth, was second to cross without incident and stood by as Micja re-crossed as before. Einna crossed successfully. Salocin with Adam tethered to him, crossed the rock face gorge without incident. Bocaj estimated that the drop would have to be approaching 120 meters and the depth of the rushing waters was unknown. Not a pleasant environment to plummet into.

Kasha and her husband, Moltov, were the last of the couples to step onto the swaying bridge. The breeze had picked up to a more constant intention and vigor. She held on tightly as the bridge creaked in defiance. Well wishes and endearments filled the air as she painstakingly and fearfully etched forward over the great gorge. Intensely, her friends watched. At last, cheers prevailed as she reached the main land and she fell into the waiting arms of Tavlo. Moltov rejoiced with a waving of his fist as he approached and tempted the dourly play of the wind. Cautiously he treaded, but with determination. Moltov was second in size to Tavlo, with as much determination. His pack was heavy; he set forth with the weight of one and half men. The stepping logs strained under his footing, but gracefully granted him his place on the main land beside his thankful wife.

Kire and Micja crossed as before, but with more determination, as the wind had increased its deliverance. Only two were left to defy the wind and the waiting white caps of the waters below. Their suspension bridge had served them well as Tavlo's design of triple wrapping each stepping log proved to be more secure, especially for the added weight each man now carried.

Songa once again made that first cautious step upon the logs as he stepped out from behind the sheltering bushes into the full force of the intimating wind. He stood midway on the bridge... when suddenly—the ground SHOOK with FIERCE GYRATION..., trees TOPPLED with a deafening BOOM..., waters RUSHED the sides of the sheer cliff, and the bridge... the bridge flipped upside down with a CREEK and SWOSH! Songa hung in suspension—dangling—only his tethered life line secured his fate from what awaited him below.

Tavlo picked himself up from the ground and charged the inversed bridge. Songa was safe, as long as his tether remained strong. Tavlo's securing tree stood proud, but across the gorge, Bocaj was dangerously re-routing the life line around another of more substantial girth. His arms pumped with adrenalin; his face contoured with grim realization that he held Songa and his heavy pack in his grip. Tavlo and the rest HAILED with support as Bocaj tried to encircle the loftier anchor of life. His legs trembled under the suspended weight—he struggled to gain his footing. Half around, then once around, and then he encircled one more time. His bloody hands soaked the rope as he attempted to knot the free end. Secured, he collapsed in pain.

Micja instinctively tethered a line to his waist and slowly edged out over the treacherous waters along, the now underside, of their bridge. Tavlo stabbed the twisted-crossed lines with a sturdy fallen branch so they could not reverse and send Micja over the side to certain death. Moltov aided Tavlo as the two men forced the lines to remain in their inverted position.

"Stay calm, Songa! I am coming!" hailed Micja.

Songa's view was obstructed by his pack as he dangled precariously by a single tether a meter below the swinging bridge. Only the sound of the fiercely lapping waters was audible to his ears. Bocaj approached the edge to see Songa swaying helplessly as the tether wedged tightly under his arm pits with the weight of his pack. Songa could see Bocaj above him in pain and bleeding. He was trying to say something to him but his pack and the waters below made it impossible to hear. Suddenly—another shake shook the ground beneath them. The fierceness was not as the one before but still with determination, which caused the bridge to sway even more. The tether tightened around Songa. Micja was tussled in the new wave of shaking. He held on with clenched fists on the twisted ropes. He remained in movement like that of a spider in the wind, without hesitation. He approached his dangling friend. Tavlo and Moltov remained resolute in holding the bridge in the inverted position; sweat moistened their garments—muscles trembled. The ladies watched Micja in horror as he risked his life for another. Where Songa's line was tied, Micja tied another, and then another, before he dropped over the side, suspended in midair facing his friend.

"Good to see you, Micja. What took you so long?" jest Songa.

"I knew you were not going anywhere too soon, so I had a refreshment before I chanced saving your bag of bones. Listen my friend...I am going to tie off your pack and then cut it loose from your back. Your tether might respond with slack so I will tie a loop around each leg and slip it around your waist. Let the pack go, we can recover it after we get you topside and right the bridge. Can you feel your arms?"

"You mean the two stumps that are holding me from slipping through to the waters below? No, I cannot."

"Alright, here goes, just follow the flow, I have you," insisted Micja.

Micja cut the webbing on Songa's new pack donated by Relaeh for this journey. Snap... snap—like that of a wide-tailed animal beating on the water. The pack dropped away from Songa. His body propelled upward, and then downward, swaying in defiance to the twisted bridge. His bloodied arms soaked his clothing from the tethering.

"Very good, my friend, you are doing fine. I shall go topside and pull you up. With the pressure off your arms, can you feel them?"

"I know I have them. How useful they are right now, that I do not know."

"When I start to pull you up, if you can help by grabbing onto the bridge, please feel free."

"I will do what I can, my friend."

Micja swung up onto the bridge and tied himself off with a shortened tether.

"Alright, my friend, I am going to turn you around so you face the bridge and me. Keep your eyes on me... All right, now..."

Micja strained to pull the much larger, Songa upward, a centimeter at a time. His body flexed on each measurable delivery, hand over hand, he pulled on the tether until Songa was in range of grabbing onto the bridge. He attempted to lift his swollen arms, almost lifeless arms...

"Try, my friend! You need to help me..." hailed Micja.

Songa made another attempt of swinging his arms up to grasp the bridge. His face declared the grimacing of pain, but his strong hands took hold. Micja pulled. Songa mustered all his strength to assist. His legs remained dangling below the bridge without a foothold. Moments seemed like hours until Micja was able to grab the back of Songa's pants and he hoisted Songa up to the flat of the underside of the bridge. The two lay motionless, one on top of the other expressing jovial intent. Finally, Micja raised his hand to acknowledge their success. The ladies exhaled a sigh of relieve and bore moisture that filled their eyes—they cried out with joy. The men followed suit cheering their fellow hunters onward. Bocaj smiled in relief as moisture clouded his vision. Tavlo and Moltov remained resolute. Their muscles ached as the bridge rebelled against them.

Micja grabbed Songa by his waist and slowly they crawled along the wavering platform. Kire and Kasha extended their hands in aid to hoist Songa and Micja to safety of the main land. Tavlo and Moltov released the branch from between the crossed lines and the bridge flipped back to its intended position sending the branch like an arrow into the depths below. The bridge bounced and swayed, and then it finally slowed to the precarious positioning of the wind. Only Bocaj remained. With bloodied hands wrapped in his top shirt, he painfully lifted his pack to his back and stepped forth onto his bridge.

Shake but No Roll

Armed with the astonishing news, of not only the workmen, but key municipal officials had vanished, Erodec and Droenal left the Din Master's office and headed downstairs to the RDDS department. Erodec swung open the door and saw sweet Landora sitting by herself.

"Good will to you, madam Landora," announced Erodec.

Looking up and seeing her young lover with another man by his side, she acknowledged Erodec, "Good will to you, Councilman. May I help you?"

"I have come in regards to your missing friend, the pregnant one. I believe her name is Yuda?"

"I do not know what to say, Councilman. She was here one day and then not the next. I went to her home with presumption of her taken ill. When I entered, she was not there. Nothing seemed amiss; garments remained in closets, utensils in drawers, and bedding was neatly folded. I did notice a sketch of Jacor and Yuda from their union was missing. I remember on a previous visit commenting on the handsome couple as it was displayed in plain view. Other than that one item... she just vanished."

"Did she share any misconceptions of belief or foretell signs of abnormality?"

"No, except she was a little anxious about the long hours her husband was enduring building the sports field."

"Concerns for his health?" questioned Droenal.

"She made no comment one way or the other."

"And her friends, Einna and Rajean, what of them?" asked Erodec.

"I have not laid eyes on them since before the revelation. Does this have anything to do with our scenario?" affectionately inquired Landora.

"UH... not exactly... we are still investigating all possibilities to disclose the nature of these disappearances," nervously answered Erodec.

With a quick smile, Landora said, "Well, let me know if I can assist you further in your intentions."

"We shall, madam Landora, and thank you for your impressions," said Erodec cordially.

The two men shuffled out of the archives of RDDS. They ascended the stairs without a word, through the rotunda and beyond the revolving doors. As they were about to take their first step down the Androicropulous' massive concrete stairs, the ground HEAVED without compassion. The two were brought to their knees. Small cracks snaked through the outside auditorium before them.

"What was that!?" questioned Droenal.

"I do not believe I have ever felt anything like that."

People streamed out of the building behind them, mystified, as they. They looked around, talked with each other and pointed at the snake-like cracks in the ground and most of all, befuddled of such intent. There was no explanation for this tremor.

As the citizens of Belcare gathered to debate the unusual occurrence, the Nalhsians recorded the shock wave that rocked the north and southwest landscape. Perched to enter the Endeavor, Master Leumas paused in stepping as a slight shift caused a momentary adjustment to the level of the Endeavor's platform. He was not fazed by what had just transpired—he had endured several in his aging years. Unaltered, he headed to confer with Madame Noir of the latest developments concerning the men of Belcare. He reached Madame Noir's lab and entered.

"Good will, Madame."

"Good will to you, Leumas. I perceive you felt the slipping of plates?"

"Nothing I haven't felt before."

"We have located the epic center to be around the old San Francisco Bay area. A 7.8 magnitude," informed Madame Noir.

"Is San Francisco still there?"

"Leumas, you are indeed in a mood."

"Oh umph! My concern is not for a little shake and roll but getting the antidote to the men of Belcare. I believe they could do more damage if untreated. One can only hope they were not in a position of danger when they got hit with the shaking."

"I am sure they will overcome any challenges that might befall them," insisted Madame Noir.

"There are several elements for us to discuss. I have been informed that Erodec would chance a meeting with Dugar on a matter of disturbing consequence. As related to me, a substance numbered 401.11 that I believe to be the warrior gene. The other concerns Relaeh in deploying communication beacons from the outer world. Dugar and Madame Ruvana have committed their allegiance in setting forth this endeavor, but as you are aware, that could be a grey area within the treaty."

"I understand your hesitation with the latter, Leumas, but as you say, they have pledged their allegiance with Relaeh, which is exactly what we had hoped for—the bringing together of two misunderstood citizens of this earth. What better alliance then best friends leading the way?"

"My problem is... I have no hesitation. My concern is that my love for these two boys is clouding my judgment and possibly forcing a standard of loyalty that may be misconstrued as my overzealousness of defrocking the Engram before natural occurrences," lamented Master Leumas.

"They have asked of you by their own free will. That is the natural occurrence you speak of. We both believe, and as we have nurtured competition, respect and love between them, it has always been their choice to develop their loyalty with each other.

"You should be pleased of this relationship... or do I detect a solemn remiss of watching these boys turn into men that has caught your stature in a quandary, my dear friend?"

"Noir...Why must you always understand my feelings before I logically deduce my own?"

"I see you as you stand, my friend. Your heart is on your sleeve for both of these boys, as mine."

"They believe I must charge a vote from the other Councilmen, but they have no knowledge that it is our allegiance that propels the continuance of the treaty. I will instruct them there was opposition, but we defended their case with fortitude and won the support of all."

"You are a wizard of intent, Leumas. Now you referenced Ruvana as Madame?"

"Yes, her standing in the community as an innovator, an inventor, a scholar of engineering, and a true loyalist to our cause has been long overdue. Her peers must recognize her outstanding achievements as a Nalhsian and as an ambassador to the citizens of Belcare," declared Master Leumas.

"Then I must set an appointment to congratulate her on her designation you have so proudly bestowed upon Madame Ruvana," lovingly requested Madame Noir.

"Let us finish with Erodec first, Noir. How shall we handle his inquiry to speak to Dugar?"

"If we inform him truthfully, how shall he react? Hmmmm, if we side step his inquiry, will he then not trust our intent in the future and possibly forge an alliance with whom we distrust. If we do speak the truth, as we have true knowledge, we could gain another alliance within the Council of Belcare. What do you propose, Leumas?"

"He is a smart man of determination who very well could assist us in our quest, if... he learns the truth as per our knowledge of known facts and not speculation."

"Very well, Leumas. Should we invite him to Nalhs where his eyes will be truly opened, and then let the mythical aberrations linger as he absorbs his vision?"

"And who is now calling who a wizard?" jest Master Leumas.

"Then inform Dugar of the affairs we have discussed and position Erodec in our visitors sector, whereby he may gaze upon inconsequential apparatuses and a flurry of activity for his intent," suggested Madame Noir. "And please, my friend, inform Madame Ruvana of my wishes to meet Her."

"I shall inform all of their forth coming challenges and our intentions, Noir."

Inception Shakes

An intimate whiff of smoke carried the fresh baked scent of pastries wafting through the valley. The fishermen were busy reeling in their nets, slightly rippling the otherwise smooth bay. The children were in school; Eittam had assigned the reciting of poems from ancient philosophers, while others were learning the whipstitch from Aivila. One young couple was trading commerce for favors of adding a room to an undersized hut, now intended for three instead of two. A kilometer from town, lying above the lazy stream, the foundry had returned to full production after a scare of abnormal weather threatened a shut down. The corn was set to be harvested in a week while the orchards still had another month or two before they would be ready. They all awaited the return of their great hunters; to hear them recite stories of intrigue and adventure, which would undoubtedly spark the young boys to learn their fathers' trade.

The passage of time was peaceful in this southwest village. Leinad sat above the village under a grand broad-leaf tree pondering the pages of his dog-eared book, while Nephets and Tomei remained inland in the higher altitude of the grazing lands.

A large bird broke the serenity when it landed on top of the village's warning bell, forcing a single 'clang'. As Leinad instinctively looked up past his ruffled pages and past the massive rampart, he noticed frenzy among the usually passive birds of the reeds. They were scattered in all directions, squawking and diving, but did not land... out of nowhere, a THUNDEROUS BOOM echoed—the ground SHOOK and HEAVED, sending Leinad rolling down the hillside. Huts RUMBLED, separating the heavy bamboo frame work from its foundation. The boardwalk HEAVED UP and DOWN like a wave. People fell out of their huts SCREAMING! Eittam stumbled to the schoolhouse's doorway, holding a child injured from a falling rafter. Aivila had a deep gash over her eye; blood ran down her face and dripped off her chin as she helped the children leave the school. The villagers who remained in the pathways, bounced off the ground like marionettes on a string. Then... calm!

People hesitated in the wake of destruction. Bodies, spread about in random configuration, slowly picked themselves up. Tears moistened their eyes, and some held an arm or favored a leg, while others with bloodied garments walked awkwardly. In the aftermath, huts were shifted askew, others had toppled completely; boiling pots still rolled side to side and emptied their contents in a *tapestry of clay*. Leinad propped himself against a strewn piece of roofing, seemingly unscathed from his tumble. He looked at the wreckage before him, and in the distance, he saw Eittam carrying a young child as she walked towards him. He gathered his staff and instantly felt a sharp pain from his shoulder where his staff would have resided. He remained.

Luckily, the infirmary had been spared any outwardly damage. Eittam climbed the stairs and entered through the doorway. Aivila was behind her with a child on each hand; she also turned to head up the stairs passing the line of other citizens who required attention. Aivila had held the honorary duty of applying her stitch to those in need. Today she also had to apply her hand for her own intent.

Inside the infirmary, Eittam cleaned Aivila's wound and wrapped her head so she could continue to help others. Aivila's eye was developing redness and had puffed, which made it difficult for her to see her work. Eittam aided the other assistant in wrapping splints that were supporting broken arms and legs. Thankfully, no one had lost their life, as they could so far determine.

As Leinad watched the citizens' line-up to receive attention, he noticed the difference in design of the infirmary compared to the huts that toppled. The infirmary had poles driven into the ground and then continued to the height where it met the roof. These poles framed each door way and window opening, and then the platform was attached as a whole to each standing pole. The bamboo had natural flexibility, thus swaying with the ground rather than toppling—a design that he would incorporate with every structure. His mind wandered as if it had its own set of eyes that lurked above him, looking down at all that had happened. He saw things clearer and thought how the village could be set out differently to take advantage of its surroundings.

~

When time permitted, Eittam took advantage to check on her father. He remained where she had seen him. She approached him. Noticing he had a distant-glazed look to his eyes. She called out, "Father... Father!"

Startled, Leinad brushed the moisture from his eyes and momentarily flashed a smile. Eittam returned the gesture as she carefully felt for any broken bones. He winced as she touched his shoulder.

"Ahhh! Is it necessary to continue my torture?"

"I will need to wrap your shoulder, Father. I cannot feel any misplaced bones, but heat is generating from this spot. I will put your arm in a binding cloth so you will not be tempted to move it."

"You will need to bind my leg as well so I may move about without my staff."

"Yes, Father, now lean on me and I will help you to the infirmary."

"How is your sister? I noticed blood about her face."

"She will be without sight in one eye until the swelling goes down. When her skill is no longer required, her head will pound and she will finally realize she is not super human."

"The determination of both of you provides me with great pride. Sons could not perceive my admiration more than what I have for you," proudly insisted Leinad.

"Come Father, I believe your head has possibly been adjusted in your tumble," jest Eittam.

Madame Noir Invites Madame Ruvana

Madame Ruvana was very nervous as She stepped off of the Endeavor and headed towards Madame Noir's chamber. Master Leumas had bestowed a great honor upon Her, and to be invited to Madame Noir's chamber alone, without point of business but merely social, She could not had imagined such pleasantries. Madame Noir's chime notified Her of Madame Ruvana's arrival.

"Good will to you, Madame Ruvana."

"Good will to you, Madame Noir. It is such an honor to meet you. Regor and Relaeh speak very highly of you, as does Master Leumas," nervously confessed Madame Ruvana.

"Please, sit beside me. Shall you take some warm water and herbs?"

"Yes, that would be so kind of you, Madame Noir."

"You may call me Noir as this is a social meeting without watchful eyes," jest Madame Noir.

"Thank you Madame... Noir. As you can perceive, I am about myself to be in your presence."

"There is no need. We are the same, two women speaking informally."

"May I say, I did not realize you are not Nalhsian," timidly inferred Madame Ruvana.

"I have asked of those I have been acquainted with to not speak of my heritage at this time of revelation."

"I shall remain, as you wish, and keep this affirmation nearest my heart."

"There will be a time for declaration and discovery. Now let us focus on you. Leumas tells me of your many accomplishments as a scientist and a humanitarian. Your intent both in Nalhs and Belcare have been remarkable."

"Thank you, Noir. I had no direct intention; it was justly conceived, partly as a desire to apply my education and to help my friends. I had no preconception that friendship would develop as it did. The ladies of Belcare are as true to my heart as my close friends in Nalhs."

"Your determination of spirit will be the standard for all to adhere," declared Madame Noir.

"You flush my face with praise, Noir. I am only one of many who have developed respect for our fellow travelers."

"Are you of a husband?" inquired Madame Noir.

She held up Her hand, "I have not had the pleasure of receiving the ring of life," shyly shared Madame Ruvana.

"Is there intent of one so lucky?"

"Dugar, the brother of Regor, has gazed upon my eyes and I in turn."

"Very well! I have not had the pleasure of Dugar's company, but my son, Relaeh, has made many references to Dugar. I did have the pleasure of Regor's assistance with an experiment."

"Relaeh is your son, Noir?"

"I apologize for the slip of tongue. I witnessed his birth and since I am without family in my little world, I perceive him to be."

"Relaeh is a true believer and as I have gotten to know him through Dugar, his intentions for the well-being of all men and women to be a single instrument in defining the new world will take him on many discoveries. That I truthfully speak."

"Ruvana, you are a woman of many endearing traits and as you speak, you warm my heart. And if I may presume, a development of our friendship would also please me."

"I am so honored once more by your consideration, Madame Noir. I am truly flattered."

"And as we have agreed upon, our distinction among our peers is not required between us."

"Yes Noir," graciously accepted Madame Ruvana.

"May I be so bold as to feel your long locks of hair?"

"You may."

"I have not had an opportunity to touch such loveliness."

"Your lady friends from Belcare did not welcome your inquisitiveness?"

"The conversation did not appear, as their need for escape superseded any desire of mine. More importantly, they are truly aware of each other's wholesomeness and display no intention of disrespect. They were quite open with me as well, and spoke of their desire for a continuing friendship."

"You may take brush in hand as it has been a lifetime ago that one has adorned me so."

"I have not done so before. You may instruct me on my technique."

Madame Noir instructed Madame Ruvana on the technique of brushing one's hair. The long slow strokes from the crown of her head to the tip of each strand. They each enjoyed the womanly companionship that had not been present in their lives. The Nalhsians had mostly adhered to the development of one's mind. It had only been since the dating of Dugar, that Ruvana had started to discover Herself as a woman. It had been wonderful. And now, She had an understanding friend in whom She may confide.

The morning slipped away as the two conversed on many topics. As each of their time was heavily scheduled they agreed to meet again, soon.

"We have much work ahead of us in preparation of launching your beacons. Leumas tells me you have unrestricted access, which you do here as well," granted Madame Noir.

"Thank you, Noir, you undoubtedly know how much our friendship means to me," shared Madame Ruvana as She placed Her arms about Madame Noir.

"And to me as well, my love. Our family grows as it should. Perhaps next time I can meet your man, Dugar?"

"I believe he would be as honored as I have been."

Madame Ruvana glowed in enlightenment as She took leave of Madame Noir's chamber. She headed straight to Her lab to check on the deployment of the Portal. As She entered, Her H-WAC had a message announcing the arrival of the Portal in air chamber 398; although, set up had not yet commenced. She attached a message of gratitude and instructed with permission to continue. Her authority had been acknowledged by all commands, as Her H-WAC was flooded with congratulatory comments. She was, however, more pleased with the admiration of Madame Noir and their immediate friendship.

As Madame Ruvana remembered Her parents as a young child, it was the custom of Nalhs to devote one's self to develop the fields of interest that would propel them through life. Most of Her friends that entered into unions did so within the boundaries of their research. She was glad that it was a chance meeting that Dugar had come into Her life. She truly believed Relaeh was instrumental in the development of Dugar's feelings for Her. Even though Relaeh was obviously a Belcarian, he held an emotional bond with Dugar and Regor, which She felt had somehow manifested a more caring nature of the two brothers. He truly was a 'Healer'.

Erodec Visits Nalhs

Madame Ruvana's appointment had now granted Her dignitary status, thus enabling the receiving of guests from Belcare. During Her audience with Madame Noir, they touched on the request of Erodec to meet with Dugar. Master Leumas had already instructed Dugar of such a meeting, but now instead of Master Leumas signing in Erodec, Madame Ruvana had the authority and the presence to assist Dugar with Erodec's questions.

Erodec was pleased to hear that his request for audience with Dugar was approved. He had set out as instructed, as the sun lit the sky in its highest position. The Portal on Conviction and 2nd always intrigued him, but the actual thought of descending into the dirt shafts without sunlight gave him a strange sense of closeness. He had wondered how Droenal could manage in *his* dinginess, but to live underground was unimaginable.

Erodec placed his hand upon a screen of intersecting lines, and then stood still as the monitor flashed about his stature. An air chamber slid open and he stepped inside. He felt the rush in his stomach as the chamber lowered into the darkness below. A slight clicking was audible as he was relinquished to the visitor's sector.

Stepping out, he looked up into an array of color with a ceiling height, he guessed, to be twice that of the Androicropulous. Where was he? This is not what he expected. People were flashing by him on platforms made for one, while moving walk-ways carried others in multiple directions. He carefully stepped over to the massive translucent-enclosed tube that descended for as far as the eye could see. Looking down, he noticed the numbers of the floors disappeared beyond 42, but could tell it ventured much farther than that. Hands tightened, almost appearing white as he held on to the side rail. An urge flushed over him with a thought that he would plummet into the vastness.

Dugar and Madame Ruvana walked over to Erodec, and watched as he rocked back and forth, as if he was overcome with anxiety.

"Councilman Erodec, are you of ill health?" inquired Dugar.

He looked away from the endless pit and replied, "Ah, no I am fine. A moment of uneasiness came over me. I am fine now, thank you."

"Let me introduce you to Madame Ruvana, a respected dignitary of Nalhs."

"It is an honor Madame...Ru..."

"Ruvana," She said as She put forth Her hand in gesture.

"I believe I have laid my eyes upon you before."

"Quite possibly at the sports field," she said without hesitation.

"Yes, during construction, you displayed a colorful array of lines about the field."

"That is correct. One of my doctorates is in Engineering. Will you join us in the visitor's lounge?"

The glass doorway swished open as they approached the newly developed visitors' lounge. Inside the brightly lit room, displays of interest lined the walls, while others were juxtaposed about the space.

"What novelties are these?" queried Erodec, with unexplainable intent.

"They are of ancient history of man, the creatures that roamed their land, and his perception of his universe," explained Madame Ruvana.

"But how do you come by these depictions?"

"Are you referring to the holographic display or the truth of nature?" queried Dugar.

Looking up to Dugar with an astonished look about his face, "I...um...the nature?"

"They are the truth of nature as written in our volumes and passed down through the generations," enlightened Dugar.

"What do these numbers mean?"

"They are of the periods of time set forth at that particular segment," instructed Madame Ruvana.

"I beg your indulgence, but I have not heard or laid eyes upon such awareness. What does this peculiar creature, with all the hair, somewhat resembling my being, signify?"

"He was discovered to have roamed the earth in 350,000 BC. There have been many forms of time that have been part of history, mainly relating to the sun, moon, and revolving planets. From the old Christian faith, the Gregorian calendar was introduced by Pope Gregory XIII in the year 1582 that most of earth adapted. The BC or AD referring to *before Christ* and *Anno Domini* 'in the year of Christ's birth' was calculated in the 6th century by Dionysius Exiguus. Thus these homo sapiens developed 350,000 years before the birth of Christ," informed Madame Ruvana.

"Who is Christ?"

"As implied by books of faith, a man of great healing powers that gave his life for mankind," stated Dugar.

Erodec looked at Madame Ruvana. "You are making my head dizzy. Why is there not any mention in our T-series books?"

"Faith and scientific fact have always been at odds. As we have not been privy to your T-series books, we can only assume that religious fact has prevailed and therefore, been set within your teachings."

"May I sit?" asked Erodec, wavering slightly.

"Yes, over here," said Dugar as he aided Erodec in his stepping.

"I came here to ask a simple question and now my head swirls in doubt and confusion."

"How may we be of assistance to you, Councilman?" asked Dugar.

"I do apologize for my seemingly flutter of mindless incapacity, but I had no knowledge of such existence as we sit here in your world, or of the past. I thought of myself to be of knowledgeable intent, but I am a mere infant to your magnitude. I truly apologize for my ignorance."

"There is no need to apologize, Erodec, but to keep an open mind of your surroundings and future perceptions."

"I have misunderstood you and your brother, and what I have learned from my teachings. You have given me renewed intention. I shall not proceed as foolish as before."

"You said you came to ask a question, may we hear what that might be?" cordially inquired Madame Ruvana.

"It all seems irrelevant, but as my companion Droenal and I have been cross referencing the DNA of disappearing citizens, we chanced a discovery of a missing portion of a strain numbering 401.11. We have been led to believe it is of an ancient design as designated by its numbering. We have no knowledge of its intent but thought it might have peculiarities to cause our citizens' disappearances."

"We have knowledge of this strain but not its name, or number as you implied, or of its intended use. It has made several of your citizens' ill, which until just recently, my brother has developed an antidote."

"Thank you for being truthful with me. We knew there was a conspiracy, but not from whom or why. The one I thought to be against me proved otherwise and the one I thought to trust, thrust a knife in my back. I know not who to trust."

"You spoke of your companion, Droenal. Is he trustworthy?" asked Madame Ruvana.

"Yes, but we are the same in the eyes of the Council. The elders control the Council, and we are to defend our teachings in meaningless exercise to appease their interest. Our eyes together have been opened by one of the workers named, Kire. By memory, he painted a portrait of Droenal and I sitting in a valley of flowers, with a view to a white capped mountain. The colors are spectacular and the image... where would he come by this if he was not a man from another world?"

"Our eyes have not seen this truth but trust in your heart that a place does exist," impressed Madame Ruvana as She touched Erodec upon his heart.

"We shall hold true to heart of what we spoke of this day, as we caution you to do as well. If a question arises of our knowledge of this missing strain, reply positively but to the intent, we have no knowledge at this time," instilled Dugar.

"How shall we stay abreast of learning of its application," questioned Erodec.

"If you learn of application, go to the Portal but do not place your hand upon the screen, just push the numbers 401.11. That will identify your concern, and then take leave as not to be discovered by watchful eyes. We will contact you," informed Madame Ruvana.

"I told Droenal of your truthful ways, as he thought the foreman might have been instrumental in the disappearance of our citizens. We have no knowledge of his whereabouts, as he seems to have vanished. I believe he has been before our eyes on numerous occasions," reflected Erodec.

"Be cautious, Erodec. Play the game well. Listen more than speaking. He who wishes to turn the tide will expose his under-belly," insisted Dugar.

"I shall, my friends, and again, thank you both for indulging me with my ignorance."

"Let us escort you to the Portal," warmly offered Madame Ruvana.

The day had been alive with triumphs. Erodec surfaced with enlightenment about him that street lamps could not out shine. His mood had changed from despair to gaiety, as he headed along Conviction towards Droenal's office.

Dugar and Ruvana headed immediately to Regor's lab, and they also telepathed Relaeh and Master Leumas of their intent. A raised cheek forming a glint in Her eye came over Her face as they moved along a walk-way to board the Weaver II.

"What is the smile for?" questioned Dugar.

"I just had a pleasantry placed upon my stature by Madame Noir," gleefully informed Madame Ruvana.

"Truthfully?" queried Dugar.

"Yes, my telepath was open to Her as we spoke to Erodec. She complimented us on our resourcefulness as one. She also wishes to meet you."

"Please forgive my insensitivity to your audience with Madame Noir. My head was with Erodec. She wants to meet me?"

"Yes, you are my man," said Madame Ruvana as She leaned Her head upon Dugar's shoulder. "She wants to make sure you are of high standards and intent," jestfully implied Madame Ruvana.

The Vision of Naturalness

Bocaj and his travelers finished that horrific day upon the suspended rope bridge with a farther ten kilometer hike. They had set camp in a shallow valley out of the wind's intimidation, alongside a fresh water stream. Taeman instructed the ladies on which berries to gather and which leaves to use in mulling a salve for Bocaj's hands and Songa's rope burns that lay about his chest. It was the consensus that this protective area would be an ideal spot to heal, at least for the next few days.

The hunters had been successful in catching fish as well as wild boar. The days remained warm but the nights dipped below a comfortable temperature for the citizens of Belcare. The repetitive temperature of Belcare displayed well for that controlled environment, but was unrealistic in the outer world where nature designated the time line for harvesting. Taeman had scribed many notes along their journey and Kire had added impressionistic sketches to aid Taeman's memory.

The ladies had been busy mending garments, and with the help of their husbands, washed the soiled ones in the creek. Not all had been work, as the ladies found a perfect spot where Kire may apply his artistic hand at portraiture of the ladies in their wholesomeness. The men had to tend to the three little ones while the ladies took leave of the camp site.

Rajean questioned an area of solitude, as they walked upstream where sun rays danced upon the waters and warmed the rocks on its creek bed. A natural cove lined with trees, with flatlands caressing the waters' edge. Kire had set his parchment on a stable limb across the waters as the ladies undressed in the glorifying light.

The ladies placed Yuda, stripped of her brace of life, upon a rock with her protruding belly as the focal point of intention. Rajean, in kneeling position, placed Yuda's foot upon her thigh, as Einna stood with hand upon Rajean's shoulder gazing towards Yuda, and the other hand touched Yuda's out- stretched arm. Kasha was behind with Yuda's long black hair following through her fingers, as Siena poured water soaking Yuda's long locks. Narfinia sat below Yuda offering a flower as a gift of beauty to her fertile being. Kire quickly sketched the bared figures before him and then added the scenery to enhance the awareness of the ladies. He was used to sketching quickly, as Bocaj was a determined man on a mission, but today, his focus was on the tender features and the warmth that radiated from the faces of the ladies as they jestfully exchange innuendos.

A moment of serenity occupied their vision of companionship, as their artist glorified their awareness upon his parchment.

The Four for Hope

Dugar and Madame Ruvana entered Regor's lab moments before the arrival of Relaeh and Master Leumas. The question on each of their minds was, how did Erodec react to the discovery of Nalhs, and, can he be trusted? Regor stood and bowed his head to Madame Ruvana. It was the first official visit Madame Ruvana had made to his lab since Her appointment.

"Good will, Madame Ruvana. I welcome you and congratulate you on your appointment. There has been no doubt in my mind that you deserve the honors bestowed upon you. I feel doubly joyful as your friendship has warmed us all."

"Thank you, Regor." She stepped to his stature and wrapped Her arms about him. "I too feel the same about you. Did you know Madame Noir wants to meet your brother?"

"Dugar?"

"I know of none other."

"Perhaps Your light will guide his intentions," jest Regor.

"Brother, I put up with the little one, and now, more from you?" infused Dugar.

Relaeh entered to catch the tail end of Dugar's remark of 'the little one'.

"Little one, you say."

Spinning around, Dugar faced Relaeh as they all jest at Dugar's misrepresented remark. Relaeh did not wait to compliment Madame Ruvana with words, but engaged in one of his infamous hugs.

"I am so proud of your appointment, Madame Ruvana. I understand your audience went well with Mot... um... Madame Noir."

"She is amazing. You are so fortunate to have Her in your life."

"We all are," insisted Master Leumas.

"I have spoken of this before. You all are my family, which I hold truer than my own breath," stated an emotional Relaeh.

Master Leumas cleared his throat, "Uhum... we better get down to business before I require a hydrostatic cleanser to dry me off."

Madame Ruvana informed them, although Her appointment afforded Her the respect of others, when they were without watchful eyes, She still was their Ruvana.

"Just curious... but when the two of you unite, will Dugar have to ask you for permission?"

"Only with which garment he should dress in," slyly replied Madame Ruvana.

"Ahahah, you are all so jestful today."

Master Leumas quickly changed the subject as he knew how Dugar and Relaeh could fence with words. "Madame, Dugar, what were your observations of the young Councilman?"

Dugar commented first, "I believe him to be a true soul who has been misguided by his teachings. He does what is asked of him because that his is duty."

"He questioned the displays of man and truly tried to understand. He apologized several times for his ignorance, but that is no fault of his. He has strong determination and appears very bright, a welcomed ally," stated Madame Ruvana.

"He did mention a numerical value for the warrior gene, 401.11, but he has no direction to its behavior. He also mentioned the *little one's* inappropriate appearances and disappearances as a possible assumption of the genes aberrations," added Dugar.

Astounded at Dugar's remark, Relaeh laughed heartily and said, "Ahahah, he believes the gene is of my deliverance and cause of the citizens disappearances?"

"Not that you delivered the gene, but that the gene caused you and the others to disappear. We did not inform him otherwise but suggested he speak less and listen more," recounted Dugar.

"A wise statement, Dugar. Did he speak of alliances or mistrusts?" asked Master Leumas.

"He did question a conspiracy upon his stature and thought of one to blame, but turned out it was another who 'stabbed him in the back'."

"His alliance is only with his companion, Droenal. I believe we all have seen them together. He is also an attractive young man," delightfully injected Madame Ruvana.

"Attractive in a Belcarian sort of way, much like our friend here," initiated Dugar.

Master Leumas cut off Relaeh before he could muster a reply. "Now boys, do not start again. What shall our next move be concerning Erodec?"

"We mentioned that if he learned of possible usage or intent of one's interest, to code the gene number into the

Anon at the Portal, and we shall return his inquiry," related Madame Ruvana.

"This number 401.11, where did he perceive this?" asked Regor.

"He did not say where, but he was of the belief it was from an ancient strain due to its minimal value," informed Dugar.

"I shall research this code, perhaps there will be records indicating its architecture and intent."

"While Regor is involved, Madame Ruvana how is the Portal planning out?" inquired Master Leumas.

"It has arrived in air shaft 398, and I have given permission for its installation. We should have more news by end of tomorrow."

"Relaeh, how is your readiness?" asked Master Leumas.

"Regor has made available the three doses per man in his cooler. He has instructed me on the insertion of the needle and I feel comfortable with his training. I also have packed extra needles as precautionary."

"And of the beacons?" questioned Master Leumas.

"Out of harm's way until they finish the work on the Portal," assured Madame Ruvana.

"So, the Portal, then the beacons, and then Relaeh will be able to fulfill his destiny."

"My destiny, Father? My destiny is to free all man and to establish a common appreciation for our two races."

"I apologize for the matter of chosen words. Of course, I meant one of your many discoveries you will need to fulfill," recanted Master Leumas.

"He does not take lightly what Madame Noir has instilled in him," defended his friend, Dugar.

"And I am the proudest of all who may claim his intentions as a product of his teachings and love," insisted Master Leumas.

"Father, I apologize to you for my impertinence. I shall charge the unknown to deliver the serum to the travelers with saving mankind as it has to begin somewhere."

"You are a good lad, Relaeh. I love you very much. I shall take leave of you young people so you may plot your journeys."

As they all in turn wrapped their arms around their Master Leumas, Relaeh's eye caught a shimmer from the frock of Madame Ruvana.

"Ruvana, what is this?" He positioned Her just right in the light, and plucked a single strand from Her person, and then held it up and commented with much surprise, "It is a hair."

"It must be Madame Noir's as I was brushing it earlier," innocently replied Madame Ruvana.

"You were what!?" exclaimed Dugar.

Shrugging off his panic, she said, "We are two women with womanly urges. I have not had an opportunity to even touch a woman's mane. I asked, and She profoundly accepted. It is not as Relaeh's...stiff and wavy," explained Madame Ruvana as she ran Her fingers through his hair..."so cute!"

Lightly brushing off Ruvana's humorous intent... "Listen all," as he held this strand of life in his hands. "Regor, you know I do not understand all your double talk when it comes to...well, whatever you do. But, if you take this hair and run it through whatever you run it through and determine Madame Noir's DNA, can you then develop a healthy patch for the repair of Her spinal cord?"

"I can isolate Her DNA and then possibly scan the records of earth, but without a growth hormone matched to Her DNA...I," he hesitated. "We...I should say Madame Noir, was experimenting with a cream that repaired skin damage in Nalhsians so we may explore more of the free world. That was a while ago and I have no knowledge of the continued experiments."

"You had a good thought, Relaeh," shared Dugar.

"I will take this opportunity, if we all hold true to our hearts the implication of doing this without Her knowledge, I will record and file the findings for possible future resurrection," stated Regor.

"As I love Her as if She bore me, I owe my life to Her. I will accept any implication that may transpire. Stay true to your heart, Regor, and appease my favor of you."

"We are four for hope and inspiration," magically expressed Madame Ruvana.

Erodec Enlightens Droenal

Droenal's office was a mere hop and a step away from Erodec imploding from the visions and knowledge he had to share. He believed Dugar and Madame Ruvana were speaking truthfully, and he hoped he had found new allies to trust, and possibly enhance his career. He believed in the citizens of Belcare, but now, with what he had seen, this knowledge could only benefit his people without prejudice.

He rushed the steps to Droenal's office and swung open the door. Only a few more steps, then ratta-tat-tat... he waited with excitement... Droenal's friendly voice inquired, "Yes?"

"Droenal, it is I... open up, please."

The door swung open to Droenal's private office. Erodec bounced in.

"What manner of your engagement do I perceive?"

"Shhhh... close the door. I have just experienced the most incredible revelation of my life. I have come from Nalhs with knowledge of our universe," explained Erodec with such excitement.

"You are glowing... what could possibly have set you in this grandeur of illumination?"

"I have seen the dawning of Man!"

"You have WHAT!?"

"Yes... Yes!" He took Droenal's arms and sat him down, so he could enlighten his friend without toppling over.

"Everything you have ever thought about Nalhs is untrue, everything! They are intelligent beyond our comprehension. They do not live in dirt tunnels but in... I do not know the words... tubes of translucents, and moving walk-ways, and flying machines. There is a city below us that thrives in ancient knowledge passed down from generation to generation. There are things that talk to you as you gaze in a box, and as you pass your hand through them, they continue to speak without harm."

"Slow down my friend, you will become of fever," insisted Droenal.

"No, my friend, I have seen the light. Do you recount the Din Master's speech of a proposed time piece, but then the idea was discarded as a hindrance to the citizens?"

"Yes."

"They know of time and a man called Christ, whose birth signifies BC or AD, as related to the order of life itself."

"You are confusing me, Erodec."

"I know, and I apologize for these outbursts, but I will try to comprehend my visions and lay them before you as I perceive. As I understand our teachings, our T-series books were transcribed as religious revelations rather than foretell tales of human invention. It seems there has been conflict between fables and truth; thus, our teachings are of truth but lack any human element of endurance."

"Could that explain why the Din Master constantly reads and re-reads the books? Is he formatting our discoveries as we know them into the writings of the books so he may understand the order in which to grow our city and advance our comprehension with fables of better understanding?"

"I believe you have set our quest, Droenal. We should prepare to re-read our books with greater understanding, then insert our experiences amongst the lines transcribed."

"And what will be the outcome?" questioned Droenal.

"A greater awareness of who we are and our destiny."

"What of the missing substance?"

"They spoke of knowledge of its existence but had no value to its intent, as we. We must not divulge our awareness to anyone. They believe whoever is of distrust will eventually display themselves."

"Did you confide in them the portraiture we found from Kire?"

"Yes... they have not seen such a vision but suggested we believe in its existence."

"Why would they recommend to us, to have faith in the truth of that vision, if they have not foreseen it?"

"Perhaps not all things can be explained scientifically; one must imagine in good faith of unexplainable occurrences."

Cheers to All

The Portal had been completed as per instructions of Madame Ruvana within Her prescribed time allotment of three days. Now they, Relaeh, Dugar and Madame Ruvana, had two days of work to set up and launch the beacons. Time was challenging their determination as the days were eighteen, thus only three days left of the masked pills given to Bocaj for the journey. The discovery of being outside of the energy dome and into the new world would be, as the three envisioned, to be without words!

Dugar and Madame Ruvana manned the accessory air machine, as Relaeh's experience qualified him to operate the larger and more cumbersome craft that carried the beacons with the installed articulating arm. The Portal was such the size as to the maneuvering of these larger machines within its chamber would be as two grains of sand in an hourglass. They positioned themselves parallel to each other as the giant tube floated the machines upward to the massive exit doors. Their excitement rose as each meter brought them closer to the new world. What would it be like? Would the canopy of the trees remain as a bluish tint as in Belcare? Would the air smell as fresh or even fresher? Would the temperature seize their bones and limit their movement? Would they float above the ground and have need to put weights about their bodies to keep them grounded?

The machines hovered as the great doors hissed open. The light filled the chamber with an instant glow, so much so as they instinctively placed adornments about their eyes. The air wafted in. It made the air of Nalhs seemingly stale and stagnant. They ventured out slowly, side by side. The colors were magnificent! The trees, such a beautiful shade of green; even the sand field radiated a whiter essence. Their new world was spectacular!

They remained hovering for a moment as they took in their new surroundings. They had just created history. Dugar and Madame Ruvana were the first of Nalhsians to recount the new world in 15,000 years! Their exuberance was overwhelming as they timidly proceeded beyond the sand field to more stable ground. Their Anons simultaneously captured each movement, each emotion, and each incredible sight, and broadcasted those sensations to the thousands of Nalhsians who had been waiting for this precise moment. Moisture filled the eyes of their peers as they forged new territories, meter by meter. Nalhs rejoiced!

Regor had taken time away from his experiments to rejoice with Master Leumas in Madame Noir's chamber.

The three displayed an array of satisfaction as they 'hailed' their adventurers. The tall one, the pudgy one, and the beauty of Belcare were overwhelmed with excitement, each proud of their own and collectively. The three would be remembered and honored as the coalition between Nalhs and Belcare, united again as one people. This mark in time was the 15th of the seventh month, 15,082 AD.

The influx of adulations over their Anons did not alter the intentions of the three. They set their machines down on the ground that Madame Ruvana declared as solid. They had work to do and no time to spoil. Lives depended on their dedication.

Madame Ruvana directed Relaeh on placement and angle of trajectory of three beacons so they could stay in a semisynchronous orbit to project a tridirectional inclination for positioning coordinates. The other three would be sent into a geostationary orbit around the equator for communication satellites. Relaeh did not question Her instructions and set his articulating arm in removal of the first three beacons. Carefully, he positioned each beacon as Dugar set its corresponding angle on the launch pad brackets. Guide lines were attached to the brackets and then secured to the ground. Within the first long day, they had physically set the six beacons. It was time to rest as the chilled night air dipped below their comfort level.

"Well done, my friends," said Relaeh.

"We do work well together," insisted Madame Ruvana.

"We are as one," declared Dugar.

Relaeh was busy pounding a thermomagnetic rod into the ground with his pneumatic hammer, and then attached a thermo-coupler to a series of hydrostatic cells. With the help of his Anon isolator in his air machine used as an energy source, the honey-combed guard surrounding the cells produced a warm glow that cast a heat band of five meters in diameter. They set their BTIs around their thermal heater and enjoyed in comfort, their first gaze upon the stars of the clear night.

"In the beginning of man, do you believe they marveled at the sights before us?" asked Relaeh.

"The stars have always been an aphrodisiac for stimulating our ancestor's imagination," informed Madame Ruvana.

"I believe it will continue to do so in the future," remarked Dugar.

"You speak the truth, my friend. I feel the need more than before to pursue my discoveries. Today was just the beginning of teasing our imaginations. Tomorrow will bring an infinite collection of new studies for our people, for our children, and for their children," shared Relaeh.

"We have broken the barrier of confinement. We need to tread lightly in its discourse and learn from our teachings of all the wrong brought about by greed and inflated stature," insisted Madame Ruvana as She tracked the soothing twinkle of the stars.

"Relaeh, might you find a woman who can harness your preposterous ways before injecting children into your sense of idealism and philosophy?"

"You say what you believe, Dugar. I have no doubt of my intended journey or my unity to a believer of truth and determination," replied Relaeh, not taking Dugar's bait for jocular interplay.

"You may hold myth of an aberration too close to your heart, Relaeh... to recognize someone's true intent."

"What do you imply, Ruvana?"

"Your love and respect for Madame Noir might cloud your direction if one does not achieve the same stature as She," clarified Madame Ruvana.

"Then, so be it. I shall be satisfied to be uncle to your children and spoil them with the desire to discover," jestfully stated Relaeh. "I shall take them with me and show them what they cannot read or feel in holographic concepts. And I shall not accept any other discourse then the unity of you two."

Dugar paused for a moment before he spoke to let the words of Relaeh dissipate into the night's air.

"I have spoken my heart out loud as you have witnessed, Relaeh." Dugar reached over to his Ruvana and placed Her hand in his. "My friend, I ask you to be witness once again, and you, my love...I ask of you on the genesis of this most glorious night, in our inaugural of the free world to unite with me as one."

"What do my ears hear?" hailed Relaeh excitedly.

"Yes...Yes, my love, I will accept your hand."

Relaeh, as excited as Madame Ruvana, opened his telepath and hailed with delight so his family in Nalhs may perceive the extraordinary delight binding his companions on this night.

"If I would have had knowledge of my silly friend's popping of this question, I would have prepared fine nectar to celebrate. I will work twice as hard tomorrow so we may celebrate with our family in Nalhs. No brother could make me prouder than what you have asked tonight," declared Relaeh with moisture about his eyes.

. . .

The morning light brought warm shimmering rays reflecting off of the droplets of dew on the broad-leaf trees. Relaeh prepared a delicious meal from his supplies he stowed aboard his air machine. The atmosphere was light, and joyful, as Madame Ruvana instructed Her fiancé, and his best friend, Relaeh, on the attachment of the RF igniters.

Before they cautiously configured the wiring, Madame Ruvana warned of possible interference with other electrical stimuli that could set off the igniters. Anons were safe, but their thermo heater had to be disengaged. Everything had to be set in place before the final connection. A malfunction, at this point, would be of certain catastrophe for them all.

The actual firing took place back in Nalhs Control Center (NCC) where they controlled the guidance of the beacons. Last minute inspection of each igniter and tension on the guide lines was complete. The activation of their air machines was of no consequence, as the system of propulsion had no deliverance from radio frequencies.

The day was clear. It would allow visual contact throughout their trajectory from the Anon placed on top of the Portal's tower. Once in orbit, the onboard Anons would display their information back to Nalhs. Systems were a go.

Upon returning their air machines back to their docking ports, a hail of adulation erupted from its sector populace. The three graciously returned waves of hopeful gestures as they stepped onto the moving walk-ways and headed for the NCC. They stepped determinedly from one deck, through Weaver II's propulsion to another, and then finally, the NCC doors swished open. Waiting patiently,

Master Leumas and Regor finally had the opportunity to congratulate them on their accomplishment, as well as, reveled in Dugar and Madame Ruvana's proposed union.

The anxiousness of detonation precluded their engagement festivities as their heightened mission was still without finalization. Codes were manifested into synchronized firing orders as each in the chamber waited for the command.

"Madame Ruvana, I share this historic day with Madame Noir, the citizens of Nalhs and Belcare, and we wish that you begin the countdown on your command."

Master Leumas handed Her one of two keys. Looking at Relaeh, he handed the other to him to insert into the control switch. They engaged the keys simultaneously and turned. A red light flashed steadily as the countdown begun. Dugar squeezed Madame Ruvana's hand as the beacons were displayed upon the H-WAC mounted in series of six around the chamber for each beacon.

10, 9, 8, 7, 6, 5, 4, 3, ignition, 2, 1... Lift off!

The Anons captured the imagery of each nose peaking forth as they propelled from their stationary station through the mist. Six ravenous beauties headed skyward with the inscription N.A.L.H.S adorned in white, as they streaked the skies in solidarity. The flashing light turned to a solid green and hails of delight filled the chamber. Within a sidereal day, the beacons would be set in orbit and ready for transmission.

A relief transcended over Madame Ruvana's stature. The technology, She felt, was old to Her standards of today, but nonetheless, She had prevailed. She acknowledged the team of scientists that endured the sleepless nights with Her across the H-WAC, so they too, could indulge in the gratitude being bestowed upon them. As experiments come and go, they would be promoted as pioneers of the new world and set in presentations in the visitor's sector, from now forward.

The late of day was no excuse for not gathering in Madame Noir's chamber. Relaeh and Regor poured liquid nectar into slim translucents, while Madame Ruvana introduced Her fiancé to Madame Noir. With the translucents filled and passed about, they raised to salute, officially, the appointment of Madame Ruvana and one more raised to the proposed union of Dugar and Madame Ruvana. Once again, they raised their translucents to Relaeh's future success in reaching the endangered men of Belcare. Such excitement for Madame Noir, as for many years, She had protested the social meeting of anyone, and now, with such joy in Her heart, She had what She had longed for... Her family.

Eve Saves a Predator

The departure from their protective cove gave way to steeper hills defined by lush green valleys. Their compass displayed a truer indication than anticipated—allowing for a more discreet direction. The ladies were holding their own, as Yuda only had to rest a couple of times in between Bocaj's scheduled rest periods. The journey was hard for men. He admired the resolute of the ladies as they trudged forward without complaint. The children seemed unfazed, and happily played with each step. They were so inquisitive of all that surrounded them—their delight was reassuring.

Bocaj had not received any messages from Relaeh. He perceived that the mountains had probably acted as a barrier and blocked any signal from reaching his symbol. They were on their own. He only had one pill each, for the six men, left to administer. He hoped there would not be any indiscretions along the way, to activate, whatever evil was injected into their bodies. He knew they would all be welcomed in Inception, and he was thankful for their friendship.

The endurance at the great gorge was beyond anything he could have ever imagined. He was thankful for Taeman, with his knowledge of healing plants that now salvaged his hands. The ladies had taken their silken-blend of undergarments and wrapped his hands in their fine cloth to sooth his pain and protect them as they forged through brush and forest. He thought of his fiery-haired lady that promiscuously cut her locks for his keepsake.

What was her intent? Does she chance my gazing upon her eyes? What of Councilman Leinad or Lady Eittam, what wrath would I encounter with such a young lass? She was certainly fine to the eyes, with hips fitting for child bearing, a waist almost as thin as my hands spread, and her delightful round and full...stop your insanity!

He looked up to see if anyone noticed his enthusiasm.

If she approaches me again, as when I took to this journey, I will no doubt have to have words imagined, to speak to Councilman Leinad. Surviving the great gorge might have not been such a feat, as to tame her spirit.

Retu was leading the travelers with Micja behind him. Bocaj noticed uneasiness about the conversations between the two. Their travels had been long and little quirks did not go unnoticed.

Yuda had expressed kicking pains as they trenched through under-brush and forged small streams. At times, she stopped, just to revel in the moment of life within her. Her friends were the dearest anyone could ask for. The men of Inception were as much as gentle souls to them as their husbands—always respectful without underlying intent. She felt they also longed for their loved ones, and she was so appreciative of their determination to arrive in Inception, where she may deliver a new life.

Retu, mindful of his point position, thought of his three off-springs and how big they must be getting. His son probably stood as he, and would desire to hunt with the men.

I will not discourage him this time. I miss his wanting gaze as he watched me sharpen my arrow tips and re-string my bow.

Aivila had given him a string made from a mixture of yarn, cut from strands of goat hair and interweaved with a thread from her mending, laced with a wax that gave the string a 'snap'. It had more power than his old style of reed. His eldest daughter would enjoy the opportunity to cuddle a newborn.

Einna, looking down at her son Adam, saw him absorbing every sight with every step he took. His wonderment would now be appeased in this new world. He would be free to discover as he so chose. Perhaps, he would discover new worlds within our earth's arrangements. Perhaps, he would take Eve with him.

Kasha watched Moltov as he walked in front of her. Each step he took twisted at her loins within. She wanted to stop and take him on this very spot; lowering herself down on him to feel his full depth and then rise to swallow him again and again. She thought of the terror of almost losing Songa, and how he jumped in to aid Tavlo in holding back the twist of the suspension bridge. His muscles shimmered in his moisture as they stood tall protecting their helpless mate.

He will be in trouble tonight, she thought. She loved his manly scent from the first time they had lain down together. His eyes peered down at hers, his hands cupped her breast as she wrapped her legs around him and thrust him deeper inside, and then finally they collapsed in pure delight. They had been together ever since, not missing one night of pleasure, that is until now.

"Kasha, are you getting a fever, you have beads of moisture about your brow?" inquired Siena breaking the thought of all.

Moltov looked back at his wife, Kasha, with a concerned stare. Her eyes meet his. She threw herself into his arms and just hung on for a moment.

Siena courted with jestful implication, "Ah, I see what troubles your thought, my girlfriend."

The other ladies smiled with the same intent as they side stepped Moltov and Kasha.

"Come, my friends, we still have a ways to go," said Bocaj, delicately.

Ahead, Eve had a peculiar smile about her face as she appeared to be observing something in the distance. Retu halted their stride, as he too, perceived movement ahead. He drew his bow with an arrow in its load. Scouting before him, two pups rolled and tumbled unaware of what danger might preclude their playfulness. A low growling sound penetrated the air and then pitched with intensity. Eve ran to the front before Retu could disarm his bow and grab the child. He motioned for everyone to stand tall and still. He softly called Eve back.

She turned to him and smiled; her intention was not to return, but to head straight for the snarling visitor. She brushed away a fern that revealed an injured, grey in color, blue-eyed creature thrice the size of Eve. A thorn the size of a man's finger had pierced its paw and forced the animal to finally collapse from loss of blood and pain. Her pups, one black and the other pure white, clambered about her and yelped with little distinction. The large animal growled with minor intent as Eve placed her hand upon the head of the injured animal comforting its pain. The animal flickered its lips, but then, licked her hand as it surrendered its power to one of luminous cognizance.

Retu approached as the animal lay still—her eyes glazed. Bocaj was helpless with his hands bound with dressing, but Micja, seeing the need to help his friend, slowly approached the wild animal with purposeful steps. He had never seen an animal of such stature, allow anyone close to it, no matter what its circumstance. Retu braced the head of the animal as Eve continued to stroke the beast's nose while whispering to her. Micja slowly placed the injured paw in his hand and with a swift movement displaced the jagged thorn. The animal had obviously been gnawing at the thorn and its leg to remove it, but failed.

Einna sprung past her husband with the same mixture she had placed upon the hands of Bocaj. They cleaned the wound, placed the mixture about, and wrapped it. The animal tried to raise her head but did not have enough strength to do so. Her breathing was laborious. Her pups tried to snuggle into her for nourishment, but Einna pulled them away and gave them to Rajean to harness. Eve looked up at Retu—moisture filled her eyes.

"You won't let her die will you?"

Retu was paralyzed by the will of this little girl's voice. How could a small thing as she, command such determination? Retu turned to Bocaj, and Bocaj in turn looked at Tavlo and instructed him to cut some branches so they could make a harness to support the animal. They could drag it along with them in safety, until she healed. Adam played with the pups.

"I feel eyes upon us," quietly shared Micja to Retu.

"For some time. Her pack is waiting for a precise moment when our guard is down," insisted Retu.

"Night fall will attract the scent of her weakness. We should alert the others if we continue to support her possible recovery," suggested Micja.

As if the pack understood their conversation, one by one they howled to inform the others of the intruder's seizure of their alpha female. Tavlo and Moltov lifted the burdened animal into the supportive sling. Lying quietly, they continued on their journey as Eve walked alongside. She continued to console the injured animal.

The sun disappeared early in the shaded valley forcing the travelers need to set camp before darkness captured their movement. The hunters built a central fire, and then several smaller ones, forming a perimeter of defense. The men of Belcare assisted in setting lean-tos and securing their provisions. Retu and Micja placed the injured animal to one side, away from their bedding. The howling had been with them all day; sometimes, so close as to touch, but the animals stayed hidden from view. Bocaj instructed his men to sharpen branches and place them in holes between the fires, protruding enough, as to make it difficult for the stalkers to jump them without warning. Would it have been better to leave the injured animal and let nature take its course? Or would that matter? The animals had the scent of humans embedded in their nostrils—their next meal.

The children paid little intent to the severity of the situation as did the citizens of Belcare. They all seemed to have no concern for the savagery that could befall them that very night. Only the hunters knew the danger and had witnessed the unforgiving slaughter that these animals could inflict upon its victims.

It would be a sleepless night for the hunters, but what they had witnessed from this little girl, was unexplainable. With arrows stacked around each hunter, for ease of release, the Belcarians took much needed rest. Perhaps, the animals smelled the injuries sustained by Bocaj and Songa as their healing was not yet complete. It was for certain, they had the taste of their fallen alpha, drooling from their saliva.

The night was clear. It made it easier to perceive their attackers—the waiting loomed. The alpha female wrestled with its fever and whimpered in its delirium. The howling all of a sudden, stopped. The men readied for the attack with arrows strung as they searched their perimeter. The smell of years of kill was embedded into their predator's fur. Not a sound, then off in the distance, the howling began all over again. Why did they not attack? What had they sensed? Perhaps, they want the choice of battle? Were they that smart?

Madame Noir's Cream

Relaeh had one last chore before setting out on his mission of humanity—to meet with Madame Noir. His head reminded him of the night before, possibly one too many hails of appreciation and admiration. Even in his cloudiness, his vision was true. Madame Noir's H-WAC chimed as Relaeh excitedly shuffled past the hissing of the door, to the awaiting Madame Noir.

"Good will, Mother. I trust Your head is of clearer intent than mine?"

"My veracious, son, you do have a vernacular way of expression," implied Madame Noir jestfully.

"Was I of ill form last night?" he asked as he hugged his Mother.

"You made many 'hails' to your unconceived nephews with a variety of chosen names as spoken into a mirror, for the contemplation of Dugar and Madame Ruvana," recounted Madame Noir.

"I was merely voicing my opinion of possibilities as we approach a new area as we need not be set in our old ways."

"So you do recount your performance last night?"

"Ah, most of it, some not so," he replied, unabashed.

"Well... your friends speak highly of you, and Dugar will make an excellent Chancellor as you requested," elaborated Madame Noir.

"Well, that indication perchance, is foggier than the rest."

"Ahahah, you certainly know how to liven a party."

"Shall I construe that as a compliment?" smiled Relaeh.

Madame Noir changed the subject.

"I have made a cream intended for Nalhsian's thinner skin, but I altered the gene structure so you may place upon your entire body. It will protect you from bites of undesirable distaste and support nourishment against the rays of the sun."

Madame Noir handed Relaeh the modified cream encased in a medium-sized flexible tube.

"Shall I apply it before my journey or if endangered by such insects?"

"No harm in applying before you depart. It should only take one application; although, I did not have a subject to test it on before now."

"I see! I am the subject of this experiment?"

"You might very well say that," smiled Madame Noir.

"I shall report any ill effects or if upon my demise, you may seek its disadvantages," liberally stated Relaeh.

"My son, I shall miss your capriciousness."

"To dispel your last statement, I shall be careful and will not endure unnecessary risks."

"I believe your intent, my son. I am relieved as to the successful workings of Madame Ruvana's beacons. We will be able to stay abreast of your journey and view your discoveries. Now wrap your arms about me before I get too sentimental, and please... be safe."

"I shall, my Mother. I love you as my own heart."

Relaeh departed with cream in hand. As he ascended in the Endeavor, he was overcome with a thought. He momentarily stopped at Deck 86—Regor's lab.

Relaeh Begins His Journey

Relaeh finally arrived at the loading docks where his friends, Dugar and Ruvana were waiting. Together, they inspected his air machine for all practical nuances possibly needed to complete his journey. Regor's serum was nestled securely at a controlled temperature of 12.22 degrees Celsius. He had food and shelter, extra garments, implements of chopping and digging, ropes and tethers, first aid treatments, even an extra manual compass (Master Leumas' contribution) in case his two other guidance systems failed. His air machine would lock on to the communication and guidance beacons as soon as he cleared the Portal.

His machine was not the fastest, but a shared combination of speed (NCC of 60 kph) and durability. Perhaps, one week or less of travel would set him within reach of his travelers as he was unsure of what he might encounter. Their collective excitement had longed for this day: *To actually step beyond the confinement of the energy dome and expand Relaeh's destiny and perception of the unknown.*

In turn, they acknowledged their good wills and sweet successes until they lay eyes upon each other again. Relaeh set his machine in the air tunnel. His anticipation of the cargo doors opening had not been squelched by their earlier enlightenment; his excitement remained as heightened as before. Floating upon the air foil, the doors swished open. The light filled his cockpit as he slowly maneuvered his lighter machine into the depths of the unknown. The doors closed behind him.

With determination, he commanded the machine into swift acceleration. He streaked past the beacons' launch pads, past the obvious camp of the newly escaped citizens, and down their path of freedom. As all machines were made for specific tooling; this one, Model S2, cruised two meters above the ground with a maximum altitude of six meters, but with the elevation came a reduction of speed. The closer to the ground the craft hovered, the greater the increase of its maximum speed, but also, to unknown obstacles in its path. His guidance system could react, but the stability suffered. He recalled a training session where he had an open-style cockpit machine sideways in a roll and had lost all his provisions. He was reprimanded for his zealousness and had to re-take that course with less enthusiasm. Master Leumas was not happy with his conduct. *Not this time, my Father. You will be proud*, he thought.

As systems flashed on in his S2's bubble-shaped enclosed cockpit, he was aware of the changes made to its design. He had the options of completely enclosed, partial enclosure, or open-style cockpit, as in his training version. It carried refined excavating operations, compared to his larger unit used at the sports field, as well as laser enhanced beams. The S2 had more carrying capacity but lacked the speed of the newer TR4 and 5's. They were fast!

His first communication was with Madame Ruvana at the NCC. They ran a series of monitoring tests as well as maneuverability. A couple of little tweaks to the directional thrusters had set its maximum performance. It was one thing to test in the controlled environment of their wind tunnels, but another in the wild of nature. Cross winds, earth density, and temperature played a key role in its fine tuning. From this point, the machine would automatically adjust for terrain and other chartable factors.

His ship's Anon sent continuous recorded images back to NCC. Comments sprung forth across the interfaced channels describing the beauty of the many islands to his west, and then, the fields and fields of brilliantly colored Tulips. The botany department indicated their amazement, and a wish for Relaeh to gather samples on his return. Relaeh reveled in the cross talk as this was all new to the scientists of Nalhs; however, he was hoping after six hours of constant chatter, they would let him soar in peace. He muted his interface, set his autopilot and reclined his seat backward. Not so much as to not be able to take in the visions of nature, but just enough to relax. His culinary digester issued him warm water and herbs, and holding up against the blue of the sky, he displayed a special treat from Madame Noir.

. . .

The freshness of the morning air succumbed to drenched whiffs of perimeter fires. Eve served liquid refreshment to her injured, moisture-soaked animal. Her fur reeked of stale blood, with a noticeable mixture of the black and white striped rodent's scent. She was alive, but barely, and no telling for how long. Her pups, in turn, stepped onto the supporting branches of the sling and immediately tumbled, unable to steady their footing. Adam sat on the ground with bowls of nourishment for each, as they happily accepted his re-direction.

As the light shone through the lush canopies, the danger from attack diminished. The hunters gathered their arrows and sheathed them, for now. But as Bocaj indicated, keeping this injured animal by their side would further slow their direction and also invite her pack to provoke a kill. That was the way of nature. Eve begged for its life with the rationale of one ten times her senior. The men of Belcare joined her request and offered to spare the hunters of the arduous task of dragging this dangerous beast. They confided that they would divide the hardship amongst themselves as it was more important for the hunters to have watchful eyes.

Bocaj deposited the last of the pills into each man's cup as they sat around the fire. It might not just be the animals they would have to watch out for—only time would tell.

They cleared their camp and once again broke into the sun shining day. It was impossible to hide their tracks as the hunters would have done under normal conditions. The simple urination of the ladies along the trail could invite unwanted guests, and now, the drag marks of the sling poles lead a perfect accounting to their whereabouts. Not an ideal situation for any of them. Drawbacks had been discussed by the hunters but there was nothing they could do to eliminate possible detection..., or was there?

The day's walk was long before they approached a sizable incline. They had to take several rests before they reached the crown, but as they all gathered on the summit, they turned and witnessed the most spectacular display of nature. The valley was surrounded by mountain ranges, with some of the higher ones to the east, still topped with a blanket of white. To incorporate the whole scene as one was breathtaking. The beauty they now beheld minimized any pain associated with the ascension of this summit. If only Kire had the time to sketch this beauty would one believe it's magic.

Bocaj decided setting camp on top of this plateau would make for an advantageous defense, if they needed it. The routine for set up applied here as the day before; although, the forest was set further back, a perimeter must be established. Just then, Einna and Bocaj felt a warming sensation on their chest. Surprised, but over joyed, they each scrambled to free their symbol from its confines. The others waited with anticipation as Bocaj's wrapped hands fumbled with the correct button.

"Relaeh!" hailed Bocaj excitedly as he pressed the button Einna had expressed.

"Bocaj, my friend, good will to you."

"Where are you?"

"Still several days away. Your tracking button has been activated and I am receiving your signal loud and clear."

The group hailed with excitement. Einna, as she jumped up and down while hugging Kasha, accidentally activated her visual accumulator.

"Bocaj, tell Einna to deactivate her accumulator. Although the view is very nice, I do not believe Moltov would approve of my view of Kasha's awesomeness."

The group hailed with increased cachinnation at hearing Relaeh's visual recounting. The mood was of joyous retrospect as they went about arranging their camp. Bocaj stepped to the side and continued his conversation with Relaeh.

"How does it go, Bocaj?"

"We have had our share of setbacks. Two of us are on the mend from our extreme encounter with the great shaking over the deep gorge. We pulled through with incredible fortitude by all. Our immediate concern, is of this vicious animal little Eve has calmed, somehow magically. It is badly injured and we fear her pack will be upon us at any given moment. It does not appear to give Eve or any of us concern, as it is still weak."

"Activate your accumulator so I may identify your scourge."

"I will inform Einna, my hands are bound with her undergarments at the moment."

"Please repeat...I believe I heard you wrong."

"Good will, Relaeh, Einna here."

"I misunderstood Bocaj's last transmission. He said his hands were bound with your undergarments?"

"It is a story in itself. Can you see the animal?"

"Yes... on the travois... it is called a wolf. They are very predatory and vicious. I would say by her size she is at least 60 to 70 kilos in weight; the size of a grown man. How did you come by this creature?"

"My daughter, Eve, approached it as it lay dying in the woods, while her two pups were trying to further expel the nourishment from her body. My Eve has a way with animals..."

"I would say more of a gift, Einna. Be wary of this wild animal, they are very cunning."

"Her only wish is to see this animal improve before we abandon her to the wild. She will have to fend for herself and her young pups after that."

"Very well, Einna. Bocaj is a righteous man, do as he says for your safety."

"Bocaj, are you still listening?"

"Yes."

"How are the men doing?"

"They are well with no incidences so far. They had their last pill this morning."

"Very well, as you keep your course and speed, I should be by your side in a few days."

"We shall look forward to your stature."

"Keep them safe, my friend, and I will see you soon."

Relaeh pondered..., *Undergarments? Now that is a story I want to hear. And Madame Noir believes I have a vernacular twist for telling stories!*

First Phase of Inception's Redevelopment

The village of Inception was recovering slowly from the incredible shaking. If the citizens were not busy in harvesting their corn, they were helping in the re-construction, under Leinad's watchful eyes, of new structures of commerce and residential residencies.

Aivila's nasty gash over her eye was on the mend, as was the return of her sight. Leinad was still favoring his shoulder, but under protest with the binding obstructing his movement.

Eittam helped many with their re-establishment and re-location to higher ground. Plateaus were cut into the ground and then stabilized with bamboo, retaining the dirt behind them. Each hut was then secured in their very own island of binding infrastructure. They could now shake without the fear of toppling over and harming its citizens with debris. New aqueducts were in the process of being fabricated for the redesign and placement of the huts. A team of builders had gone to the north to harvest sturdier trees, honed them into smaller slats and then bound them with vines in a circular configuration. The new aqueduct fed these barrels with fresh water gathered upstream. The higher installation added increased pressure at each dwelling for improved domestication and sanitation.

Trenches were slated to be dug to lay the newly cast pipes, for delivery of waste from each residence to holding barrels that would be treated with grubs and fauna, and then redistributed to their growing fields. The village was taking on a new and more sustainable presence.

Nephets and Tomei finally returned from the higher grazing lands of the east with stories of wonder resulting from the shaking. A new fresh water lake opened up and almost swallowed them in its making. Where their experience was positive, they could not believe the destruction of Inception. Nephets joined Leinad's well thought-out plans of implementation with as much determination as his friend. The two were a team!

Aivila, as she sat with her sister partaking in a meal, wondered how one's heart could be held in suspension for almost one third of a year.

"Your exaggeration expressing a year when it is merely four months is a selfish wrong that propels your state, my sister."

"I realize my intent but nonetheless my aching takes hold without my presence of mind," complained Aivila.

"Focus on our re-development; time will be absorbed in your actions rather than idleness."

"I do not perceive my time as idle in the light of the day. It is the darkness that occupies my sadness."

"Aivila, stay with me in my hut and we will plan the life you will share with Bocaj. We will dream together of children and our large huts to protect them, the discovery of lands beyond our vision, the growth of Inception with multiple classrooms devoted to special assignments, and a community of women sharing our experiences. We will close our eyes with love and future discoveries. What do you say?"

"My sister, I love you with all my intent. I will do as you say so I may clear this shadow and restore the light within. Your inspiration of words and gesture has always delighted the people around you. I believe your chosen one will shine with the same light as you. That, I truly believe."

"Even now you shine as before. It has not been easy with all that has happened, but I believe as never before, we shall become the women of our mother's intent."

"Have you had anymore visions of Bocaj and his men?"

"My bones have been stressed and as I lay at night they hinder my sight. We will need to reset our bath so we may indulge in the warmth of the healing waters."

"I shall aid in its setting. Perhaps under the window so we may gaze over the waters as we pamper ourselves?"

"You have implied a wonderful design. We shall do as you wish," remarked Eittam with a smile on her face.

The two nestled in their resting chamber as they had done as children—each with the security of the other, with arms held tight.

A Single Droplet

Deck 86 was a flurry of activity. Regor had summoned Master Leumas, Madame Ruvana and Dugar for the witnessing of an experiment light years ahead of their time. With a single droplet, Regor transformed the anxiousness of the room into an overwhelming collection of joyous recounting, applauds, and cachinnations that turned into liquidized moisture streaming from their eyes. The implications were momentous! They stood in Awe.

Forging New Waters

Bocaj awoke abruptly with the sound of the wolf mimicking a child's speech. He gathered his wits and quickly jumped to his feet as did the other hunters. Eve giggled as the wolf, with her head raised slightly off of the travois, offered its interpretation of a *thank you* in a deep rolling growl. Her body remained still as it tried to muster enough energy to lick Eve about the face in appreciation. The men looked at each other in amazement; her pups yipped with understanding. Who could have foretold this wonderment? They knew of only one that had powers beyond a natural man and she was in Inception. They were in agreement that they had never witnessed such intent as this. The wolf returned its head to the travois, as Eve gently fed more nourishment to her. The air had been still of howling—that had the hunters questioning the beasts' intentions.

The others jostled from the warmth of captivity from their BTIs as the image of Eve and her beast silenced the usual morning chatter. In soft voices, they mulled around the fire, prepared their first meal, and watched Eve with her new questionable friend. Striking camp was of lesser intensity as to not disturb the resting animal. With all packed and slung upon their backs, Moltov offered to be the first to bear the travois. The summit was short lived as the vision before their descent offered the relief of a long flowing river at the bottom of the next valley. There was no question in each hunter's mind of their next forging.

~

The pathway was cumbersome to navigate between the healthy growths of trees, but they did offer the needed buffer before one might tumble with momentum. At places, they had to remove their packs, and had to hoist those down the steep embankment to protect their stature from toppling head over heal. The animal was lifted hand over head, from one to another, as if it was a prize of fortune. They slipped Yuda into a tether for her ease, as her tummy was enlarging daily. Every second day now, Kasha readjusted her strapping to accommodate her increased size. Whispers were, Yuda may be off a month, as her belly was indicating a possible birth on the journey. Yuda insisted her child's first vision would be of Inception; the hunters admired her courage and strength.

As the morning sun approached its apex, the travelers had reached their intended area of interest. Thankfully, the grasslands were secured without marsh; this made for easy rolling of timber as the hunters hurriedly cut, honed,

317

and reefed mid-size trees. The rest of the travelers set camp for a possible two-day stay, whilst they ready their floating barges. They would take to the river as far as it allowed.

Bocaj indicated to Relaeh their decision to travel the waterways. Relaeh fixed their position on his air machine's internal Anon display for guidance. Everyone's spirits were high, and even more so, now that they would be free from trudging through bush. It seemed as though Regor's pills had remanded any doubts Bocaj might have conjured. Relaeh instilled his concern as they were only meant as a mask and not an antidote. Relaeh had to sign off as he approached a great divide with rushing waters below.

~

Relaeh set his machine upon the ground as he ventured forth to inspect the gorge before him. Placing his adornment about his eyes and activating its zoom feature, he saw his friends' swaying bridge. It was quite the feat for the hunters, without aid of modern technology as his. Regardless, it was no use to him, as his machine required more substance in width to remain afloat in the air. Even water had more structure, but how to descend these sheer cliffs? He could do a free fall and then quickly activate his thrusters; something he would have considered in the past. But his machine was heavier than his training version and he had promised to his friends to lessen his initial impetuous decisions to a more informed responsible determination. If he did not carry the traveler's life serum, he might have chanced his first inclination. That decision, however, would require a shut down of the chiller as he would need maximum power to regain control. Life was becoming more of a challenge the older he got. *What will be my outcome when I reach my 40th year? I will need those mobility chairs just to move my spirit,* he thought as his mind jest with him.

Relaeh decided to search the cliff-line for a lesser elevation, even if it put him farther from his intended direction. Bocaj had indicated the men were without episodes; therefore, he had the extra time to follow the river upstream, and hoped the ground would give-away to a more suitable crossing.

. . .

Bocaj and his men finished the first two of three barges they would tether together; seven on each with the middle barge carrying the wild animal. One child on each barge tethered to one of their parents. Eve would be on the middle barge as her determination was responsible for the injured animal. Two hunters on each, as their experience were mandated in case of anything that might need the swiftness of intent. Bocaj was not leaving anything to chance. They had come too far and there were a lot of lives at stake, and one that had yet to have a chance.

What struck Bocaj humorously was the fact that Kire, the mildest of his hunters was actually more experienced on the water then the rest. His father was a master fisherman who was instrumental in the design and construction of Inception's boats. Kire had learned well from him as he naturally took charge of the tethering and formal shape.

The first barge was set with a point with doubling of tangents to form a ram if needed, while the others remained rectangular in shape. Each was then outfitted with longer, thinner poles, transversely set apart and hung over each side, with another of lighter dimension secured to them. Kire called them as his father—outriggers. Their intent was for stability from side to side, if turbulence was encountered. His father had designed these protrusions for when they ventured beyond the sandbar into the open seas.

The night brought brisk talk among the travelers. Retu, as a father, remarked of Eve being of such tender years, shared a parent's responsibility to secure the animal from any inappropriate behavior. She had to understand that sometimes, the will of nature dictated what must be done. Eve acknowledged what Retu's intent of speech indicated; however, her 'Lady' would cause no discourse. Retu smiled and shook his head in wonderment of this child. *What would be her destiny? And the boy? They seemed to communicate without moving their lips or uttering a sound, yet they independently did things that complemented each other's movement.* He could only recount his children. Each needed direction... and daily.

Micja came over to Retu, and as he was about to speak, Retu inferred his intent, "Yes, I feel them as well."

Immediately Eve looked up to Retu and flashed him a big smile. He understood.

Yuda asked Kasha and Siena to aid her in removing the brace as she was experiencing some discomfort. The light of the fire radiated on her imposing belly—her beauty was glowing. The ladies decided to enjoy the warmth of the night and to indulge in the flow of the river. Stripped down to their natural state, they frolicked in the water and without hesitation or intention, they hailed the men to join the naturalness of the soothing waters. Respectfully, the men accepted. Standing guard was Bocaj and Songa, the children, her Lady, and two pups.

Ancient Waters Beware

Relaeh had spent more time than he had anticipated heading east before he found a suitable point to cross. He had to raise the complete bubble of his craft as the swish of the air turbines set to fill his cockpit with a soaking of water. He now had to re-establish his forward direction as he had no recounting of the land's display. His charts were of ancient times; although, as he passed over this indignation, his Anon charted what now appeared before it. Some of the areas had to be completely re-designated.

This area must have been severely compromised by such intensity, he thought. *What would have caused such upheaval?*

As he hovered at the entrance of a tributary, his Anon projection screen overlaid the mapping of old, and displayed the river's name as Willamette. It showed a great length heading south. He thought this riverbed suited his needs. He lowered his machine to the rocky embankment to gain extra speed. There would be little interference as there were at least four meters on each side before it gave way to grasslands. *It was not rocket science...*, he smirked to himself. *Ruvana would appreciate that slight of words.*

With controls on manual override, he swiftly accelerated along the riverbed and caught a shallow pool of water inlaid amongst a sunken depression. It flared into the air as a tail on a bird.

Relaeh was enthusiastic as he traced the river below him. At this speed, he could easily make up the time he had spent being responsible.

. . .

At water's edge, they pushed off the first of the barges, and as it hit mid-stream, the tether caught the second, and the second invited the third. They were coasting along with the current as Kire had predicated. Smooth...only the occasional redirection with their standoff poles was needed to keep them true. They were making at least thrice the time as walking. Perhaps Yuda's will of having her baby in Inception as she declared, would come to fruition as long as the waters stayed true to their intention.

As the westward grasslands moved past with distinct observation, Retu felt it, Micja felt it, and little Eve smiled as she cuddled the giant mass of fur.

All was not leisurely as they floated downstream. Three men took up post on the leading barge, and four each on the other two, while one man at a time was able to sit and rest before the rotation started again. Bocaj's injuries were being attended by Einna who removed her undergarments from his hands. The swelling had subsided and the lesions had closed, but they were still tender to touch. Another day without chores was her order, but she knew how far that would go. Bocaj was a determined man. He promised her not to do anything to further add insult to injury. She sounded like his mother, Tomei, who always insisted he take better care of himself and not to be so impetuous.

Kire studied the rock formations and the fish habits of the river basin as they floated by. When the rock formations increased in size, the river seemed to pick up speed and the fish were not as abundant. Conversely as the rocks multiplied but decreased in size, the river slowed and the fish appeared many fold. *An interesting phenomenon,* he thought. Sharp bends as they had perceived on the initial leg of their journey, usually foreshadowed uncontrollable rapids; this was what concerned him. They would be vulnerable. Their barges were not intended for rushing rapids.

As daylight dipped below the mountain peaks, Retu spotted a cove ahead. It exhibited an easy tether to the mainland without fear of predators seeking a meal of fresh human. The distance from shore acted as a safety perimeter that would allow them to stay aboard at rest without their usual ritual of defense. Only one man needed to be aware at a time; each would take one hour of post. As they guided their poles with determination, their barges eased out of the main stream and floated in the calmness.

. . .

Relaeh nestled his machine alongside the river's edge perched atop the flat surface of a giant boulder. The night sky showcased thousands of stars twinkling above. Opening his cockpit, he reveled at the magnificent view while his Anon captured and transmitted streaks of light as they passed through the sky. *The wonderment of nature was in all its glory. How could anyone who had perceived this nature deny its beauty from others?* Somehow he needed to persuade the Council of Belcare to relinquish the lives of its citizens from the grasp of the Engram. In his slumber, he realized what his Father had been saying about his destiny and his fulfillment of many discoveries. His mind wandered as he thought of Madame Noir, and how She had forsaken Her life for his. Trapped in that chair, yet She was so positive. There was no mistake of Her younger beauty as She radiated in Her mid-years. Her husband must have been devastated on Her loss—all because of him. *The years I cannot replace. Perhaps after this mission or the next, I will further my discoveries to*

323

Bocaj's village in search of possible whereabouts of Her family. At least I shall return to Nalhs with the satisfaction the men of Belcare will be able to continue their journey without fear of the injustice thrust upon them. He closed his eyes.

. . .

As they sat around the fire enjoying the tranquil night, Yuda recounted the inquiry of Councilman Erodec at the RDDS.

"You are saying that Erodec knew of a missing strain?" queried Salocin.

"Yes...as I witnessed, Landora had given him a document indicating a numerical transcript of a missing unknown strain."

"Why did he not approach your husbands of his findings?" asked Bocaj.

"He seemed bewildered of its intent, and there were whispers of a failed speech in the council chambers that might have made him uneasy," explained Yuda. "I believe him to be a good man, perhaps misguided, as we all were."

"I look forward to Relaeh's stature. Perhaps he may share his knowledge of the councilman and what has transpired," remarked Bocaj.

"Let us hope all stays calm," shared Retu.

"We have had some excitement along our way. The men seem calmer as we proceed," related Bocaj. "We all should get a good night's rest. Tomorrow will bring new adventure, I predict."

The travelers picked up their blankets and headed to the barges. One man stayed on point, even though the air had been quiet of any disturbing sounds; another reason a seasoned hunter stayed alert. Sometimes it was not what you heard that instilled fear, but what you did not. Lady remained quiet as her pups weaned nourishment from her.

Micja was the last sentry on post and as the dawn broke he readied the fire for their first meal. One by one, the travelers leisurely welcomed the new day and commented on their restfulness, while lying on their BTIs as the water rocked them to sleep.

"Eve, your Lady seems more spry this morning," said Micja.

"Yes, she is responding well to Father's concoctions."

"I believe your father's knowledge of roots and plants will serve Inception well. Will you follow his course?"

"He knows the power of many healing plants. My destiny has not yet presented herself," replied the young Eve, as if she were twenty.

Others around them who heard the conversation smiled at the little girl's answer. Her astuteness was beyond her meager tenderness. A mere babe in the arms as she stood now, but her abilities propelled this five year old with astonishing grace.

With their barges prepped with properly tethered provisions, they pushed off once again and entered the mid-stream's determination. Adam remained tethered to his mother Einna, while sharing responsibility to keep a watchful eye on the two pups. Eve was on the second barge with Lady, who was tethered down to her travois. Each day, Lady's determination was getting stronger. Her recovery would not be long before her safe release. Rajean cleaned and re-wrapped Lady's leg as the animal started to declare her independence.

"Be still Lady, Mama is not finished."

The animal succumbed to her words with the occasional lifting of her head—her steely blue eyes watched every movement.

. . .

Relaeh awoke with the vision of six, brown-skinned animals drinking water from the river's side. His Anon informed him they were called *Deer*, and the one with multiple horns protruding from its head, was the male. They were not bothered by the machine as it lay motionless upon the rock. His movement inside the cockpit startled them only slightly, and only enough to move farther down the river bed. Relaeh wondered at their reaction when he swished by them with a mere hiss. He waited long enough, he had to go. With a swish and hiss, he passed by them and he headed down river again. They appeared unfazed, and without fear. They remained.

The coordinates on the S2 indicated the travelers had increased their speed of travel. Relaeh was not gaining as much ground as he wanted, but still, he was making some headway. The landscape was changing as he darted in between fallen trees and large boulders. The grasslands were turning into reddish dirt cliffs, but for now, he was still able to hug the bank's line. Larger bodies of water opened up and then slimmed to higher peaked rock walls and then relaxed again to wide open waters in a series of four groupings. It was beautiful, as he swished on top of the water delivering huge sprays of water behind him.

. . .

Kire mentioned to Bocaj that the river was narrowing and growing deeper with radically larger boulders displaced beneath them. Their speed increased as the river narrowed, and as it seemed to end, they rounded a bend and delved into flushing of water. A thundering noise sounded ahead of them as they now had got caught in a vortex of swirl, bouncing them side to side. Kire looked behind and saw the ladies had set to all fours hanging on to their tethers as the men braced themselves against the forces.

Kire directed his craft with his pole...off one boulder then another, the others still in tow. Up and then down, from one side to another, the barge bounced aimlessly down the rushing waters towards the roaring sound. Hailing loudly, Kire screamed, "HANG ON, WE'RE GOING IN!" They dove down one slope... the bow caught water... soaked Kire and the others... and up again, relentlessly they pounded on. The boulders shouldered each side, as the river narrowed to impossible passage. Scraping the bark from their arc, they squeezed through, and dove down into the next hole of swirl. The second barge smashed its outriggers, sending them flying aft, missing Retu, but as he turned, he watched the branch snatch Moltov and Jang off their corners and propelled them deep into the rushing river behind. Kasha and Siena screamed with intent as their husbands disappeared into the depths. Each followed as the first, each barge battered by indignation, receiving blows after blows, hurling them through the angry waters. Suddenly, out of the white foam, one surfaced, then another—eyes darted above the water line.

Moltov and Jang associated the screaming of the ladies as - "Sarge, hold on! Knuckles grab the pole..." Upon the barge were not the friends of Belcare, but dressed in an ominous black, nondescript uniforms with black smudges smeared under their eyes, stood assistance from ancient times. The two men cautiously looked around for enemy fire before they accepted the hand from their fellow team member.

. . .

Relaeh was quietly cruising along when suddenly, a piercing clang set off his emergency notification channel from Einna's panic button. He slammed off the persistent noise and answered immediately.

"Einna...What is wrong?"

"Our worst nightmare!"

"Explain."

"We went through a terrifying spot on the river. Moltov and Jang got knocked off the barge by an outrigger that broke away from the middle barge. When the waters eased they surfaced as two very different men."

"Where is Bocaj?"

Einna whispered, "On the lead barge."

"Are you safe?"

"They are questioning our intent with great determination."

"Who is speaking to them?"

"My husband, Salocin."

Relaeh switched channels on his Anon.

"Regor, do you receive me?"

"Relaeh, how are your leisurely travels?" jestfully inquired Regor.

"Not so... have you any information to 401.11?" frantically asked Relaeh.

"I have isolated its intent as a 1972 strain drawn from a specialized rescue team operating in a place called Vietnam. There was an Operation Thunderhead, spearhead by the U.S. Navy Seals from a vessel called a submarine named USS Grayback, to recover escaped prisoners of war who were be held at the Hanoi Hilton. They were to enter the Red River. Their command ship was the USS Long Beach." informed Regor.

"Anything else I should know?"

"Not all made it."

"Thanks, Regor."

"Einna... hand your symbol to whomever you believe is in charge," instructed Relaeh. "Tell him this is Command."

The soldier accepted the strange apparatus, from Einna, and listened.

"Soldier, this is Command Central from the USS Long Beach, do you copy?" forcefully stated Relaeh.

"Yes, sir."

"Stand down, soldier... mission abort. Do you copy? Operation Thunderhead... abort."

"Sir, we have civilians..."

"They are a special ops team, soldier... from another division. They have authority. Do you copy? Do as they request."

"Yes, sir."

"Good... pass the communicator back to the Colonel."

"Command wishes to speak to you, Colonel."

"Yes, Command."

"Einna, what do you think, will that calm them for now?"

"I believe so, Command. I'll have some of our allied citizens' join in and try to relax the situation," shared Einna for all to hear.

"Very well, Einna, I have no other instructions. Do your best," directed Relaeh.

"Yes, sir, I understand. Out."

She turned to one of the warriors and said.

"Good, sir, you have blood about your head. Let my assistant clean your wound."

"Yes, ma'am... ah Colonel".

"Relax soldier, you both are in good, safe hands here," instructed Einna with a soft but stern intent.

"Ma'am, what division are you from?"

"Belcare."

"Belcare, Belcare, I've heard of it," affirmed soldier Jang.

"I believe...I believe..." he placed his head into his hands and rubbed his temples.

"You believe what soldier?" inquired nurse Siena.

"Knuckles, the lady asked you a question?"

"Knuckles?" questioned nurse Siena.

"He has lightening hands like Bruce Lee, ma'am," informed a soldier from the ancient past.

"And you soldier, what is your status," lovingly asked Kasha.

"I'm...I'm..."

"Moltov, my love... you are Moltov... my big strong husband. And I am your loving wife Kasha. Do you recount my presence?"

He looked into her caring eyes and weakly said, "Kasha... yes my wife, Kasha."

He buried his head between her awareness, and moisture conjured in her eyes while the hunters watched with great intent.

Relaeh lowered his air machine below recommended air travel. He hovered at speeds never before obtained in a S2 craft, 72 kph. His determination overruled his own safety to save his comrades.

A Lingering Scent

After three days of considerably calmer waters and stable significance from the travelers, the river's passage ended just beyond the remarkable red bluffs. As they recounted from their journey, these massive mounds of lavish red color, had been nothing they had ever witnessed of nature, only the vibrancy of Kasha's hair. Much jocular intent was jestfully implied that her origin of birth must have been carved from these hills. The atmosphere had transformed from intense drama to calm interludes.

Leaving behind their floating carriages, they once again took up on foot. Lady was determined to join their walking, albeit with a limp, with her pups in tow. There seemed to be a developing mutual respect between Retu, the great hunter, and Lady. Eve closely monitored Lady's intent. Bocaj's prized possession, his symbol, had somehow been ripped from his neck as they bounced through the rapids. Only Einna possessed their communication between the two worlds. The range of Einna's symbol was not as favorable as the larger displacement of Bocaj's, but with any luck, it would be enough for Relaeh to track their whereabouts, that is, the closer he got to them.

The mountain ranges had been left behind as rolling hills with a definite arid intent now laid before them. What concerned the hunters now, was, the eyes that had been following closely. Lady was not up to her full strength and her intent was uncertain if her pack joined her. Would she defend the humans or take part in a fresh meal?

Eve had made a peculiar gesture of touching everyone on the arm as they walked along. No one really took notice except Retu and Tavlo as they had shared the last five days aboard their barge. Eve's intent, although slight, was questioned by the two. Bocaj had indicated that another week of travel would confront them, before they would set eyes on their home of Inception.

Yuda's condition was laboriously increasing and they required frequent unscheduled stops. Still, morale was high as they trudged forward.

. . .

The NCC asked Relaeh to increase his ground clearance and decrease his speed. He muted his air ship's Anon. He thought he would be placed on leave to pay for his insolence, but his actions could be defended, if needed. He had already zipped past, a clearing where the travelers had created their barges. He was on their trail and wound with the river, full speed ahead.

Bocaj's signal was increasing to where Relaeh thought he should be almost upon them. He slowed the S2 as he approached the rushing rapids. He clung to the narrowed banks until he glided over a set of precariously placed branches that were lodged amongst boulders, to where a signal was emitting from the waters below. He hovered and searched the area around him. In the depths of the river, Bocaj's symbol gleamed as the light refracted off of it. It would have been a simple retrieval for his electromagnetic lure, but the material had no element of carbon, thus a painstaking grabbing of pinchers as the river's current defied its success. Relaeh felt like he was at the grand festival in Belcare during the twin moons' celebration, toying with a child's game as set by one of the hawkers. Finally his pincher made contact. It clasped on and he slowly raised his prize to his air ship. Tapping it off, he sped away without signal, but with gut feeling. Soon, he hoped, he would be in range of Einna's symbol.

. . .

After walking many kilometers, Bocaj decided, since the sun still sat at a decent height in the sky, they should make camp. They took shelter near the last remaining trees, as before them lay a vast landscape of nothing. The sun was unyielding, and they were thankful for the shade that had dotted their journey. A full moon was approaching, so night travel would be preferred rather than the intensity of the daytime heat. The travelers would wait out one day to prepare for the following night's travels.

As they began to set camp, Lady disappeared, leaving her pups to Adam. There were whispers among them of her intent—possibly reestablishing her presence with her pack. The trees were parched from the heat of the sun, and their fallen branches made for quick fueling of the fire. Retu and Micja geared up with their bow and arrows to search the area for fresh game. Suddenly, with absolute silence in her step, Lady returned with a long-eared game in her mouth. She dropped it at Retu's feet and then took off again. Five times she repeated this practice until on the sixth return, she gathered her pups and set the fury animal between them, away from the humans. The hunters sat in disbelief. If they had not witnessed this gesture from this vicious animal, no storyteller could convince them that such wonderment could transpire. They enjoyed a wonderful feast, thanks to Lady, as the night air closed around them.

~

As the fire light reflected the piercing blue eyes of Lady, her GROWLING and HOWLING awoke the travelers. She stood with fur raised and head lowered, searching the shadows. Retu made his way to her side. Her lips peeled back baring her massive teeth, and her throaty growl switched to a high pitched HOWL as her nose acquired a distinct scent. The hunters gathered in a broad circle, protecting their comrades, bows in hand and arrows set as they too searched the shadows for movement. In the far distance, Lady's invite set shrills reverberating in the night air. She HOWLED again. As the slight breeze changed direction, Lady articulated her neck following, sniffing, and caught the hint of some thing. She let out an ominous GROWL, fluttered her lips, and then, she made a quick whine and a flick of her nose as she nestled her face into Retu's leg. Warmly, Retu placed his hand upon Lady's head, and caressed her. Lady broke from Retu's attention and with a rolling growl, stepped to the ridge of the circle, lay down, crossed her forelegs, and listened. Three hunters set point while the others rested—it could be a long night. Luckily, the keen scent of their fierce predator was on their side. Whatever loomed in the darkness, better beware.

. . .

The morning light offended the eyes of the tired travelers. Bocaj, Retu and Songa had spent the hours before daybreak discussing the early break of camp. They felt they needed to take advantage of the cooler morning hours, and then re-set camp before the heat of the day. Whatever disturbed Lady in the wee hours, was probably still lingering. Bocaj wanted to keep traveling to put distance between them and Lady's nemesis. They made haste and set course.

Lady nudged Adam as if to say, *take care of my pups*, as she then turned and took up the rear behind the last man, Tavlo. Tavlo had been stalked before by a predator, but this time he felt secure in her presence.

The morning air was dry and hot. Their garments were soaked with moisture before the sun hit its apex and their movement was slowed because of the relentless heat. A patch of reeds ahead indicated, at least at one time, a presence of water. As they slowly proceeded, the reeds opened up to a small pond that invited their needs. They disrobed willingly and plunged into the relief of the waiting waters. Lady guided her pups to the water's edge before she lay belly deep to cool her frame.

Premonition Two-Fold

Eittam startled Aivila as she awoke with moisture about her body, trembling.

"My sister, what troubles you?"

"That same dream from long ago. He runs with fear in his eyes. Beasts are ripping apart human flesh. Arrows and spears fill the air. Many men are causing much bloodshed..."

Eittam buried her face into her hands and tears flowed from her eyes as she gazed up at Aivila.

"Bocaj...is it Bocaj?"

"I had not seen Bocaj before I awoke," grieved Eittam.

. . .

Madame Noir's eyes opened starkly. She gasped as She sat up quickly, causing pain about Her legs. What dream was She foretelling? *Why was Relaeh running so determinately? What harm has approached him?* Madame Noir swiveled off of Her BTI into Her awaiting chair. She contacted Master Leumas, wakening him from a sound sleep.

"Noir, what is it? I hear trembling in Your voice."

"I fear for Relaeh. Can you contact him?"

"Yes, of course. Of what shall I discuss with him?"

"I do not know. Tell him to be careful. I have had a dream."

"I shall not insult You with a mother's intuitive heart ache of absence, but he has made no communication of any harm or warning of such. His journey remains fruitful without discourse, except for the two who feared their near drowning," informed Master Leumas.

"Maybe not, but please ask for my sake of his safety."

"I shall do as you ask, Noir. Now go back to sleep and I will inform you after I have spoken with Relaeh."

"I shall rest, but my sleep has been removed from my body," declared Madame Noir.

Master Leumas programed his H-WAC to patch through NCC to Relaeh's air machine. It buzzed, again, and again. Finally...

Wearily, Relaeh answered, "Good will."

"Relaeh how goes your travel?" queried Master Leumas.

"Father, is Nalhs on a different time than the new world?"

"No... Madame Noir is concerned for your safety. She has had a frightful dream and has woken me to ask of your health," he said feeling slightly foolish.

"Father, I am fine. I perceive I shall be upon our travelers this very day."

"Good, I shall inform Madame Noir to your status so that I may continue to enjoy my rest," jestfully implied Master Leumas.

"Thank you, Father, good will to you."

"Oh Relaeh, the commander of the NCC wishes to speak to you on your return."

Master Leumas informed Madame Noir of Relaeh's status and reluctantly did not discuss Relaeh's garish movements commanding his air machine.

The Hostile Engagement

As Relaeh zoomed past the abandoned barges, he picked up a weak signal from Einna's symbol. The rolling hills and sparse vegetation were but a blur as Relaeh pushed the limits of the S2. The heat outside his nicely chilled cockpit was building as the sun rose.

. . .

Downwind they lay, waiting for their next meal. They watched as their nourishment frolicked in the water—spears in hand.

The warm breeze abruptly changed. Lady stood tall, her hair rose about her neck. She GROWLED with more intent then the night before. She HOWLED anxiously as she raised her head high. Taking note, the travelers scrambled for their bows. Confused, the ladies looked about them. The children ran and hid amongst their packs as *egregious creatures* leaped from cover and plunged forward toward the dazed travelers.

Lady instinctively jumped with determination and fiercely ripped the throat open of one of the mud-clad humanoids. Bocaj and his men rallied with swift arrows dropping the first barrage of invaders. The ladies encircled their children with broken reeds in their hands, and readied for the next strike. The invaders surrounded the camp and came at them from all sides. A spear found Lady in the hind quarter as she de-throated another, collapsing with teeth buried in her victim. SCREAMS of war-cries echoed through the airwaves as the mud people approached strong and fervently.

The travelers were outnumbered many to one man. An invader slithered through the ladies defense and secured Yuda in his grip. Einna plunged a reed deep into his side. Dropping Yuda, he turned to face Yuda's protector, saliva dripped from his disgusting face. The men of Belcare came alive! *Knuckles* leaped into the air, and with a roundhouse, kicked the invader in the head. Spinning, he delivered another, and with exacting might, he swiftly enacted an open palm into its throat. The creature dropped to its knees and fell backwards.

The six Belcarians swarmed together with the deliverance of ancient warriors. Hand to hand, they reconciled the advances of the creatures. One by one, the humanoids fell to the ground. The hunters' arrows downed only a few as the hordes gave them little time to redraw their bows. Vigorously they engaged, arms clashed against sharpened spears, blood spewed from open wounds.

The hostile mud people were relentless and without fear as they continued their surge. Kire took a spear to his shoulder, which dropped him to the ground. As the perpetrator moved in to finish him off, *Sarge* reacted with an elbow to the back of the *its* head, SNAPPING its neck just as another grabbed for him. Sarge spun out of its grasp, bent its arm, SNAPPED it in two and lodged the exposed jagged bone into its heart. With a warning SCREAM from Einna, *Nick* side-stepped a thrusting spear, broke it in two and thrust the remainder into the back of its skull before it could reach Einna. Tavlo with his great strength picked up an attacker and body slammed him across his knee, breaking the intruders back.

Through the reeds, with the wind to his back, he ran, he ran as fast as he could with glaring determination in his eyes. Relaeh sprung from a downed body, and inflicted a precise punch to the jaw of an egregious creature. As it fell backwards, he hammered its knee with a crashing side kick leaving the leg L-shaped. Kasha ended its misery with a reed penetrating through the eye into the center of its brain. It heaved and twisted before it lay motionless. Relaeh joined Bocaj, and side by side, they fended off more foul creatures. The smell from their wretched breath disgusted them.

Suddenly, Eve stood up from her hiding place, raised her arms skyward, and without warning, Lady's pack leaped out of the reeds unto the backs of the mud people. They fiercely ripped off limbs, and predatorily dissected their windpipes. They left the 'it' creatures squirming— blood spouted in the deluge. Snarling, and with massive teeth bared, the wolves forced the remaining few cannibals to retreat leaving their wounded for dead. The wolves wasted little time in ending any movement that still occupied the defenseless injured.

The wolves gathered around their fallen alpha—tainted blood dripped from their mouths. They watched her lie, wincing in pain as the spear wavered in her thigh. Bloody noses poked at her to get up. Eve, SCREAMED with horror while she ran to her fallen Lady. The warriors, pumped with adrenaline, set to approach the fallen animal. Instinctively, the wolves turned and snarled at their offense. The ladies grabbed their warriors and tried to calm their influence. Retu and Relaeh advanced cautiously, talking as they moved among the wolves to Lady's side.

"We need to stabilize the animal so her pack does not get any ideas that we look good to eat," explained Relaeh.

Eve, already at Lady's side, cried with heartache, "Do not die Lady. You cannot die. You lived once, you can do it again," she insisted as she stroked Lady's forehead.

"Kire, how are you doing?" hailed Relaeh as they moved closer to the injured wolf.

Kire lay in pain. His blood started to pool around his injury. Bocaj, the ladies, and with Tavlo's help, calmed Kire as the two men removed the piercing spear with a distinguishing SLURP as it ejected.

"Ugh...I have felt better," he said shivering in pain.

"Eve," gently called Relaeh. "We need for you to stand aside while we try to remove this spear."

Loudly Relaeh hailed, "Ladies, in my machine there is a red bag with a white symbol on it. Please fetch it and bring it to me."

Yuda was on the ground breathing heavily as Narfinia and Siena tried to calm her.

"I'll be fine," she insisted. "...just need to work out my anxiety." She rubbed her heightened tummy in a circular motion.

Kasha returned with what Relaeh asked for.

"Now Retu, I will remove the spear while you hold the wolf still. After, I will inject her with this medicine. I have bandages to wrap her. She will fall into a sleep. We will use her slumber to inspect the wound without her upsetting her pack."

"Does anyone know how to inject a needle?" inquired Relaeh.

"I can," insisted Narfinia, "I have worked at the medical hall."

"Good, take the blue one to Kire and inject him, now," said Relaeh, calmly but directly.

Narfinia did as she was asked. Kire's shivering started to subside as the fluid slowly entered his body.

"He might talk a little out of character... that is normal. Let him ramble, keep him awake," insisted Relaeh.

With a determined upward motion, Relaeh ejected the spear from Lady. Sponging the surfacing blood, he quickly injected the numbing solution. She rested her head in the reassuring hands of Retu, his scent permeated her nostrils, she snorted. Her pack milled about restlessly.

"HUSH...," cried Eve.

With the conviction of her words, they settled down and watched attentively while the humans inspect their fallen alpha.

As they had no chance to re-robe before the mud people attacked, the travelers stood in all their glory, wounds displayed, and mud-caked. Retu and the others looked at Relaeh with wonderment. Where moments ago his wounds bled as theirs, now bore, hardly any influence of damage.

"What powers do you possess?" asked Retu in disbelief.

"I have none that I am aware," reflected Relaeh as he turned each arm about to reveal the disappearing wounds. "Madame Noir insisted I put a cream about my body for the protection from insect bites and the ravishing rays of the sun."

"That is quite the insect bite cream you adorn," jest Bocaj.

"Yes indeed... shall we place it about your wounds?" queried Relaeh.

"If it works on us as you, we shall have no need of bandages, my friend."

"Wipe your injuries clean and then apply lightly," instructed Relaeh.

The wives helped their now mellowed husbands cleanse their wounds. Each applied lightly as instructed and within minutes they started to heal as Relaeh.

Carefully moving Kire, they inserted a dab of cream into his wound and then upon his shredded skin. His wound was of much greater intensity thus the response was not as forthcoming as the others. Relaeh injected a small amount into the gaping hole in Lady's thigh. They would have to wait for results as each had lost a lot of blood.

The wolves remained vigilant. Sitting as sentinels, they protected their alpha without interest of the dead remains ravaged through the brutal fighting. Repulsed by the indignation of the mud people, the travelers washed the rest of the foulness from their bodies in the reddening pond. They decide to leave as soon as possible. Lady needed to be transported as before on the travois, but instead of dragging her, they hoisted it upon the air machine. Kire would also enjoyed his slumber state in the air machine until they reached their next camp ground. Irreverently, the heat battered their bodies, decreasing the speed with which propelled them forward towards Inception. The S2 hovered slowly behind the travelers—the pack closely followed it.

Relaeh instructed NCC of what had transpired and his possible continuing journey with the travelers. He asked of them to inform Master Leumas as he awaited his suggestion for further assistance.

They Wept

The screams of horror had been transmitted to Nalhs via the S2's Anon. Only spasmodic images revealed the anguish of the fighting as seen through the reeds separation. Nalhs watched and listened in disbelief.

Madame Noir and Eittam wept with their vision of the chaos. Master Leumas tried to comfort Madame Noir as Aivila held her sister tightly, and powerless.

After the Chaos

Regor, Dugar and Madame Ruvana were numbed by what they had witnessed. How could there be such violence embedded in those creatures? And what liberated the travelers from the vicious nature of the animals? What or who controlled their spirit? Regor contacted Relaeh and asked if he could take a blood sample from the creatures and possibly from the injured animal as well. There was so much to learn of this new world. As they had Relaeh's attention on the Anon, Dugar inquired somberly, "Relaeh, my friend, how are you?"

"My wounds have healed magically as have the travelers. My hands remain sore. I have not stuck another with such vengeance."

"Your stature has not been harmed," interrupted a tearful Madame Ruvana.

"I am fine, Ruvana. Kire is not doing as well. He suffered a sharpened reed to his shoulder piercing through to the other side. He is calm with the drug for now. We shall watch his vitals closely as the night befalls us."

"Madame Noir has suffered an attack on Her visionary perception. Master Leumas tends to Her now," informed Dugar.

"If She is of ill health on my account, tell Her not to worry, I am fine. The travelers are shaken, but in good spirit. Narfinia is versed in medical necessities and can administer the antidote if Master Leumas requires me to return?"

"He has shared with us for you to continue, if you so choose. Inception is but a two or three day journey from your current location, if we have plotted Bocaj's recount precisely," insisted Madame Ruvana.

"We will determine our direction upon first light. Yuda, I believe, will need transportation. She is as big as a double chamber," jestfully shared Relaeh. "I have no measure of her tenacity to have continued as she has."

"Tell her I miss her and send my love," affectionately offered Madame Ruvana.

"I shall. It seems we are stopping. I shall correspond after we have settled."

John F Russo

Bocaj motioned for Relaeh to place his air machine into the indicated circle. Relaeh lowered his machine. As it silently shut down, one of the larger wolves that had being following them, pure white in color, stepped upon the side of the air ship with anxiousness, but also curiosity. He nosed Lady with intent.

"Not so hard," remarked Relaeh.

The animal rolled a growl and looked at Relaeh with piercing blue eyes.

"She is yours, is she?" intuitively queried Relaeh.

Lady returned a weaker growl as Retu and Relaeh lifted the burdened animal from the air ship. They placed her to the side, away from the confusion. Her pups gathered upon the travois seeking nourishment until, one by one, the white male picked them up in his teeth and delivered them back to Adam's care. He HOWLED and with a quick snarl, the pack disappeared into the long shadows of the evening's setting sun. The attentive male lay beside his injured female and waited.

The travelers wearily set camp and forewent the usual jesting and idle conversation. It was decided that three guards shall deploy at two hour intervals, including the men from Belcare. The hunters rightfully conceded that they were no match to the hand-to-hand combat they witnessed that day. Although the men had calmed, it was apparent their awareness remained greatly heightened. Relaeh thought it prudent not to start the injections until they were out of danger—their reassuring talents might be needed again.

"What do you make of these animals, Retu?" inquired Relaeh.

"I believe Eve has a charmed force with them. She touched us all before the battle as if she instinctively knew or comprehended Lady's awareness. She and the boy have remained calm throughout this journey, like seasoned hunters. I can only speak from experience with my children, this nature is not natural. And what of you? They have no bother with you either."

"I cannot explain your truth, my friend. I am as perplexed as you. My destiny seems to change daily. My awareness increases as I share my discoveries and I know not why," related Relaeh in confidence.

"I have heard whispers that you are the chosen one to unite all of the land. You are the Healer," reported Micja, interrupting.

"I have been relayed a destiny. We shall see what transpires, my good fellows," lightly jest Relaeh. This was not the time to be expressing philosophical idealisms.

"Bocaj!" hailed Relaeh. "I have something for you."

Dismissing himself politely, Relaeh treaded over to his air machine and produced Bocaj's symbol.

"This is twice you have offered me this symbol."

"Yes and twice you have accepted," replied Relaeh. "We will need to make a harness like Yuda's to keep this keepsake about your stature."

Relaeh, with his implied humor, broke the dulled atmosphere as usual. The travelers, realizing their solidarity, regained their co-mingling of jocular overtones, and spirited conversations flowed as the night set in.

As the travelers lay on their BTIs and looked at the starry night, Relaeh offered Madame Ruvana's request.

"By the way, Yuda. Madame Ruvana sends Her love to you."

"Madame ... Ruvana?" Questioning whispers circled the camp in the revelation and good will afforded to their friend as the white male rolled an acknowledging growl.

Last Night on the Trails

For the last two days, Yuda had enjoyed the carnival advantage in Relaeh's air machine. Kire was sitting up, but still weak, and Lady, as they lifted her off the machine for the last night before entering Inception, welcomed her pups. Rowdy, the white male as Relaeh had named him for its constant rolling of growl, gently placed its mouth around Relaeh's hand and pulled him to his Lady's side. Relaeh accepted the gesture and bent down onto one knee. The-would-be predator licked his face in appreciation.

There was much jubilation, as according to the hunters, their homes lay within a short morning walk over gentle sloping hills. The children played with the pups as the mother and father lay beside each other and watched the interaction with the humans. The journey had been hard, but the gains rewarding, and the stories would be plentiful for the ears of the citizens of Inception.

Tomorrow would no doubt bring new awareness and offer its own challenges for the citizens of Belcare and Relaeh, but tonight, song and dance had everyone in a blissful state. Relaeh, with Narfinia's help, began the first of three injections for the inflicted men. Soon Relaeh would take leave of his fellow travelers, and head back to his home and friends of Nalhs.

The warm night welcomed the bond from the flickering fire, as husband and wife shared tender moments concealed under light linens. The soft whispers brought smiles to the hunters knowing that tomorrow's eve would bring the same enchantment to them.

Relaeh drifted in the sounds of pleasure never before heard. He wandered into the sun-filled marigold field, and as he lay with a grand smile, a faceless figure draped her long ravenous locks about his face. She tenderly kissed his cheek, and then his chin, and then his lips parted as her moist lips met his. He felt her weight pressed to his body as they nestled as one. His dream was as vivid as one could imagine and slowly as she touched his chest she heard her name being called out...

"Eittam...," (softly at first) "Eittam, what are you dreaming!?" exclaimed Aivila.

Eittam awoke in wonderment as she too felt the warmth of the sun in the field of marigolds.

"I... I..." failing to understand the meaning she said,

"I have met him."

Act III

Welcome to Inception

Inception Celebrates

Leinad and Nephets walked past the newly enlarged and re-enforced infirmary on their way to the docks. A flurry of hustle and bustle filled their vision as they meandered down to where their newly considered commercial street began at the crossroads of the main pathway that lead north. They stopped there with drawings in hand and a ball of measuring twine to transcribe the distances of this intersection onto their plans.

Northward, at the top of the slight incline, the sunlight reflected off of her silver highlights. Two large predators stood with heads down observing their next meal. Leinad and his friend Nephets, noticing their image through the glaring sun, hailed to the citizens in close proximity to take to their huts and gather bow and arrows as adversaries approached. Aivila rushed out of the infirmary upon hearing her father's demand and ran to his side. They witness the unusual preoccupation of the predators as they sat and looked back from whence they came.

A head bobbed up and down from sight with each step he claimed, until he stood in full view with the predators on each side. He paused and then began his step downward as another figure followed him, and then another. The figures came to light in the shade of the tall palms. Aivila SCREAMED with delight as Bocaj led his men toward home. Within a flash of a firefly, Aivila exploded with the speed of a panther, each step more powerful than the last. Bocaj opened his arms wide with a clenched fist of red strands dangling. She leapt into his arms forcing him to fall backwards onto his pack. Wrapping her legs around him, she adorned him with kisses. The men gathered around and clapped and hailed. From the lower street came the cry of two young children.

"Papa... Papa!" Retu turned to see the vision he longed for most—his son and eldest daughter as they ran to his side.

The citizens rushed their wayward hunters with gleeful wishes, unfazed by the sentries that still adorned the top of the hill. Still more came over the ridge, two by two, and then children as well, with pups in tow. At last, a mysterious machine floated in the air with Kire and two unknown faces. The two adult wolves followed behind.

The word quickly spread of the return of their hunters as a gala procession herded them into the center of the village to the long house. The celebration would be of a magnitude never experienced in Inception. The farmers were instructed to bring bushels of corn for the heating pots, and fruits, fancy red, green and yellow would be displayed. The long tables would be dressed with fresh cut flowers, and herdsmen and farmers would shed their tools for instruments of sound, so proclaimed Leinad. Bocaj and Aivila walked arm in arm as two proud peacocks as the crowd lined the street welcoming the return of the hunters and the unknown travelers from a distant village. The wolves remained close to the air machine, not bothered by the hailing of the crowd, but kept a keen watchful eye.

As the crowd gathered into a circle around the long house, Leinad motioned for the crowd to quiet down. Relaeh set the air machine within the circle and helped Yuda and Kire maneuver to solid ground. The wolves remained at his side. Taking his son by the hand, Nephets proudly lead him to the top of the landing of the long house.

"Citizens of Inception," he said with tears in his eyes. "I welcome the safe return of my son and his fellow hunters."

The crowd exploded with cachinnation and cheers as Nephets held Bocaj tight. Bocaj and his fellow hunters waved their arms triumphantly.

Wiping the tears from his eyes, Nephets hailed with excitement once more. "I know you all want to hear their tales but first let us meet our men's companions so we may celebrate as one."

The crowd again broke out in loud cheering and once again Nephets had to quieten them. Bocaj commenced with introductions of his fellow travelers.

"Before I begin, let me say this. These people speak the truth as we. Their heart is tender and their determination is strong. Their talents are many, and most of all, they are our friends."

Again the cheers ignited. Bocaj waved his hands to settle them down and introduced each one by name as they took the landing beside him.

"I, we, welcome you to Inception, and from now on, you will be known as citizens of Inception. Let their names be written in our registry!" proclaimed Bocaj.

Cheers flared once more. He paused for their adulation that was being bestowed upon the new citizens. Bocaj motioned the citizens of Inception to listen once again.

"At last, the soul of our brigade, the one that pulled us all together and saved our lives, the one with knowledge beyond our imagination, the man who commands this floating machine, whose destiny I believe shall touch all of us, whose name has been whispered as the Healer, my friend, Relaeh from Nalhs."

Relaeh approached the landing—the two wolves followed.

"And another mention, if I may, our fierce companions, Lady, the grey one and Rowdy the white wolf who leaped to our rescue only a few short days ago. You will want to hear stories by little Eve, I assure you."

Reaching the top of the landing, the two grappled each other in tradition. Bocaj introduced Relaeh to Leinad and to his father, and as they grappled a strange phenomenon stirred in each. As Bocaj looked around, he asked his father to the whereabouts of his mother. Nephets related that she was with Eittam in the far valley with some of the children on a nature excursion, but insisted she would be back in time for the grand feast.

Leinad took the command and said, "Citizens, today, as my dear friend has said, marks a special day for all to recount. But we also must make haste to build accommodations for our new citizens. On tomorrow's light we will plot their home to their needs. And even I, as an old man with poor vision can see, their needs will be forthwith," jestfully implied Leinad as he looked at Yuda.

The crowd acknowledged the directive from Leinad with glowing cheers.

He continued, "But tonight... we shall all celebrate!"

Rowdy let out a bellowing HOWL and several rolling growls as the crowd applauded his intent. Relaeh rubbed the predator's head as it rested against his leg.

The crowd dispersed as arrangements had to be attended to for the grand feast. Aivila led the new citizens to the infirmary as this was the only place with enough beds for all; besides, it would not be long before Yuda would be in need of one.

Bocaj took Relaeh to his hut, with the family of wolves who followed behind. Relaeh's excitement for Bocaj and his men, for what they had accomplished, was a humane gesture of goodwill. He guided and protected the travelers as their own, and now, he introduced them into his society. That trust was the soul of a man of great determination. Bocaj was a good man, that he had witnessed, and the citizens held him in the highest regards. Relaeh could not be happier as he thought of his friends and family in Nalhs, and he wished, possibly one day, all would be one.

The moment for retrospect quickly vanished when Aivila bounced into the hut. Her love for Bocaj, as Relaeh observed, was quite obvious as she had wrapped her arms around him many times. His reaction was similar but with a slight hesitation. Her interruption might have appeared childish but her excitement over Kasha's fiery red hair bound the two together as sisters. Neither had witnessed such vibrancy in another and their ages were only a couple of years apart in Kasha's favor. As quickly as they entered they now exited, a whirlwind of flowing garments and youth.

"She, your Aivila, I believe holds you dearly in her heart."

"We have not spoken of intent of gazing upon each other's eyes. It just happened."

"If I may be so bold, you appear as in love, but you hesitate being forthright."

"It is not my intent to not display my caring. It is that I have not asked permission from Councilman Leinad or Lady Eittam. I fear their discourse as Aivila is a mere eighteen years." respectfully replied Bocaj.

"But she has made no hesitation in front of her father and I preclude her strong will has stated her course previously."

"I had no preconception of her intent until the day we took upon our journey. She took my dagger from its pouch and cut these strands of hair and placed them in my hand." Bocaj raised his hand with the tuff of hair still tightly secured.

"But you have kept them with you for these many months of travel. I believe you are as taken with her as she with you. Your hesitation lies in fear of her sister then?"

"Councilman Leinad is a good man and my Father's best friend. Eittam has powers that can foretell and perception of inner spirits that could make a normal man dubious of engaging in the household of Leinad."

"Ahahah... You fear her sister's powers that she might foresee a troubling spirit within you, and therefore, as her duty to her sister, compromise your intentions?"

"You do have a way with words, my friend. Wait till you have the pleasure of conversation with her. She can anticipate every word before your mind has thought it."

"I shall look forward to the honor. When shall I meet this temptress?"

"She is not a temptress, but a seer. She has a kind heart, beauty beyond compare, and determination that will recount your life back to infancy," jest Bocaj.

Relaeh shook his head back and forth and placed his hand upon Bocaj's shoulder.

"My friend, our worlds might be from different beginnings and you have witnessed much of Aivila's sister, but I tell you with truth, as I stand before you, there is only one who has such power, and She remains in Nalhs."

With a lighthearted intent, Bocaj declared. "Let this be my fore warning to you."

The two companions continued their bantering as they ready themselves for the adulation that would comprise this day's events.

The other travelers' moods were of similar jocular intent. They jest over the design of the beds that were so endearingly offered to them. But, they had their BTIs to implement upon the boards of discomfort. At some time they would have to introduce their gift from Relaeh to the citizens of Inception for their own BTIs. Their sacks of lumpy dried grass that they now endured would most certainly receive a different application. Salocin and Moltov also endured with humor the design of the village, but conspired not to be overzealous. They had witnessed intent of implementing a more suitable layout, and commented on not having the resources of Nalhs.

The ladies laughed and giggled as they *pomped and prepped*, and scrubbed off the latent woes from the travels. Hair was washed and styled, and securely hidden in one of the heavy packs, unbeknownst to the men, Siena retrieved a colorful tray of eye and face adornments. This was a necessity for any woman to bring on a lengthy journey to unknown lands. Although, the ladies here in Inception seemed to possess natural beauty, and some apparently had instruction on adornment about the eyes; nonetheless, their preconception of their new home, inspired by the hunters, made no mention of such luxuries. Their husbands would appreciate their concerns now that they had safely arrived in Inception.

~

Tomei and Eittam had bravely survived the inquisitive young minds that questioned every leaf, every insect, every flying moth, and every wisp of air. They were delighted with the children's interest, but next time they would port pencil and paper for them to sketch their findings to alleviate the tedious, never-ending but's, why's, and how comes.

One by one they dropped the children off at their huts so they could ready themselves for the beginning of the late afternoon festivities. Tomei's hut came first; the ladies hugged and bid farewell until later. The infirmary was a bustle of moving bodies and joyful exhilarations. Eittam passed with a smile upon her face. Bocaj's hut was farther down and set higher on the hillside. She thought as she walked past, it would be good to see him and took delight in her sister's joy. As she continued on her walk, she felt eyes upon her. Finally, she neared her hut next to the solace of the ocean.

Relaeh, peered through Bocaj's doorway, and mustered a double take as a woman on the lower road passed by his sight. Her stature was blocked by huts set along the pathway's edge for a further glimpse. Her hair resembled the woman in his dream, but that was an aberration brought on by the passions of the travelers the previous night. He brushed the vision out of his mind as Bocaj and he left the hut for the long house.

"Do you have your symbol, Bocaj?"

"Always," declared Bocaj reaching into his shortened tunic.

"Then display it proudly and activate the accumulator so our friends in Nalhs may take part in this grand day."

~

Eittam entered her hut where Aivila excitedly awaited.

"My sister, did you see him? He looks handsomely!"

"Are you referencing Bocaj?"

"Yes, of course. My lover to be," shared Aivila as she held her hands to her heart.

"I did not, but as I passed by his hut, I felt eyes upon me."

"Ohhhh, have you seen his friend? He is handsome like Bocaj."

"No, I did not see anyone, just perceived a watchful eye."

"There is a lady named Kasha that resembles my fiery hair," added Aivila. "I placed them all in the infirmary for their use until other arrangements can be made."

"I heard the cachinnation as I walked past. Everyone in the village is talking about the travelers and the tamed wolves belonging to the man with the floating machine."

"Bocaj called him their Healer. His name is Relaeh from Nalhs," informed Aivila.

"Their healer? As in our men and the travelers or as the travelers' medicine man?"

"I do not know, he mentioned his station as he introduced him on the landing."

"I shall look forward to meeting this charlatan with the mysterious machine."

"I do not believe that was Bocaj's intent. He spoke highly of his knowledge beyond our imagination and of his quick wit. You may find him charming, my sister."

Eittam hugged her sister and with lightness in her response, she clarified her sister's statement.

"Let me be the judge of his intent and nature, my young one. Now let me ready for today's activities."

"Very well, Eittam, but beware. Shall I adorn my eyes with berries of green or blue?"

"Green, my sister... to compliment your hair and your fiery personality. Take Bocaj of his senses so his eyes do not wander elsewhere. And I shall adorn with blue, to soften the glare from our visitor's intent."

~

Further in the village, Nephets was pacing up and down as Tomei readied for the jubilation.

"My husband, slow down, you will wear a spot of weakness in our landing."

"I cannot. My excitement of seeing my son as he led his hunters down the road with the travelers behind will stay with me forever. He made me so proud I can hardly stand in one spot."

"Yes, I can see your excitement. I can barely sit as still as an owl, prepping myself before gazing into his eyes. My son has been gone for four months without word to his well-being. I could not survive another disaster as we did before."

Nephets walked over to his wife and as she sat, he placed his arms about her tightly.

"Aivila made no hesitation in declaring her intent." He paused and with jestful recounting, he said, "She laid the poor boy onto his back like a turtle upside down and smothered him with kisses." Laughing loudly now, "It was magical but a comical sight you had to witness."

He wiped the moisture from his eyes, "We are fortunate that our son has a woman like Aivila in his life. I have faith he will do right by her."

"She is strong-headed like Leinad. It shall be an honor to share their lines. Now, let go of me, my love so I may finish these adornments about my eyes."

"You are beautiful as you be with no need of further adjustments, my love."

The Festivities Begin – The Gift of Life

Leinad had stayed in the long house organizing all of the preparations. It would be a welcoming like no other. He was thrilled that Bocaj had returned safely, and now, if providence would play its role, the nuances of his young daughter would be his burden to share. With mist in his eyes, he was thankful for all their safe return and longed to hear tales of his old city.

Bocaj and Relaeh from Nalhs arrived in time to share in the re-positioning of benches and long tables. It was important that everyone would be able to fully observe the head table. As he counted the seating, he was perplexed on the order. "Should Aivila and you sit by me or should Aivila sit with your family at the other end? What is the protocol?"

"Councilman," interjected Bocaj. "Why not disperse us all among our fellow citizens at each table, thereby introducing our new residents and eliminating the embarrassment of misalignment."

Relaeh added, "We could periodically switch chairs in a revolving manner in between speeches and servings to further add to Bocaj's design."

"That would be allowed?" questioned Leinad.

"We have no testimony to what is right or wrong, so let us enjoy the companionship with all," cheerfully said Bocaj.

"Let us break up these long adjoining tables to a haphazardly placement, perhaps angled from the center like spokes of a wheel, opened in the middle so you and Bocaj's father can instruct the proceeding. Others might be afforded the chance to relate stories of the journey, while others may voice the goings-on from Inception," elaborated Relaeh.

"This is the time we need Madame Ruvana to swish a layout from her control module," laughed Bocaj.

"Madame Ruvana... control module, what talk is this?" queried Leinad.

"We have much to share with you and Father. We are enlightened men, thanks to our friend here." He patted Relaeh on the back.

Working together, the men tweaked their idea to a more desirable layout that would make Madame Ruvana proud if She would be in charge. The twelve tables favored the sundial. The main table held prominence in front of the Grand Chair of the Council, the others placed accordingly with food displayed respectfully at three and nine. Citizens that arrived early, aided with the set up, and then, they directed others to leave the end seating of each table empty for the hunters and their families, and the new citizens with their children. Smooth as clock work!

With most gathered and enjoying the welcoming back of their adventurous friends and the acknowledgement of the new citizens, Leinad stepped into the circle to open the ceremonies. He looked about the room with pride. He observed Aivila was snuggled into Bocaj's side, while Yuda rubbed her belly as she discussed her need of assistance with Retu's daughter, who, by the way, was beaming with delight. His friend Nephets sat with his lovely wife Tomei, and Relaeh from Nalhs was caught up in delightful conversation with another young couple who were expecting their first child. But where was Eittam? This was not like her to be late for anything. In fact, she was usually the one overseeing everything. What mischievousness was she up to?

"Ladies and Gentle Men let us begin with the welcoming back of our adventurous hunters, Bocaj, Retu, Micja, Songa, Tavlo and our son of the arts, Kire."

The crowd cheered with feverish cachinnation. Some placed their fingers to their lips and made a trilling sound while others hailed loudly with banging on the tables. He raised his arms to quiet their intent. Leinad continued.

"With their discoveries, we have the honor of welcoming new faces to our clan..."

Again, the cheering filled the long house like never before. Leinad continued loudly over their excitement.

"...As you witness, the boys, Bocaj and his friend Relaeh from Nalhs, have conceived an ingenious seating arrangement so all may intermingle and enjoy the atmosphere to its fullest." The crowd eased their intent. "First let us give thanks to the forces of nature that have summoned us all together." He paused as each guest grappled in tradition with the next. "Let us take food and sweet nectar, and after, we shall exchange tales of what has transpired."

The crowd gleefully accepted Leinad's direction as food and chatter occupied the lips of its citizens. Bocaj excused himself from his table and gestured to Relaeh to meet his mother.

Nephets and Tomei stood for the introduction as Bocaj declared, "Mother, this is my friend..."

As Tomei gazed into Relaeh's eyes, a daunting warmth seduced her body. As in a void, her lips quivered with his name secretly being whispered for her ears only - *Trebor,*

Trebor, my lost son. How can this be? Her eyes misted as she graciously accepted his outstretched hand—his lips moved as she struggled to understand.

"It is an honor to meet you. You should be proud of your son. He is a good and fair man, a born leader."

Weakly, she said, "Yes... thank you Relaeh from Nalhs. I look forward to more talks on your... your circumstance."

Excitedly, Bocaj grabbed Relaeh by the arm, "Come Relaeh, I want to introduce you to some other close friends."

Kissing his mother on the forehead, Bocaj dragged Relaeh around the tables for others to meet. Nephets detected a strange fluctuation in his wife's voice, and inquired, "Tomei, you are weak. Are you of ill health? Please sit."

She looked up into Nephets' eyes and with a tremor in her voice and she said softly, "He is our son."

Nephets' concerned manner gripped his face and questioned his wife to what she had just said. "What do you speak of?"

"I do not know how, or by what manner, or what fate has turned to bring our son home?"

"You are speaking the truth? Perhaps it is the joy of seeing Bocaj in such fine spirits that blinds your vision?"

"I have no explanation," tearfully added Tomei.

While Relaeh, Bocaj and Aivila were at the far end of one of the tables, Eittam slipped into the room. Her slender body was draped in a crimson cloth that caressed her curvy wholesomeness and her ravenous hair barely concealed what must be left to imagination. On the way to her father's table, she stopped to chat with friends. Relaeh, in an interlude from jestful conversation, looked up and briefly captured a vision of his aberration as she once again disappeared within the crowd. Standing still, searching the room, Aivila broke his concentration.

"You look like you have seen a shadow of death?"

"Um, no… not death but definitely a shadow."

Once again, Eittam appeared.

"Ah, you eye my sister, Eittam," jestfully acknowledged Aivila. "Let me introduce you to her."

Placing her hand in his, she stole him away from the table. Bocaj looked up with concern, and then, he saw Eittam who was standing with others—she radiated in her beauty. He nudged Songa as the two stood with arms crossed, and watched with smiles on their faces. Kasha tapped Siena, who was sitting at the next table as the two witnessed Aivila, in her glowing stride as she led Relaeh slowly through the crowd toward Eittam.

"Eittam!" called out Aivila. Turning around she faced her premonition, her stature stood tall as she gazed into the eyes of Relaeh.

Relaeh fell back in disbelief, only saved by one of the guests from not collapsing to the ground. The constant chatter of the room hushed in anticipation.

"What is this treachery before me? You stand tall and straight." He gently raised his hand softly touched her face. "Your skin is soft and young. I don't understand. Are you the temptress, the chameleon that steals images from one's vision for your delight?"

The room beckoned with quiet horror. Bocaj rushed to Relaeh's side as did Leinad and his friends, Nephets and Tomei.

"What delight do you speak off, you arrogant man? We are true as the sun and moon. I do not deceive you or mock you. I am my Father's daughter. You speak a falsehood upon my image."

"Relaeh, what do you speak?" questioned Bocaj cautiously.

"She steals my vision of my Mother from Nalhs."

"Your mother?" questioned Leinad, "You know of another whose image is of my daughter?"

In the comfort of Nephets' arms, Tomei tearfully declared in a mild tone, "This is our lost son—this is Trebor!"

If a pine needle would drop, it could be heard throughout the village. Whispers of the name, Trebor, echoed throughout the building.

Relaeh turned with moisture misting his eyes. "This dream cannot be. What aberration have I slipped into?"

Once again Leinad asked impatiently, "Relaeh from Nalhs, do you know of another that shares likeness of my daughter?"

Quietly, weakly, and confused, he said, "Yes."

Eittam with lessening composure, hailed loudly, "You know of my mother?"

"Is this knowledge of years past?" rapidly questioned Leinad.

"No, just before I started this journey. She is our respected Oracle and scientist. She is Madame Noir."

An escape of air exhaled from the mouths of the crowd.

"Can it be true?" weakly questioned Leinad as he was guided to a chair. "After all these years, Noiram is alive?"

Eittam threw her arms about her father with unrelenting tears as Aivila dropped to her knees, and comforted her loved ones.

Relaeh turned to Tomei and Nephets who were standing in disbelief.

"Bocaj did not mention your names upon introduction. Madame Noir spoke highly of you both and declared to me only months ago of my true heritage and circumstance. I have only recently met Her face to face. I believed through all my years as a student of Nalhs, She was Nalhsian and not as the same flesh as I."

Tomei instinctively wrapped her arms about her long missing son. She was drenched in tears of joy—Nephets cradled the two.

Bocaj stood with an astounding look and then realized loudly for everyone to hear, "You are my brother!" He hailed excitedly with arms triumphantly pumping the air, and then, compassionately joined the others.

The crowd had tears streaking their faces and now laughter as they joined in on this wondrous re-union of the most unlikely souls.

Suddenly, in the mix of excitement, from the back of the room, a SCREAM broke the joyous atmosphere. Yuda, holding her tummy, looked down and revealed a pool of fluid beneath her. Einna and Rajean quickly ran to her side. Jacor and Moltov helped her stand as Aivila told them to take her to the infirmary. Each step brought excruciating pain as they headed for the doorway. The men crossed arms, and with aid from Songa & Tavlo, they carried her to her destiny, only a short distance away.

Eittam feeling the anxiousness of Yuda hiked her crimson cloth to her knees and rushed past the entourage as did Aivila with Bocaj and his brother Relaeh, following suit.

~

They cleared a clean space from a raised table, and Bocaj set a BTI for the comfort of the incoming patient.

"Have you done this before?" questioned Relaeh of Aivila.

"I have," said Siena, with Einna and Rajean by her side. "We can deliver her child."

The men carefully placed Yuda on top of the table. The women stripped Yuda of her garments and set a warming blanket upon her awareness.

"Bring me boiling water and clean cloths," instructed Siena. "You will be fine my love, just breathe slowly until I tell you to push."

"Yes ma'am," deliriously replied Yuda.

"Aivila, wipe the moisture from Yuda's face. Einna, her body runs with fever, we need to cool her down," insisted Siena.

"Ahhhhgg," screamed Yuda.

"Calm, my love, I need you to listen to me. Can you hear me?"

Yuda motioned with her head that she understood what Siena was telling her.

"When I tell you to push, I want you to push as hard as you can, understand? We need to place some cool cloths about her side. She is abnormally hot. The BTI can only adjust 10 degrees. She needs to be cooler."

"She will be all right?" asked her husband, Jacor.

"She is a strong woman; she will be fine," declared Siena.

"Yuda, I can see its head. Push now, Yuda, push now."

Yuda, with all her might bore down while she squeezed her husband's hand turning her fingers white.

"Breathe, Yuda, one, two, three, push Yuda, push."

Siena gently cradled the baby's head as Yuda bore down once again. Siena pulled the child's shoulders as the baby cleared Yuda's passage, then the attachment cord followed by its perfectly formed feet. "It is a girl!" The room cheered with delight as Siena ushered the little one to Rajean for cleansing. Yuda remained with a grimacing look on her face—blood flowed from within her. She faded into unconsciousness.

"YUDA!" screamed Siena.

"What is happening?" asked Jacor as he still had a hold of Yuda's hand.

"I do not know. I have not witnessed this before."

Relaeh pushed past Siena and listened for Yuda's breath. He beat on her chest, then back to her breath. Again he beat on her in a rhythmic session. He opened her mouth and breathed into it; then listened... nothing.

"Bocaj, give me your symbol now." Hastily he activated the panic button, "Hold it over Yuda. Father, can you hear me, Father, are you there," he shouted.

Over the symbol, he heard the soothing voice of Master Leumas.

"Relaeh, what upsets you so?"

"Father, I need instruction. Yuda has lost consciousness giving birth. Her heart has stopped!"

"Use the chillers' auxiliary probes," announced Master Leumas, calmly.

"Yes, of course. Eittam, run like the wind and bring my machine here," commanded Relaeh as he pumped Yuda's chest trying to resuscitate her.

"I have no knowledge of its workings?" frantically said Eittam.

"Place your hands upon the sensor pads of the command seat and open your mind; use your will to command its direction. You can do it. I believe in all my heart, you are the one..."

Eittam rushed out of the infirmary and ran as fast as she could. She jumped into the waiting seat and placed her hands upon the sensor pads of the arm rests. The machine illuminated around her. Perplexed, she scoured each dial and gauge for enlightenment. She repeated Relaeh's instructions in her mind.

"Will...in all my heart, you are the one. Will...I need to will it to my command. How do I will it? Open my mind, relax Eittam, and open your mind. I will you to lift."

The machine responded—it hovered. The concerned citizens who stood on the landing awaiting news of Yuda gasped, as she commanded the air machine with her will.

"To Relaeh's side, I command you."

The machine turned instantly to her desire to be by Relaeh's side. It moved silently, and hovered above the ground to where Relaeh awaited. She bounced off the steps of the infirmary with a degree of uncertainty before setting it down.

"She is here!" alerted Aivila.

"Tell her to twist out the black and red probes from the chiller in a counterclockwise direction. Do not touch the probes together," wearily expressed Relaeh as he continued to try to resuscitate Yuda.

"In a what?"

Bocaj understood Aivila's confusion, handed his symbol to Einna and darted out of the room to Eittam's side. He grabbed the probes, and twisted as Relaeh instructed—out they came. Carefully, he entered the room as the probes flickered between each other. He passed them to Relaeh.

"Stand back! Do not touch anything on Yuda. Jacor, let go of her hand, now," he insisted.

He touched one probe to her heart and then brought the other to her side...it sent an automatic jolt through Yuda bucking her body. The friends jumped back in amazement. Again he placed them upon her slicken, motionless body.

The energized probes zapped again. Yuda's body jumped with welcoming intent. Relaeh listened...

"She's breathing!" He exclaimed wildly.

Handing the probes back to Bocaj, he cupped her face with his hands and whispered to her. All of a sudden, feet appeared from whence the baby girl had just expelled. Yuda's natural size could not support this type of delivery—the body was stuck.

"My Anon," he shouted to Bocaj. "...get my Anon in the machine."

Bocaj swiftly darted out of the room while holding two precarious weapons in his hands. He relocated them back into the chiller and grabbed Relaeh's Anon from the multiplex command socket. He rushed to his side.

"Siena, place your fingers inside and feel for any obstruction."

Siena did as she was told and felt under the baby's protruding legs.

"I cannot feel any entanglement."

"Hold on. I will make an incision below her canal with the laser from my Anon. It will be easier on her recovery then being ripped apart."

Relaeh made a laser incision below Yuda's birth canal and with his bloodied hands, he handed his Anon to Eittam who stood to his left and in awe.

"Now Siena, together, let us pull gently."

The baby began to slide through the enlarged canal. He was noticeably... a boy.

"I believe he wanted to test the waters before coming out," jestfully announced Relaeh as the baby boy cleared Yuda's birth canal. He displayed the boy proudly.

The friends teared in delight as they heard the first cry from the new born. Relief overwhelmed them as Yuda opened her eyes to the questioning stares of her entourage. Jacor broke down in a wailing cry of exaltation. Her babies, gently wrapped, were placed in her arms, one on each side, to suckle from Yuda's nourishment. With arms about each other, they gathered around their treasured friend and observed the miracle of life.

Over the symbol, they heard cries of joy. Madame Ruvana offered Her love and welcomed the joy in being able to be part of Yuda's giving of life. Master Leumas, Relaeh's beloved Father, imparted with his praise.

"Well done, my son. One of your destinies is now fulfilled - the gift of life."

Eittam Gazes Upon Relaeh's Eyes

The entourage departed from Jacor, Yuda and her twins; her rest was now the element of concern. Before leaving, the ladies agreed to each take a post by her side, in case of any other complications. Einna's Anon symbol was programed directly into Madame Ruvana's in Nahls. The day's discourse had many twists and turns, some of joy, of uncertainty, of love and disbelief, of near death, and the gift of life; certainly the most profound day in Inception's short history. There were many more questions and longing answers that needed to be satisfied this night. Not all could wait till the morning light.

One by one, the entourage re-joined the festivities at the long house after a quick cleansing and change of attire. Eittam's sultry dress would have to be for another occasion as she re-dressed in less provocative wear and Aivila donned a simple frock, but still revealed much of her awareness for Bocaj's delight. The two walked arm in arm, back to the long house where Aivila's lover waited on the landing, while inside, Relaeh conversed with Nephets and Tomei. Each shared the joy in their expression and in their voice as they admired their son - a man with a destiny beyond their scope of understanding, but one they would happily share.

Aivila and Bocaj walked with hands entwined and searched out Leinad. Eittam sauntered to the man in her dreams. The crowd quietened to a mere hum as the last time the two met, their conversation was not so genteel. Standing above him, Eittam reached for Relaeh's hand; he obliged. They stood facing each other and gazed upon each other's eyes and deep into the light of their souls. She lightly pressed her body to his, and graced his face in her hands. She pulled him nearer, her lips touched his, and he responded holding her tight, feeling each curve as she pressed against him. They embraced in a slow passionate kiss, his heart ached and his head felt light. Quietly they stood with no other sounds around them. Their world was unfolding as it was meant to be. It was their destiny.

The crowd hailed in cachinnation barely distinguishable to their ears, until Bocaj and Aivila barged to their side, and shook them back to reality, and announced their proposed union.

In Nalhs, Master Leumas sat in the recovery chamber beside Madame Noir, each with tears in their eyes, hand in hand, as they watched the feed from Bocaj's symbol. Her beautiful daughter, Her aging husband, Her old friends, and Her son... Her son, who had given Her back Her dignity and Her life with his unselfish discoveries.

There was much to celebrate in Inception, as in Nalhs. Some of the excitement would have to be shared on another day, as today belonged to Relaeh and his birth family. Her friends, Nephets and Tomei, deserved his attention as their pain was Her only joy, their forced denial of his years was Her salvation - rest Inception - rest Nalhs.

Infectious Nature

Clear heads had been sacrificed as the previous night's celebration afforded too much indulgence in sweet nectar. The early morning tropical air, however, did relieve the agonized senses with its sweet, moist smell... or, was it her scent that occupied his being? Her body lay still, nestled into his, with her hand upon his, cupping her firm roundness. Her hair messed like that of the decoy in a field, and Relaeh's spiked like a preposterous creature. She sensed his first awareness of the day. She pressed back against him. His loins swelled with desire. She was a temptress; she was his temptress. She came to him in a dream, and now, he shared her bed, in the flesh.

He kissed her neck and down her back; she reacted to his movement. Slowly they made love, sharing the dream they already shared in the marigold field. She had known from her first premonition that he was the one, but not wanting to disrespect her vision, she unselfishly discarded her desires to focus on others. Her father had assumed correctly when she recounted her vision to him on the docks. But now, she was his and he was hers; tightly she held him, tightly...she gasped.

An untimely knock and the voice of her father ended their pleasure.

"Eittam, may I enter?"

"Um, Father, gives us a moment, please."

Leinad waited patiently with a grand smile upon his face.

Tying a robe about her, she courted her father, "Yes Father, what may I... we... um Father my tongue is tied, what pleases you this morning?"

Leinad entered to a decoy of nature; he smiled, his manner was of sheer joy.

"Ah, my daughter, your image shows well," jest Leinad. "Relaeh mentioned I might have a private conversation with my wife. Is he of better endurance?"

"Father, his endurance is no concern...," she paused. "...of either of us," she said returning her father's intent.

"Good... good for you both. It seems I have men of integrity sweeping my daughters off their feet. I had thought one of lesser persuasion might calm your mischievousness but you have gallantly chosen one of equal impetuousness to fulfill your desires."

"Father, you know in your heart we will serve each other best."

Relaeh stepped forth with a robe of Eittam's, only tied at the waist, as his broad muscular shoulders did not fit the sleeves. Leinad broke into uncontrollable laughter as Eittam turned to witness her father's vision.

"If you think the two of you can insult my nature, trust me, better have tried and failed."

"I have no words, my son," said Leinad as tears of laughter misted his eyes.

"I am glad you do not have an Anon or know of its use to display images to my friends in Nalhs."

"You mean this symbol?" replied Leinad holding it up.

"Aha...I see I will have no relief from this family either; however, my good man, yours does not have an accumulator on it. So, I will beg your forgiveness of my appearance and kindly excuse me while I dress more formally."

"My love, within a day you have chastised my nature, bloodied my gown, made love to me, and now you bring such laughter to my spirit, I may need Aivila to stitch my sides together."

"I have been told I have an infectious way." smiled Relaeh.

"I shall wait for you at the long house, my son. I am an old man who has not laughed like this in a lifetime."

Leinad's step was lighter than he thought possible as he strolled through the streets to the long house. Not too far away, he heard the cries of little ones wanting their mother's milk - these sounds of life added to his delight. Already on the landing, his best friends, Nephets and Tomei waited. They greeted each other in a binding hug, foreheads pressed together as if transferring the years of pain into a glorious re-union. Eittam's promise that Bocaj would endow them with great wealth on his return, the magnitude of this treasure, she had no comprehension until last night.

The Truth of Family

Not all the excitement was reserved for Inception; although, they had plenty to be joyous about. Master Leumas, in his infinite wisdom, and solemn declaration to his duty, offered to Regor the title of 'Chief Medical Research Advisorate'. This honor was the highest decree to one's accomplishments offered in Nalhs. His superlative dedication for research in spinal reconstruction and gene manipulation afforded him the title, 'Master' and recognition from his peers. Master Leumas had also offered to Dugar, internship to his position as the next Consulate General in studies of Education, Communication, and Speaker for negotiations and stabilization between Nalhs and the re-builders of Earth. Nalhs responded to these appointments with welcoming adulation. The dream of their forefathers was nearing completion, as the future of earth now depended on the resourcefulness of its new citizens. Nalhs had watched the birth of a new humanity, one that was accomplished through co-operation, love, and intuitive design. The stage was dressed for a new beginning.

In the confines of her recovery chamber, Relaeh's Anon compassionately relayed a holographic display of a private conversation between Madame Noir and her long lost husband.

"My love, words cannot describe my joy for Relaeh's discovery of you. In my heart, I knew you prevailed but your whereabouts and our communication abilities would not serve us until now. I have so longed for your arms about me," tearfully affirmed Madame Noir.

"Noiram, my heart too was shattered. The pain of not having you beside me and thinking of your unconscionable disappearance haunted me nightly. Your daughter... our daughter, Eittam, was my only constant belief of your nature, as she is of you. Without the two of them, I would not have survived these tumultuous years."

"Two?"

"Yes, we have two daughters of absolute delight and I perceive it will not be long before we share the designation of grandparents to Aivila and Bocaj. My darling, how can we meet and be one again?" he questioned longingly.

"Technology is changing every day here in Nalhs. I must believe we will be together soon. I have heard of Bocaj. He was here in Belcare with the other hunters. Relaeh spoke of him."

"He is more than that, he is Nephets and Tomei's second son, your Relaeh's brother." announced Leinad.

"You speak the truth?"

"Yes my wife, and your daughter Eittam, the sunshine of my life, shared her bed with your Relaeh. Oh my wife, this very morning he brought such height to my spirit as he was dressed in one of Eittam's night garments. The boy had me in tears."

"He is a man of many talents. I love him as my own."

"At first sight of Eittam, he mistook her likeness of you as an insult against his Mother," informed Leinad.

"I asked him out of love if he would call me as his own. I had no preconception that Tomei and Nephets would be his first discovery. I meant no disrespect."

"They did not perceive it as so, as you saved the boy and watched him grow. No one can take that away from you. You are still his mother in his heart as he has known no other."

"If destiny permits, we will have him as our real son," emotionally stated Madame Noir.

"And I will be proud to have him as a son."

"My husband, I remained loving you so through all the hardships; we shall be joined as our destiny was meant to be. But if I may, would my daughters be available?"

"Of course, my love. Let me secure them for you. They are on the landing waiting for you as well."

Excitedly, the two sisters entered the long house and rushed over to where the Anon rested.

"How do we speak on it?" queried Aivila of Eittam.

"I do not know. Do as Relaeh did when he was speaking to his father."

"Um, good will?" queried Eittam. "This is Eittam and my sister, Aivila."

The Anon once again displayed an array of holographic delight.

"Eittam and Aivila, my daughters, I am so profound with joy, my words, I can barely express," cried Madame Noir as she witnessed two grown women before Her.

"Mama!" blurted the sisters in unison.

"Your image is as Father has recounted many times and that I dismissed as his forlorn for you. I disbelieved his assumptions to our likeness - please forgive my impertinence."

"My daughter, you had no way of knowing the truth as I just realized that same vision, as you. I have wondered many times of your health and vision."

"Mama, this is my sunshine, Aivila, and very much your daughter in spirit."

"Mama," cried Aivila, "I have realized no other and as Relaeh spoke of you, I am as honored as he, to call you my mother."

"It will be our destiny to be together as a family, that I assure you," said their endearing Mother.

"Aivila, Your Father tells me of your intent with Bocaj. I look forward to witnessing your union. Perhaps Relaeh can adjust his accumulator to record all the joyous recounting."

"And why can you not be part of this? Relaeh has the knowledge to command his air machine. Is there no other that can perform this task?" voiced Aivila.

"I believe Relaeh has not spoken to you of my situation. I have been without use of my legs since the terrible tragedy befell us. I could only go a few hours without re-energizing the fluid to my lower extremities. As it stands, my outcome for relief is undetermined," explained Madame Noir.

"I apologize for my impetuousness. I, we had no knowledge of ill health," stated Aivila.

"Relaeh is a trustworthy man as I asked of his silence to anyone whom might inquire. Eittam, your Father tells me you have feelings for Relaeh?"

"I had a premonition of his image but discarded it, and then on meeting him he denounced my likeness to you, but once we joined together with Yuda's plight, I knew he was the one for my heart. And after Father left us this morning, he rushed out to the garden and picked flowers to adorn my table."

"He learns very quickly, my love. You have obviously stolen his heart. I could not be happier for both of you. Is my son near?"

"Yes, Mama, I will fetch him," said Aivila.

John F Russo

"Eittam, hold him tightly and dearly, he is not like normal men; he has many destinies to fulfill. Your challenge will be to assist him in his discoveries."

"I know, Mama. I share the same dreams as you."

"Mother," hailed Relaeh as he bounced in.

"My son, you have honored my request of you."

"It appears I have been honored by others for only doing what destiny has transcribed. I merely fell into this discovery, although, beyond anything that I could have imagined has declared itself before me. I gaze upon the eyes of your likeness with uncontrollable desire, not of just the flesh but of heart. I see her soul surround her, as you, and her peace is consoling to my intent, Mother."

"You make us proud. Leumas cannot gather words to inspire you as he sits here with moisture about his eyes. You will need to speak to him later when his composure resets."

"I shall, my Mother. Tell my Father I love him and I shall correspond in a couple of days."

Eittam and Relaeh gazed upon each other's eyes and held each other tightly. His mission was to help the men from Belcare with the antidote his friend Regor had constructed, and yet, here he sat in the arms of one so beautiful, in a distant village basking in the tropical air, meeting for the first time, the parents that bore him, and the realization that his friend was also his brother.

Relaeh's Anon flashed, and as he acknowledged its intent, Regor, Dugar and Madame Ruvana excitedly explained that because of Relaeh's insistence, a discovery that had identified the original DNA was instrumental in Madame Noir's surgery to be successful. Soon, she will be able to walk again. Moisture displayed rolling down their faces as the morning sunrays glistened off of a tear-drop as it followed its destiny. It was filled with hope, and love, and enlightenment, for tomorrow's discoveries shall soon be told.

Two Months in Passing

It was a glorious day that Aivila and Bocaj had picked to reinforce their love for each other in their union. Relaeh stood beside his brother Bocaj, and of course, the beautiful Eittam stood as maid of honor for her sister, Aivila. What could be more appropriate? Relaeh's excitement, however, was not only for his brother's union, but privately, he smothered a secret that would soon display itself.

The villagers: Yuda, with one twin nestled to her chest and the other bounced in the arms of his father, Jacor; Salocin and Einna kept Eve by their side, as Adam stood next to her and his mother Rajean, while her husband Taeman, admired his display of flowers. Siena, with her one year, almost two now, daughter, and husband Jang, whispered to Moltov and Kasha as Sirius and Narfinia talked with Retu and his family. The other hunters stood next to Relaeh, while Kire stood apart, and sketched the scene for prosperity while also adjusting the Anon. They all gathered to witness this union, on the hillside of Inception, across from the main intersection, above the creek that flowed through to the coral blue waters. The palm trees responded to the gentle breeze, as the proud Councilmen Leinad and Nephets with his wife Tomei, offered words of endearment to the young couple before them.

"My beloved daughter, Aivila, as beautiful as you stand today, let no day pass with a heavy heart, but reconcile your love as you see before you. Life is precious as you are well aware, and now, as you have chosen to begin a new life with Bocaj. We all stand here today to celebrate this union, as the two of you declare.

"Bocaj, you accept Aivila and all of her whimsical charms, to love her and hold truth to your declaration by this union..."

And before Leinad could finish his passage, rising into his vision, above the northern incline, appeared a new model SR5 air machine as it rushed towards them. In a solitary gasp, all eyes were on the approaching visitors as the machine came to rest beside the attendees.

Stepping out—tall and proud, Dugar offered his hand to the slim, curvaceous Madame Ruvana, who in turn aided a podgy old man navigate the landing ramp. With respect, Regor folded his arm peculiarly inward so a reaching hand could entwine. She stepped out onto the ground of Inception, without further assistance.

"I trust we are not too late, my husband?"

Anon...

John F Russo

The Author

After years of setting aside this profound urge to write, to create characters of higher standards rather than what was seen and heard on the controlled news sources, I deliberately introduced a society that was misrepresented by hearsay—the Nalhsians, and the humanistic need to control a society that had lost all reason—only to be—like a puff of air.

The Belcarian society was just that. A society mixed and matched by a computer, uneducated to past events and controlled by an oligarch disguised as a man of peace, and blind to the world that existed beyond their merger existence held tightly by the oppressors. Sound familiar?

This first book, The Perplexity of Engram, was designed as a trilogy. The characters names as described by Madame Noir talking to Relaeh, "...you spoke their names as into a mirror." Each name was flipped to read backwards equaling the shift and flip of the magnetic poles. "and = dna"

Something to think about: what if everything you were taught was a lie!

Books controlled by the government (as seen today), insurance companies controlling doctors and your health, politicians setting prices and standards by ingesting superfluous wealth from industry, and banks setting a rating system that holds no bearing, all of these mark the decline of a democratic society.

Website: johnfrussoauthor.com

John F Russo

Interesting Facts

While living on the west coast for over twenty years; including Vancouver, British Columbia; San Diego, CA, and Puerto Vallarta, MX (only 6 months); I was well aware of tremors and shakes, and the damage, shifts of tectonic plates could cause. With the help of Wikipedia, I was able to pinpoint these areas of concern.

There are many realities that we dismiss, or are unconscious of their existence. The San Andreas Fault, the most famous, along California moves an average of 37 mm (1.5″) per year. The New Madrid Fault line has the ability to affect Illinois, Indiana, Missouri, Arkansas, Tennessee and Mississippi and possibly has the potential of splitting the USA in half. The Afar Desert in Ethiopia, Africa could birth a new ocean; look up Tim Wright, a geophysicist with University of Leeds, UK.

Another interesting source was reading, although, not understanding, the National DNA Index System (NDIS) found on swgdam.org.

I have always admired Art Deco Architecture. When researching a suitable character for my "Androicropulous", I again turned to Google, and found a photo of a building I thought, would be ideal. With the aid of my loving wife, Lori, she found it, not in Boston, where I had been looking, but in Vancouver, BC. I knew exactly where it was on Burrard Street, which turned my story 180 degrees.

The Marine Building from Wikipedia: Look it up...

Google: 355 Burrard Street, Vancouver.

Wolves: Rowdy, the name my uncle gave to his white wolf that he found, as a pup, in the interior of British Columbia.

He weighed about 150 lbs. and yes he actually laid his head against my knee so I could stroke his head. He was poisoned by a neighbor.

His roll of growl and mannerisms were taken from our Akita, who was also pure white and mistaken as a white wolf.

The "J" in Belcarian language is silent.

There are many innuendos in this book; some are email addresses of friends, names of real places, slang, sayings from TV shows, a description of a country's flag, and parts of poems I have written or titles of stories to yet write.

The segment title 'et al' refers to Bocaj's travels away from his home of 3 months but also my journey with them of writing this novel to that point.

Madame Noir makes a comment to Relaeh about his toasting to Dugar and Madame Ruvana naming their children as 'spoken into a mirror'. Character Salocin is actually my grandson's name backwards 'Nicolas'. Try the others...

I felt we needed new words to replace our common words that we use to describe something. For example, video; it is all digital now, see if you can find a video camera. In 15,000 years they will not have video monitors, but who really knows. Maybe the sequel book will reveal more interesting facts.

The warrior gene numerical significance is the segment number from my Roget's 4th edition for 'Gases'.